THE PLAYWRIGHT'S HOUSE

THE PLAYWRIGHT'S HOUSE

A NOVEL

Dariel Suarez

 Red Hen Press | *Pasadena, CA*

Book layout by Vivian Rowe

Library of Congress Cataloging-in-Publication Data

Names: Suarez, Dariel, 1983– author.
Title: The playwright's house : a novel / Dariel Suarez.
Description: First edition. | Pasadena, CA : Red Hen Press, 2021.
Identifiers: LCCN 2021000793 (print) | LCCN 2021000794 (ebook) | ISBN
    9781597091145 (trade paperback) | ISBN 9781597098809 (epub)
Subjects: GSAFD: Suspense fiction.
Classification: LCC PS3619.U328 P57 2021 (print) | LCC PS3619.U328
    (ebook) | DDC 813/.6—dc23
LC record available at https://lccn.loc.gov/2021000793
LC ebook record available at https://lccn.loc.gov/2021000794

Publication of this book has been made possible in part through the financial support of Jim Wilson.

The National Endowment for the Arts, the Los Angeles County Arts Commission,
the Ahmanson Foundation, the Dwight Stuart Youth Fund, the Max Factor Family
Foundation, the Pasadena Tournament of Roses Foundation, the Pasadena Arts &
Culture Commission and the City of Pasadena Cultural Affairs Division, the City of
Los Angeles Department of Cultural Affairs, the Audrey & Sydney Irmas Charitable
Foundation, the Kinder Morgan Foundation, the Meta & George Rosenberg Foundation, the Albert and Elaine Borchard Foundation, the Adams Family Foundation,
the Riordan Foundation, Amazon Literary Partnership, the Sam Francis Founda-
tion, and the Mara W. Breech Foundation partially support Red Hen Press.

First Edition
Published by Red Hen Press
www.redhen.org

MIX
Paper from
responsible sources
FSC
www.fsc.org   FSC® C011935

To Ali & Nati

Andrea: "Unhappy is the land that breeds no hero."
Galileo: "No, Andrea: Unhappy is the land that needs a hero."
                                                    —Bertolt Brecht

For us, a revolutionary people in a revolutionary process, we value cultural and artistic creations in regards to how they serve the people, in regards to what they contribute to man, in regards to what they contribute to man's vindication, to man's liberation, to man's happiness. Our assessment is political. There can't be aesthetic value without human content. There can't be aesthetic value against man. There can't be aesthetic value against justice, against well-being, against liberation, against man's happiness.
                                                    —Fidel Castro

Chapter 1

The show was a success.

It was no surprise to Serguey, who during the past decade had seen his father direct over a dozen plays to critical acclaim. Still, he was delighted to witness Felipe's greatness come alive in *Teatro Mella*, one of Havana's premier venues. The audience applauded and cheered, calling for him to be brought onstage. A smile materialized on his father's lips as he took the last few steps up the side stairs. For a man of fifty, he moved sprightly. His graying hair shone elegantly above his thick, dark eyebrows. His eyes gleamed under the lights as if filled with tears. He stared at the crowd, saluting those he recognized. The cast held hands behind him, forming a human fence, and bowed in appreciation. He stopped for a moment and blew a kiss in Serguey and Anabel's direction. Serguey gave him a thumbs-up. In the periphery of his vision, he could see that his wife had blown a kiss back at his father. She continued applauding with fervor, her whole body stirring the contours of her dress. Serguey smiled at the genuine thrill in her reaction, spurred by the fact that her sister, Alida, had just made her acting debut.

The actors and Felipe took one final bow. The curtain glided down, and his father placed a hand over his heart as his figure disappeared. The lights became brighter, illuminating the yellow banisters of the theater. Their undulating design mimicked the motion of waves rushing toward the stage. The murmuring crowd inched gradually up the aisles, leaving a sea of red chairs behind. Serguey and Anabel remained in their seats.

"Alida was wonderful," Serguey said. He took his wife's hands. They were exceptionally warm, as if heated by fire.

"I'm so proud of her."

A couple in their late teens was attempting to pass them in order to leave their row. Serguey and Anabel stood, springs squeaking as they pushed up the foldable seats. The girl's canvas bag snatched on the armrest of Anabel's chair, abruptly yanking her shoulder. Anabel slid the strap off politely as they traded a demure look. The boy, already in the aisle, went to assist his girlfriend a little too late, resorting to a timid stroke of her shoulder. He did a double take at Serguey and hesitantly asked, "Do you know the director?"

Anabel gazed at Serguey in mock amazement, implying his connection to the director made him important.

Serguey chuckled and said, "He's my father." He pointed at Anabel, then at the stage. "Her sister played the *Pedagogo* in the first act."

The couple bobbed their heads and brought up their hands—a recognition and a goodbye. They stuttered their steps until the girl shoved the boy and he got his feet fully in gear.

As if the interaction had been a mere daydream, Serguey turned to his wife and said, "Were you nervous when Alida came on?"

She sat again. He did the same.

"Nervous? I was dying!"

They waited until most of the venue cleared, both of them absorbing the relative calm that immediately follows the raucous collective experience that is theater. Now he could focus more easily on the details. Anabel had put on her favorite clothes for the occasion: a navy cocktail dress that accentuated her breasts and narrow shoulders. The silky fabric fell tightly over her body to the base of her knees. On the way over, Serguey had wanted to run his fingers down her back, rest them atop her curving butt, maybe a little lower. Instead, Anabel had looped her arm around his elbow.

With the seats now practically empty, he looked around and shouted, "Hello!" He listened carefully for his echo. "I used to love doing that when I was a kid," he said to Anabel. "My dad would bring me to theaters during dress rehearsals, and at the end of the night, when everyone had left, we'd sit and scream our names at the ceiling. Dad said he'd done the same inside a few cathedrals in Spain when he traveled there."

Anabel said, "I wouldn't be surprised if he did it during Mass."

"I don't know if he did, but he got kicked out of the one in Toledo."

His father was a daring man, Serguey knew, and this was especially true of his work. THE GREATEST DIRECTOR OF OUR GENERATION? had been the headline of a recent article in *El Escenario*. It made the case that Felipe's bold approach to his craft—his willingness to break away from the norm in the contemporary stage—had solidified him as an "innovator" and "artistic genius." He'd decided to reject adaptations of Greek, Shakespearean, nineteenth, and twentieth-century classics to concentrate on the original work produced by his trusted playwright, Mario Rabasa. He'd incited a trend that, in some critics' view, defied recent decades of Cuban theater. Serguey couldn't help laughing at the praise, even if he agreed with it at some level. The article had been printed on the heels of the announcement that Felipe would be presenting Virgilio Piñera's *Electra Garrigó*—the play they had just watched—a 1940s Cuban parody of Sophocles' *Electra*.

So much for original material.

Serguey pictured his father pacing slowly around his living room, flaunting a copy of *El Escenario* at his friends. He'd be looking into each person's eyes as he passed them, claiming that such academic and critical nonsense stood in opposition to art, that he was now doomed to personal failure and subsequent misery, since, when one thought about it (here he'd raise both his voice and the magazine in his hand), the focus had been placed on him and not what truly mattered: his creative work.

"No artist can receive such attention and remain pure," he had likely said. "Not while he's alive." He might've paused and added, "And if they're going to write such idiocy, why put a question mark? It's insulting!"

Serguey also knew that a handful of those friends—the ones who had been around when his father was little more than a young, insecure playwright— would be fighting back smirks and chuckles. Felipe had been a playwriting professor for the better part of a decade. As a graduate of the Instituto Superior de Arte, he had written his share of reviews and critical essays for national publications, dissecting plays with a mixture of objectivity and flare.

His father was an exceptional artist, Serguey had no doubt, but he was also the most contradictory person he had ever known.

The heavy base of the curtain billowed in shifting shapes: the stagehands' night wasn't over. As a child, Serguey had helped clean after several shows, sweeping and placing props in their respective boxes. Occasionally, an actor would mount him on his shoulders and walk him to the front edge of the stage. Serguey felt as if he were floating over the chairs, his belly tingling like it did when he zipped down a slide. Seeing the inner-workings and aftermath of a performance didn't detract from his enjoyment of the plays. On the contrary, it enhanced it: what to him seemed so commonplace during cleanup had the ability to create a spectacle, a fantasy that was as real and unforgettable as the parading *Muñecones*—giant, expressly hideous puppets—during Carnival.

The few people left inside the venue had assembled in small groups at the end of the aisles. They spoke and gesticulated with passionate urgency. Even their grins and gazes were exaggerated, as if the characters in the play had taken possession of their bodies. A spurt of laughter with an infectious pitch spread from the back of the room. Heads began to turn toward a red-faced woman, her body bending under the weight of her own wild glee, as she tried, uselessly, to cover her mouth.

Anabel leaned her head on Serguey's shoulder, unaffected by the noise, then straightened suddenly and scanned the seats. "I think Victor's gone. Can we go?"

Serguey had already seen his younger brother exit the theater, though he'd dissimulated by pretending to inspect other faces for acquaintances. He took Anabel's hand and led the way.

The lobby was packed with more of the same: animated conversations amalgamating into a dissonant choir. Serguey recognized some people here, but none that he felt obligated to greet. As he and Anabel squeezed their way through, he saw a lip-pierced young woman declare, "This is the best version I've seen."

They emerged onto the sidewalk and decided to linger under the marquee. The night was humid and breezy. The traffic on Linea Street flowed with ease, as if propelled by the soft wind. The bottom of Anabel's dress fluttered against her legs. For a moment he visualized himself lifting the hem, titillated by the thought of how his fingers might feel against the fabric, how they might glide across her skin.

She stared at him. He could tell she'd noticed something in his eyes, because she smiled and slid her own fingers across his hip. He turned away, feigning innocence. A bus was blocking the driveway that flanked the building. Beyond it, walled up in a parcel of land that had been unkempt for as long as Serguey could remember, trees rustled with an unhurried, cadenced harmony. He inhaled as if he'd just risen from underwater and looked to his right. Victor was standing against a column, lifting his cigarette in acknowledgement. Serguey nodded, his lungs slowly deflating. Victor took two deep drags, then discarded the cigarette butt and stomped on it.

"Please be nice," Anabel whispered, pulling at Serguey's cuffs.

Victor joined them. He was wearing a black V-neck T-shirt, the bottom of it fitted over an absurdly big belt buckle. The burnished vestiges of a recent shave coated his cheeks. "You didn't have to wait so long," he said. "I got out as soon as the curtain went down."

"You're still here." Serguey dipped his eyes at the words engraved on the buckle: GUESS.

Anabel grazed Victor's smooth cheek with hers, making a kissing sound. "How are you?"

"'Not in jail,' as my brother would say."

Serguey shook his hand, more for Anabel's sake than Victor's. "So you finally came to one of Dad's plays."

"I'm becoming a cultured man." Victor scratched his throat and grinned. "I actually helped finance the cost of materials to build the set."

"Look at you, benefactor and everything."

Anabel said, "If you two are going to be like this, I'm going back inside."

Serguey interlocked his fingers with hers. "You're right. This night is about Dad and Alida."

Victor fished another cigarette out of his breast pocket but didn't light it right away. "Your sister was amazing," he told Anabel, glancing at the venue's entrance. "Hopefully they'll be out soon."

Serguey stared at the glass doors of the theater, counting the seconds. As if telepathically summoned, Felipe and Alida appeared an instant later. The group exchanged hugs and kisses, their voices overlapping in lively hellos and congratulations.

Felipe said, "Isn't this a miracle? My two boys together!"

"Yes," Anabel said. "They've been singing each other's praises."

"Well, what did you all think of Alida?" Felipe asked. "'Who needs ballet when you can act like that?' is what I'd say."

Alida bent her knees in a graceful bow. She was shorter and slenderer than Anabel, but had the same dark eyes, dark hair, plump cheeks, rounded nose. Serguey sometimes called them "teddy bear sisters." Anabel absolutely abhorred it.

"We're very proud," Serguey said.

"It's all thanks to Felipe," Alida said. She ran one hand down his ribs, the other bracing the small of his back. "He's a tough director, but there's a gentle soul underneath."

Felipe pretended to be annoyed. "No sentimentality, Alida. You're a better artist than that."

She laughed. "See what I mean?"

Anabel looked at Felipe. She stiffened her lips into a diminutive smile. "Are the other actors happy with her?"

Alida flushed with embarrassment. "Anabel!"

"They've been together a while, no? I don't know how they feel about an outsider."

Serguey was amused. Anabel was brazen. No hairs in her tongue, as the saying went. Victor was shaking his head emphatically, approving of her candor.

"Your sister's grown up now," Felipe said. "She can handle the drama."

"He's kidding," Serguey said. "Of course they like her."

Anabel grinned. She excused herself and snatched Alida away from the men, pulling her hand and inclining her face close to her sister's. Serguey hadn't experienced this kind of sibling intimacy with Victor, not even as children.

Victor said, "Dad, I'll see you back at the house."

"No, no. Let's have a drink!"

Victor embraced him. "Some other time, *viejo*. I feel like walking." He tapped Serguey twice on the arm, then walked toward Anabel and Alida and kissed them goodbye. Continuing across the road, he lit up his cigarette and blended momentarily into the shadows of Linea Street.

"Why don't you talk to your brother?" Felipe asked.

Serguey sighed. "You know it's not that simple."

"We need to do something together. Maybe a lunch at the house. You haven't been there in ages."

Victor and I have barely spoken in eleven years, Serguey wanted to say. He let out, "I don't think our problems can be fixed over lunch."

"A father can hope."

Serguey observed his brother again, now visible under the glare of a streetlamp. Victor hopped briefly into the gutter as four young tourists—blond-haired, pale-skinned, swank-clothed—walked in the opposite direction. His burning cigarette rose to his mouth as he swiveled his head and climbed back onto the sidewalk. He was, without a doubt, eyeing the ladies in the group.

"At least you got him to come," Serguey said, still staring at Victor. "He even dressed up a bit."

Felipe's eyes, aimed at the distant shape of his youngest son, glinted with fatherly pride.

Serguey spotted Victor lifting his arm. A man on a small Suzuki motorcycle pressed his brakes and swerved across the opposite lane, pulling up to the curve. He put his feet on the pavement while the engine idled. The visible entrails of the motorcycle seemed covered in soot or rust. The man bumped Victor's elbow, pointing with his other hand at a large bag attached to the luggage rack. The front wheel slid limply to one side, the headlight emphasizing a grin of recognition on Victor's face. He peered into the bag, then saddled himself onto the backseat and knocked on the man's helmet. The man bent forward and straightened the wheel, the engine revving and clanging as he accelerated in the direction from which he had come.

Serguey turned to his father. Felipe was looking at the lobby, his hands clamped and twisted together in front of his chest.

"So *Electra Garrigó*?" Serguey said. "I remember you saying you'd never do it."

Felipe unlocked his hands and smiled. "It was out of respect for Virgilio, but I got over myself."

"You might be the best director in the country. You can do whatever you want."

"I've had my fun with that."

"I suspected you would. In all seriousness, the play was spectacular. So much energy."

"Thank you." Felipe kissed his oldest son on the forehead. "Get the ladies. Let's have dinner."

Serguey struggled not to wipe the smidge of saliva his father had pasted on his skin. "What about the actors?"

"I've taught them that family comes first. Besides, they see me every day."

Serguey didn't reply, distracted by a man who had exited the lobby and was moseying in their direction. He sneaked up behind Felipe and shook him.

"I see you're hiding from your fans." The man was tall and slender, his lips buried under a thick moustache. His face shone with a fine luster, which Serguey associated with imported lotion or aftershave. He wore a cream-colored jacket with black elbow patches and a striped shirt underneath. Serguey no longer felt overdressed in his own suit. He figured the man was an actor, his clothes a kind of costume.

"This is Mario Rabasa," Felipe said. "My dramaturge."

Serguey introduced himself. "I recognize the name. You were mentioned in the article."

"In passing," Mario said. "Your father got all the glory." He leaned into Felipe, regarding Serguey with playfully narrowed eyes. "He's not as handsome as Victor, but definitely more refined. More intelligent. I can tell just by looking at him."

Felipe slapped the dramaturge's stomach. "Please forgive Mario," he said to

Serguey. "He has a thing for young men, and he's not afraid to humiliate himself and others in order to show it." Addressing Mario, he added, "My son is happily married."

"It's fine," Serguey said. "I'll take it as a compliment."

Mario widened his eyes. They were like a pair of giant marbles. "You've raised your children well."

"You don't have to tell me." Felipe gripped the bottom of Serguey's neck, just above the collarbone, halfway between a caress and a choke.

"A few of us want to take you out for drinks." Mario spread his arms dramatically, his hands pirouetting like a dancer's. His shoulders, temporarily exposed, looked scrawny in the confines of the puffy jacket sleeves. He glanced up and down the street. "There's got to be a place in this city where starving artists can invite their director to celebrate." He dropped his arms casually. "Serguey and his wife are welcome to join."

"Thank you," Serguey said, "but we'll pass."

"I've already made dinner plans with them," Felipe told Mario.

"Anabel and I have to be up early tomorrow," Serguey lied. "Go enjoy yourselves. We'll have dinner soon."

Felipe protested, but Serguey insisted that it was best for him and Anabel to go home. Resigned, Felipe called the women over. He hugged them and praised Alida once more.

"I'll call you tomorrow," Serguey said to his father.

"Please do."

Felipe and Mario headed back into the theater. Almost immediately, they had a new set of spectators. The dramaturge positioned his outstretched fingers below his ears and opened his mouth in a mimed frantic scream. Three young, drably dressed men shared an identical laugh, one of them miming his own excitement back at Mario. An older woman with dyed red hair in a polka dot dress grabbed Felipe's elbow with the supple, confident manner of a personal guide. She picked something out of his hair, which caused Felipe to smile.

"Are we good to go?" Anabel said.

Serguey nodded, and they started down the sidewalk. The women picked up a conversation they'd been having about the play and the crowd's reaction. He walked behind them, paying more attention to the sound of their footsteps. Home wasn't too far away. Only nine blocks. It was best to let them relish the moment without his intrusion, enjoy the refreshing weather. Alida would be spending the night. She had left a change of clothes at their place that same morning.

Then, like a slow motion reel, Serguey watched a boy not older than seventeen bump into Anabel's shoulder as he tried biting into a slice of pizza. Following the impact, the boy clutched his food, which jutted from a paper sleeve. Only after he had secured his late-night snack did the boy glimpse at Anabel.

No apology came. Instead he grinned and said, raising the slice above his forehead, "These aren't free, honey."

Anabel sneered but said nothing. She and Serguey had an implicit accord to avoid public conflicts.

Alida had made no such agreement. She said to the boy, "Are you blind or just an idiot?" With this she began to turn away from him, as Anabel had already done, but not before glancing at Serguey.

"You should watch where you're going," Serguey told the boy in the deepest voice he could conjure.

The boy chewed off a piece of the slice with a smirk, staring back at him. Serguey inhaled the warm, piquant smell of cheese, tomato sauce, garlic, and oiled dough. For an instant he was transported to 1986, his first memory of tasting pizza. It had been at a government-sanctioned cafeteria, the waitresses always sour and in a hurry, a legion of flies hovering over everyone's plates.

The scent of the boy's slice, here on the street, was much more enticing. He had bought it with convertible pesos, the equivalent of American dollars. An expensive treat.

"Don't get mad," the boy said, casting a suggestive glimpse at the sisters. "Looks like you'll be eating better than me tonight." He didn't wait for a response—he wasn't looking for a confrontation. He ambled away with bouncy steps, his baggy jeans exposing the elastic band of his underwear. A gray T-shirt was draped over his neck like a towel.

Anabel and Alida had resumed their conversation. Serguey allowed himself to ignore the boy, struck now by the purposeful layering of emotions when Alida had briefly looked at him. He wondered if her acting skills allowed her to manipulate her expressions in such a way. There was no layering with Anabel. At most there was subtle withholding, which he could usually decode. He appreciated and preferred his wife's straightforwardness. Even Victor's. His father was an adept actor himself, and that had often not been beneficial to Serguey. He knew, for instance, that Felipe's dinner idea had been largely a performance piece, thus why he'd declined. His father's words had a propensity for emptiness, after all. He loved to profess family unity, only to merrily scamper back to the world he truly loved: the theater.

Part of Serguey, however, regretted not having accepted the invitation. The oily aroma of the boy's pizza had remained somewhere inside his nose. It prickled at the back of his tongue. With the family together, Alida's debut, Felipe's success, they could've splurged, having a reason to. And without Victor there, Serguey could've bragged about his improving situation at the Ministry of Foreign Affairs, about the Sweden assignment—his first trip abroad—which he was on the verge of obtaining. Felipe would've celebrated it, even if just as a formality or segue to his own boasting. But Serguey wasn't about to change plans, to plunge himself into the capricious endeavor of convincing Anabel to sacrifice private time with her sister. He simply hoped that they would want a full meal when they got home.

Approaching a street corner, Alida hurried to a nearby lamppost and used it to stretch her legs. They tensed and folded like malleable rubber.

Anabel said, "First a performer, then everything else."

"Don't make fun of me," Alida said. "This play has me thinking. I might want to be a serious actress instead of trying out for ballet again when this is over."

The straggling voices of strangers reached Serguey's ears: a swarm of six or seven, most likely students. They were dissecting technical aspects of the play, what they saw as the director's brilliant artistic variations on previous versions. Serguey felt saturated, fraught with irritation. He'd suddenly had enough of his father and *Electra Garrigó*. He quickened his steps, catching up to the women.

"I've been around theater most of my life," he told Alida. He watched her and Anabel's expectant faces for a few seconds before adding, "If I were you, I'd stick with ballet."

CHAPTER 2

At eleven in the morning, the sun blazed overhead. The chairs on the balcony, unprotected by shade, were hot enough to singe skin. Serguey carried one into the living room to let it cool. He sat on the sofa to read the newspaper and drink a cup of coffee he'd just prepared. At the end of the hall—past the master bedroom, the bathroom, and a second bedroom where Alida had spent the night— Anabel stood by the dinner table, removing weeks-old sand from her beach bag. The laces of her two-piece swimsuit peeked out from her shorts and tube top.

"Hurry up, beautiful," she said to her sister, who was still in the bathroom.

Serguey chuckled softly, not wishing to be heard. Alida's presence always brought out a more jovial Anabel. His job, the apartment, their plans, it was all very serious and demanding. They constantly had to handle themselves with decorum, show the world that they were wise beyond their years, deserving of their status and good fortune. This wasn't easy for Anabel, as she often had to keep her outspoken temperament in check while listening to the boring chatter of insecure men. With Alida, she didn't have to worry about any of that. They were both brash and honest. They could behave more immaturely. They could be silly and obnoxious, even rude if they wanted. Blood ties at their age could excuse a lot.

The bathroom door opened, and Alida came into view. She was wearing a pink bikini bottom and a blue top. She held onto the doorframe, put a hand on her hip, and stuck her butt out.

"What do you think?" she asked Anabel.

"Whorish."

"Prudish!"

Serguey caught himself staring at Alida. Her skin was slightly darker and slicker than her Anabel's, her thighs trimmer and more muscular, splendidly tautened by years of exercise. Nonetheless, there was a striking resemblance in the shape of their bodies. It had been a while since the last time he'd seen this much of his sister-in-law. He let out an inadvertent cough, and both women looked at him.

"Your wife feels threatened by her younger sibling," Alida said. "Isn't that sad?"

Serguey didn't know what to do except force a smile.

Anabel rolled her eyes. "We're going to be late."

The sisters had agreed to take advantage of the sunny forecast by heading to a tourist-only resort near Guanabo Beach. They had already arranged for Manny, one of Serguey's colleagues, to drive them. He was their ticket in. Anabel was hoping her younger sister and Manny, the handsome son of an eminent government official, could hit it off. Anabel had, Serguey now thought quite regrettably, befriended him at a Ministry of Foreign Affairs' party. He'd been excruciatingly charming. His compliments were like a magician's handkerchiefs—varied and neverending, and to Serguey's taste, a little played out. He owned a car, to boot. Not a Soviet-era Lada or Moskvich or Volga, the kind Serguey would be ecstatic to have, but a black, wax-shined, four-door Peugeot. Not even Dr. Roberto Gimenez, Assistant Director to the Chief Legal Executive at the Ministry and Serguey's boss, could claim ownership of such a vehicle.

Serguey had originally been included in the plan, but he insisted they go alone. He wanted no part of Manny, whom he thought a bad match for Alida.

"You can gossip without having to worry about me," he had said to Anabel. "Plus I have to prepare for a Monday morning meeting."

"You're the only person in your office who works on Sundays," she told him. She knew how to criticize him without outright attacking him.

"You know I'm still trying to prove myself."

Anabel walked away and said nothing, as if the conversation had concluded with her last statement.

"Cover yourself up and get your things," she now said to Alida. "We have to meet Manny downstairs in ten minutes."

"*Si la envidia fuera tiña,*" Alida sang in a made-up melody.

"Yes, we're all very jealous."

Perhaps it *was* jealousy that predisposed Serguey to the whole Manny arrangement. Manny was two years younger, and a life of comfort had already been laid out for the guy. He had mastered, quite exceptionally, a smug grin to go with it. A very punchable face, Manny had. Born into the right family—his father was the head of Havanatur, Cuba's tourism monopoly—with just the right amount of ass-kissing in his personality. He embodied the perfect upper-class individual of the communist state.

Considering how far he himself had come, however, Serguey was aware of his own hypocrisy in resenting a spoiled brat like Manny. He and Anabel lived in the heart of El Vedado. That fact alone would impress plenty of his childhood friends. Their ten-story building, freshly painted and garnished with Cuban flags hanging from several rails, stood highest for a few blocks. It was like a decorated tower, an emblem, as many things tended to be in Cuba. The balconies were long enough to hint at the desirable size of the apartments. There were only four units per floor, a locked entrance to a clean lobby decorated by bamboo palms, and a fully functional elevator. By El Vedado standards, the building was considerably appealing. By Havana standards, it bordered on luxury.

How he'd gotten the apartment wasn't as admirable. The place belonged to his boss. Gimenez had been a well-regarded defense attorney-turned-government official whose bourgeois relatives survived the Revolution unscathed. They had supported Castro's clandestine fighters at an opportune time, and unlike other affluent families who were ransacked or betrayed by the new regime, they were rewarded. Gimenez's sister, a lawyer at the Cuban embassy in France, had lived in Serguey's apartment with her husband after the building was finished. That was until she got a job as a law professor at the Aix-Marseille Université. Unbeknownst to her brother, she decided to defect. (Why she'd done it, Gimenez had never said.) Perhaps out of personal umbrage or for political reasons, he lost touch with her. Soon after, he offered the place to Serguey—his favorite protégé—rent-free as a sort of wedding gift. He had no one else to give the apartment to, he explained, and Cuban laws didn't allow him to collect rent.

"The furniture is included," he had boasted, "though you're welcome to change it."

They didn't, of course. It was a rare kind of Cuban inheritance: a loan, bereft of familial history. The delicately worn quality of the three-drawer chest-like TV stand, the squared glass center table, the upholstered dining room chairs, they were lovely and valuable in their own right. In time he and Anabel could take emotional possession. When Gimenez gave them the keys, she hadn't been able to contain her tears. Very few people their age could live so comfortably and with so much, especially without having to pay for it. In a communist economy, bequests—almost always meager in nature—were more about subsistence than remembrance or extravagance. What Gimenez had given them was the equivalent of lottery winnings. He and Anabel were among the luckiest twenty-seven-year-olds in the country.

The sisters were now in the dining room, stuffing their beach bags with towels and sunblock. Sure that he wouldn't have a last minute change of mind, Serguey took hold of the chair he'd brought in with one hand, his coffee cup in the other, and walked cautiously to the balcony. From here, on the seventh floor, he could see the graying, puddle-ridden rooftops of neighboring structures: clotheslines flapping in the wind, wiry antennas with reflectors like lengthy whiskers, moldy water tanks and abandoned tricycles. Still, the view was a huge improvement over his childhood neighborhood in Santos Suarez. In the distance, flags wavered and snapped above schoolyards and medical buildings. Looking to his right, cars and buses trudged down Avenida Paseo toward Malecon, where high rises and hotels occasionally impeded a view of the sea. The air felt crisper, the streets and avenues wider in El Vedado. In Santos Suarez, everything felt aged, narrow, squalid. The sidewalks were riddled with cracks. Street corners had been converted into temporary garbage dumps, refuse piled so high they resembled gigantic anthills. Initially everyone complained about the smell, about the lack of decency. After a while you couldn't help throwing your own trash into what had become a symbolic monument—a communal middle finger to whoever dared call Cuba a pristine, exemplary island.

"It's a sad example of how, sooner or later, people give up," Felipe had told his sons in an ironic lecture, himself a culprit in the trash epidemic.

Living in El Vedado, there was a sense of having been liberated, of being tangibly separate from the more disheartening side of Cuba. Serguey was aware of this, and as much as it might border on betrayal—considering his father and brother belonged to that other side—he was proud of what he had accomplished.

He sat opposite the railing, his ankles drenched in sunlight, the coffee still hot to the touch. A couple of hours before, he had called his father. He wasn't pleased with how he had dismissed Felipe the previous night, even if his old man had been faking. Presenting *Electra Garrigó* at Mella Theatre was a big deal. If dinner wasn't a feasible option, lunch was the least he could do. Anabel had whispered these last words to him in the bedroom, and they'd stayed with him like an accusation. But Felipe hadn't picked up the landline. Serguey had tried again a half hour later with the same result. Victor had, at some point, bragged about getting his father a cell phone, its own form of luxury, especially for a theater director—nowhere near the top of Cuban society's money-making strata. But as far as Serguey knew, it had been another one of Victor's hollow,

I'm-the-cooler-brother pledges. The home phone was the only way for Serguey to reach Felipe.

Calling for a third time with no response would irritate him, so Serguey gave up the idea. Best to wait for Anabel and Alida to leave the apartment, he thought, and proceed with the rest of the day on his own terms.

He inhaled the coffee's aroma as if the drink's bitterness could magically undo the bitterness in his mind. He succeeded in tempting his taste buds, but before he could take a sip a loud knock came from the front door. He remained quiet for a moment, expecting to hear Manny's voice. Why hadn't he just honked, the standard car-owner's "hello" in Havana? Serguey went to the railing and glimpsed down at the street; he couldn't locate Manny's Peugeot. There were plenty of spaces for him to have parked it.

As he approached the door, he was halted by a second, sturdier bang. Someone was slamming the oversized knocker. They were doing it with such force that the wooden frame of the door rattled. He decided not to look through the peephole for fear that his face might be struck.

"Who is it?" he yelled, but no one answered. He fumbled with the lock and finally opened the door.

It was Victor.

"What are you doing here?"

Victor pressed his right forearm against the wall and chewed his nails. His hair seemed to have been slopped in water. His eyes were panic-stricken. "I need your help."

Victor had been in trouble before, but he'd never appeared this nervous. "What happened?"

"It's Dad. The police took him this morning."

"The police? I've been calling—"

Victor's voice was suppliant. "This is some fucked up shit, Serguey."

He clinched his brother's wrist. "Where did they take him?"

Before Victor could answer, Serguey noticed his neighbor, Carmina, stealing out of her apartment across the hall. Her hair was wrapped tightly around a set of rollers.

"Is everything okay?" the lady asked.

"Yes, Carmina. Sorry for the noise." Serguey turned to Victor. "Come in."

They hustled inside, and Serguey locked the door. "What the hell happened?"

Victor sat on the edge of the sofa, biting his nails again. A streak of wet dust crept down his throbbing neck, his Adam's apple ascending and falling like a pump. "There was a cop and two guys in civilian clothing. I'm sure they were from State Security. They said they had orders to arrest him."

Serguey stalled, struggling to remain composed. "What was the charge?"

"They didn't say."

"So they just took him?"

Victor didn't look at his brother. "They searched the house, took his typewriter. They threw all his paperwork and notebooks in boxes, confiscated the paintings and books." Victor retracted his fingers from his mouth. "Then they barged into my apartment and took my laptop. They fucking knew what they were looking for."

"You didn't ask why?" Anabel said. She and Alida had come to the living room. Alida's eyes were welling up with tears.

Victor raised his own eyes in her direction. "Of course I did. One of them said they were aware of my record and would take me in if I interfered. Dad told me to stay put and shut my mouth. I've never seen him so serious."

"Did he tell you anything else?" Serguey said.

"When they shoved him into the car, he mouthed that I should call Mario."

"Mario?"

"Dad's friend. The dramaturge."

"I met him last night," Serguey said. "Why him?"

Victor sighed, embarrassed by his answer. "I don't know."

Anabel asked, "Do you have any idea what your dad might have done?"

Victor shook his head.

"Maybe it has to do with the play," Alida said, her voice shaking.

"I doubt it," Serguey said. "The Department of Culture would've been involved." They were all standing stiffly, arms close to their own bodies, hands near their mouths. They might as well have been at a hospital's waiting room, a loved one down the hall undergoing a high-risk emergency procedure.

Victor stared expectantly at Serguey. "What do we do?"

Serguey felt his brother's gaze and those of his wife and sister-in-law fixed on him. He thought about his father, about where they might take him, what they might do to him.

"Serguey . . ." Anabel said.

Her voice sounded like a demand, like an admonishment for his hesitation. "Did you call Mario?" he asked Victor.

"With what number? They took *everything*, including Dad's phone book. I don't think he realized it when he told me to call the guy."

"Can't Serguey call someone?" Alida asked her sister.

Anabel looked at him. "Can you?"

Victor said, "I wouldn't have come here if I had somewhere else to turn."

"You did the right thing," Anabel said, giving Victor a reassuring nod.

Serguey resented her assumption, considering Felipe's arrest could cause problems for Serguey at the Ministry. Mostly, he resented everyone's belief that they could depend on him to call someone and magically solve the problem.

Victor bobbed his head as if he were sitting in a rocking chair. "If you knew the details of my record, then you'd understand why I can't go around asking questions."

Serguey glared at him. "Oh, I know everything about your record."

Victor stood. The rim of his nostrils contracted as he squinted. "What's that supposed to mean?"

"It means I know everything about your record."

"Did Dad tell you—"

"Victor," Anabel said, grasping his shoulder. "Relax."

Victor faced her. "You know, it makes sense that your husband would study law. All he does is judge people. Here I was thinking he could use that knowledge to help his own family. He never gave a shit, so why would he start now?" Victor moved toward the door. Holding on to the knob, he said, "I'm sorry for bringing you *upsetting* news. I'll figure out what to do about Dad. I'm sure you'll hear what's going on through the grapevine."

And with that he was gone.

Anabel gaped at Serguey, blinking as if her eyelids could form words. "Don't you let him go."

Serguey stood silent, his hands balled into fists. His neck was hot, his chest heaving. His voice, however, was low and deliberate: "He's very good at it."

"At what?"

"Making it seem like it's someone else's fault." He gave Anabel a look of condescension. "Making people take his side."

"It's not about him. It's about your father."

"It's not that simple. I can get in trouble at the Ministry. I have to consider—"

"You do what you have to do." Anabel stepped away from him and hugged her sister. "We'll deal with the consequences."

"I'm really sorry," Alida said to no one in particular.

That snapped him out of his anger. He nodded nervously at her. The sisters walked slowly down the hall.

Serguey threw himself on a chair by the balcony entrance. The towel that Alida had draped over herself suddenly fell, and she bent down to pick it up. He was unmoved by her fine skin, her firm thighs, the strange familiarity of her body. He extended his hand to the rotary phone on the circular table between him and the sofa and dialed Gimenez's number. He cleared his throat, humming to himself as he had seen actors do before taking the stage and as he now always did before a presentation at work.

CHAPTER 3

His boss's home was a handful of blocks past Mella Theater, on the eighteenth floor of a modern white building, its pristine exterior not yet sullied by the city's soiled air. The balconies, for distinguishable flair, had been painted bright orange. The elevator rails always looked polished, the floors mopped to a shine. According to Gimenez, there was a mutual understanding between the residents that the common areas must remain clean. This had stood out to Serguey, who was used to collective disdain even in his own building. Getting an apartment in such an exclusive location, the doctor claimed, was quite a process, unless you had a recognizable family name. Reputable television actors, a museum director, the Transportation Minister's oldest daughter—these were Gimenez's neighbors, whose homes Serguey had to pass on the way to ask for help.

The lobby was empty as he waited for the elevator. He was surrounded by an understated chemical odor, remainders of the kind of cleaning products his and Anabel's family never had access to. The elevator doors gaped with a soft groan. He stepped in and pressed the corresponding button. The doors had begun their slide when another man stuck his arm in. He stood next to Serguey, expecting him to select the floor.

"Which one is it?" Serguey said, skipping formalities.

The man shook his head in appreciation. "Fifteenth." He had a perfectly cropped beard, as if meticulously clipped with a tiny scissor. His hair, with sporadic strips of gray near the sideburns, was parted to one side. The doors shut, and Serguey could smell cologne, which, for some reason, he linked to the color green.

"You've been running?" the man asked.

Serguey felt a sudden chill on his face, where sweat had accumulated. "I walked here."

The man lifted his hand toward Serguey's neck, a gold-plated watch sticking to his furry wrist. "You're going to ruin your collar."

Serguey didn't bother to look at it. "The wife will take care of it." He had learned at the Ministry that poise and authority always went over well with men of power.

The man smiled, and Serguey noticed he had feminine lips. "Do you live in the building?"

A cunning question. Gimenez could recite the names of all the residents. No way this man, concerned about a perspiring intruder, didn't know them as well. "I'm here to see Dr. Gimenez."

"Ah. Tell him Carlos says hi. I haven't bumped into him for a couple of weeks." The man got off the elevator shortly after, the scent of his cologne staying behind, out-welcoming its stay.

Serguey began to feel nauseated, his chest tightened by the upward movement of the elevator, but was relieved the moment he exited and the odorless air of the eighteenth floor hallway greeted him.

He knocked on Gimenez's door, which the doctor opened with a courteous smile. A green kitchen towel was draped over his left shoulder. He motioned Serguey in. "Follow me to the dining room," he said. "I've got something on the stove."

He had insisted on the phone that they speak in person before getting into details. Just like Felipe, his boss had a proclivity for the spectacle that is face-to-face human interaction.

Serguey stepped through the lavishly furnished living room—hand-carved wooden chairs and a glossy leather sofa, none of which seemed meant to be sat on and which Serguey was always afraid to touch, and three exotically stenciled vases on a glass shelf, which Gimenez asserted were from Egypt (except for the one instance when Serguey had caught him telling a superior in his office that they were from Morocco). He walked past framed degrees and diplomas set at various heights along the hall, snaking like a stream of musical notes that announced your impending arrival at the dining area. The layout was similar to Serguey's apartment, though more spacious and elegantly adorned. A long wooden table stood in the middle of the room, decorated by a basket of artificial fruit, a gift from a Canadian ambassador.

"He knew our fruits are better than theirs," Gimenez had told Serguey, "so he gave me something that looks better than ours."

An old cupboard with sliding glass cabinet doors rose against the wall. A set of sparkling wine glasses, assorted in color, lay arranged like museum pieces inside it.

The last time Serguey had visited, the apartment was filled with coworkers, a get-together organized by Gimenez to celebrate his birthday. In an unforgettable night (now considered legendary at the Ministry), he had commanded everyone to stand behind their assigned chairs and sit simultaneously at the imperious wave of his hand. He drunkenly professed his love for Italian women as the night wore on and called Serguey his "son" with a sniffle as a parting note.

The inviting smell of butter and garlic on fresh seafood wafted from the kitchen. Serguey watched Gimenez stirring a big pot of yellow rice. Despite the man's age, his hair was still brown and thick. His posture and movements, like Felipe's, rivaled those of a younger person.

"Take a seat," Gimenez said, his back to Serguey. "You don't mind if we speak like this until the food's ready, do you?"

"Not at all." Serguey pulled out a chair.

"So what's the matter? You sounded worried when you called."

"It's my father. He's been arrested."

Gimenez tossed the kitchen towel from one shoulder to the other, like swatting at a fly. He tapped the large spoon on the edge of the pot, set it down on the counter, and turned around. "I'm sorry, Serguey. *That* you should've told me on the phone."

"I wasn't sure . . . it's a very private matter."

"I understand. I'm glad you came to see me. Has he been charged?"

"I'm not clear about it yet. I don't even know where they took him."

Gimenez wiped his hands on the towel and threw his weight against the doorframe. "That shouldn't be difficult to find out."

"I considered going to Section twenty-one in Marianao, to the State Security building."

"They won't tell you anything. If you get too nosy or confrontational, they'll throw you in a cell. Those guys don't mess around."

"That's why I came to you."

Gimenez shifted his body so that his spine aligned with the frame. His faraway gaze, a thinking man's veneer, gave Serguey hope: his boss was interested.

"Why do you think they arrested him? Your father's a playwright, correct?"

"Used to be. He's a director now."

"Ah, yes."

"Well, as I said, the details are a bit blurry. My brother was the only one present when they came for him."

"Victor, right?" Gimenez caressed his own chin, committing to a full display of clout. "He's the one who's been in jail."

Feebly, Serguey nodded.

"I'll make some calls tonight, when people are home. I'm friends with some of the guys on the fifth floor at the Ministry, in the State Security wing. I'll see what I'm able to find out, and I'll give you a call. You can take the day off tomorrow. Try to meet with your old man. Unless . . ."

"Unless it's political." Serguey figured it was best to get it out of the way, before it began festering, before it became like a curse no one wanted to speak out loud.

"That would complicate things." Gimenez pushed himself off the doorframe. "But you should cross that bridge when you get there. Maybe they just want to interview him."

"With State Security handling it?"

"It's possible. Has your father ever been in trouble?"

"No. His work doesn't involve politics."

"I see."

"He's well respected."

"Right, *El Escenario*," Gimenez said with a reserved smile.

Serguey had told him about the article in passing, but Gimenez was bound to log these kinds of details. Convert them into weapons, he might've said, as good litigators should. He knew damn well that Felipe was a director, just like he remembered that Victor had been in jail. Serguey stared at the table, preferring not to acknowledge his boss's subtle derision of his family. He had never touted them; he perhaps had even complained about them in the past to share in the inconsequential smugness of the office. But his father and brother as subjects of wry mockery now bothered him.

"Do you want a drink?" Gimenez asked.

Serguey hesitated. "Sure."

His boss retrieved a bottle of cognac from the bottom of the cupboard and two glasses from the top. "Got this in Marseilles," he said, pouring a glass for Serguey, the other for himself. "Anyway, if the charges are serious, if they're political in nature, don't dig too deep. Be certain you're standing on solid ground. I'm aware he's your father, but one false step and your career could be over."

Serguey let a flood of cognac slither down his throat, embracing the sting in his nose and eyes.

"You're very talented, Serguey, and you have Anabel to worry about. What does she think?"

"About what?"

"About what happened."

"She's distraught."

"That's not what I'm asking."

Serguey considered lying, withholding. Coworkers once warned him (at the time, he figured it was out of jealousy) that Gimenez had fired two previous protégés: one for showing up unprepared to a meeting and embarrassing him, the other for failing to disclose that an uncle had successfully processed the paperwork to get him to the United States. The latter, the coworkers said, saw his trip delayed six months, having to get by without a job, as a result of a Gimenez's phone call. Should he admit that Anabel was willing to risk Serguey's job, their status? Should he give his boss reasons to doubt him? Those protégés, of course, hadn't lived in the apartment. Neither of them, as far as he knew, had been called "son."

"Family comes first," he finally said, refusing to betray his wife.

Gimenez drank his cognac. "You have a brave woman by your side. But it is our job to be lawyers, not heroes." He grabbed the bottle and offered a refill. Serguey declined. He poured more for himself. "However, I got to where I am in part because of my family, so I know what Anabel means."

"I'm going to help my father," Serguey said, infusing authority into his words.

"I understand." Gimenez gulped down half his glass, then said, "When I was your age, things were different. Back then, if your father's issue had been political, he would have no shot. Today the game is different. Between you and me, it's very winnable, but you need connections and luck."

"My brother thinks I have connections." Serguey stared at his glass. "I have you, but not much else."

Gimenez chuckled. His cheeks and forehead were smudged by the rosy hue of mild inebriation. "I'm no connection, believe me. I'm a washed-up attorney with a cushy job. Go back to your brother. Ask him who he knows."

Serguey resisted a grimace. "Victor knows delinquents." He had the feeling of having said something similar about Victor before.

"I know your brother is a sore subject, but family comes first, right? You can't be prideful if you really want to do something for your father. I'm still going to make my calls and get back to you. I'll be reaching you on your landline, so make sure you're home."

Serguey thanked him, tapping his glass as if he were flicking a marble.

"Now, have lunch with me," his boss said. "I'll give you some food to take with you, that way Anabel won't have to cook today."

"I really should go. I'll get something on the way home."

"A quick lunch. You can tell me more about your father. I have no one I can reach until later today. I don't like calling people at work. You don't know who's listening. Besides, if you show up too soon, they won't let you see him." Gimenez went to the kitchen. He brought out plates and silverware and placed them on the table in an almost ceremonious way.

"Let me give you a hand," Serguey said.

"Nonsense," Gimenez said. "You're the guest."

CHAPTER 4

The trip back to his apartment offered no consolation. With all the uncertainty, he couldn't calculate or strategize. There was no argument or concrete plan to put into practice, no list of scenarios and he could logically consider. What Serguey had was a sensation akin to fear incessantly gnawing at the walls of his stomach. There was frustration, teetering between calamity and self-pity. What was haunting him was merely abstract, a heavy dose of *Why me? Why us?* As if the universe had anything to do with it.

Mostly, he felt sorry for his father. His illustrious career—his life as he had built it—could be over. At this very moment Felipe could be in a dark cell, bloodied and beaten, and here Serguey was, feeling sorry for himself, hanging on to his mentor's goodwill, to the promise of a phone call that wouldn't be made for hours. A stain on his record, as this had a chance of becoming, could keep Serguey from ever achieving Gimenez-like status. Regardless of what Anabel said, whatever she might convince herself of, the ramifications for them were unavoidable: the son of a political prisoner had to be doubly patriotic in a country where ideals superseded the individual, where the red on the flag superseded the red in your blood.

Serguey chose the sidewalk reached by sunlight at this hour. It would have been a perfect day to spend at the beach. It would have been a perfect day if Victor hadn't knocked on the door. Now he would have to go see his brother, no matter what news Gimenez's call brought.

On Paseo Avenue, he slowed his pace toward an old lady who regularly sat on a wooden chair selling roses and sunflowers out of a grungy bucket. She liked to grin, as if proud of her missing teeth, at anyone who examined the flowers for more than a second, especially tourists whose empathy occasionally led them to overpay. Serguey had never heard the woman speak, though he didn't think she was a mute. Was it a sales strategy? If she had been a character in one of Felipe's plays, he might have written that slinging words with her tongue—eroded by years of regrettable speech—could drain years from her waning life. Maybe this was what the occasional tourist saw, or the local men who dropped change in her hand while crooning her name, which now escaped Serguey. (If he had been asked to guess, a gun pressed to his temple, he would've called her Lazara.)

He and Anabel had strolled by her many times, saluting with what they thought were gracious glances. They hadn't bought a flower, and as he lingered now by the bucket, he was embarrassed. The woman exhibited her epic smile, and all of sudden Serguey felt as if he were staring at an Orisha in the flesh, willing to forgive him for his past transgressions. (Felipe might have written this, too.) Serguey didn't believe in saints or gods, but if help from the beyond was somehow possible, if karma was real—if in fact the universe had something to do with what was happening—surrendering to the irrationality of the moment couldn't hurt. He fished out his wallet and picked half a dozen roses. He handed the money to the lady. She folded it into a tattered, zippered handbag, which she then placed inside her bra, above her low-hanging breasts. Serguey didn't want the flowers for himself or Anabel. Roses would go unnoticed on a day like today. His purchase, as he intended it, was an act of goodness toward the old woman, whose skin was like a burnt raisin and whose income, judging by the floppy flowers, barely fed her. The roses were an offering, so he gave them back.

As if expecting them all along, the lady grabbed the thornless stems and, grinning again, plopped them into the bucket.

When Serguey arrived at his building, he was met by a handwritten sign on the elevator's door: broken. please use staircase.

Was life mocking him? Should he have kept the roses?

He found Victor sitting on the steps leading to his floor. He almost laughed, as if everything on this day had been a hilariously elaborate set-up.

"What's this?" he asked, noticing dismay on his brother's face.

"I just couldn't go back to the house."

"Why are you out here? Anabel didn't let you in?"

"I knocked and no one answered. Your neighbor said she saw them leave." Victor rubbed his right knuckles repeatedly in the palm of his left hand. He'd done this as a child whenever he was anxious, whenever his mischief was in danger of being discovered. "Did you find anything out?"

"My boss is going to call. We might not hear from him until tonight."

"Can't we go to someone else? Maybe we can check some prisons and police stations."

"Victor, if I'm going to help, I'm doing it my way. Chances are we might not be able to see Dad for a while."

His brother thrust his hands into his pockets. "I get it. We have to be patient."

"We have to be smart."

Victor looked down at the stairs, then at Serguey. "Do you mind if I stay until your boss contacts you?"

"Come on," Serguey said.

The living room and balcony were empty. Serguey called out Anabel's name to no response. He rushed down the hall, incensed by the thought that the sisters had inexplicably left with Manny. Serguey exhaled when he saw Anabel's beach bag sitting on their bed, her two-piece bathing suit bunched next to it.

She'd left a note on the kitchen table:

I'm taking my sister to her place. We'll talk to her roommates to see what they know. One of them is an actor in your father's play. I decided not to call your cell phone just in case. Be back soon. Love, Anabel.

Victor read the note over his brother's shoulder. "That's a good idea, not calling. That's why I came in person."

"This isn't East Germany," Serguey said. "We aren't dealing with the Stasi."

"How do you know they're not listening?"

He dismissed Victor's insinuation, crumpling the note.

Victor snatched a chair and sat. His nail biting and knuckle rubbing had been replaced by a strange calm. "I've been doing some thinking," he said, "and with Dad, this could be political."

"Why do you say that?" Serguey said.

"He's always having people over at the house."

"He's done that since we were kids."

"Yeah, but we knew those guys. Stuck-up artists talking about art and shit. Now I don't know half the people who walk in. Sometimes Dad asks me if I'm going to be around. I didn't make much of it until today. I just thought he wanted space to work on his plays."

"He never told you anything about those people?"

"The old man and I live in different worlds," Victor said. "My apartment's separate from the rest of the house. What the fuck are we going to talk about? I mostly let him do his thing. It's his house, and I'm always out and about anyway. I usually don't even bring women to my place, which is a pain in the ass. I have to borrow Kiko's guest room for a few hours, and that asshole listens through the wall. I know it."

Serguey rolled his cell phone between his palms like an oversized die. "I thought you were more involved with Dad's projects. You gave him money for *Electra Garrigó*, didn't you?"

"I did, but I wasn't *involved*. I heard him talk about not having funds for a big prop or something. He seemed like he really needed it. I had fifteen dollars with me, and I offered them. I made it sound like a big deal last night to mess with you. Anyway, Dad usually turns down stuff like that from me, but he took it this time. He gave the money to a guy who was there. Don't know his name. I think he was a carpenter."

"Goddamn it, Victor."

Victor shuffled Anabel's note against the table's surface like sandpaper on ragged wood. "I'm embarrassed about the whole thing, okay? I know I'm supposed to be aware of what's going on. I'm supposed to protect Dad and give a shit all the time."

Serguey tried seizing the note from his brother. "That's not exactly what—"

Victor slid the note closer to his body. "I have my own life. I just fucked up. People know when they fuck up."

Serguey desisted. "I know, I didn't—"

"I don't need you to judge me. You think it's easy for me to come here and ask for help? I'm used to solving things myself."

Serguey skipped a few responses that came to mind. He simply said, "Dad was taken. That's all that matters. Forget the rest." He gave Victor a moment to speak further, but he appeared satisfied.

Serguey dialed Anabel's number.

Victor shook his head. "You're still going to call, after she told you not to?"

"She didn't say not to. And they should've stayed here. It's safer."

Anabel didn't pick up. Frustrated, Serguey dropped the phone on the table.

"She's smart," Victor said, leaving the note next to it and walking away to the living room.

Serguey thought about texting her, but he decided that, at this point, he might as well wait. He had to resign himself to a lack of control over the circumstances. He prepared some linden tea, grabbed two glasses from an overhead shelf, and stirred two teaspoons of brown sugar into each glass. He listened absentmindedly to the clinking of the spoon. He realized that the gravity of his father's arrest hadn't truly affected him. A son should've been devastated, terrified, irate. He hadn't instinctively rushed to the nearest police station, as Victor had suggested, or the State Security offices, as he had contemplated. He wanted to believe there was no reason to panic, not until Gimenez's call. Worst-case scenario, he thought, they shut down the play and ban Felipe from directing on a big stage again. Men of his father's prestige rarely went to prison. The government seemed to know that stripping artists of their work—of their voice, as Felipe referred to it—was punishment enough.

Serguey saw his brother standing on the balcony, watching the city. He was wearing a pair of Ecko Unltd jeans, white Adidas sneakers, and a Nike T-shirt. He looked like so many young men in Havana, men who prided themselves in the brands stamped on their clothes, their spiky, overly gelled hair, the cell phones clipped to their belts, as if these things signified a superior ability or advantaged position—the mark of a shrewd mind, *con chispa*, or family in another country, *en el yuma*. Or both.

The sun, now somewhere behind the building, wasn't as oppressive as it had been in the morning. The brothers sat in the balcony holding their respective glasses, which were dripping from the humidity.

Victor sipped his tea and frowned. "You should've put some rum in this."

"I try not to drink alcohol."

"You mean to tell me you have no beer in this house? No Havana Club? They have to give them out like bread at your job."

Serguey drank his tea slowly.

Victor chuckled. "You're worse than Dad."

"What do you mean?"

"You've got his smug attitude. But even the old man drinks beer and tells dirty jokes now and then. You're too fucking uptight."

"I don't think of it as uptight." Serguey finished his tea and rested the glass on a narrow patio table, a gift from Gimenez.

"What do you call it?"

Serguey raised his eyebrows. "Mature? Serious?"

"Boring, conceited, out of touch." Victor delivered the words with an emphatic rhythm. He meant each one, carefully selected, and he wasn't finished: "How does Anabel put up with it?"

Serguey allowed an instant of silence to settle between them. It was hard to deny his condescension toward the world Victor knew. Did his brother see it as contempt? For some time now, Serguey had been able to elude many of the gritty, dispiriting aspects of life in Cuba. There was the hunger and sickness and persecution, the "aspirin to cure everything" and "only pair of shoes" and "inner tube rafts" reality of it, which was no longer *his* reality. There was the deadpan bureaucracy, which he regularly circumvented thanks to his connections, and the endless imperialism-bashing speeches and stodgy political discussions, which he avoided by watching films and American television shows on his DVD player. There was a pervasive, deeply entrenched lack of hope in Havana. He recalled perceiving it in his teenage years, when the Special Period was at its worst. This attitude had not only prevailed, but it had gained strength. Victor was closer to it. He saw it and lived it every day. Serguey didn't have to, not from this apartment, not in the places he and Anabel frequented thanks to Gimenez. He no longer had to buy pizza from government establishments or grungy street vendors—as Felipe had done for him and Victor—when his boss often took him to fancier lunches near the Ministry. He could treat the flower lady on Paseo Avenue as an ornament, like most tourists did, while in Victor's neck of the woods she would be a social case, the neighbors' responsibility. He didn't have to hop on the back of some street hustler's motorcycle, make a living selling stolen goods in the black market like his brother. Serguey's ambitions, particularly after he had met Gimenez, were all branched from a singular goal: to remove himself from the Cuba most people knew, the Cuba in which he'd grown up, in which his father and brother still lived. He wanted to join his mentor's Cuba, to have it be his. He'd begun to get a damn good taste, and now he wanted to remain.

"If you don't like the tea," he finally told his brother, "don't drink it. Linden calms me when I'm nervous."

He couldn't bring himself to drop his armor and shield, not after years of contention. Why give Victor the pleasure of highlighting his hypocrisy? Why let himself be openly criticized, when his brother had always shown contempt for his accomplishments, an unwillingness to respect his job, to appreciate what he and Anabel had built together? It was Victor asking him for help, not the other way around. Serguey was the one with the connections, with the means to make a difference. He was the one in the fortunate position, with the imminent ability to have the city at his disposal.

And why should he negate what he'd worked so hard to achieve? Wasn't that what most Cubans aspired to: some kind of relief from the drudgery and scarcity of communist life? He had chosen to see Havana for its beauty and enduring heartbeat: Spanish fortresses and lighthouses turned into museums; centuries-old churches and cathedrals; wrought iron gates and fences encasing colonial-era houses and courtyards; cobblestone roads leading to open plazas or cul-de-sacs, large balconies and eerie lampposts watching you along the way. There was a tropical, communal spirit that buzzed in the parks of El Vedado, in Old Havana's narrow streets, at bodegas and bus stops in each municipality, and in almost every inch of sun-drenched shoreline during the summer. There were theater, film, and book festivals; African-themed music and costumes; children flying kites and *chiringas* from rooftops; old men fishing along the esplanade or playing dominoes on street corners; the unbearably loud, smoke-spewing trucks carrying resilient commuters; the ringing of bicycle bells as workers sped into and away from roundabouts and hurried home.

He didn't dare paint this picture to Victor, however. His brother's response would be swift: Havana was more than a romanticized collection of historical and cultural images. Serguey wouldn't argue against this point, but he could dispute there was nothing wrong with viewing the city this way, and more importantly, that the lifestyle he had started to attain was its own form of survival. It was a triumph, in fact, deserving of respect and yes, even praise, not derision or envy or spite. It was proof that the system, for all its flaws, could produce success stories.

In admirable form, Victor chugged down the entire contents of his glass, then forced a burp. "Still tastes like crap," he griped, putting the empty glass on the balcony's ledge.

Serguey watched the glass as if it were a toddler at the edge of a pool. "Be careful."

"What?"

"You'll knock it over."

"See, that's what I'm talking about." Victor surveyed the street from above. "There's nobody down there. This neighborhood's dead."

"You'll hurt somebody."

"And they'll put me away for good."

"Give me the glass."

"What if I throw it? You afraid your neighbors will file a complaint?"

Serguey jolted from his seat in anticipation. The pugilist in his brother was getting ready to unleash a barrage. "Victor, give me the glass."

Victor grabbed it and stretched his arm into the open air. "It'll just be a splash."

"Don't you dare!"

"Just a little splash."

Serguey seized Victor's wrist.

Victor laughed wildly, surrendering the glass. "You're one sad human being."

Serguey ground his teeth, showed the glass to his brother as if it were a rock, and said, "I should smash it on your head."

Victor stopped smiling. His top lip quivered with rage. He got close to his brother's face, their warm breaths daring each other. "What I hate most about you is that, no matter what you say, you don't have the balls to do it."

The sound of jiggling keys and a turning lock interrupted them. Serguey moved away from Victor. The door opened, and Anabel entered.

Serguey approached his wife and kissed her. "How's Alida?"

Anabel chucked her bag on the center table. "She's more composed now. I convinced her not to tell anything to Mom and Dad. I don't want them worrying."

"Of course."

"What did Gimenez say?"

"He's calling tonight. Victor didn't go home, as you can see."

His brother waved from the balcony.

"Are you staying for dinner?" Anabel asked him, massaging her temples.

"Are you inviting?"

Serguey said, "Anabel, I don't think—"

She cut him off: "This isn't the time, okay?"

"All right. Did you find anything out?"

"The actors are as clueless as we are. Alida's roommate seemed really scared. They don't know if this is going to wreck their careers. They're also really worried about your father."

"I'm sure they are."

"Don't be cynical, Serguey. Alida cares, and I'm sure her friends do too."

"I know she does. That's not what I meant." Serguey looked toward the balcony. Victor was leaning against the railing, his back to them. "You should've called me," he told Anabel, his voice hushed.

She sighed. "I was just trying to be careful."

"Don't listen to him, Anabel," Victor shouted without turning. "You're smart."

Anabel flashed a halfhearted smile. She kissed Serguey, tapped his chest, and took the glasses from him. She dipped her nose into one of them. "You gave your brother tea?"

Victor's voice called out: "He's a sadist!"

❦ ❧ ❦

Serguey assisted Anabel as she reheated Gimenez's paella in a pot. She added more rice, red peppers, and canned sausages Serguey had been given by the stockroom supervisor at work. She sautéed *habichuelas* and fried a few plantain slices. Their generous food supply was also a result of his boss's kindness. Gimenez never hesitated to let Serguey get his hands on goods primarily allotted to supervisors at the Ministry. Serguey often carried boxes and bags to Gimenez's car, already aware of what portions his boss had proffered him.

Victor was napping on the sofa, his snores audible from the kitchen.

"How's he holding up?" Anabel said.

"Not sure." Serguey scooped plantains out of the frying pan with a metal skimmer. "He's edgier than usual, but so am I."

"You're the one who needs to keep a cool head."

"He's not a child, Anabel." Serguey dug out the last two pieces of fried plantains too brusquely, hot oil dribbling onto his hand. "Damn it!" he cried. The plantains flew off the skimmer, ricocheted off his pants, and stuck like snails to the floor.

"Neither are you," said Anabel. She fetched an ice cube from the freezer and wrapped it with a dishcloth. "Keep this against the burn. Let me finish here. Go lie down for a few minutes."

"I'm fine. Let me clean up."

"Go to the bedroom, please. And change your pants. Sprinkle some talcum powder on the grease stains."

Serguey didn't want to argue with his wife in front of his brother. He didn't want to give the impression that there might be cracks in their relationship, especially since, to his mind, this wasn't the case. He left the kitchen in silence, used the talcum powder as she had asked, and waited in bed, eyes shut, until she came to get him.

"Go wake your brother," she said, "and tell him we're eating in the living room, so you can be near the phone."

They used faded doilies Anabel had inherited from her grandmother to hold the plates. She and Serguey ate with forks. Victor ate with a spoon, chewing like a ravenous dog.

"Love what you did with the rice," he said to Anabel, his mouth full.

Anabel said, "The good stuff came from Serguey's supervisor."

"People in high places." Victor swallowed vigorously and quaffed his water.

Serguey put on a scowl, disgusted. "Dad could never get him to close his mouth. He's never had manners."

"I like to savor everything. Anabel's a wonderful cook. It isn't my fault."

Serguey regarded his own plate for what felt like a long time before he took the next bite.

After dinner, Victor and Anabel washed the dishes. Serguey waited by the phone, growing impatient. Outside the apartment, dusk was graining into night. Specks of white and yellow lights from the hotels hung statically in midair. They were a contrast to the unlit windows of the smaller residential buildings, windows that seemed, in an alluringly bizarre way, like hollow sockets on an ancient face. Serguey considered the possibility that Gimenez might not call. Victor would give him the insufferable "I told you so." Their inactivity, disguised as patience, could go from wise to egregious in an instant.

Victor's exalted voice and what he perceived to be his Anabel's giggles mingled with the clanking of metal and porcelain. The water rushing through the faucet and spiraling into the drain muffled their words. Serguey turned on the radio, which stood behind the phone. Industriales had lost their game, suffered a 9–2 pounding to last place Sancti Spiritus. He had made the right decision not following them this season. He lowered the volume and for an instant wished that Alida were present. She didn't know him well enough not to have faith in him as a problem-solver, as a family leader. He could comfort her. They could talk baseball and ballet and acting. Anabel and Victor's conversation—its chirpy intimacy fueling Serguey's envy of his brother's talent for charm—could become harmless white noise. Instead, he was holed up, chained by inertia, gradually recognizing that they might ultimately fail their father, that Victor's cheerful attitude and his own unwillingness to act might sooner or later reveal that they cared about Felipe only so much.

The images Serguey had been trying to suppress the entire day came at him in excruciating succession: his father in the back of a car, a gun aimed at his chest, being driven to a prison in another province; his father crying, pleading, or worse, fighting back and losing, again and again. Maybe the system had already swallowed him up into that growing darkness Serguey had labored so fervently to escape. He looked through the sliding doors at the night sky, dusky and indeterminate. The phone sat beside him, silent and useless. He was suddenly convinced that this day had established the makings of a disaster.

In the brief time he'd worked as a defense attorney, prior to Gimenez's recruitment, Serguey had listened to more experienced lawyers, men he respected—red-eyed, half-inebriated, with loose ties barely hanging from their shirts—talk about clients who'd been abused and raped, their families threatened and shamed. One of the lawyers had said, "In Cuba, the music is so amped up, no one hears the screams." At the time, Serguey had tuned out all of it. For a Cuban lawyer wishing to keep his sanity, the absence of first-hand experience was sufficient reason to reject the peripheral truth of his own practice. However, words that he had once dismissed as exaggeration now made him shudder. He'd been nudging that volume louder and louder.

He pressed his hands into the cushions of his sofa and watched their impressions dissolve. The apartment was silent, the water no longer running. He began to stand, but he heard Anabel laugh and Victor say, "What an asshole!" They were walking toward the living room.

As he sat back down, the phone rang. He picked it up.

"Good or bad news first?" Gimenez said.

"The good news."

"He's still in Havana. Calderas Prison. The bad news, it's political."

Serguey's eyesight blurred. He felt as if a rock had been stuck in his throat. "What's the charge?" he choked out.

Victor and Anabel huddled close to him, straining to hear Gimenez's voice. Serguey raised his hand, telling them to retreat.

"I don't have many specifics," Gimenez said. "I was told that you should go to the prison tomorrow morning. You probably won't see him, but at least they can give you a date and time. There's an interview process. That's what they're calling it. The guy you want to speak to is José Manuel Montalvo. He's a retired colonel who works for State Security. He was described to me as 'not very bright, but not unreasonable.' That's all I got. I'm giving you an indefinite leave so you can take care of this."

Lawyers under contract at the Ministry didn't get indefinite leaves. If Felipe was indeed a political prisoner, he was now like a disease-carrying patient whose family had to be corralled, observed.

"Am I fired?" Serguey asked.

"We'll talk about it later," Gimenez said. "For now, I have to ask that you please keep my name out of this."

"Thank you, Roberto." The name sounded awkward in Serguey's tongue. "For the food as well. Anabel enjoyed it."

"I'm glad. Good night."

Serguey hung up. He looked up at Anabel and Victor. "They have him at

Calderas. It's political, so they won't let us see him tonight. We'll go tomorrow morning."

Victor scratched his head. "Not as bad as the Eastern Combine, but Calderas sucks. I met someone who did ten years there. He went crazy."

"What do you mean 'political'?" Anabel asked Serguey.

"It means they want to fuck with him," Victor said.

"Or that he did something," Serguey said.

Victor started to pace, rubbing his knuckles. "They're messing with him."

"It makes no difference."

"He's fucked. *We* are fucked."

Anabel hugged Serguey.

He waited for her to let go, then stepped toward the balcony, gazing down at the city below. He was searching for inspiration, something outside the astringent air in the apartment, the buzzing of Gimenez's voice in his eardrum.

"If it's the one honorable thing I do in my life," he said to himself, "I'm going to get him out."

He had so little faith in his words, he had to repeat them.

CHAPTER 5

The bubbling and spurting had ceased, the coffee already served by the time Serguey and Victor went to the kitchen. Serguey could sense the cumbrance of the newly-formed bags under his eyes as he stared at the dark liquid. He had tossed in his bed, trapped in a purgatory between sleep and alertness for most of the night. He had gone to the bathroom twice, though he didn't really need to. His appearance in the mirror was worse the second time. He had splashed water on his face, attempting to wake himself, but his body moved as if loaded with drugs, his mind skipping like a record: it's over, it's over, and he could do nothing else but return to the bed.

"I'm sorry if the coffee tastes funny," Anabel said. She was standing barefoot by the stove, wearing a sunflower-patterned nightgown. "Did Serguey's underwear fit you fine?" she asked Victor.

Victor sipped his coffee. "They're uncomfortable." The bravado was gone from his tone. "Not the best thing for a day like today, but I guess I have no choice."

Serguey blew into his cup and stirred it carefully.

Anabel said to Victor, "Let your brother handle things, okay?"

"Yes, ma'am."

"I mean it. If he ends up in trouble because of you, you're going to deal with me."

Victor drank all his coffee and gave the cup back to her. "He's the lawyer."

Serguey scoffed. "Which in this case means exactly nothing."

Anabel pushed her lips to Serguey's stubbled cheek. "You should be on your way already."

He drew her close and kissed her mouth. "I'll see you soon."

Serguey hadn't asked anyone for a ride. The authorities could interpret a mere favor as collusion, and what assurance did he have that a person involved in helping him wouldn't crack under the pressure of a system willing to punish the slightest sign of dissent?

He and Victor had half a century of history working against them.

With no car at their disposal, they had to take two buses. Brimming with morning commuters, the second bus grinded to a halt a handful of stops before their destination. People congregated outside by the door, jeering and hissing. The driver, slack-faced, checked behind the wheels. Eventually he waved his hat and told the crowd the vehicle was out for the count. People converged on him, one man telling him that he was a mechanic. The driver opened the rear hatch. The parts, tubes, and cables were coated by smut, some of it so black that it gave the appearance of charring, as if the bus had been on fire. The mechanic tinkered with some cables and clicked his tongue.

"Burnt all the way through," he said. "Ride's over, people."

The brothers walked on an empty road, far enough from both the city and the sea for foreign investors and the government to bypass development. Nearly three desolate kilometers later, they were at the prison's entrance. The white walls of the complex had lost their luster. The cylinder-wrought bars casing the windows had corroded like bad plumbing. The front gate and name of the prison, however, were freshly painted—the letters slanted and curved, as if handwritten. The surrounding streets were barren, blanketed with dust and rocks. The remnants of two adjacent buildings had been picked apart, used for basic renovations and repairs, a common practice in Havana. It was as if the area had been leveled and Calderas had survived, proud of its sturdiness and scars. *The heartbreaking resilience of a neglected place*, Felipe had written in the last play he'd authored, referencing Havana. Serguey had never been inclined to revise the phrase, to change it for himself: it spoke for every weathered ounce of brick and mortar still standing in the city. What lay inside Calderas, that was another story. He had visited on several occasions as a defense attorney. On his last visit, he had ridden on a bicycle carrier, his briefcase nestled between him and the man who was pedaling—his client's good-hearted nephew.

Serguey presented his credentials to the guards at the gate and explained that his father was being held there. "I'm looking for Colonel Montalvo."

The guards patted him and Victor down. One of the men, sporting a fishbone-shaped scar on his forearm, frowned and said, "Go ahead, comrades."

At the sign-in desk, they provided their IDs and gave Felipe's name. They were required to fill out a form and be searched once more.

"Montalvo will see you now," the desk clerk said. "Officer Yenier here will escort you."

Serguey felt a growling in his stomach, but it actually made no sound. They followed the officer through a long corridor, opposite a group of cellblocks.

Serguey whispered to Victor, "Let me do the talking."

Victor closed his eyes and nodded.

A series of rectangular windows offered a passing view to the shabby courtyard below. The open space served as the prisoners' recreational area. The basketball boards and hoops were missing. All that was left were the cement posts spearing up, the tops slightly bent. Serguey had heard a story about an inmate who'd tried to hang himself from one of the posts, putting on a show in front of the entire complex. The guards did nothing but watch the man fail miserably. They were so amused that they didn't punish or isolate him. Instead they asked some of his fellow inmates to give him more shoelaces and encourage him to repeat the attempt, just for a laugh. Looking at the posts, Serguey saw that the angle at which the top of the structure bowed did not allow for any leverage. It was obvious that a rope or cord wouldn't hold without sliding down.

Montalvo's office was consistent with the rest of the prison. His desk and chairs were small and worn. The ceiling was in need of repair. Brown stains, smelling of tobacco, smattered the floor like squished roaches. A large photograph of Fidel and Che Guevara, both wearing berets and decked in military attire, hung from the wall. A pale Cuban flag curtained the window behind Montalvo, projecting shards of red, white, and blue over his head, like a kaleidoscopic halo. What was left of a cigar was jammed into the corner of the colonel's mouth. His hands were on the top of his head, allowing Serguey and Victor a view of the round sweat blots in his armpits. The escorting officer stood next to the colonel, his countenance grave as ragged stone. Just like the suicidal inmate with the shoelaces, Serguey surmised, they were putting on a show.

"How may I help you, comrades?" Montalvo asked, the cigar waggling in his mouth.

"We're here to see our father."

"You're Serguey, right?"

"Yes."

Montalvo grinned and shot a glance at the escorting officer. "He looks like a Serguey, doesn't he?"

Yenier remained unfazed.

The ex-colonel looked back at Serguey. "I'll get to the point. Your daddy's in big trouble. He pissed off people so high up, I'm still trying to get them out of my ass."

"What did he do?"

"The question is *why*. The only reason you and your brother were allowed in here is that we're hoping you'll tell us."

"We don't know anything," Victor said.

"I highly doubt it, but I respect the sentiment. I have a father too. Bastard used to hit me with a belt, but here I am, so he must have done something right."

Serguey said, "Colonel—"

"That was in another life. Call me Montalvo."

"I apologize. Montalvo, I'm a lawyer, so believe me, I know these are special circumstances. We would appreciate it immensely if you'd let us see our father. We're willing to cooperate in any way we can. We just want to make sure he's okay."

Montalvo put his feet down and his elbows on the desk. "I thought you'd be smarter than this. You've just implied there's a chance your daddy's not okay, that we've hurt him. I'm no lawyer, but what you just did can be interpreted as questioning state authority. You have no faith in the system? Hell, that almost makes you a counterrevolutionary!"

"That's not what he said," Victor put in.

Montalvo chuckled. "I'm surprised you're letting your brother talk."

"I'm asking for a favor," Serguey said. "You can jot me down as his lawyer. A routine visit. It can stay between us."

Montalvo again glimpsed at the escorting officer. "You see that? He's trying to build trust. He doesn't understand that not all military people are stupid. All right, you boys sit down."

Serguey and Victor hesitated.

The ex-colonel widened his eyes, and the brothers obeyed. He stood up, the tri-colored halo now shining around his shoulders and arms. "Felipe Blanco, to put it simply, is in deep shit. He's been an active participant in subversive activities for quite some time, and we have proof. The list of things he's going to be charged with makes *War and Peace* look like a pamphlet. He's not getting out any time soon. It's black and white. He fucked up."

Montalvo stopped, letting what he'd just said settle in. The weight of it overtook the room. Serguey had dealt with military men before, but never of Montalvo's rank, and not with such puny leverage to offset their authority. He stammered for a moment before Montalvo cut him off.

"Despite all this, you boys are in luck."

Serguey controlled his exhale, waiting for the obtuse but reasonable man Gimenez had described to take possession of the ex-colonel's body.

"For some reason," Montalvo said, loosening his features and inciting a dash of optimism that made Serguey stir in his chair, "I've been asked to make this black and white situation a little gray. If you cooperate, and by that I mean you tell me what you *really* know, we can make some considerations, maybe even exceptions."

"We don't know anything," Victor said, frustrated.

Montalvo looked at Serguey. "What's it going to be?"

"We don't know anything," he said, emboldened by his brother.

"Don't insult me," Montalvo said. "You don't want to piss off this State Security officer, believe me."

Serguey was frozen, without words. The thought gagged him further.

"You're an educated man," the ex-colonel added," so you should appreciate this. I had a detainee once—a writer, actually, kind of like your daddy—describe me as a veritable nightmare. Since then, I've been trying to live up to it."

Serguey had nothing to barter with the ex-colonel. He had no choice but to stand his ground. "We got nothing."

"Not a thing?"

"No."

"You sure?"

"Yes."

"All right." Montalvo went to Yenier and tapped him on the back. "Take these comrades to the front desk so they can be on their way. There you'll be told to come back in a month to visit your father, though by then he might be transferred to another province." He spread out his arms like a large bird approaching ground. "I'm at the mercy of the system I've devoted myself to."

"You mean these two?" Victor angled his head at the photograph of Fidel and Che.

"Wait." Serguey coughed to unlodge his throat and repeated, "Wait."

Montalvo smirked. "Happens every time."

Serguey got up. "Let's cut the bullshit." Victor made as if to join his brother, but Serguey motioned for him to stay seated. "If you had anything on us, you would've picked us up. You would've come to us before arresting our father. You would've searched my place, told me to sign some kind of statement."

Montalvo's smirk was gone. "I can still do that. Your brother has five arrests.

I can make it six and ensure this one sticks. I can bring your wife in. What's her name, Anabel? Maybe she knows something. Or maybe her sister knows. She works with your father, doesn't she?" The ex-colonel slammed his palm on the table and began to walk back to his chair. "Now that I think about it, I'll just call the Ministry where you work and ask the State Security department there to interview everyone who's been in contact with you for the past six months. I'm sure they're going to love that."

Serguey moved toward the desk. "You extended the courtesy of talking to us so we would volunteer some information, to see if we were desperate enough. Victor's right. We have no idea what the hell our father did. We don't snoop around his private life, so we have nothing to trade. All I have left is to ask you, not as a lawyer but as a son, to let us see him. We just want to leave here with the peace of mind that he's fine. That's all."

"Goddamn, Serguey," Montalvo said, smiling again. He retraced his steps and grabbed Serguey's collarbone near the neck, much like Felipe liked to do. "I had you pegged all wrong. You're the sentimental type."

Serguey felt as if in mid-air—a mix of weightlessness and panic hurtling through his body. Anabel's voice kept ringing in his ear: *Do what you have to do.* "With all due respect," he heard himself say, raising his shoulder against Montalvo's touch, "I don't care what you think of me. What's my father accused of, exactly? What has he done? Is he even here?"

"Brash!" Montalvo clapped. "I like it. No wonder you're about to land an embassy assignment at such a young age. And you've done it all with a counter-revolutionary father right under your nose. It's unfortunate. Tragic, really. A criminal for a brother and a dissident for a father."

"Let's go," Serguey said to Victor.

Montalvo said, "We're not ready to divulge the specifics of Felipe's case. But he's here. I have him in an interview room waiting for you two. Yenier will accompany you."

Victor chuckled and shook his head.

"Thank you," Serguey said, with a smidge of respect for the ex-colonel's performance.

"I didn't lie. Your father *is* fucked. He'll tell you so himself. I'm just hoping you can convince him—as his lawyer or as his son, I don't give a shit—to cooperate. And don't think that because you called my bluff, I can't call yours. You *do* know something, and I'm going to find out what it is. Maybe a visit to your lovely wife is in order after all."

Victor took a step toward Montalvo.

Serguey held him back. "I understand. I'm aware of how this works."

Montalvo spit the moist butt of his cigar on the ground and flattened it with the heel of his boot. "You have no idea."

⁂

At the end of a long corridor, they made a right. Soon they were in a small, bare room, hugging their father. Felipe looked disheveled and reeked of sweat. His eyes were inflamed, the skin around his lips bloated. Serguey was relieved to see no bruises or scars. He'd heard of political prisoners beaten so badly they'd lost teeth, suffered broken or fractured ribs, spat blood for days. Some hadn't been given medical attention, despite documented histories of chronic ailments. Luckily, Felipe was a healthy man for his age.

Yenier, who'd taken a spot in one of the corners, was watching all of them diligently.

"I told you not to involve Serguey." Felipe said this to Victor so wearily that it didn't carry the weight of a reprimand.

Victor screwed up his mouth and looked down.

"Dad, don't be stupid," Serguey replied. "What have they done to you?" He didn't trust a visual appraisal of his father—there could be hidden injuries, strategic places where they'd beaten him.

"They haven't touched me. I just haven't slept."

"Did they interrogate you?"

Felipe blinked laboriously, as if it required agonizing exertion. "What do you think?"

"*Viejo*, what the fuck's going on?" Victor asked, stealing a peek at Yenier. The officer wasn't trying to hide the fact that he was there to listen.

"Did you speak with Montalvo?" Felipe said.

"We did," Serguey said.

Felipe scratched his eyes. "They think I'm involved in something, some kind of dissident organization."

"Why do they think that?"

"It's a mix-up. That's what I've been telling them. I'm just a theater director."

"A mix-up?" Serguey said, incredulous.

"After this, I won't be able to direct a play in my own living room."

"Now you got the space," Victor said.

It took a few weak breaths for Felipe to speak. "How much did they take?"

"Everything. Typewriter, books, paintings, your boxes."

"Years of work, out the window." Felipe sighed with profound heaviness, as if a vital part of him were leaving his body.

"What do you want us to do?" Victor said.

"I want you to let me deal with this myself. There's nothing you can do." Felipe rubbed his eyes again and let out a faint groan.

"Did they use pepper spray?" Serguey asked.

"Hey!" Yenier said, leaning forward. "Watch your mouth."

"It's fine." Felipe lifted his hand defensively. "No pepper spray. I'm just tired. They told me I'm getting some food when we're done here. I want you both to go home. Victor, you be a model citizen from now on, all right? Serguey, go back to your job and Anabel. I'm going to reason with them. I'll call a couple of people in the Department of Culture who will vouch for me."

"I can contact them for you," Serguey said.

"Not necessary."

"I'm a lawyer, Dad. Let me help." As he said this, Serguey was immediately aware that he was embarking on a pointless mission to convince his father. Felipe was a theatrical man in every sense, keen on sacrificial acts. He had a proclivity for martyrdom, for keeping distance and touting self-reliance, for mapping out a reality in which all roads led back to him, always on his own terms.

"Serguey's right," Victor said. "Don't be stubborn. I'm sure there are things we can do."

Felipe grabbed their hands. "I'm happy to see you two together. If that's the only good thing to come out of this, it'll be worth it. Now, get out of here and go back to your lives."

"Do you know what's happening?" Serguey said, fighting his own instinct to give up the argument, to give up altogether and leave his father to his martyrdom. "They're talking about sending you to another province, not letting us visit for months."

"Smoke and mirrors. I'll be released by the end of the week."

"What if you aren't? What are we supposed to do, move on like it never happened? What if we don't hear from you again?"

"I tell you what, if a month from now I'm still incarcerated, you come see me and tell me how wrong I was."

"Can't you stop being such an arrogant idiot?" Victor said.

"We're not afraid of these people."

"Tell us how we can help," Serguey said.

"This will ruin you, Serguey. It's a misunderstanding, nothing more."

"What the hell are you talking about?"

Felipe rubbed his eyes vigorously. "It's the pepper spray. They used it."

"Out!" Yenier said, pulling Felipe toward himself, then to the door.

Serguey put his arms out. "Hey, easy!"

"Let him go," Victor said, raising his fists. "You son of a bitch!"

"Do anything stupid," the officer said, "and we'll put him and you in the hole for a week. You want that?"

"Easy," Serguey repeated.

"Go home," Felipe said. "It's a mistake."

Yenier dragged Felipe out of the room. He called a guard over and asked him to take the detainee back to his cell. He signaled for Serguey and Victor to exit the room.

"You touch him, and I'm going to fuck you up," Victor said.

"Victor, stop it," Serguey said. He began to lead the way down the corridor. His father had mentioned the pepper spray on purpose. He was sure of it. Montalvo didn't want the torturing of a respected theater director to become news. Now his father could be paying the price for revealing what he had been forbidden to say. As he walked, Serguey stole another glimpse at the courtyard and pictured the old man hanging from one of the cements posts, the other inmates mocking and taunting him. He refused to lose his head. His father's decision would be for nothing if he and Victor ended up in a cell. He advanced toward the prison's exit, quickening his pace with every stride.

"You have no idea how we can get to you," Yenier said. "Montalvo doesn't bluff twice."

"We can't leave Dad in here," Victor said.

"Do you want to join him?" Serguey said.

"We can't leave him!"

"He doesn't want to be helped."

Victor stopped. "Where's Montalvo?" he said to Yenier. "Where's that motherfucker?"

The officer shoved him along. "You had your chance."

Other officers had gathered at the reception, brandishing weapons. The black metal of the rifles, the wooden sheen of the magazine and handguard made Serguey think of the Cuban militia, of marches and the images of war shown on television during the Cold War, when he was a child. His skin became suddenly sensitive, to the point of pain. Victor thrashed his arm around, trying to free it from Yenier's grip. The officer had shoved his hand under Victor's shoulder, hoisting him up like a bar drunk. Another officer began to thrust the butt of his rifle into Victor's back. Finally, he desisted as Yenier carried him outside. Serguey kept his arms up during the jostling, impelled along by some of the other men.

As soon as they passed the front gate, Victor yanked Serguey's wrist. "You coward!"

"Not here," he replied. "Shut up and move."

CHAPTER 6

Serguey had a few devices of his own to offset his brother's lifelong perception that he was a coward: his intellect, his reasoning, his foresight. These qualities had, at times, commanded respect from Victor, whose reckless impetus made him deficient in them. On the way to the bus stop, Serguey explained what they had to do. Arguing with Yenier or Montalvo about rights or family was useless. It would only get them thrown in a cell for public disturbance. If they were goaded into physically retaliating, they might not see the light of day for a week. It wasn't clear whether Felipe would be officially charged, whether a trial would take place. If these things were to happen, State Security would bring in a puppet lawyer; the trial would transpire behind closed doors. There would be no case anyone could make against a politically motivated accusation, not without losing their job. There would be no other entities that could intervene, no individual that could defy the government's ubiquitous will.

It took a summary beckoning of his reserves for Serguey to remain resolute. He had to apply the same method he'd had all these years: willfully ignore what was inherently and morally wrong with the system and continue onward with the aid of practical solutions.

"But if they don't charge Dad," Victor said, naively hopeful, "they have to let him go."

"If they tag him a dissident, they can hold him indefinitely."

"Can't you request to be his lawyer, like you told Montalvo?"

"I work at the Ministry now. I can't officially act as his attorney." The brothers' feet slammed the ground somewhere between a speed walk and a full sprint. "And if I try taking them to court some other way, they'll bury me. They can plant anything on me, and who's going to prove it's a set-up? I've seen things, Victor . . ."

They had to figure out what they could on their own. If legal recourses didn't suffice, they had to consider all possibilities, explore all avenues. Cubans prided themselves on their ingenuity, the product of a sound education in a nation with scarce resources and even fewer freedoms. He and Victor had to be crafty to obtain results without being jailed.

"First, we have to search Dad's house," Serguey said, "in case they missed something."

Victor stared at him in silence. The passage of time, it seemed, had eroded Serguey's familiarity with some of Victor's gestures and expressions. Holding his brother's gaze, as he could do now that he felt in charge, he couldn't guess what the next words out of Victor's mouth would be.

"I thought you were going to say we should wait," Victor said. "Or that you were done with us."

Serguey couldn't fault him for the thought. Victor's fears were justified: he and Felipe hadn't been a priority for a decade. Still, Serguey didn't want to give hollow promises or demonstrations of commitment. "I can't just plunge," he said earnestly. "I have Anabel and my career to consider. I know it sounds selfish, but this whole thing can fuck up what I've been trying to accomplish."

"It's not selfish." Victor lowered his jaw and swallowed. "We *are* screwing up your life."

The brothers stood motionless and stared at one another. The unequivocal rumble of an accelerating bus resounded behind a tall fence and the copious crown of numerous trees. Serguey and Victor broke into a sprint, the bus slugging by just as they turned the corner onto the main street. Commuters at the stop signaled to the driver, allowing Serguey and Victor to catch up. The next bus, they knew, might take ages to come.

Heading into the city early in the route, there were empty seats. The driver swerved to the middle of the road, and the brothers staggered toward the rear. They sat on the last row, their heads resting on the back wall. For the next three stops, hordes of people piled into the bus until it reached maximum capacity. The driver started to allow in only the same amount of commuters who got off. Victor gave his seat to an old man with a cane, who'd made his way patiently to the back, at times anchoring himself on other bodies, pitifully riffling for a generous soul. A decade prior, Serguey thought, he wouldn't have gone more than two rows before a civil act had him sitting comfortably. Nowadays, men pretended to be asleep just so they wouldn't be bothered. As a discreet form of social complaint, Serguey offered his spot to a middle-aged nurse, whose bag kept slipping from her shoulder. She thanked him emphatically. The gangly man standing next to her had breathed heavily and shot her a surly look when the bag fell on his foot. Now standing, Victor told Serguey to switch sides so he could be adjacent to the man. He too had noticed. Victor then asked the stranger if he could have a cigarette. The man brought his hand to his shirt pocket, an uncertain look passing over his eyes.

"All right," he said at length and took one out.

"Can I have one for my brother?" Victor said. "Rough day, you know."

The man dawdled, mumbling something about one being enough.

"Come on, comrade," Victor said with a rigid smirk, "don't be stingy."

The man handed Victor another cigarette. At the next stop, he wriggled his way out. Victor showed the cigarettes to the nurse.

"You want them?"

She laughed. "Sure," she said and put them in her bag.

A couple of stops later—the heat inside the vehicle already acquiring unpleasant, smothering smells—Victor leaned into Serguey and asked, his voice apologetic, "Do you think you'll lose your job?"

The idea of his brother feeling guilty for possibly wrecking his life made Serguey's stomach churn with self-loathing. Victor was ready to deal with what was coming. Serguey owed him honesty, at least to this particular question. "If I do, I'll lose the apartment too. Anabel's parents are nice people, but going back to their place will be rough."

"You guys can come live with me."

"Funny."

Victor waited for the squealing of the brakes to cease as the bus neared a street light. "I don't blame you for leaving, Serguey. I just didn't have the luxury of a choice."

"Do you really want to do this now?"

Victor sighed. "No, you're right."

Serguey stared out the open window. A boy on a bicycle was hanging on to the ledge, wanting a faster ride to his destination. A colorful tattoo wound its way down his right bicep to his elbow. His bronzed skin sparkled in the sun. His eyes squinted under the mid-day glare with a mischievous focus, the kind of dogged expression sported by those who spend most days at the mercy of Havana's blistering roads. His features were inscribed with the tenacity and ruggedness that Serguey associated with Victor and those his brother knew. Like the man on the motorcycle, this young boy seemed an integral part of the streets, like he might at any point be waved at by a friend, a confidant, an accomplice. Did he also think of himself as not having the luxury of choice? Were the bicycle, the tattoo, the tenacious gaze, inevitable—the only path left for those who, like Victor, had found no other way to subsist?

Victor glinted in the direction of the boy, then turned to Serguey unemotionally. "Make sure you call Anabel when we get to the house," he said. "She's going to have your balls if you don't."

❧❧❀ ❊ ❀❧❧

They got off the second bus at the intersection of Juan Delgado Avenue and Herrera Street, four blocks away from the house. More than a year, Serguey thought, since the last time he'd been here. As they waited to cross the road, he recalled the days he and Kiko, his best childhood friend, had walked by this stop on the way to and back from their middle school. They had often bought peanuts from a street vendor. The man's front teeth were missing, and he always wore the same pair of tattered pants and camouflage fanny pack. Restlessly, he waded into the rush hour crowd getting off buses, the peanut-packed paper cones raised aloft like a torch. Some called him Titi, alluding to Los Van Van's "La Titimanía." His salt-encrusted peanuts had no equal. The packages were the bulkiest Serguey and Kiko had ever seen. They definitely got their money's worth.

A newspaper stand, shaped like a kiosk, had stood at the edge of the block. The person who'd worked in it, Norton—a black man who Serguey's classmates claimed was a hundred years old despite not looking a day over sixty—had passed away a few years before. The kiosk had subsequently been shut down for good. The same newspaper, dated May 15, 2003, was affixed to the window for months until the stand was disassembled. As teenagers, Serguey and Kiko loitered by the side window, where Norton taped the sports section of the *Granma* newspaper. They browsed through the baseball scores, looking to see if Javier Mendez had hit a home run or if Lázaro Valle had thrown a complete game. On the rare occasions when Norton forgot to post the new issue, the boys pestered him so they could borrow the sports page.

"Can't give it to you," the old man would say. "You'll rip it."

Norton had read the scores out loud to them. After a while, he began to memorize the numbers before Serguey or Kiko asked. When Industriales suffered a bad loss or their favorite player had struck out multiple times, he teased them: "They can't hit a melon with an ironing board!"

Serguey missed that kind of banter. No one in his office followed baseball. If they did, they wouldn't talk about it the same way as Norton. There was no flavor, no irony or personality behind their remarks. The cordiality and overall tone of importance everyone displayed at his workplace had originally appealed to him. He had felt part of a distinguished world, a world whose language and appearance created the illusion of success. In a country where the illusion itself was as close to the real thing as most could get, he'd been delighted. But now he couldn't help wondering if, in courting that illusion, he had lost the substance of things.

As the brothers stepped across the avenue, Serguey saw two men immersed in a lighthearted debate. One of them, who looked curiously like a younger Norton, smacked a rolled-up newspaper on the other's chest each time he made a point. The other slapped the back of his right hand on the palm of his left, staring with his head skewed at a downward angle, his eyes compressed, questioning each argument. Serguey then noticed his brother hastening toward the newspaper-wielding man and playfully punching him on the shoulder.

The man smacked the newspaper on Victor's shoulder in return. "*Licenciado!*"

"I'm in a hurry," Victor said, rejoining Serguey, "but I haven't forgotten about you."

"I know, *hermanito*," the man said. "*Tranquilo.*"

Turning into Herrera Street, Victor told Serguey, "A bit of a shit talker, that guy, but he's loyal."

"Is he related to Norton?"

"You mean deceased Norton? That's Yunior, his grandson." Victor closed his fist and shook it in the air. "Always with the fucking newspaper." Serguey wished that Victor had stalled with the men for a bit. Maybe he could have asked Yunior about Norton, see what memories might spring from it. But Victor's steps had become determined, rushing down Herrera faster than Serguey would have liked. At the end of the block, a group of bony, shirtless kids were kneeling on a parcel of dirt between the sidewalk and the road. One of them used a sturdy twig to carve a sloppy circle, inside of which the boys began to place marbles just as the brothers passed them. Serguey remembered having weeded out, with Felipe's doubtful permission, the rectangular plot of land in front of their house so he and Kiko could play *quimbe* with their marbles, or *fanguito*, which only required mud and a large nail. In Serguey's block in El Vedado, there were no parcels of dirt on which to play. Now that he thought about it, the immediate area neighboring his building seemed devoid of children. Whatever sections of land were available had been planted with a tree or bush of some sort, always maintained and supervised by a senior citizen who treated kids as a farmer might treat crop-infesting mice.

Serguey stayed a couple of paces behind Victor, scrutinizing the homes on either side of the street. Although some houses had been refurbished, the majority looked as they had a decade or more ago, each with its own decrepit vibe, its own history. In this part of the city, bare concrete showed on facades so clustered they allowed little to no view beyond them. The heart of Havana— in contrast to Serguey's own lofty neighborhood—had gradually transformed into deplorable sleeping quarters for all who could fit. Block after block it was the same: backyards and garages had been turned into rooms and apartments for sons and daughters, brothers and sisters. Generations of people clumped together, waiting for the elders to die off so they could claim the homes for themselves.

Your next-door neighbor knew your secrets. There was no avoiding it. Their windows opened right across from yours. To escape the sultriness of their residences and the smothering presence of relatives, people poured into the streets: kids played ringer; men argued and wielded newspapers. There was a constant coming and going, the kind of bustle that makes a place seem gregarious, nomadic, restless. A few preferred to sit back and observe, watching life unfold around them like a familiar film. They sat on the steps of their homes, or—like the large woman who was now gaping at Serguey as she sipped brown-sugared water with a cat curled up by her swollen ankles—they swung on a rocking chair, grim-faced and forbearing, hoping for something, anything, to distract them from the repetitive nature of existence in the entrails of a communist nation.

In the corner of Herrera and Milagros stood *la casa de los muchos*. Its foundation was slightly elevated, surrounded by a wrought-iron fence topped with thick spikes, some of which were missing. The lawn was well-kept. The walkway consisted of concrete slabs laid in a zigzagging pattern. The yellow-painted exterior, though admittedly in bad taste, had no visible chips or scratches. Rumors alleged that between twelve and fourteen people shared the house's three bedrooms and two bathrooms. How they maintained the home in such good condition was as big a mystery as the family name. Everyone simply called them *los muchos*, the many, after an infamous gang in the municipality of El Cerro.

In all the years he walked by this intersection, Serguey hadn't seen a single person entering or exiting the place. *Los muchos* might as well have been ghosts. He and Kiko never dared to snoop around. There was a story of a young boy who'd thrown a rock at the door, only to be chased by six *muchos* of different ages and sexes. He'd been caught two blocks down and dragged by his hair back to the house in humiliation so he could retrieve the rock and take it with him. Others said that it'd been three people, not six, and that the boy wasn't brought back but instead beaten with a jump rope until he got away.

Closer to his father's residence—number 709 on Herrera—the homes weren't as enigmatic. Serguey knew exactly who lived in each and, for the majority, the stories contained within their walls. To his right was Francisco and Magalys's two-story house. The first floor had a garage, where Francisco stored his company's Toyota van, and a game room, highlighted by a foosball table. He and Magalys, now in their sixties, didn't have any children. Francisco worked for an Italian corporation that helped finance the construction of hotels in Cuba. Magalys was employed as secretary for the director of a clothing distributing company out of Panama, a Muslim man Magalys had nicknamed "Ahmed the Sultan."

The couple liked to host their poorer nephews and nieces from Alamar. One of them, Carlito, sometimes invited the neighborhood children to play video games behind the garage. In addition to the foosball table, Francisco owned two color TVs, a VHS player, a Sega system, an Atari 2600, and an impressive collection of board games. No one else in Havana seemed to have such a bounty. Serguey and Kiko kept an eye out for visitors at Francisco's during the summer, knowing Carlito would occasionally stay with their uncle and aunt for weeks at a time. Even little Victor had joined in the fun.

Farther down, almost at the end of the block, was José El Bola, an old, crusty-skinned man with a bulging goiter on his neck. José slept in a shed encased by large tin sheets, which he had turned into walls. He sat perpetually on a wooden chair by his front door, smoking previously discarded cigarettes from a stash he'd put together. José had also wrangled up stray dogs and took care of them in his yard. Once a day, at about 5:00 p.m., he released them. The animals ran like maniacs around the block for a good quarter of an hour, knocking over cans and trampling the few weeds the children hadn't yanked, before returning to their owner at the sound of a whistle. The children screamed and laughed,

climbing onto porches and up trees, not out of fear but rather looking to enter-
tain themselves, pretending the dogs were dangerous. Whenever José forgot his
routine, one could hear the agitated animals slamming and scraping their paws
against the tin sheets.

José sold guava pies for a living. They almost always had ants crawling in and
out of the crust. Serguey had eaten the pies a couple of times. They weren't bad.
You just had to break the pastry and make sure no ants were stuck to the filling.

"What do you do when the pies have too many ants?" Kiko asked José once.

The old man went into his shed and returned with a large plastic bag full of
crumpled pies. "The dogs love them."

⁂

The brothers ascended the stairs to their father's porch. The second step was still
chipped in the shape of a very small, upside down Italy. This was the same chip
Serguey had been gazing at the week of his fourteenth birthday—on what was
then about to become an extraordinary night—while he waited for some friend
or another. Felipe was in bed with a migraine, Victor somewhere in the house
mesmerized by the flaring screen of a Nintendo Game Boy. Serguey had gotten
it in a week-long trade with a classmate, giving him a photographed version of
the Kama Sutra, which Felipe kept between a large hardcover Bible and a set of
outdated encyclopedias on a bottom shelf. Victor had begged Serguey for the
Gameboy so persistently, he agreed to lend it to him on just the second night.
The street was empty. Neighbors were holed up in their homes—shedding the
misery of their day by scooping water from a bucket and dumping it on their
heads—before jaunting out for some cool-breezed banter. As if out of a fog,
a girl in a tube top and Lycra shorts walked up to Serguey. He had seen her
saunter by for the past few days, but he had no idea who she was. In the poor
lighting of Felipe's porch, she introduced herself as Yusimí and asked him if he
had a girlfriend. He said no (Anabel had yet to enter this particular frame of
his life). Yusimí's skin, as he recalled it now, was like Alida's, but her eyes were
an intimidating dark green.

"I've looked at you a few times," she said, her voice devoid of excitement or seduction, "and I think you're the most beautiful boy I've ever seen." She extended
her hand. Serguey's heart was hammering the scraggy bones in his chest. He
feared that its feral beating would show through his plain T-shirt. He presented

his hand floppily, wishing to possess the courage to say something suave, to rise above her on the steps and avidly stare down at her green eyes.

It turned out he didn't have to. She led him to the pitch-black gap between Felipe's house and the next. She pulled down his pants and asked, "Is this okay?"

He nodded absurdly, unable to see her face just inches from his, then said like a wisp of smoke, "Yes."

She began to stroke his penis, his erection stiffening quickly. "You're a man now," she whispered, again and again, then asked him to warn her when he was about to finish.

Seconds later, he did, and she took him in her mouth. He grasped at the porous cement wall, almost fainting, the aching pressure in his buttocks and prodigious sensation in his penis causing a slight bending of his knees.

Yusimí stood, released a wet moan, and said, "Was I the first?"

He nodded, and she walked off swathed in a bout of giggling laughter.

Days later, after failing to see her around the neighborhood, Serguey heard the friend with whom he'd traded the Kama Sutra brag about losing his virginity to a Yusimí. "She called me a man," the boy said with a stupefied grin, which, to Serguey, was the most hideous thing he'd ever witnessed. It was this fragment of the memory that greeted him as he planted his foot on the miniature shape of upside down Italy, which, looking closer at it, had lost its Sicily.

He had told Anabel about the encounter, though in that version he'd rebuffed Yusimí's advances. Anabel had shared similar stories about naïve sexual excursions with boys in her block, but nothing as explicit as what Serguey had experienced. Had she lied too? Did she have anything like these porch steps, paved with graphic memories? One day, he told himself, he would tell her the true story.

He unlatched the small gate and swung it open. Victor overtook him, keys in hand. The history of this house Serguey knew best. It had belonged to Felipe's father, Joaquin Blanco, a sculptor and art professor before the Revolution. Joaquin had served fourteen months in an internment camp alongside writers, musicians, architects, and professors in the late 1960s, for declining to participate in a government project to propagate communist-inspired artwork throughout Havana. While at the camp, he contracted hepatitis and never really recovered. He died a few years later, when Felipe was only fifteen.

Felipe hadn't told his sons how he truly felt about his own father's death. Once, as Victor lay asleep next to him while in the living room Felipe and a few artist friends drank from a bottle of mint-flavored alcohol—the smell of which had invaded the house like imported toothpaste could overtake the inside of Serguey's mouth—Serguey heard his father say, quite solemnly, that Joaquin's passing had been "preventable." A young Serguey hadn't been able to pin down who or what exactly Felipe was blaming, but now he was convinced that it'd been the government. The newly implemented communist system had placed Joaquin in a precarious, unmerited situation. Mistakes had been made after the Revolution: even Fidel Castro agreed to this in an interview, admitting that the camps had been an error, though the words *crime* and *gulag*, which those familiar with the conditions used to describe them, didn't come close to absconding The Commander-in-Chief's lips. The tragedy didn't lie in Joaquin's debilitating hepatitis but rather in the unnecessarily cruel treatment of people who saw things differently, who wanted to be true to their politics in a time of uncertain change. Where most would compromise or assent, Joaquin had been steadfast. Serguey interpreted all of this from the other thing Felipe had said that night about his father: "He had balls the size of a bull's, the kind I wish I had." Serguey had rarely heard his father speak such plainly vulgar language to describe people, least of all a loved one.

Felipe also chose not to speak at length about these events with him or Victor. He preferred to focus on Joaquin's artistic life, on what he saw as the man's legacy. He described him as a virtuoso with his hands, capable of molding anything into a beautiful sculpture.

"He saw what others couldn't," he liked to say in his more melancholy moments. "Can you imagine having such a gift? I work with other people's words, with someone else's vision. He was pure. His work was truly his own."

These were the only instances in which Serguey saw the pompous, proud Felipe refer to his own work as inferior, as somewhat unworthy: when he was comparing himself to his father.

Serguey suspected (and the arrest had intensified this suspicion) that his father had always wanted, to some extent, to embody Joaquin. As a young playwright and professor, Felipe had published two controversial papers lamenting the pervasive presence of Socialist Realism in the arts. He called for a more fluid relationship between politics and theater. The result, he argued, would be a broader, more diverse role for theater in Cuba. Playwrights and directors could offer an array of methods and topics to help shape the island's artistic identity, unburdened by the inherent limitations of political views. It had been a risky endeavor, considering that Joaquin's history could influence cultural authorities to tag Felipe an ideological threat to the nation. But Felipe, unlike his father, had been tactful and conciliatory. In the tone of his essays, he was careful not to ruffle any feathers, especially when it came to the government. He credited the advantages of practicing theater in a country whose system made it easily available to the masses, and described himself as indebted to such a system. He had been measured and cynical and passively academic. Serguey questioned whether Felipe had grown tired of assenting, whether—at age fifty—he had finally decided to be type of bull Joaquin had been.

From his abbreviated interactions with his father, in which an inebriated Felipe was always willing to reminisce more freely, Serguey had learned important details about his family's history. These conversations caused him to conclude that Joaquin's death had, in fact, set in motion a series of events ultimately leading to the death of Serguey and Victor's mother.

Serguey's grandmother, Maria Estela, a seamstress whose religious family left the country the minute the word "socialism" escaped Fidel's mouth, struggled to make ends meet after Joaquin's death, while Felipe continued his education. On more than one occasion she considered selling several of Joaquin's belongings, but Felipe wouldn't let her. He saw his father's possessions as a goldmine of memories. He was attached to them in a way that Serguey had never been to either of his own parents' things. On the tenth anniversary of Joaquin's death, while taking flowers to the cemetery, Maria Estela was hit by a bus and died instantly. By then, a woman named Irene had moved into the house with Felipe. She was pregnant with Serguey.

Felipe vehemently swore, to anyone with the gall to imply the contrary, that this was not the reason why he married her, that they were deeply in love.

In his bedroom, Felipe had placed—next to a photograph of himself, Irene, and the children at a playground in Lenin Park—a black-and-white picture of his mother, a close-up of her unassuming face and shoulders, with a tiny cross hanging below the crevice of her neck. Joaquin was nowhere to be found on the nightstand. Felipe had other ideas for his father: he'd hung an enlarged picture of him above the headboard, making it the first thing people saw upon entering the room. In the imposing photograph, Joaquin was hunched over his workstation. His fingers and the hairs on his arms were caked in mud or paint. His head sloped downward, his eyes peering over thick-rimmed glasses at the indecipherable shape of a sculpture-in-progress. This was the god his father had decided to worship. This had been, from the very start, what doomed Felipe and Irene's marriage.

Serguey and Victor's mother was a strong-willed woman, but she never saw

Herrera 709 as her own. Felipe refused to let go of his father's possessions, his fervor deepened by his own mother's passing. The living room was flanked by Joaquin's favorite works, some of them nude women who—according to Irene—seemed to stare deridingly at her. (Serguey remembered her covering the statues' heads with dishcloths while she cleaned the living room.) With Joaquin's book collection neatly organized in two huge cases along the wall, there was little space for Irene to decorate. She had to turn down the furniture that her uncle, a carpenter, offered as a wedding gift. Irene and Felipe slept in Joaquin's bed, used his dresser and nightstands, sat on his sofa, and ate dinner at his dinner table. Every night, she had to face that large photograph, a reminder that, in this house, art always took precedent.

Once Felipe's writing career began to take off, loneliness gradually consumed her. Six-year-old Serguey and three-year-old Victor were her only company. During her evening walks around the neighborhood, when she would push Victor in a stroller, she developed a relationship with a neighbor's son. He was an amiable and flirtatious young man, temporarily staying at his parents' near the end of the block, two homes down from José El Bola. The man's name was Raidel. Serguey hated it, especially the singsong way his mother would say it. Thanks to his father's connections, Raidel had been appointed as a funeral director at age twenty-nine. Death was a part of life, he sometimes said, as if that were profound. But it seemed to work on Irene. She started an affair with him. She would leave Serguey and Victor in Raidel's parents' living room, telling them that they—the adults—would be in the bedroom discussing the details of his work, which the boys were too young to listen to. She carried on with the affair for months before she told Felipe she wanted a divorce.

"The entire neighborhood knew," Felipe told his sons years later. "I was so wrapped up in my plays that I genuinely thought they were just friends." Here he laughed the most absurd laugh Serguey had ever heard. "The handful of times I talked to the guy, I actually liked him."

On a rainy morning, Serguey remembered, his mother had taken him and Victor to their new home—to Raidel's home. After hugging his sons and telling them he'd see them soon, Felipe had sat at his typewriter, clad despondently in his underwear, slamming away at the keys. His body, Serguey could see, tensed and shuddered as if under electric shock. He didn't acknowledge Irene while she nudged the boys out of the house.

"This isn't easy for me," she told him from the threshold. He continued typing, and even at his young age Serguey knew that, despite the lack of words, his father's non-reaction had been its own form of response.

As they walked up to the car, Victor started sobbing—silently, sedately—wishing to avoid attention. Irene swung the backdoor open, and Victor clung to Serguey's hand, tugging at it slightly.

"He doesn't want to go," Serguey said, or later recalled himself saying.

"Get in." Irene's weary stare implored her eldest son to help her. Nodding, she said, "This isn't easy for me," as if he could understand this better than his father.

Victor didn't resist when Serguey led him into the boxy vehicle.

"Did he make a show?" Raidel asked, glimpsing at the boys. For some time Serguey erroneously thought that he'd been referring to Victor.

"Just go," Irene said.

The clouds and downpour did not relent. The wipers streaked the foggy windshield with every swipe, the sound of which seemed to soothe Victor's crying. Rain stuck to the top of Irene's cotton-like, brown hair. Serguey was so bewildered by the strangeness of the moment that he simply gazed at the back of his mother's head, water from her hair sliding down the passenger seat. He waited for her to turn around, to change her mind.

She never did. Instead she repeatedly took Raidel's hand after he switched gears.

The period they resided at the man's home was foggier than any of Serguey's dreams. He remembered it in snippets: their mattresses were hard, and Raidel forbade standing or jumping on them; if Victor peed his bed, Raidel placed a large plastic cover underneath him the following night (the friction gave Victor rashes, which Irene then treated with talcum powder); the next door neighbor, a decrepit woman whose window was always agape, owned a small dog who barked constantly and only stopped when its owner yelled, "Muchi, you'll be the death of me!"

Irene never expressed any doubts about the move. She had no idea that her new boyfriend would stab her to death within a year in a drunken rage—in front of her sons—while screaming that she was an adulterer and a whore.

Serguey and Victor saw Irene gasp for air like a goldfish, blood pooling under and around her body. Muchi, the crazy lady's dog, yapped and whimpered two walls away while the boys cried. Finally, neighbors came and took them. A black woman, who occasionally gave little bags of hard candy to Irene for her sons, kept screaming, "Hang that *desgraciao*!" For some hours Serguey actually believed, in his shock and confusion, that someone had tied a noose around Raidel's neck and dangled him from a tree, as he'd once seen in a Western movie.

It did, in fact, take three days for the police to find Raidel. He was asleep on someone's roof by a dove coop, his mouth severely blistered by exposure and excessive intake of alcohol, a block away from the funeral home he managed.

The tragic nature of existence, Serguey had heard someone say, is that we repeat history despite the warnings. In the legal community, precedent mattered for a reason. It was a sign of things to come. In regards to family, Serguey was no stranger to what might lie ahead with his father. He was no stranger to the possibility and subsequent realization of loss. "Try losing your mother when you're seven," he had always wanted to say if questioned. Now that he thought about it, Victor had been four. Serguey remembered trying to understand what it must have been like for his brother, how the discovery of death had come too damn early for him. He remembered thinking about it infrequently, images of his mother's body, the adults' copious tears, sitting in a room with Victor while listening to a psychologist with a hideous beard, asking them about where they thought their mother was now. They were memories too visceral for rational thought to prevail.

At the time of Irene's death, Serguey internalized the pain of losing her, thinking only of pleasant moments as if they were tokens, like something stashed under a pillow. Kids at school asked about her death, hoping for gruesome details, but he and Victor refused to speak about it, even among themselves. Victor got into his share of scuffles with boys who'd say "*tu madre!*" as a way to offend him. Throughout the years, Serguey repelled the desire most people get to explore their family's past. He chose to look forward, a decision that was solidified after meeting Anabel at age sixteen. His memory of Felipe and Irene as a couple was hazy and bleak. Serguey didn't recall his parents kissing passionately. He hadn't walked in on them making love—as he had done with his mother and Raidel on a night Victor had wet the bed—or seen his father snuggle close to her at the movies. He remembered Felipe chiefly for his absence, showing up late with a friend to discuss edits on a play, missing birthdays, dinners. What exactly Irene must have felt in her isolation, he couldn't imagine—he had been too young to know her well enough for that. But he understood, despite the horrific consequences, why she left the house.

Felipe had reassured the boys he loved their mother to the end, despite everything that had transpired, despite her betrayal. He cried when she passed, he said, although the boys hadn't seen him do it. One of the tragedies of life, he also told them (tragedy became the operative word for anyone referring to Irene's murder: family, neighbors, police) is that no matter how hard we fight it, there are things we cannot control. It's part of the excitement and the fear. It's what makes us care for everything a little more, because we don't know when we'll lose it. On his more nostalgic days, he'd quote Shakespeare, spellbinding the boys with the sound of the words, not explaining their meaning.

Serguey remembered their home taking on a lively atmosphere following the last session with the child psychologist, when Felipe told his sons they had to turn the page toward a new life, cherishing the positive memories of their mother. During weekends, instead of making good on a weekday promise of a trip to the beach or the zoo, Felipe hosted dinner parties for his colleagues. People acted out scenes from their favorite plays and made fun of the obtuse administrators at the cultural centers where they worked. Once in a while someone would bring an acoustic guitar and play *Nueva Trova* songs. Felipe, however, rarely let his boys be a part of the celebrations, which made the few times he allowed them to remain particularly notable. Serguey recalled the laughter, the smoke snaking up from the ashtrays, he and his brother dancing for the crowd. These moments had washed over the otherwise dull, solitary lives they led under their father's supervision.

As with Felipe's current predicament, he hadn't wanted to involve his sons in his personal affairs. During their childhood, he had given them fleeting kisses on the head, dismissive sighs at their misbehavior, quick waves of the hand in the mornings. He had, very seldom, shown them books, paintings, played them music—Antoine de Saint-Exupéry's *The Little Prince*, Picasso's *Guernica*, Bola de Nieve's *"Ay Mama Inés"*—but he never related them to their actual lives, never linked what he shared to their daily struggle of growing up motherless. It was as if he believed that exposing young boys to art would be curative and edifying on its own. He never discussed his own work, either, not in the dim light of their bedroom or the ash-ridden air engulfing his writing desk, intimate places where their young minds would have been perceptive, prone to remember. He reserved himself—the vulnerable Felipe, the thoughtful and authoritative Felipe—for his circle of artist friends, for the stage he directed. Serguey and Victor had spent their lives watching like intrigued spectators, wondering about this figure that was their father.

✦❧✦

Victor unlocked the front door, and they entered. The living room was too dark for such an early time in the day. The bookcases were still there, though the books were missing. A couple of shelves had slid off their supports, forming a triangle with the shelves below. The sculptures of naked women were scattered on the floor, their heads and legs broken off. State Security hadn't just toppled them—they'd demolished them. The walls felt bare, rectangular lines of dust marking where the frames had been, like a looted museum.

"The paintings too?" Serguey said.

"Those fuckers," Victor muttered.

The brothers tiptoed around the shattered statues into the kitchen. The fridge had been plundered. It smelled of stale ice and fish.

"At least they kept it plugged in," Serguey said.

They began the search in Felipe's bedroom. All the pictures were gone. It wouldn't be beyond the realm of possibility, Serguey considered, for the authorities to use Joaquin's framed photograph as evidence that Felipe admired a former counterrevolutionary. It wouldn't matter that the image was of one of the people who'd brought him into this world. If anything, the connection made the evidence more convincing: Felipe was just like his father.

The mattress and box spring were leaned against the wall. They'd been gutted in several places. Pieces of dirty cotton were strewn here and there, rendering the air viscous and allergenic. Victor tripped on a drawer and cursed. Serguey felt a fit of sneezing coming on. The mirror had been detached from the dresser and smashed on the floor. The closet doors were open, mounds of clothes disgorged as if from a torn sack. The light was still on in the bathroom. The contents of the medicine cabinet had been dropped on the sink. Some of the bottles had broken, leaking their guts into the drain. There was a powerful odor—a mix of alcohol, ammonia, and cherry—exuding from it.

"You didn't tell me it was this bad," Serguey said. "We're not going to find anything."

"We should at least pick everything up and clean a little. We might get lucky. I got a mop in my apartment."

"You're right." Serguey sneezed into his own hands. "If all we can have is the appearance of dignity, so be it."

"I don't care about dignity. I just can't be tripping over all this shit every time I walk in here."

"If Dad's locked up for a while, you're going to be in charge of the house."

"I don't know what ideas you got in your head, Serguey, but this place will never be mine. I don't want it."

"I don't believe that."

Victor exhaled and curled his mouth to one side. "Please follow me so I can give you a broom."

His place was dark and stuffy. He'd built it as an addendum to the house with the help of a friend and the proceeds from the sale of cases of stolen booze. Serguey had bought a couple of bottles himself through Felipe.

"To assist in the cause," he had told his father.

The bottles he gave to Gimenez.

Felipe had insisted that Victor stay in the house's second room, but Victor wanted more privacy. As a result, Felipe turned the space into a guest room, though as far as Victor was aware, it was rare that anyone actually slept there: stacks of posters advertising Felipe's plays had hijacked the bed.

Serguey had twice been inside Victor's diminutive apartment, but as he walked in now he barely recognized it. The modern furniture, the scent of vanilla candles, the low ceiling and narrow layout: they were slightly strange, like his brother's facial expressions. An acoustic guitar hung on the far wall. African-themed ornaments lined a bar counter that Victor had thrown into the design at the last minute. "One of my proudest achievements," he said the first time Serguey visited. "How many people can say in this part of Havana that they have a bar in their living room?" The African figurine in the middle had a small body with a large penis aiming upward at a 45-degree angle. "I sometimes stir the guests' drinks with it," Victor had joked then, too. These things Serguey did remember, and as he did, the place felt more familiar.

"Smells good," he said.

Victor was struggling to retrieve the broom and mop from the slender cavity between his fridge and the wall. "I always keep a candle going," he shouted back, "in case a lady stops by. I have to enhance the experience, give a strong first impression. I don't have a big home, you know."

Take away the pleasant scent, Serguey thought, the cutesy bar and the exotic ornaments, and this was a clammy cave. A hideout. A tacky addition to a complicated past. Complete detachment is what Serguey had sought and achieved. His home had plenty of light and brisk air. More importantly, it was not an extension of anything. After all, Gimenez wasn't family.

"No television?" he asked Victor.

"I have a portable DVD player. I keep it tucked away."

"Has it gotten that bad in the neighborhood?"

"It's gotten bad everywhere." Victor emerged from the kitchen, broom and mop at either side, like lances. Sweat was starting to drip from his forehead. "It just takes longer in your neck of the woods."

"You're lucky they didn't trash your place."

"They went through it, but I guess they didn't have it in for me as they did with Dad."

Serguey lifted the African figurine and aimed its penis at his brother. "Looks like they barely touched it."

Victor took a quick gander around the apartment. "I fixed it up a bit before I went to see you. I'm lucky I didn't have any merchandise, but something tells me they wouldn't have cared about it."

"DVD players are not under the State Security's jurisdiction." Serguey put down the figurine. "That's more local police."

Victor stuck out his bottom lip and huffed, foolishly attempting to get rid of the sweat. "I don't remember you being this funny."

"I don't remember you ever cleaning anything. You take the mop. I got the broom."

They spent the next hour picking up the mess and cleaning the floors. Serguey opened the windows to let the sunlight cast its bright warmth on the old house. As they toiled, Serguey searched for anything that the State Security guys might have missed: a book, a piece of paper, a postcard.

He found nothing.

Inevitably, with all that was missing, the house felt incomplete. The living room was studded with empty stands. Serguey put the statues' remains in a box. The government looters had had their way. What better method to dissuade people from straying into the foggy terrain of dissidence? The trade-off was categorical: dissent, and forgo everything you've ever owned. Their entire childhood—the house where a hyperactive Victor constantly bumped into furniture and stumbled over blocks of paper, where Serguey stared at paintings for long stretches, hoping to see if the people and objects in them moved, where he and his brother chased and swiped at their father's cigarette smoke as it floated like a genie fleeing a bottle—it had started to crumble. Serguey couldn't help momentarily regretting the distance he had created for himself. As he sat at the edge of his father's sofa, some of him wished he and Victor could be children again, roaming inside the house like curious animals. To amuse Felipe's friends, Victor would stroke the statues' breasts and flick their nipples, cackling like a madman to disguise his embarrassment. Serguey impressed everyone by reciting numerous titles in Grandpa Joaquin's book collection, which he memorized like the countries in Felipe's globe. (The globe had been discarded after Victor knocked it over, cracking a chunk of the Sahara Desert and the Middle East.)

Now that the house was quiet and he was older, everything seemed smaller. He wondered how so many people had come together without destroying the furniture, which looked used and scraped, but with presentable character. Felipe would have probably said "with a sense of depth, of ancestry." He'd certainly had his way: this was an artist's home. The playwright's house, as people in the neighborhood had called it. Serguey had no idea if that was still the case. He glanced at his brother. Victor was fidgeting with the broom and mop, trying to get them to stay put against the wall. Serguey questioned whether he'd ever possessed anything resembling Victor's cackling laughter to hide his own embarrassment—the embarrassment that now overtook him for not knowing, for having removed himself so effectively from his past.

Victor hurled the broom and mop onto the floor and wiped the sweat from his forehead. His brother suffered from what Felipe called "profuse perspiration." Any kind of physical activity ended with a soaked shirt and a dribble from his chin like a broken faucet. It'd begun at the worst possible period: Victor's early teenage years. The first time Serguey brought Anabel home—both of them sixteen and Victor only thirteen—Victor had been racing with his friends for some hours around the block. As he trotted into the house, his drenched T-shirt over his shoulder and his face engulfed in sweat, Anabel giggled at the sight.

"Is this your little brother?" she said.

Serguey grinned. "The one and only."

"Were you swimming or something?" she asked Victor.

Victor's sunburned skin turned even redder. He hesitated for a second before scooping a handful of sweat from his neck and flinging it at his brother, who recoiled and cursed. Anabel shrieked with laughter.

"Ask your boyfriend," Victor told her as he walked past them.

Victor had been a lot skinnier then, though crude and brash already. He took off his T-shirt now and swabbed his head and chest with it. He'd grown a lot more muscular, as if his body had caught up with his attitude.

"You've been working out?" Serguey asked.

"For five years. You like what you see?"

"You're the muscles and I'm the brain."

"Whatever you got to tell yourself. I'm going to fry a couple of eggs and warm up some leftover rice so we can have lunch. I'm starving."

Serguey stretched his arms on the sofa's backrest. "You're cleaning, you're cooking, you're working out."

"And you're talking shit." Victor pitched the dirty shirt at his brother. "Bring Dad's fan from the bedroom. I can't eat with this heat."

A few minutes later, they were sitting at the dinner table, clanking their spoons against the bottom of their plates. The fan rattled like an engine behind them.

"How old is that fucking thing?" Victor said.

"You live here. You should know."

"I think it was Grandpa's."

"It was."

With his mouth full, Victor said, "I forgot to give you a fork. Why didn't you tell me?"

"This is fine. Anabel's the one who prefers a fork."

Victor smiled condescendingly, flashing pieces of food on his teeth. Serguey took one last bite and placed the spoon on the table. Victor gulped down the remaining water in his glass, then drank Serguey's.

"Give me your stuff so I can drop it in the sink," he said. "I'll wash it later."

Serguey lifted his plate. "Man, you're ready for marriage."

Victor exhaled disdainfully. He seemed prepared to retaliate, but the phone started ringing. He waited for his brother's reaction.

"I'll get it," Serguey said.

They hurried toward the living room. Serguey picked up the receiver.

"Felipe?" a fraught voice said on the other side of the line. "Felipe?"

"Who's this?" Serguey said.

"Victor?" the voice said.

"It's Serguey. Who's this?"

"Oh. Do they still have him? Is your dad in prison?"

Serguey raised his eyes at Victor. His brother shook his head, indicating he had no guess as to who it could be.

"What are you talking about?" Serguey spat into the phone.

"Please just tell me if he's still in prison."

"Either you tell me who you are or I'm hanging up."

The voice sighed. "They still have him, don't they?"

Serguey lowered his tone. "Mario, is that you?"

"Let me talk to him," Victor said, snatching the receiver from Serguey. "Hello. Hello!"

Victor continued yelling, his fingers choking the handle, but the line was already dead.

CHAPTER 7

It was a miracle that Victor hadn't smashed the phone. He'd grabbed the nape of his neck and gone to Felipe's room. He was standing at the foot of the bed, staring at the wall where Joaquin's photograph had been. This is why he'd come to Serguey. Victor wasn't made for patience, for meditation. He drowned in his own rage, let his helplessness consume him. When he was twelve, he had chased after a boy who'd stolen his favorite marble and ran with a heckling laugh to the refuge of his own home. Victor parked himself in front of the porch, seething with tears, shouting in a rabid voice for the boy to come out, accusing him of being a chicken.

"I'm going to fuck you up," he mumbled to himself repeatedly after a while, unwilling to leave despite the neighbors telling him to do so.

The boy and his mother, everyone found out later, were afraid to return the marble. The woman had shown her face on the window, and as soon as Victor saw her, he clamped the porch rail and shook his body as if he were being electrocuted, a raspy scream spurting through his teeth. He didn't want the marble. He wanted justice. He wanted to inflict pain. The ordeal took close to an hour, until someone went and got Felipe. The neighbors recommended that he enroll his youngest son in some kind of psychiatric program. Victor's wrath wasn't normal, they said, not for a boy his age, especially considering how well-behaved Serguey was.

Felipe replied that maybe no one should take Victor's fucking marbles. To this day, that'd been the only time Serguey saw his father curse at another adult.

The electric socket dangling above Victor's head in the bedroom was missing the light bulb. Felipe preferred to use the bedside lamp, one of the few objects State Security had left intact. Years ago, a rounded bulb was suspended in midair, the socket attached to a cord that shot down from the ceiling. Serguey had imagined it to be a microphone, amplifying their voices, recording what took place in this room.

"Let's talk at the table," he said.

He didn't wait for Victor's response. He went to the dining room, sat at the far end, and fixed his eyes on the bedroom door. He wanted to prove that he could still lead.

It worked. Victor followed him, his aspect more serene as he sat across from his brother. The food-smeared plates were close to the edge of the table, where they'd been left. The turbid dregs in the glasses, like powdered pills stirred in water, oscillated as Victor dragged his elbows.

"If that was Mario," Serguey said, "he knows what's going on."

"Yeah, but I don't even—"

Serguey lifted his hand and shut his eyes. Victor understood the cue and stopped talking.

"We'll figure out a way to find the guy," Serguey continued, "but right now we need to decide what we can do for Dad."

"That's what's killing me: I don't know what's the best thing to do."

"Stop feeling guilty, Victor. I wasn't even around when all of this happened. *You* were here." Serguey did his best to channel Anabel: "The rest doesn't matter."

Victor combed his eyebrows, another nervous tic. "So what's the plan?"

Serguey tapped his splayed fingers on the table. "No one's going to print anything about Dad. They won't mention him on television or the radio." The government controlled every communications medium, every mass media outlet, every newspaper. Information always came with one angle, one bias in Cuba. Felipe's name would be brought up only if they wished to make an example out of him, and in that case, the obstacles could be insurmountable. "I've been thinking—and I don't really want to do this, because I'm not sure it'll work—but we should reach out to people outside the island."

"Like who?"

"Anyone who can take up Dad's cause. Maybe we can do it through someone here. Like Caseros."

Victor shifted his eyes aimlessly, as if trying to peer inward, delving into the recesses of his memory. "I have no idea who that is."

"He's a blogger. His name's been thrown around the office. He got fired from *Juventud Rebelde* years ago for criticizing communist bureaucracy and corruption after the Special Period." Serguey had also seen Caseros's name in the papers, though not in the same publication where he'd been dismissed. A scathing piece had dubbed the blogger the tip of the iceberg of a new online dissident movement bent on spreading lies about the system. The article excluded any explicit information that could send the few curious readers with internet access in search of such blogs. Instead, it'd focused on exposing Caseros as a disgruntled quasi-journalist on a mission, a morally and politically reprehensible online activist who blamed his personal failures on the country which had supported him from an early age. "The problem is," Serguey added, sagging his head apologetically, "I'm not sure what's the best way to contact him."

Victor planted his hands on the table and rose. "We go to Kiko."

"Kiko?"

"He knows all kinds of websites and that Twitter thing people in the United States are using." Victor shoved his chair under the table and chuckled repentantly. He'd been joggled out of his haze. "I've always made fun of him for spending so much time with computers."

Serguey got up gradually. "Can we trust him?"

"We've known him since we were kids. The guy used to be your best friend, no?"

The arched rim of Serguey's ears heated up with shame. "He was."

Victor seized everything from the table and ditched it in the sink.

Serguey trailed him to the front door. "What's Kiko doing these days?"

Victor waited for Serguey to walk out onto the porch so he could lock the home. "He's mixing CDs or something. I don't know, I'm not that much into music. He has a girl in Mexico. He hasn't said it, but I'm smelling that he's trying to leave the country."

Serguey put his hand on Victor's chest as his brother turned and housed the keys in his pocket. "Then we shouldn't bother him. We can mess up his plans."

Victor smiled, full of confidence, and descended the steps in two long strides.

⚜⚜⚜

In June of 1989, perplexing news stopped the country in its tracks: Cuba's highest decorated soldier and certified Hero of the Revolution, Gen. Arnaldo Ochoa Sanchez, had been accused of, among other acts, treason. During a televised Military Honour Court and subsequent trial (something rare in Cuba, where serious governmental matters were usually dealt with behind closed doors), a docile, bespectacled Ochoa humbly declared that the accusations made against him—drug trafficking with the Medellin cartel, illegal arms and sugar trade with Angola, diamonds and ivory smuggling—were all true. With a slumped head and childlike aspect in his stare, he said in a soft, defeated voice (some speculated that he'd been drugged by Castro's people during the entire proceedings) that he couldn't explain exactly why he'd betrayed his country. While trying to acquire arms to strengthen the Cuban military, he explained, one thing regrettably led to another. The one biting assertion Ochoa made was that some of the other men suspected of involvement, as well as witnesses who'd testified, including senior officers in the Ministry of the Armed Forces and Ministry of the Interior, had distorted the facts in order to save themselves.

On July 13, after being found guilty—his sentence ratified by a Council of State led by Fidel Castro—Ochoa and three other officers were executed by a firing squad. Fidel went as far as to publicly call some of the men "sons of bitches" for involving his brother Raul in their statements and claiming that there'd been "mitigating circumstances." Ochoa's body was dumped in an unmarked grave in Havana's historic Cristobal Colon cemetery. Hordes of top officials, heads of police, immigration, and counter intelligence officers were fired or demoted. A few other people went to prison. The Castros cleaned house. Numerous rumors dispersed among the population, though no one ventured to state them openly. One alleged that the Castros' top-notch counter-intelligence unit had to know what Ochoa was up to from the start. Another said that Raul, who'd been close friends with the well-liked general for decades, saw him as an adversary for succeeding Fidel, so he tapped Ochoa head of the Western Army in order to conduct the background check that coincidentally revealed the general's unpardonable crimes. The most popular rumor went like this: Fidel had discovered plans of a potential military coup by Ochoa and his men, and without wasting time he put on a theatrical display for all to see.

Whatever the truth, one thing was clear—regardless of who you were, you didn't fuck with the Castros.

Soon after, the Soviet Union joined history as another failed state, and the Special Period in Cuba began. A different kind of political oppression, though just as effective as executing widely known officials, inhibited the populace: shortages. Food, water, electricity, clothes—they became commodities. The new patriotic stance was to embrace lack of possessions and access to services as a worthy sacrifice for the Revolution. The US embargo became the chief scapegoat, the reason for the acute poverty in Cuba. The flexed arm of Imperialism was hell-bent on subjugating the small, heroic island. To speak out against its government was to sell yourself to American ideals, to endanger the safety of the country's commanders, to incite civil unrest. The number of dissenting voices grew despite this, however, emboldened by the decaying economy and political restrictions. By 2003, Fidel turned his attention to political activists, and what was later termed the Black Spring transpired. Seventy-five people, including journalists, writers, librarians, and democracy advocates, were jailed and sentenced in the blink of an eye. Many were sent to prisons hundreds of kilometers from home to secluded locations. A law student at the time, Serguey had avoided any articles or conversations dealing with the cases.

"I don't like to get too deep into politics," he'd say carefully, aware that he couldn't dismiss political positions outright without arousing suspicion.

Where did Felipe's arrest fit in all of it? Was he now a fundamental part of a questionable national history, the latest addition to an interrelated thread of persecution? These were the questions in Serguey's mind as he and Victor walked toward their friend's apartment. Serguey wasn't aware of any recent executions, like it'd happened with Ochoa, but the possibility of it remained in the nation's psyche like a stain. The rules since then had become unspoken among the population. Very few knew what exactly was happening to arrested dissidents, but everyone knew what *could* happen, and that was enough.

Kiko's apartment was four blocks away from Felipe's house, on the second floor of a once-green building, now unappealingly gray. It stood across Vento Avenue, technically in the municipality of El Cerro, home of Cuba's premier baseball stadium—the decaying *Latinoamericano*; the city's first aqueduct, whose moldy stone wall lined parts of Via Blanca Avenue like a fortress; and myriads of slums and youth street gangs.

Whenever asked where he lived, Kiko claimed that it was in 10 de Octubre. His friends weren't shy about correcting him.

"You're on the wrong side of Vento Avenue," they teased.

On an August afternoon (Serguey and Kiko must have been twelve years old), while returning from a game at the stadium, an overweight young man called Kiko and Serguey over to a park bench and asked to see Kiko's digital watch. It'd been a gift from his father: a large, colorful face on a brown plastic strap. The young man said, "I ain't gonna take it" when Kiko hesitated in presenting his wrist. Serguey saw two shifty figures behind a tree and without thinking bellowed, "Run!"

And run they did. Serguey only got one look at the pursuant group—they must have been four or five boys—as he and Kiko sprinted for half a dozen blocks before realizing the gang had given up.

This had been Serguey's only brush with the supposedly rampant crime element in El Cerro, though he'd been to the stadium ten or fifteen times. To indict an entire municipality because of a few bad seeds, he thought, was a ridiculous stretch. But reputation, savory or unsavory, was like an irremovable tattoo in Havana. A history teacher had once told him, "Build a reputation and go to sleep." Serguey interpreted it to mean that the image he created in other people's eyes, once there, would be permanent. The opposite also applied: the fact that the strip of buildings in and around Kiko's block was safe didn't keep him from being badgered about living in dangerous El Cerro.

Serguey and Victor climbed a set of stairs and moved briskly past two doors before reaching Kiko's apartment. Serguey leaned on the iron decorative railing, the balusters shaped like thunder bolts, and waited anxiously for Victor to knock. His brother pounded his fist like a hammer.

Serguey clutched his forearm from behind. "You really have to stop that. You can't go acting like a caveman at every person's door."

"You don't understand. Kiko sits at his computer with headphones on. He can't hear shit." Victor banged on the door again. "Kiko, you asshole!"

In a few seconds, a young man with black hair twirling to the bottom of his ears appeared. A pair of earphones was clasped at the base of his neck, covering his collarbone like an immense stethoscope.

"Holy crap!" he said, lunging forward and smacking Serguey on the chest.

Serguey embraced him.

"I didn't know you were in love with my brother," Victor said, standing on the doorsill. "I would've brought him sooner."

"You've got to come to terms with it, man." Kiko receded and shook Serguey's hand. "He was always the cooler of you two. Besides, it's been what, three years since I last saw you?"

Victor said, "Almost four, actually. Six if you go back to the last time he was in this apartment."

Six years ago, Kiko's parents still lived here. Serguey recalled them speaking about a *permuta* on his last visit, an official exchange of domiciles. Cash under the table often played a part in the transaction, but it usually came down to space versus location. Serguey's apartment, if he owned it, could have easily been swapped for a spacious three- or four-bedroom house with a yard in this part of the city. But giving up a location in El Vedado only made sense if you had a big family. As for Kiko's parents, Serguey wondered how and where they had found a new place without having to give up this one.

"You're keeping track?" Serguey told Victor, bothered by his brother's insistence on underscoring how inattentive he'd been.

"Purely for historical purposes," Victor said.

"Four years." Kiko shoved his fingers like a wide-tooth comb into his hair and scratched his scalp. "You'd figure we would've bumped into each other somewhere."

"My brother doesn't go out much," Victor said. "Not as much as us hustlers."

"Havana's a big city," was all Serguey could muster, tapping his heel against the bottom of the railing.

Kiko took them inside. He brought chairs so they could sit by his computer desk. Serguey considered his friend's new hairstyle, which had previously been shorn military-style. He considered the eyeglasses by the monitor, which had to be new, the headphones, the small mixing board on the corner of the desk, the unrecognizable furniture, wooden and lacquered, the seats and backrests woven like straw hats. The friend he had known—old-fashioned, dapper, mild-mannered Kiko—had transformed, only vestiges of his old self remained: the unrestrained smile, the cheerful gleam in his eyes at the sight of friends. Genuine expressions of delight. Kiko loved being around people. Felipe had once said that knowing someone as a child meant that you would know something of theirs forever, that not all in a person could be done away with, no matter how much one dressed it up or tried to hide it away.

Kiko and Victor lit up cigarettes and offered Serguey one. He declined. Kiko began speaking about a music project he was involved in, a rap group with jazz influences. He was mixing their latest CD. It was clear that Victor had taken Serguey's place in the friendship. Maybe it had been that way from the beginning. Maybe the age disparity was the only meddlesome factor at the time.

Kiko's parents had moved out to Regla, he explained, across the harbor, to care for Kiko's maternal grandmother.

"It's been a crazy year," he said, crossing his legs and dumping the excess burnt ash from his cigarette into an ashtray on his lap. "My grandmother's dementia is getting worse by the day, and my dad had a heart attack three months ago."

"Damn," Serguey said. Though he sincerely meant it, he felt hollow, even fraudulent, when he added, "I'm so sorry." He sat up and stared gravely at Victor. How could his brother have thought it sensible to bother their friend, when it was obvious his own family seemed to be in a bind?

"It's fine," Kiko said. "Dad just had to retire early. He helps around the house and has more patience than Mom does with my grandma, which is crazy, because they didn't have a great relationship when they were both healthy. I guess chronic illness can bring people together." He inhaled and immediately exhaled the smoke from his cigarette and perched it on the lip of the ashtray. Serguey didn't know what to say. Kiko continued, "Your brother has been good support, if you can believe it."

Victor raised the corner of his lip and gazed at Serguey's shoes.

"A couple of weeks ago," Kiko said, "he brought them a pound of ham. It made their week. He's convinced my dad to join him in some shady venture, you know, to give him the illusion that he's doing something."

Serguey looked at Victor. "So you really *are* a philanthropist."

Victor shrugged and glanced at Kiko. "He'd do the same for me."

Kiko put out his cigarette and carefully deposited the ashtray on his chair as he got up. "You thirsty?" he asked, walking away to the kitchen without waiting for a response.

The conversation Serguey suddenly wanted to have with his brother couldn't be carried out here. He wished to learn the specifics of how Victor and Kiko's friendship had developed, the sorts of favors they'd done for each other, the deals they'd been involved in, how much Victor had gotten to know Kiko's parents. More precisely, he wanted to know if Victor had not just usurped Serguey's position in their relationship but surpassed it.

Serguey skimmed the living room to distract himself. Kiko had hung posters of Queen, The Beatles, Bone Thugs-N-Harmony, Tupac, and Los Aldeanos. Serguey recognized the first two artists. (Felipe sometimes played *A Night at the Opera*, *Abbey Road*, and *The White Album* on the weekends during his friends' informal visits.) An old record player was propped on an inverted decorative crate in the far corner, flanked by two boxes bursting with records. Serguey could make out the first album cover in the box closest to him: Irakere.

He was going to ask about it, but then he heard Kiko's voice from the kitchen.

"Victor, is your brother deaf?"

"What?" Serguey said.

"Do you want a beer?"

"No, thanks."

"Victor, is Heineken okay?"

"Better than what I usually have at my place."

Kiko returned, and they popped the beers open. He asked Serguey if he didn't mind taking the ashtray and placing it behind him on the computer desk.

Serguey took an elusive peek at his brother.

Victor wet his lips with beer and said, "Kiko, we're here because we need your help."

"And here I was thinking it was because you love me." Kiko sat and crossed his legs again. "What's going on?"

Victor described what had transpired since the previous day: the arrest, Gimenez's advice, the conversation with Montalvo. He mentioned that they wouldn't see Felipe for another month, that Mario had called, but they weren't able to get anything out of him. Kiko listened raptly, his face taut with dread and sympathy. He set his beer can on the floor and jammed his fingers into his hair, this time pulling and coiling it almost like a chignon at the top of his head. When Victor paused to let him respond, he released the hair, which fell back haphazardly into place, stiff strands remaining at odd angles.

"That's heavy." He stroked his chin forcefully, like trying to peel a scab. "I had no idea."

Kiko was worried, but Serguey could also detect a twinge of curiosity in his tone.

"You hadn't heard anything from the neighbors?" Serguey asked him.

His friend's answer came swiftly, effortlessly. "I've been holed up in here mixing the CD. I even told my girl not to show up until Friday. No distractions, you know."

"Isn't your girl in Mexico?" Victor said.

"That's another girl. It's complicated." Kiko dropped his head and then looked up, his hair flopping behind his ears. "I'm sorry about Felipe. He was like an uncle to me growing up."

"It's fucked up," Victor said.

Serguey said, "My brother says you might know some people who can give us a hand. Someone with outside connections who can get Dad's story in the news, online, the radio, whatever. We're not asking you to get involved. Heck, I wouldn't have the nerve to ask that after being such a shitty friend. Just point us in the right direction."

Kiko seemed to mull over Serguey's appeal and made as if to talk, but Serguey wanted to lay the cards on the table first.

"I was thinking Caseros," he suggested. "I've heard his name thrown around at work. He seems to have a lot of pull."

"Caseros?" Kiko said. "No way. That guy works for State Security. Shit, he might know Fidel and Raul personally at this point."

Serguey leaned his elbows on his thighs, his body bent forward. "Really?"

Kiko and Victor also leaned in. To an outsider's eye, they might as well have been sitting at a campfire, telling horror stories. In truth, they were making sure their conversation didn't leave the walls around them.

"I'm exaggerating about him meeting the Castros," Kiko said, "but have you read his blog?"

"I don't have access to any of that. Internet is restricted for people like me at the Ministry, and I can't log on at home with the laptop they gave me."

Kiko's closed-mouth smile was redolent of their childhood, when he would approach Serguey and Victor with that same expression—a smile that might be smug on others, but in Kiko's lips, gracious—and imparted some scientific fact he had learned from his father, a high school geography teacher who loved geology. "All of Caseros's stuff is very general," he said, "very abstract." He picked up his beer and took a swig. Kiko was comfortable now, enthusiastic. "He thinks he's a poet, but he's terrible. Writes a lot and says nothing. Last year, he started traveling. He went to New York and Madrid to some journalism convention. Do you think if he were a real threat, if he really had pull, they'd let him loose like that?"

"Caseros a rat?" Serguey whispered, half to himself.

"Let me put it this way: if it were my dad's life that depended on it, I wouldn't go to him."

Serguey was not ready to give up his disbelief. "Doesn't he criticize the government? I mean, he's got everyone in my office fooled, then. And I'm talking people who've read his blog."

Kiko finished his beer and put the can carefully next to his chair's leg. He lifted his hands with the swagger of a cool professor about to give a critical lecture. "Think of him as a plant. He posts his diatribe about corruption, lack of food, the black market, the failure of the Revolution, but he doesn't point any direct fingers. He doesn't call for any revolt. He's just reporting what he sees or what other people tell him. Maybe they arrest him a couple of times, make it look like they're persecuting him. All the while he knows exactly what he can and cannot say. That's why he writes in such poetic prose. His posts are short, three or four paragraphs at most. You know how romantic and intellectual some Cubans are, or pretend to be. They read something that *sounds* good, and they don't really pay attention to the missing subcontext, to what's not being said." Kiko tilted back, pausing to revel in the precision of his logical reasoning. "We were all fooled by Fidel, so why wouldn't we be just as fooled by those who pretend to be against him?"

Serguey swallowed, too embarrassed to comment.

"Anyway," Kiko continued, perhaps to spare him, "Caseros gives the illusion that there's some freedom of speech in Cuba. That's how the government sees it. But if you go to him, you run the risk of being reported to the authorities. He'll tell those assholes exactly what you and Victor are planning to do or say, and before you know it, you're locked up. Caseros will write about it like it's a short story, but he won't lift a finger to help you."

Serguey nodded in appreciation. He had nothing to counter Kiko except his skepticism, which, if he were to let it take the reins, might lead down a path of isolation and helplessness. He had to trust him, take a chance.

"Who do you have in mind?" Victor asked. He seemed to know where his friend was going next.

"Claudia Bernal."

"Who is she?" Serguey said.

Kiko bent to grab his beer can but desisted mid-effort, remembering that it was empty. "She's been involved in a lot of stuff. She knows the human rights people, people in the Catholic Church, and definitely people in Miami. I studied with her at the Polytechnic. She was a computer engineering major. Believe me, she was already militant back then." He chuckled at his own recollection. "If anyone knows how to propagate information the right way, it's Claudia. I can vouch for her."

Serguey asked, "How soon can you reach her?"

"Give me a few days. I have to be careful so that none of us gets in trouble, especially her. She's been arrested before, and not like Caseros. She's been beaten and threatened. They've confiscated her computer, and she's had to start from scratch. They're scared to mess with her too much, though, because she knows how to document abuse better than anyone, and she's not afraid to publish names."

"I met her once," Victor said. "Kiko and I were hanging out somewhere in Centro Habana. She definitely likes him."

Kiko ignored him. "I'll serve as the link for now," he said to Serguey. "After she gets in touch with you, you can take it from there."

Serguey contemplated his friend, the audaciousness and ease with which he'd proposed this Claudia as the solution. They were running out of resources. If placing unconditional faith in Victor's decision to embroil Kiko was what it had come down to, he had to commit. He said, "Thank you," then showed his right palm as a cautioning sign, "but please tell her not to do anything without talking to me first."

"Sure thing."

Serguey ruminated on whether he should be frank with Kiko. Four years of non-existent contact didn't justify his curiosity about his friend's political interests and access to information that was forbidden to most Cubans. But again, as an unofficial lawyer to his father, he had a responsibility—to consider all angles and probable mistakes.

"How come you know so much about blogs?" he asked, modulating his tone. Not the smoothest way to phrase it, but the question had already left his lips.

Kiko wasn't upset by it. There was no look of surprise, no throat clearing or coughing, no averting of the eyes. He opened his mouth but then closed it, perhaps searching for the most believable way to couch his response. He stood and went to the kitchen. Serguey heard the refrigerator's door gasket unsticking, then the clanking of bottles rattling when the door closed. Kiko returned with a new beer can and sat again. He made a pistol out of his hands, the can serving as the grip, and pointed it at Serguey. "Do you know what percentage of Cubans have open access to the internet?"

"No idea."

"Less than five percent." Kiko cracked the can open and drank. "The government publically states that over twenty-five percent of its citizens have access, but that number is inflated. It includes restricted access, the kind that only lets you see national websites and databases. That's what doctors, engineers, academics get at their workplaces. It doesn't really count."

Ash from Victor's cigarette fell on the floor. Kiko scoffed genially at Victor's attempt to sweep it with his foot. He addressed Serguey.

"The places where you can get decent connection are internet cafes, which are government owned, require identification, and cost between two and five dollars an hour. That's what, almost a quarter of a monthly salary? Or you can sit in a hotel lobby if you have a tourist connection who will pay for you to sign on. Then, they block all the blogs that originate from inside the island, so you can only see what international sites are publishing. All of *that* material they can dismiss as imperialist propaganda."

Serguey mimed a pistol at Kiko. "So how can *you* read the national blogs?"

"Like with anything, there are ways around it. You need to figure out how to bypass certain obstacles through a secure network. Once you do, there isn't much risk of someone spying on you because the government knows there just aren't many people inside the country reading these blogs."

This time it was Serguey who moved his lips but didn't speak.

Kiko asked, "Have you heard of *Operation Truth*?"

Serguey couldn't recall where he had heard it, but it sounded familiar. It most likely had been at the Ministry.

"Right now," Kiko said, "they have about a thousand students from the University of Computer Science looking for anything that relates to Cuba's government online. It's structured into several divisions: monitoring specialists, information analysts, and counter-responders. It's like a cyber-militia. They attack the bloggers personally and try to discredit them. They defend the regime to make it seem like the dissenter is a traitor. I think it got started through the *Unión de Jóvenes Comunistas*, so it trickles down directly from the top."

Serguey marveled at Kiko's wealth of information. He wondered whether his friend couldn't usually converse about these things, whether he'd taken this opportunity as a way to vent.

"How do you know all of this?" he asked him.

Kiko hoisted his beer as if it were a prize. "I still have friends at the university."

Serguey deduced that Kiko's access also came from those associations and not just from his technical knowledge. He swiped his eyes over the posters and vinyl compilation and figured that this might be what Kiko did in his spare time: host friends, Cuban jazz fusion humming from the record player, discussing technology and politics with cold beer in the pit of their bellies. But meddling deeper into Kiko's life would verge on cynicism and disrespect. Serguey himself knew as much as the average person: home connections were prohibited; independent Wi-Fi networks required so many permits that they were impractical to set up; public internet access at schools, hospitals, and libraries was excruciatingly—and after Kiko's explanation, he now suspected purposely—slow. If Kiko had found a way to sidestep and outwit the system, he should be celebrated, his privacy revered.

"We have one cell phone provider for the whole country," Kiko said, pressing the moist-glazed can against his cheek, "and it's state-controlled. Social media's exploding around the world; all that data and traffic is very difficult to oversee and regulate, so it's just easier to dissuade use by not giving people an option. It's fucking wicked, but it's genius. They haven't maintained this government for five decades out of sheer luck."

As Serguey processed Kiko's explanation, he hankered for a beer himself.

Maybe just putting his forehead to a cool, moist can would do the trick. "So the people at my job talking about Caseros—"

"They might've been testing you, to see if you knew or had read something. Why the fuck does an employee of the Ministry of Foreign Relations care about a blogger?"

"Unless they're State Security," Victor said. He finished his beer and crushed his can, burping.

"Don't!" Kiko swatted at Victor's hand, but he was too late. "I give the cans to a buddy of mine who makes decorative pieces," he told Serguey. "He sells them to tourists in Old Havana."

"You're still giving cans to that bald guy?" Victor said.

"He's a San Alejandro graduate. Amazing talent. He just hasn't made any headway through the proper channels."

Victor held up the mangled can. "Tell him it's an abstract."

"There's another thing," Serguey said. He had no idea whether his intuition that Kiko's technical knowledge could facilitate locating Mario was right, but if his friend turned out to be their only ally, he might as well consult him. "Dad told my brother to call Mario, the dramaturge, when he was being arrested. I get the impression that he's also my dad's best friend. Victor doesn't have the guy's phone number, and State Security confiscated all of my dad's stuff. So I was wondering if you knew—"

"Did he call your cell or the landline?" Kiko asked.

Victor squeezed whatever little pockets of air were left inside his beer can. "Landline."

"If you can get his number," Kiko said, fluttering his lashes with confidence, "I might be able to do something with it."

Encouraged by the response, Serguey nodded vigorously. Looking to buy time and process some of what Kiko had laid on him, he asked his friend about his parents, about whether his mom had also retired. He expressed remorse for not being informed as to his father's condition, for not visiting Kiko or his folks more often.

"Leave that for another day," his friend said. "They remember you fondly and will be happy to see you whenever you go."

"I'll take you when Dad's ordeal is over," Victor said.

Serguey let his brother have his moment of moral superiority. "I should have time then. I doubt I'll be able to keep my job."

Kiko rucked his forehead, his pained look meant as a form of solidarity. "The minute those guys at the Ministry find out, they're going to investigate you."

Serguey felt the urge to ask for the beer, to taste its bitterness on his tongue. "I'm hoping my boss will intervene."

"The guy who told you where Felipe was?"

"Yeah."

"How well do you know him?"

"The apartment where I live is actually his."

The expulsion of air from Kiko's nostrils shattered Serguey's hope that he should trust Gimenez. "All the more reason for him to watch his own back."

"Serguey and Anabel are practically family to him," Victor put in.

"If that's true," Serguey said, "I'm not sure it's a good thing."

Kiko tucked his Adam's apple under his chin. He advised the brothers to get calling cards for their cell phones. "You can get them at any ETECSA branch or the post office. Those calls are untraceable."

"I told you I wasn't paranoid," Victor said to Serguey.

Serguey wasn't convinced. "Do you really think they're listening?"

"You never know," Kiko said. "G2 doesn't need court orders. I'm surprised they didn't come to you before they arrested your dad. They usually work the family first. That's what Claudia says. Anyway, use the cards as a precaution. You get your own code and everything."

"Why would G2 get involved with my father?" Serguey held Kiko's gaze and watched his friend swallow.

"If it's anything political . . ."

Until that moment, Serguey hadn't believed that G2, Cuba's Intelligence Directorate, could possibly be involved in Felipe's case. G2 meant the Soviet Union, the C.I.A., espionage. For many people, however—including several clients of Serguey's former colleagues—it spurred another kind of fear, a more recent and homegrown one. Serguey had heard stories: a cousin of a cousin who'd been electroshocked to a mumbling existence. But just as he had pretended to have faith in the Castros' leadership, he had behaved as though State Security was a standard, if harmless institution. They had offices above his floor at the Ministry. The people who'd ridden in an elevator with him for months, exchanging polite good mornings and commenting on the receptionist's delicious coffee, they were willing to extort, maybe even torture, behind closed doors. Serguey was horrified by the thought that he'd shaken their hands and engaged in their small talk because he hadn't conceived he or his family would ever be targets. The deplorable nature of prison life, the one he had witnessed, he could chalk up to isolation, poor supervision, the military mindset of the guards. But persecution bore a more menacing undertone, a level of oppression that once exposed to, you couldn't ignore, not with your own father a political prisoner.

A wearied Serguey thanked Kiko for all his help. As the brothers readied themselves to leave, Kiko asked Victor to wait outside.

"You've always been smitten by my brother," Victor said.

Kiko shoved him to the entrance while laughing. As he pushed the door, Victor called out, "You two deserve each other!"

Kiko told Serguey that he understood how serious the situation was. "I won't fuck this Claudia thing up."

Serguey tendered his hand. "I've been an asshole, Kiko. But I know I can trust you."

His friend pressed it firmly. "Your brother and I are good friends, but I'm not stupid. You're the one who can really help your dad."

Although he was flattered, Serguey felt saddled by the responsibility. The longer he went without replying, the more desperate he became to break the tension. "Victor says you listen through the wall when he brings a girl over."

Kiko laughed. "Your brother says that to everyone. Truth is I give him my spare key and leave. I usually go to see my parents when he's here with someone. The couple of times he's been to Regla with me were because he'd been stood up."

Serguey shook his head.

"Your brother's an eternal prankster," Kiko said. "He never really grew up. Then again, most people in our generation didn't. You're an exception."

This facet of Kiko—the recalcitrant idealist, the system-bashing blog reader and enthusiast—was still new to Serguey. He hadn't witnessed its natural progression, its tentacles taking hold of his friend's worldview. To be called an "exception" hurt him, even if Kiko hadn't meant it as an indictment or criticism. The people with whom Serguey worked and kept company over the last few years were people whose objectives and successes fell neatly in line with the system. To be looked at and judged by those outside this exclusive environment made him feel part of the problem, a comrade of those who'd imprisoned Felipe and caused Joaquin's death, a traitor to those with whom he'd grown up.

"Nothing to do for the rest of us but drink, screw, and tell jokes," Kiko said. "This country's gift to its youth."

Serguey thanked his friend again and told him that he would await his call.

As he and Victor went down the stairs, Serguey saw a boy and a girl on the sidewalk approaching the building. The boy was bare-chested, his collarbone like two perfect branches holding up his neck. He was wearing white-and-blue Hawaiian shorts that covered what had to be fist-sized knees. The girl, her feet shoved loosely inside flip-flops, wore a fluorescent green spaghetti strap top with a red school uniform skirt. Her knees, possibly broader than the boy's, peeped out below the hem. The colors of their sparse outfits darted beautifully next to one another as the boy held on to the pooled string of a kite. There wasn't playful happiness on their expressions but rather a kind of concentration associated with an unfinished task. Were they on their way to sell the kite? To return it? To prove to a friend that theirs flew better? Serguey watched them turn into the building next to Kiko's and vanish behind the sidewall.

He looked at Victor and told him he was going straight home. No need to go back to the house. Victor promised him, at his request, that he would stay put until Kiko spoke with Claudia and a meeting was arranged.

Serguey walked past the building where the kids had entered and, to his disappointment, he didn't see them. He wondered if they were on their way to the roof, to take advantage of the afternoon breeze. Serguey had flown a kite once, slicing the web of skin between his thumb and index finger when a relentless draft dragged the kite away from him. He went home with tears in his eyes, a meter of cord still attached to the twig he'd used for leverage, a burning sensation at the center of his bloody cut. The cord had snapped, and another boy had run faster than him after the kite, pilfering it from a low-hanging telephone pole and claiming possession under street rules. Felipe told him that he should pick a more brain-stimulating game, like chess or Mastermind. Flying kites and playing marbles always ended in fights. Felipe was right: Serguey wanted to punch the other boy in the face, rip the kite to shreds. But he could never do it, he told himself, not with an injured hand, or without Victor's help.

CHAPTER 8

Anabel had prepared sandwiches. She'd scraped mustard from the bottom of the jar Gimenez had brought them on his last visit and smeared it on top of the ham. She topped it off with a slice of lettuce for crunchiness, just as Serguey liked it. She was looking to give him temporary satisfaction, to be mindful of the small pleasures left for them. She was sensing the insidious approach of change, Serguey assumed, and she wanted to retain matrimonial gestures, packed with love in their simplicity. It was either that, or she intended to make a demand and wanted him in a favorable mood.

Regardless, he was grateful. He shared with her in detail what'd happened at Calderas. Montalvo knew about his Sweden assignment, so he feared that the State Security Department at work was already monitoring him. He told her about Kiko and Claudia and how that might be a start. Things just needed to get moving. He had purchased two calling cards on the way to the apartment. Leave nothing to chance, was his new attitude. Give them nothing that they can use as evidence later.

Anabel listened straight-faced, barely touching her sandwich. When he asked her if she wasn't hungry, she replied that she would save it for later. She took Serguey's empty plate, brushed the breadcrumbs into the garbage bin in the kitchen, and dumped the plate in the sink. Her own plate she put in the fridge.

A demand it was.

As she walked back to the dining table, he asked her, "What's going on? And don't say 'nothing' because I know that isn't true."

She sat next to him. "I don't want to play the wife-at-home role on this one. I want to help. I want my opinions to matter. I know Felipe's your father, but he's my family too."

"Who says you can't help?"

"I'm just pointing out how I feel."

What he saw as protecting his wife, she saw as exclusion. Still, he was surprised. Anabel was seldom selfish about her feelings. "Where's all this coming from?"

"You shouldn't tackle your problems alone. I know you have your brother, but quite frankly, and you know I like him, he isn't the brightest bulb in the box."

"Victor's smarter than you think," he said instinctively. "And of course I want your help. But it's not like you need to go with me everywhere."

She began fidgeting with her fingers. "I just want my opinions to matter."

"You already said that."

"I think we should go to the Church." Her eyes met his, then she withdrew them to her own hands, watching her fingers continue to fiddle with an invisible object.

She should have opened with that, he thought. "The Church?"

"My parents are friends with a priest. My mom believes he's assisted in getting people out of prison before."

"You mean political prisoners?"

"Some of them, yes."

She had fallen for the set-up. "You've already told *your* parents that *my* dad is a political prisoner?"

She crossed her arms. "What was I supposed to tell them? My parents aren't communists, Serguey. They know how this country works."

Serguey shoved his chair back as he got up. "So they have no respect for what I do."

Anabel's mouth twisted into a mien of anger. "Don't pretend like they don't love you. They're very happy for us. They might be religious, but they don't judge other people like that, especially their son-in-law."

Serguey clamped two fingers to the bridge of his nose and lifted his head. Through a narrow gap in his lips he released a prolonged hiss, meant to signify deep irritation. A feeling of déjà vu suddenly swept over him. He realized he was imitating his father, hoping to maximize the effect that his histrionics might have on his audience. He dropped his arms inelegantly and said, "The Church could be problematic, Anabel. You know how the government feels about it."

Her eyes were pinned on his. "And how do you think they feel about bloggers?"

"I can keep my name out of it."

"You can do the same with the Church. You can trust my parents."

It took a moment for him to reply. "We can't go around involving people. If all this backfires, then who knows what route the river of shit that will follow is going to take?"

"What's the alternative? Hope that some woman you've never met gets Felipe's story to the right people? Are you going to walk into a police station and demand your dad's freedom?"

"If that's what it takes."

"Maybe what it takes is going to the Church. We have to take risks. We have to be willing to sacrifice everything." She tilted back and raised her eyebrows. "If you play it safe, you won't forgive yourself, and then I'll have to deal with *that* for the rest of my life."

He had no retort. He sat still in his chair and laid his hands on the table, gazing at the opposite wall. "Do you really think it'll make a difference?"

She shrugged. "I don't know. But—"

"But we have to try."

"We've been dealt a shitty hand. We have no choice but to play it. We've always been that couple: whatever has to be done, we do it. With your dad, it can't be different."

He sighed. "Let me sleep on it, at least."

Anabel took his hands. "Thank you."

At night they made love. Another small pleasure. More than anything, it felt like release to him, as if all his tension and worries had been momentarily exorcised from his body. He thought of a joke, as the double-entendres were not lost on him, but he refrained, not wanting to cheapen the moment. He let Anabel snuggle close, her cheek on his sweaty shoulder. He loved how her skin felt when it was wet: warm and slippery, as if it could slide into any position until their bodies locked. She wasn't shy in bed. Quite the opposite. She was brazen, self-assured. The first few times they were intimate, Serguey wondered whether she'd find him too passive, too hesitant, and whether this would cause her to grow bored of him. He caressed her body, always stealing looks at her face, searching for signals. Apparently she enjoyed it, never discouraging him. Occasionally, she proffered him an indicator—the subtle thrust of her pelvis, the palpable tightening of her thigh, the sensual arching of her back. She'd licked her own lips once. It had been reactionary, not something to entice him. He naively thought this only occurred in movies. He was thankful. Perhaps he'd gotten better at it, though he'd been too abashed to ask her.

As Serguey turned off the bedside lamp, he sensed Anabel's hand crawling to his pelvis.

"I'm spent," he told her.

She recoiled her hand. "It's okay." Her voice was lambent, like a drifting ember in the darkness of the room.

"Are you sure your mother's fine making an appointment to see the priest?"

She repositioned her head on her pillow, the way he knew she did when she was readying herself to sleep. "The only reason she didn't make it already," she said, "is that I warned her not to until I'd spoken with you."

"Good."

"And we're going together."

He scrabbled for and kissed the edge of her mouth, still moist from the sweat. "Of course," he said. "Together."

It was during instants like this one, in the placating space of their bedroom, where he could isolate his thoughts as he could her scent or her slightest movement, that he felt most blessed to have her by his side. It was here that he could reflect on what she had forgone for his sake. Anabel had had dreams of her own when they met. She wanted to be a psychologist. She attended the University of Havana for a year before being burned out—as many students were—by the insufferable load of Marxism-Leninism courses.

"They feed you so much bullshit," she told Serguey in confidence. "It's like they want you to quit. I'm interested in psychology, not politics."

She took a handful of courses and got her license to teach elementary school math, a job that was in high demand. She figured she could land one quickly, somewhere near their home, and do that while Serguey's career took off. Then came the vague promise of a secretarial position if Serguey got the Swedish Embassy position. That'd been six months prior. Anabel chose to quit after two years of teaching. She wanted to be available in case the opportunity presented itself. That's what she told her husband, though Serguey suspected that it was because her menial salary, like that of most Cubans, didn't justify the amount of work.

Now, Serguey knew, his window to travel might be closing, and Anabel was sacrificing just as much as he was.

This is what he opted to tell Gimenez the following morning, when, as Serguey did a second set of push-ups on the balcony while Anabel slept, the phone rang with a call from his boss. Gimenez began with a sequence of polite questions about Felipe's condition.

"All things considered," Serguey replied, sitting stiffly on the sofa, his muscles throbbing from the exercise, "he's doing fine."

Gimenez expressed what Serguey would have described as overstated gladness, and then told him that he had phoned to let Serguey know that he was holding down the fort in regards to the guys on the fifth floor.

"They're curious about your involvement," his boss said, "but that shouldn't be surprising. I told them you've been given a week-long leave of absence so that you can clear up everything on your end."

"Right," Serguey said, his own tone a bit inflated. "Thank you." The neurons on his brain conditioned to carry and transmit legal knowledge were telling him that "clear up everything" was coded language. It was more than advice. It was a warning. "I just want to make sure this won't affect my Sweden assignment." He stood, holding the telephone cord like a fishing line, gradually releasing the tension as he peered down the hall. "Anabel is really worried. This is an opportunity for both of us."

"And that's what you should keep in mind," Gimenez said. "Can I expect you back next week?"

Serguey twirled the cord with his fingers. "Absolutely."

"If you need anything, I'm here for you." There was a gap in his mentor's voice, filled by the sound of shuffling papers and a drawer slamming shut. Edging his mouth closer to the receiver, it seemed to Serguey, Gimenez said, "Tell Anabel that."

Serguey collapsed slowly onto the sofa. His arms now ached from fatigue. Letting go of the cord, he lolled his head back and responded, "I will."

CHAPTER 9

Not long after he hung up, Serguey found himself turning the front lock and facing Alida. She had knocked so lightly that he was half-expecting an empty hallway as he swung the door open.

"Hey," she said and kissed his cheek. A whitish pigmentation had formed in the margin of her eyes, which Serguey attributed to oversleeping. "Any news on Felipe?"

He closed the door before responding. "They have him at Calderas."

"Is he okay?"

"I think so," he lied, not wanting to trouble her.

The slabs of her eyelids retreated as she moved her face toward his. "Are they going to release him?"

"I'm not sure what's next." He momentarily caressed her arm just above the wrist to offer assurance. "But I'll figure something out."

She inscribed an atmosphere of hope on her features, then grasped his elbow and began leading him to the sofa. "I'm having a hard time at my parents'. I tried going back to my apartment, but my roommates are unbearable. All they do is complain."

"Must be driving you crazy."

"It's exasperating." She slumped on the sofa, same as he'd done minutes prior, sprawling her legs over the armrest. "I'm already a wreck over this whole thing."

Anabel was still in her nightgown when Serguey saw her come out of the bedroom and plod sleepily toward him.

"The world ended and I was asleep," she said.

"I didn't want to wake you," Serguey said.

"I heard you talk a little while ago. Were you on the phone?"

"Gimenez."

"What did he say?"

He glimpsed at Alida. She had burrowed her face in the nook of her right arm. "He's holding down the fort," he told his wife, "says we shouldn't worry. I have a leave of absence for a week."

"Good," Anabel said. She kissed him on the mouth, then stared at Alida, shaking her head. "It's like having a disabled child." She shifted her eyes back to Serguey. "I got coffee brewing. Help me bring some to my *languid* sister."

In the kitchen, she inquired about the call. "Has the Sweden assignment fallen through?"

"No," he said, perhaps too assertively. "State Security did ask about me, but Gimenez took care of it."

She regulated the fire in the gas burner. "What are you going to do?"

"About my job?"

"About your father."

He had to be upfront with her. "I want to help, but I'm worried that—"

"Don't," she said, her face mutating into a defiant expression. "You don't half-ass helping your father."

She opened a cabinet behind him. He slanted his head out of the way, a sugared scent (did it come from her hair or behind her ear?) stimulating him. She snatched three cups, the ceramic tinkling as she slid her index finger inside the handles and carried them like whopping rings.

The stovetop coffee pot began to gurgle, and she turned off the gas. She filled the cups, little streams of smoke twirling past the rim with a smell that seemed to expand Serguey's airways.

"Why are you so adamant about this?" he asked her. He wasn't questioning her motives. Rather, he was hoping that her reasons, compiled with his own, were sufficient to convince him to forget his job. "I understand we have to help my dad, but why are you so willing to give everything else up?"

She placed the pot among the two rear burners. "You shouldn't worry about other things while you do what you have to do for Felipe. If you start weighing the Sweden assignment and your job against your dad, regardless of what happens, in the end you'll regret it."

"I understand, but this is my career, our apartment, our future. We can't just dismiss it."

She gave him a stern look. "Don't you have a leave of absence? Use it to do what you can."

"It isn't that simple."

"It is."

"I'm falling asleep!" Alida shouted from the living room.

Anabel grabbed two cups. "Get your own," she told him.

He didn't say much while they sipped their coffee. He wanted to ask Alida about her roommates, about their gossiping and griping. She seemed relieved to be with her older sister again. They were huddled together on the sofa, holding their cups and gazing at nothing in particular. He offered to play a movie for them on the DVD player. Yet another gift from Gimenez, though he believed that his boss had taken it from a batch of international donations at the Ministry, like many of the department directors did. Anabel said she wasn't in the mood, but Alida went from languid to giddy, unloading her cup on the center table and rubbing her hands.

"Do you have anything that's not American?" she asked. "I don't like those action and special effects movies."

"We have a few European films." Serguey looked at Anabel. "Are you okay with that?"

"Fine with me." She pleated the flaps of her nightgown between her legs and said to her sister, "His father got him into foreign movies when he was young. He doesn't watch often, but when he does, they're usually European."

"We have *Dancer in the Dark*," Serguey said. "I don't know if that'll be too depressing."

"No, not that one," Alida said. "I love that movie, but it's too sad. I need something more uplifting."

"How about *Amélie*? I also have *Cinema Paradiso*."

"*Amélie*! I've heard about it but haven't seen it."

"Play it," Anabel said, disinterested. "She'll like it."

Serguey sat on the balcony while the sisters watched the film. The French words in the background began to meld with the soundtrack. He'd looked up the composer's name, Yann Tiersen, and asked the person at work who usually got him movies—the head of the mailroom, whose cousin managed a music and video store in Homestead, Florida—to get him anything he could find by Tiersen. This had been months ago. He'd completely forgotten about it. Listening to the music again, he regretted not having pressed his coworker. How easy it was to forget something you liked. How fleeting beautiful things could be when your thoughts were elsewhere, when daily life took precedence. He wondered whether his father had ever had such a deliberation. He must have. Artists were often hampered by these questions—about beauty and the ephemeral nature of life.

Serguey stared at the drifting clouds. The Cuban sky, he had to admit, was as blue as blue could get. Did people in other countries think the same about snow and white, forests and green? The soothing music from the movie was gone. Serguey got a sickening feeling that he might never get to see snow or a real forest, that he would live and struggle and love and die on these streets without knowing what lay beyond the water bounding the island like an electric fence. That was the true tragedy of life, he decided: to live longing for other things in a country that rewarded sameness and servitude, ruled by tyrannical cynics of a breed worse than Gimenez, where politics was in everything and everyone. A country kept alive and miraculously made vibrant by hopeless artists like his father.

There was a bout of laughter, both from the characters in the film and the sisters. If Serguey were a smoker or drinker, this would've been the perfect time to indulge. But he wasn't, so he got up and told the women he was going to get a newspaper.

He picked up a copy of *Granma* in a container-turned-kiosk around the corner on Twenty-third Avenue. Gustavo, the scruffy-haired attendant, asked Serguey why the sullen expression.

"Not my best day."

"I've had plenty of those," Gustavo said. "Too many if you ask me."

Serguey perched himself on a nearby concrete wall, his feet barely above the sidewalk, and snapped the paper open. There were multiple articles on an upcoming summit to be held in Havana. Fidel, now habitually named "The historical hero of the Cuban Revolution," had already met with some officials. In the picture next to the article, his scrawny face and bristle-shaped beard seemed too large for his neck. He looked impassively ahead as a female official, her neck craned forward, held him by the elbow. Change their clothes and you had an old patient with his nurse. This had been the revered leader of the Revolution. The man adored and cursed by so many. Like the rest of the country, he had finally decayed. The stalwart symbol of Cuban communism had become a parody, and yet the system persisted in spite of him.

For years, Serguey heard rumblings about a new Cuba, about the regime's entropy and Fidel's rumored flagging health being a harbinger for change. But at work, he saw that after Raul was made leader, no drastic measures were taken. Even Gimenez had undergone a stressful few weeks, waiting to hear on possible reshuffling at the Ministry, an infusion of younger blood at the top positions. As it turned out, Raul didn't want to rock the boat. Serguey wondered if the population still expected adjustments, the implementation of new freedoms, passed out like candy at a school. Or had they become irrevocably jaded, as they should be?

The sports section of the newspaper talked about the Venezuelan baseball league. Nothing of interest to him. In the Culture page, there was an article on restorations done for the next Book Fair and another on a Salsa Festival in Santiago de Cuba. No mention of Felipe, of course. Political prisoners were never mentioned in the press. In Cuba, the label didn't exist. Enemies of the state paid by Yankee imperialism? Plenty of those. Perhaps in the artistic circles the news of Felipe's imprisonment was not news anymore. But no one would dare print anything about it, not in a government-sanctioned publication.

Serguey flipped to the Science and Technology section. He found a column on the advancements of data collection in Latin America and the Caribbean, titled "Reducing Childhood Hunger, One Number at a Time." A computer program had been developed by a group of Canadian computer scientists—in coordination with Cuban affiliates—that could process data to determine the precise nutritional deficiencies in certain regions. The idea was to target the kinds of food that should be delivered to these areas in order to not only treat hunger but to do so more effectively. This fascinated Serguey, the notion that a specialized field could have such large-scale ramifications. In practice, the proficiency of the computer program would be limited by the logistical, political, and legal realities of multi-national projects, the latter being somewhat familiar to him. Nonetheless, it *could* make a difference. What purpose did *he* serve? He had never bothered himself much with existential reflection, but there was no escaping it now. He needed to make sense of what he was doing, plunging into a muddy hole whose muck he might never be able to wash off.

The Sweden assignment was nothing like the data collection project. He'd be drafting small-scale documents, offering legal advice to lower-level embassy administrators. Anabel would work as a secretary. It would be a start, he knew, not the final landing spot for them, but who, beyond themselves, would they be helping? Beyond a trip abroad, the acquisition of business clothes, and personal connections (one of Gimenez's favorite phrases), what would they gain? To do so now, with his father in prison and his brother teetering on the brink of an arrest himself, would be unforgivable. He was incapable of such a betrayal.

A horn's blaring scream reverberated through the air. A stunned Serguey watched a bus driver poke his head out the window and yell at a man speeding away on a motorcycle. Was it the same man from the night of the play, the one with the bag who'd given Victor a ride? He couldn't tell, but it was possible. One often saw the same people in Havana, like ghosts ensnared in a looping afterlife. The motorcycle was not a Suzuki, however. Serguey could swear it was a German MZ 250, ubiquitous in Cuba, not in the best of shapes.

"Almost hit him!" Gustavo shouted from the kiosk. *"Que come mierda."*

People on the opposite sidewalk were peering down the avenue. They thrashed their arms about in disbelief, appalled by such carelessness.

A man wearing a St. Louis Cardinals cap yelled to the driver, "Good reflexes there, chief!"

The MZ's engine faded into a distant shifting of gears. Had the accident happened, the motorcycle would've been crushed under the grille, the man's mauled body landing by Serguey. He had seen enough of those for one lifespan. No sense in sitting around, waiting for another calamity to settle at his feet. He folded the newspaper under his arm, jumped off the wall, and hastened back toward the apartment. He was going to ask Alida about her roommates, about what they'd been saying. He was going to pressure Kiko to set up the meeting with Claudia as soon as he could. He was going to urge Anabel to stay on top of her mother until the meeting with the priest had been arranged. More importantly, he was going to prove to himself that he was all in.

Climbing the stairs to his floor, he heard his neighbor's lock click. The door opened and Carmina stretched her head out. As soon as she saw him, she said, "Serguey, may I speak with you for a moment?" Her hair was a collection of small cylinders. The rollers had done their job.

"Sure, Carmina."

She approached him as if they were about to conspire against the rest of the building. "You didn't go to work today?"

"I'm working from home. A special assignment."

"Ah. You must be doing well if they trust you to stay at home."

"They trust me, all right."

Carmina lowered her voice. "The reason I wanted to speak with you is that you missed last night's neighborhood watch. You and Anabel have been so good about it since you moved in, I was just wondering if everything's okay."

"Anabel wasn't feeling well, so I decided to stay home." Lying wasn't enough. He either had to show remorse or assure Carmina that he would follow protocol. "I'll report it to the CDR," he added. The family in charge of the Committee for the Defense of the Revolution lived at the end of the street. There was one in nearly every block—civilian eyes for the authorities, sniffing out black market trades or suspicious activities in exchange for preferential treatment. Serguey had only seen his committee's members during one of the scheduled neighborhood meetings, which Anabel usually attended.

"Oh, how's she feeling today?" Carmina said. "I can bring her some lemon tea. I also have some cough medicine."

"There's no need."

"Nonsense. I'll bring her some right over." She began to walk away.

Serguey clamped her elbow as delicately as he could. "Honestly, Carmina. There's no need."

She stopped, a note of apprehension in her eyes. "I saw Alida come in with you earlier. She's taking care of her sister, huh?"

Serguey sighed. "I don't mean to be rude, but I really have to go."

"Of course! And don't worry about the CDR. I'll report it myself. You take care of your wife. She's a keeper."

"Yes, she is," he said, his back already turned.

❧❧❧

He cooked a quick lunch while the movie ended. He reheated leftover rice, sliced an avocado, and made scrambled eggs with cubed ham. He also poured two Tu-Kola cans, Cuba's brand of soda, into three small glasses. Anabel and Alida were pleasantly surprised. They drew the center table closer to the sofa and asked Serguey to lay down the plates and glasses, which he'd brought in a large serving tray. He took a chair from the balcony and sat across from the sisters.

"Don't take this the wrong way," Alida said, "but this kind of lunch makes it easy to stay with you guys. I can barely get any decent food with my acting salary."

The soft drink and the ham were indulgences. Serguey couldn't pretend otherwise. "I've been fortunate at work," he said diffidently, mixing his portion of scrambled eggs with the rice.

"Whenever you come over," Anabel said, sitting cross-legged, her plate perched on her thighs, "we'll feed you right."

Serguey wondered how much longer that would be true. He didn't say it, however, preferring not to ruin the pleasant ambiance.

"That was a good movie," Alida said. She batted her eyes discreetly at him.

"Yes," he said. "Funny too."

"*Amélie* reminds me of my roommates, how they usually are."

Was she simpering now? He wasn't sure, but she was clearly trying to engage him. She waited for him to respond.

"How come?"

She snuggled back deeper into the sofa, settling into the conversation. "They're very whimsical and happy like that."

"And you're not?" Anabel said.

Alida puckered her brow. "Is that how you see me? That isn't so bad. Anyway, Dosiel, for instance, always smiles really wide and is the sweetest, most innocent guy despite being tall and strong. I'd go for him if he wasn't gay." She picked out two pieces of ham with her fork and slid them off the tines with her teeth.

Serguey saw an opportunity to pry. "Is he one of the people who's been complaining?"

"Complaining about what?" Anabel said.

He realized his wife hadn't overheard the conversation between him and Alida when she'd arrived. He swallowed his food, a sensation like heartburn thumping in his chest. "Alida told me that it's been hard for her because her roommates are griping about what happened."

Alida explained that it wasn't just her roommates. The majority of the actors in the group had been inconsolable, some because they loved Felipe and were concerned about him, others because they figured their careers might be affected. Theater directors could be afraid to take them in, especially those who had a lot to lose. A rotten fruit infects the ones around it, she'd heard someone say.

"My roommates aren't saying that," she clarified, "but a few of the other actors are. I hear all this and end up with spider webs in my head. I love Felipe and don't want anything bad to happen to him."

"I know I asked you this before," Serguey said, "but does anyone suspect why he was taken in?"

"No, but they think that Mario has something to do with it. He's been missing since Felipe got arrested. No one can get a hold of him."

"Do you know where he lives?"

"I think he's from Miramar, but I didn't have a lot of interaction with him during rehearsals. It was mostly your father and a few of the other actors."

"You have to find him," Anabel told Serguey. "He *has* to know something."

Alida chimed in, "What did they tell you at the *Consejo Nacional de las Artes Escenicas?*"

Serguey discarded his plate at the corner of the table. "Does he work there?"

"That's where he and Felipe get their paychecks."

Serguey was embarrassed for his oversight. No matter how much of an independent artist his father was, he had to answer to somebody. He'd been allotted a great rehearsal space. He'd staged his latest play at *Teatro Mella*. Despite his claim that he hated elbow rubbing, some must've been involved. There was also payroll, administrative compliance, censorship, accolades. Everything was attached—some way or another—to the government. In Felipe's case, it was the National Council for the Performing Arts, which belonged to the Ministry of Culture.

The maddening irony was the location: the main branch was a mere seven blocks away from the apartment. He had seen it several times. A yard bordered the building, a pre-Revolution mansion that'd been transformed, like dozens of others, into a public establishment.

He was too ashamed to offer Alida a reply. With a supplicant face, he asked Anabel to take care of the dishes. He washed his hands and mouth, and checked for food stains on his clothes. He picked up his key, cell phone, and wallet and said he'd be back soon.

"Call if you're going to be late," Anabel said.

He promised her he would.

⚜ ❧ ⚜

He walked into the council building to find the lobby empty. He fanned his head in search of someone who could assist him. He perceived voices behind doors and up the stairs, but he didn't want to intrude, causing a bad first impression. At one point, it was so quiet he could hear flies buzzing on a crumb-flecked plate that'd been left on the reception desk.

He didn't see anyone for fifteen minutes. At last, a couple of middle-aged men entered the lobby. One of them was holding a briefcase, the other wearing a white shirt that domed over his large stomach like an igloo.

"Excuse me," Serguey said. "Do you know where I can find the receptionist?"

The men paused. The pudgy one stared at his companion, bewildered. The other vacillated, opened his mouth as if to speak, then raised his index finger, telling Serguey to wait. He trotted to the nearest door, opened it slightly, and uttered something unintelligible.

Turning back, he said, "They'll be right with you." He nodded at his companion to join him, and both men disappeared up the staircase.

A young woman emerged from the office wearing a cream-colored blouse and a lengthy brown skirt. Her hair puffed out of her head stunningly, like soft coral. A tiny hoop earring protruded from the corner of her bottom lip. She couldn't be more than twenty-five.

"Yes?" she said with a smile.

"I'm looking for Mario Rabasa." Serguey remembered Mario's last name from *Electra Garrigó*'s program.

The woman's smile dissipated. "He's not here."

"Do you know where I can find him?"

She shuffled some papers on the reception's desk. "Who's asking?" Her question was sharp. She wanted him to know that she was uncomfortable.

"I'm an old friend of his." Serguey dithered, then appended, "My father and Mario work together."

The young woman contemplated him, as if attempting to determine from his appearance whether she could trust him. "Mario hasn't been in for some time. We don't have information as to his whereabouts."

Too formal, Serguey thought. Too rehearsed. He leaned over the reception desk and coaxed his voice into an imploration. "Look, I just need an address, a phone number, anything. I just need to talk to him."

The woman surveyed the lobby. Satisfied that no one was listening, she leaned forward herself. "The police took everything. They've interviewed people here. I'm not supposed to talk about Mario." She waited a moment, and then asked, "Is Felipe Blanco your father?"

"He is."

She took a deep breath. "I'm sorry. I can't help you." She threw the fly-picked plate into a trashcan, averting her eyes.

"Listen, listen," he called to her. "What's your name?"

She looked around again. "Vivi."

"Vivi. That's beautiful. Listen, my name is Serguey. I don't want to go knocking on doors without knowing who's behind them, okay? Just tell me who worked with Mario. Point me to the right office. I won't mention your name, I swear." He suggested a scenario: "I walked in. You weren't at the reception . . ."

She began rearranging the papers again.

"Just show me the room," he insisted. "I don't want to make a scene."

She released the papers and said softly, "Second floor, last door on the right."

Serguey rapped his knuckles on the desk as a way of thanking her. He dashed up the stairs, rushed down a corridor past the briefcase-carrying man and his stocky companion, who were still chatting, and slowed down as he neared the door the young woman had indicated. He knocked, and a tall, lanky man with eyeglasses appeared.

"I was on my way out," the man started to say, tucking his shirt in. He halted at the sight of Serguey. "I'm sorry. I thought you were someone else."

"I apologize for barging in like this. May I ask your name?"

The man squinted behind his glasses. "José Parra. Administrator in charge of Human Resources. And you are . . . ?"

"Could we speak in your office?"

"What's it concerning?"

"Please, can we speak in private? I think it'd be best."

"Not until you tell me who you are and why you're here."

"My name's Serguey Blanco. I'm Felipe Blanco's son."

The man rammed his hand against Serguey's chest. "You need to leave."

"I just need to know where I can find Mario Rabasa."

"The authorities already took all the information. You'd have to check with them."

"A phone number, an address, that's all I need. Please—"

"If you don't leave now, I'm going to call the police."

Serguey glared at him, tightening his jaw and fists. "My father was a colleague of yours, a respected director, and you're going to dismiss me like this? I'm trying to find out what happened."

"Your father wasn't a colleague."

"Oh, right. You're in human resources. Where are the artists here?" Serguey started down the hall.

The man clasped Serguey's arm. "Your father's a counterrevolutionary," he said, inflating the sound of the words. He wanted to be heard, Serguey could tell. He wanted to be witnessed disposing of an unwanted parasite. That would get him points with his communist paper-pushing superiors. "He tarnished this center," the man continued, "and those who collaborated with him."

"You're a fucking joke," Serguey said.

Parra softened his tone. "Do you know how long it's going to take before we can breathe without someone listening to our breaths? State Security already interviewed half the building. Your father was beloved here. He was trusted. He was given preferential treatment and awards, and he shit on all of us."

"Mario's address," Serguey said, calmer now. "That's all I need."

Parra ignored his plea. "Mario's another selfish prick. I hope they've taken him too."

Perhaps it was the man's non-threatening lankiness or the petty intonation of his last words that made Serguey swing his right hand at him. There was a quick thud. Parra whimpered, bringing his fingers to his top lip. Stunned, he wiped away a pinch of blood. He widened his eyes and looked over Serguey's shoulder at the two men, who'd been observing the exchange.

"Call the police!" he yelled with half his mouth.

The corpulent man waddled into an office. The taller one dropped his brief-case and charged at Serguey, who'd released his anger with the punch and now, spent of bravery, cringed and hoisted his forearm as if wielding a shield. The man latched on to Serguey's arm and pulled. Parra, apparently over the initial shock, put a headlock on him.

"Sons of bitches!" Serguey shouted as they forced him down the stairs. People had already congregated in the lobby, standing to the side like a crowd at a parade. Vivi appeared to be refuging herself behind the reception desk, glancing at him with restless eyes as she wrote something down.

Approaching the front door, the man pulling Serguey's arm said, "Let's pin him down until the police come."

Panicked, Serguey threw an elbow at Parra. He let go enough for Serguey to release himself from the tall man and scurry down the stairs. He ran for a couple of blocks, reminded of years before, the amalgam of flurry and distress he'd experienced while running away from the boys who wanted to see Kiko's watch. Eventually, he looked back. No one was chasing him. He stopped to catch his breath, keeping his heart's thumping echoes from jamming his throat. He threw his body against a wall, buttressing himself with his left palm to keep his knees from folding. Despite his fear, he was partially roused by the scuffle. He'd needed no convincing, no persuasion from Anabel, no example set by Victor: he had scolded and punched Parra of his own accord, forced himself to act instead of calculate, to viscerally take a stance.

A few minutes later, just as his breathing and heart rate began returning to normal, he saw Vivi's abundant hair rushing in his direction. There was no one with her. He wasn't sure if he should still flee but decided not to when she lifted her hand, asking him to wait. She handed him a piece of paper the moment she reached him.

"Call her," she said, seizing an inhaler from a pocket in her skirt. She gave herself a shot before adding, "She should know about Mario."

Serguey looked at the paper. There was a phone number and the name Vilma in clunky lettering. "Who is she?"

Vivi took another shot. The hiss of the inhaler prompted him to gently cup her elbow.

"She knows Mario. I have to . . ." She pointed over her shoulder with her thumb, then paced away from him and back toward the Cultural Council building.

He secured the paper inside his pocket and shouted a "thank you," but Vivi didn't turn.

CHAPTER 10

Serguey could understand, even in a moment of belligerent frustration, how Felipe's arrest had blemished his colleagues' names. In some ways, Felipe had betrayed them, jeopardized their futures. His father had taught him that during the Mariel exodus in 1980, people egged the houses of those who were leaving the country, sometimes spit in their faces. Some did it out of spite and jealousy, sure, but there was no denying that a few had done it out of necessity. If they didn't show their camaraderie with such zealotry, who was to say they wouldn't come under suspicion? Who was to say they wouldn't wake up one day to find their own front walls slathered with yolk, their porch floor peppered with sticky shells, the rancid smell not clearing for days? Even Parra had raised his voice, hoping to be heard confronting a dissident's offspring. Serguey grasped that, for the foreseeable future, the mere mention of his own name and relationship to his father would elicit this kind of reaction. He was a walking plague. He also knew that sympathy for his father's colleagues would have no legal bearing. It would get him no leniency if the police showed up at his home for assaulting Parra.

He chose not to share what'd transpired with Anabel and Alida. He simply told them the people at the council had declined to speak with him and insisted that he leave.

"State Security really scared them," he said, relieved that the sisters weren't feeling inquisitive. He spent the rest of the afternoon fretting a call at the door. He took his post-dinner coffee on the balcony, stealing glances at the street, dreading the sight of rotating lights, the wail of a police cruiser. He kept fiddling with the paper containing the phone number in his pocket. Could he trust Vivi or the Vilma woman whose name she'd written? Should he tell Anabel? Should he ask Alida if, by any chance, she'd heard of this Vilma? While omitting Parra from his version of the council trip, he had also omitted Vivi's gesture. It was too late now, he thought, deciding that he would wait until the next day to call the woman. He needed time to weigh his options, to act rationally and not lose control again as he had with Parra and the other man. If the squabble at the council had stirred interest from the authorities, or if someone had seen Vivi chase after him, reaching out to the woman too soon could work against him.

Evening had swallowed El Vedado. On the nights when the scheduled power-outage hit their neighborhood, the distant lights of El Melia Cohiba and Riviera hotels became starkly visible. One section of the municipality glowed and sparkled, the tall streetlamps of El Malecon forming a luminous barricade, while the other lied dormant in a sprawling darkness. Energy had to be saved, the government had lamented since the beginning of the Special Period. Petroleum shortages called for sacrifices to be made.

Those who lived close to a lighted area often migrated to a friend's home to watch the nine o'clock soap opera. It wasn't rare, on evening walks, to see a crowd bundled up against a window, gasping and murmuring at the drama unfolding on a generous stranger's television. When the power went out in Santos Suarez, people sat on their front porches in search of fresh air. Late night conversations unfurled, full of political jokes and hysterical laughter, the only way to keep madness at bay in such heat. All was forgiven on these nights, like a rant from a drunk who bites his tongue in the sobering morning. If the administrators in charge of the power grid weren't feeling merciful and stuck to the full eight hours, entire families carried their mattresses out and dreamed under the stars. They rose from their slumber with whistles and celebratory cries when the power finally returned. Felipe didn't allow Serguey and Victor to sleep outside. Perhaps as a form of protest against his father, an older Serguey and Anabel had slept on the balcony one night at his request, their own private camping trip.

Beyond the hotels was the sea, remote and dark. Presently, a strong wind gust pelted him, making him aware of how high up he was standing. Anabel had lost a sun visor cap once out here, propelled away from her like a balloon. Serguey was reminded of Milan Kundera's *The Book of Laughter and Forgetting*, the last book he'd read before leaving his father's house. In the novel's opening, politician Vladimir Clementis had lent communist leader Klement Gottwald his hat to shield him from the cold as they stood on a balcony. Years later, when Clementis was accused of treason and executed, he was erased from the photograph that existed of him and Gottwald. Only his hat remained. What would remain of Serguey when he could no longer stand on *this* balcony? Anabel hadn't taken any photographs, and neither had he. No one would write his small story, so insignificant before a large world. Maybe a wind gust could swoop him away and drop him somewhere in a dark patch of the city, into a more grounded life. Maybe it was already happening.

When he was a teenager, Serguey overheard Kiko's mother telling a friend that a woman in Alamar had plunged from a fifth-floor balcony with a four-month-old baby in her arms. The baby died, but the woman survived. She blamed her cheating husband for it. The man was indifferent. He left the woman and moved in with a younger one, or so the story went. Serguey couldn't avoid imagining what it would be like to leap off from such heights. He wondered about the unthinkable pain that would greet him upon landing, if the shock of the impact would even make room for pain. He wondered whether he'd hold his breath, whether he'd even be able to breathe. He imagined that the woman must have really wanted a way out, choosing such an act of letting go.

He felt a hand caressing his shoulder and then retreating. Alida smiled at him, resting her elbows on the balcony rail. She'd taken a shower, her hair still wet and dense. Anabel had lent her a pair of shorts that were too wide. She stretched her right leg until she was able to touch the sliding glass door behind her with the tip of her toes.

"How come you're always doing that?" he asked.

"I'm afraid that if I don't, I'll lose my flexibility."

He stared at her leg, lithe and firm. "How's the ankle?"

She pursed her lips, deliberating her response. "It's tighter than it used to be, but otherwise it's fine." She put her leg down and extended the other.

"I'm sorry about this whole thing with my dad. I know you're very talented, and the show was going well . . ."

"Please, Serguey. There's nothing to be sorry about. If it weren't for your dad, I wouldn't have had an opportunity to do theater."

"It's still unfortunate that it affects you." He was apologizing on behalf of his family, for the toxic influence they'd become. "It was selfish on his part if he knew that whatever he was doing could get you and the other actors in trouble."

She lowered her leg and stood elegantly on her toes, her hands gripping the rail. "I'm sure it's more complicated than that. You shouldn't resent him."

"I'll try not to." The sound of his voice sailed away from him like the airplane lights behind Alida, scudding across the sky with rote intermittence.

"What I need is a change of venue," she said. "I need to start over."

"There's got to be other theater groups in the city you can audition for."

She looked at him, vivacious, earnest, open. "I want to leave the country." Her hands jerked up and down, refusing to release the railing, like a motorcyclist changing speeds.

What response was she seeking from him? Her eyes seemed exposed, yet unafraid of his gaze in return. "Are you just saying that?"

She laughed, as if he had uttered the exact words she was expecting. "I'm not stupid. I know it won't be easy. The hardest part is going to be telling Anabel and my parents. It's been in the back of my mind, even before my injury. Now I'm sure I want to do it."

"One's never sure about something like that."

Her hands stopped. "I am."

Serguey was taken aback by the shattering simplicity of her answer. "Where would you go?" he challenged.

She didn't balk. "One of the actors in our group was talking about how Felipe might try to land us a show in Miami. He's supposed to know some people in the theater scene there, people he worked with who left for good."

"You can't count on that. I have no idea if he's ever going to get out of prison."

"What I mean is, Florida seems to be a nice place for me to try. I have to get out of here. If I stay, I'm going to end up with my parents, no job prospects, listening to my mother chirp about getting an older boyfriend or going to church. You don't get many second opportunities in this country, not in the arts. I look at what happened to your dad, and it scares me."

"Tell me about it," he said.

She appeared confused by his statement, but she accepted it nonetheless.

"Tell me about what?" Anabel asked, wriggling between them. She'd come furtively.

He waited for Alida to answer.

"I was telling Serguey that I'm thinking about leaving the country."

Serguey was impressed, proud of his sister-in-law. She was going for it, then and there.

Anabel laughed. "Another impulse?"

"No. I'm dead set on it."

"Where are you going to go, Ali? We don't have family anywhere."

"Dad has a cousin in Orlando."

"He and Dad barely talk. He's not going to help you."

Serguey pondered how he'd react if this had been Victor. He liked to think that he'd be supportive, but in truth, he'd have no faith in his brother's aptitude to lead a proper life in a foreign city.

"How do you know?" Alida said. "Have you asked him? I know you guys are happy here, but not everyone has what you have."

"Yes, we have everything," Anabel said.

"You're doing better than most people."

"Alida, you're too young to be on your own in a strange country."

She pounded her own chest, her vocal chords vibrating with acrimony. "I'm twenty-three years old."

"What are you going to do over there? Do you think someone will just hire you as an actress?"

"I can study, get a waitressing job. I'm good with languages. I can fend for myself in English and Italian."

"Ha! You're delusional." Anabel stole a glimpse at Serguey. "Are you listening to this?"

He wavered, but he was too inspired by Alida's candor. "She should do what she wants. She's an adult."

Anabel swung her entire body. She locked her arms below her chest and glared at him with something that resembled, if only for an instant, intense aversion. He'd committed a cardinal sin, and he knew it. But he felt the need to be honest, out of solidarity for his sister-in-law.

"The two of you should discuss it alone," he said preemptively, "but in my view, if Alida's sure she wants to leave, none of us should question or try to stop her."

He didn't wait for Anabel's explosion. Instead he went to the bedroom, her glare trained like a laser at his back. He had already been reckless today, so he figured it was fitting to end on this note. She would scold him soon enough for not siding with her, call him irresponsible, and maybe she'd be right.

He shut the door halfway and turned on the bedside lamp. He stripped down to his boxer shorts, but not before placing Vilma's phone number on the nightstand. He grabbed his cell and, without caring for the time or planning what he would say (he did clear his throat and hummed), he dialed. Three rings later came a "Hello?"

"Is this Vilma?"

"Yes. Who am I speaking to?"

"My name is Serguey." He paused, but the woman didn't reply. "I'm Felipe Blanco's son."

"Oh!" Her voice spiked, waggling like a voltage needle. "I'm sorry about your father. He's a good friend."

"Do you know Mario Rabasa?"

Vilma's tone leveled out. "Yes, he's also a friend." The word "friend" she pronounced as a question.

"I need to get in touch with him."

"I see." She paused. "Do you think we could meet?"

Serguey walked to the edge of the room and snuck his head out the door. Anabel and Alida were still arguing on the balcony. "If you could just give me a phone number or address, I'd really appreciate it. I won't say who gave it to me."

"We think Mario's gone."

"Who's *we?*"

"I don't have his address," she said pointedly.

"What about his phone?"

She started to release her words more quickly, as if someone was approaching her. "It's disconnected. Let's meet. Where do you live?"

"That's all right," Serguey said, sighing. "Thank you for not hanging up on me."

"Serguey, I'm a friend of your dad. What I'm telling you about Mario is true. But maybe we can help each other. Maybe I can help your father is what I mean. Where do you live?"

State Security, he was certain, had his address already. Giving it to Vilma wouldn't change much. And at this stage she was the only connection to Mario. "Do you have something to write my address down?"

"I've got a good memory," she said.

Not long after he'd hung up, he lay in bed with the lights off and the door completely open. He could hear Anabel's voice rising and dipping. The sisters loved each other, cared about each other. Love did not allow half-measures, incomplete truths. What a luxury it was, the ability to passionately and freely articulate and dispute and be heard. The ability to be close and feel close to your family.

He wanted to stay with their conversation, let his thoughts be escorted by their exchange. But drowsiness overtook him. He was exhausted. In a short while, their voices, candid and musical in his fading consciousness, lulled him to sleep.

⁂

As he watched it unfold, he could intuit that it was a dream, the impossibility of the scenario: Alida was on the bed—not *his* bed, but *a* bed—nude except for her black panties. She was on her knees, her feet twined like an X behind her. Her breasts mirrored Anabel's, but not her hair. Not her face, her thighs, her ass. She was smiling at him. Seductively. She took his hand and steered him out a door.

"Not in there," she said. "They'll catch us."

And maybe it *was* his bedroom they had left behind. They were running by a row of bathroom stalls. She drew him into one and hooked the latch. She removed her panties. He was already pantless, though he couldn't recall taking them off. She took hold of his penis and put it inside her. The bathroom door clattered. There were voices mumbling and hushing each other, as if trying to spy, ears to the door.

Frightened, he woke. He stared at the ceiling of his bedroom—his real bedroom—and almost cursed out loud.

He slid his hand into his boxers and confirmed his erection. He glanced at Anabel. Her back was to him. He listened to the subtle hiss of her breathing, watched her hair mantling the edge of her pillow. She was in a deep sleep. He began to touch himself, struggling to not shake the bed. He sealed his eyes and tried to remember the dream he'd just had, the crude details. He tried to picture what it'd be like to have sex with Alida in a public bathroom stall. How rushed and careful they'd have to be. He began to speed up his hand, holding his breath as much as he could while his heart rate increased. His entire body was tense, primed for a considerable release.

Then Anabel shoved her hand under the sheets and wrapped her fingers around the head of his penis. She'd rolled over on the bed, and he hadn't detected it. It took him a few seconds before he could speak.

"I'm sorry," he said feebly.

"Why didn't you wake me?"

"I didn't want to bother you. I thought you'd be mad at me."

"Why are you like this?"

"I had a dream about you. I couldn't help it."

She kissed his neck and glided slowly to the foot of the bed, hauling the sheets over her upper body. She took him in her mouth. She then discarded her underwear and mounted him, tossing the sheets on the floor. He lay there, grunting and stroking her breasts. She stifled his mouth with her hand, muffling his moans. Toward the end, he shut his eyes again, an image of a bathroom stall and a nude Alida flashing briefly in his mind.

Anabel let her torso fall on his, her nipples grazing his chest. "You owe me," she whispered in his ear.

He felt abashed. His ears were flushing, his limbs tingling with pleasurable enervation. He was a sexually satisfied man, which meant he was a tired, selfish man. Once the urge had left the body, making love became a responsibility, no longer an impulsive display of affection and desire. As his puffing chest decreased its movements, he began to search for a source of energy within him, a second wind. If he didn't reciprocate, it would signal failure on his part, a failure magnified by the dream he'd just had, the dream he'd used to orgasm. He reminded himself that just because he experienced immense gratification and satiety, it didn't mean Anabel had experienced the same. He should make an effort and not give excuses. He shouldn't be a selfish man.

She straightened up and said with a smile, "I don't mean tonight, but you owe me."

She was letting him off the hook. Alida sleeping in the guest bedroom, on the other hand, was a different story. Serguey found his sudden sexual fixation absurd, especially considering the circumstances. Had it been seeing Alida on stage? Did hearing Felipe's praise make her appear to him more a fully flourished woman than his wife's younger sister? Or was it her adventurous desire to leave the country, or her physical likeness to Yusimí, the girl from Felipe's porch steps? Maybe it was her whimsy, the capricious and unpredictable ways in which she treated her own body. Her marked youth.

Though not as childish as Alida, Anabel had been physically expressive when they'd met. The night he lost his virginity to her, she let him take her from behind and come quickly, his uncontainable teenage urges jetting from him in a choking, exhilarating burst. She performed oral sex until he was ready again, this time asking him to lie on top of her. Their bodies interlocked, his pelvis pressed to hers, and he let her swerve, sink, and raise her hips until she collapsed with a sensual giggle. He could remember feeling pleased, as he'd remained primed and patient, tasting her breath and sensing her nails digging into his back. As a reward, he witnessed something wonderful: a woman's orgasm. It was not like his friends had described or as he'd seen in pornographic movies. It was more intimate, more contained and yet more powerful. She boosted up her legs and rested her ankles on his shoulders. He didn't last long despite it being his second time, but he immediately understood that Anabel would be more than a girlfriend. She'd be a teacher, more aware and secure than he was.

All these years, he had been a fortunate man. This night, his wife had given him another gift while he'd behaved like a liar. A traitor. He could never see himself with someone like Alida, and yet the dream was there. The fantasy.

Anabel went to the bathroom to wash up. He waited his turn, questioning why, of all possible moments, his mind had picked this one. His father was in prison. His own career was probably on the verge of derailing. His comfortable apartment could be stripped away. And here he was visualizing an impossible and unwanted affair. He moved to the edge of the bed, his eyes adjusting to the sliver of light at the bottom of the bathroom door. He listened to the gushing faucet and was overtaken by the need to urinate. He commanded his body to get up, but it disregarded him. He was weak. The eternal victim. All he'd ever fought for was his job, and that was only after Gimenez had forged an easy path for him. He hadn't done anything noteworthy for his wife, for anyone. No true sacrifices.

Anabel opened the door and, without asking, left the light on for him. She was massaging her own hands, waxing them with a lotion whose tangy scent he hadn't grown accustomed to. This is what he'd given his wife: things, objects that now seemed to him a portent of a ruined future. He felt like apologizing, like calling himself a fraud. But he was too weak even for that. He locked himself in the bathroom, one hand on the wall as he stood over the toilet. Muscles moved involuntarily throughout his limbs. He flushed his waste and washed his hands, evading his reflection in the mirror. He splashed water on his face, on his dry mouth, some of it moistening his tongue. His muscles ceased their twitching. He dampened a towel and cleaned his penis. The light bulb above him blinked, and in a couple of seconds he heard the small fan in the bedroom come to life. As usual, she had switched it to the rotating setting, so that the air could cool them both. He gave himself a moment to breathe. He loved Anabel with all his heart, but the fact didn't absolve him, it didn't make him a better person. It was her love, her loyalty, that made it all worthwhile. If he had to fight for anything, it was to never forget that.

He exited the bathroom and climbed slowly into bed without lying down. He searched for her hand, and when she took his, a tiny circle in her pupils shining up at him in the dark, he told her that a woman named Vilma was coming the next afternoon to talk about his father and Mario.

"Okay," she said, not withdrawing her hand.

He leaned his head on the pillow and told her about the fight with Parra and about Vivi too.

CHAPTER 11

The next morning, Anabel accompanied Alida to her apartment so she could stuff a bag with clothes and bring it to El Vedado. They agreed that she should stay in the spare bedroom for the time being. She didn't want to search for another job until Felipe's situation was resolved, and being around the other actors wasn't a healthy choice—and possibly an unsafe one: the net of government suspicion could be widely cast.

The women had already returned when Vilma paid her visit. She introduced herself as Vilma Carrero, and the man who was with her, to Serguey's surprise, as José Angel Despaigne. She explained, standing at the door, that José Angel was also a colleague of Felipe's and an acquaintance of Mario.

"We've all been playwrights and theater directors at one point," she said, tilting forward and lowering her voice, as if working in theater were some sort of secret cult.

Serguey figured Vilma had been afraid to come alone. Donning a serious face, he let them in.

Vilma looked to be in her late forties. She had perfectly combed black hair that fell straight down her back. She wore white-rimmed glasses, and her ankle-level skirt stretched and folded as she walked. José Angel, possibly ten years Vilma's elder, was bald and prick-skinned. A pen was clipped to the chest pocket of his striped shirt, which needed a good ironing. He had droopy eyelids, his vision slightly askew, giving the impression of subservience or social anxiety. Serguey wondered how much help Vilma expected him to be if indeed she had brought him out of apprehension.

Anabel gave them each a cup of coffee. They accepted and celebrated it, as was customary in Cuba. Alida remained somewhere out of sight in the apartment. Serguey refrained from mentioning her, in case she preferred it that way. Vilma described how she'd learned about Felipe's arrest through a critic and professor, a mutual friend. She was beside herself. It was incomprehensible for someone as admirable as Felipe, she said, with his artistic capacities and selfless personality, to be degraded and persecuted by the brutes at State Security.

"Felipe's too clever to immerse himself in politics," she said, dismantling Serguey's suspicion that maybe she and José Angel had been involved in whatever had landed Felipe in prison. There was still a chance, however, that the whole thing was an act, that they were testing the waters.

"I was stunned," José Angel contributed with a shrug, his eyes fixed on Serguey's television set.

"We all were," Vilma said. "Really."

Serguey told them he appreciated their concern. Vilma replied that she was already discussing the possibility of drafting a formal statement with many of her colleagues, asking for Felipe's release.

"None of us have been able to find out the reasons why they went after him," she said.

"Me neither," Serguey said. He was holding off on asking about Mario. He had to test the waters as well. "I'm as much in the dark as you are. They won't tell me anything."

Vilma seemed disappointed. "Felipe has a lot of fans. But what I'm hearing is that people are confused as to what's going on." She paused and tapped her knees together. She relaxed her features, looking almost defenseless. "You've got to admit it's effective. No one wants to go around asking too many questions and getting themselves arrested."

"It's difficult," Serguey said.

"It's also appalling. There has to be some integrity left. If we keep allowing the government to push us around, what will become of us?"

He appreciated her solidarity, but indignant Cubans were a dime a dozen, and Vilma's tone was far from earnest. Public outcry had always been monitored and cowed. Protests and demands were as rare as apples or decent yogurt in Havana. Serguey did not for an instant believe that Vilma and her colleagues were really writing a formal statement. "It's easier said than done," he replied as a way to divest her of responsibility for Felipe's situation, refusing to cast aspersions.

"I won't argue that," she said. "But still."

He wanted to inquire about Vilma's exact relationship with his father, but he found it imprudent. Their friendship could be genuine, after all. His father seemed capable of that. Serguey had no obligations with Mario, on the other hand, no matter how much of a friend the men were, so he asked Vilma about him.

"Do you have his number?" he said.

"It's disconnected, but I'll give it to you." She fished inside her drawstring canvas bag and retrieved a pocketbook.

Serguey saved the number on his cell phone.

"No one can find him," Vilma said.

"I think he might've left the country," José Angel said with what sounded like an involuntary sigh.

"Well, we don't know for sure," Vilma said.

Serguey asked her, "Has someone mentioned that possibility?"

"It's all conjecture. I heard he hasn't been in his house since your father's arrest. Another playwright who is good friends with him told us."

Serguey put away his cell and looked at the door.

"Do you have a plan for helping Felipe?" she asked quickly. "Anything we can do?"

He crossed his arms. "I'm exploring several options. My brother and I got to see him. He seemed fine, in a manner of speaking."

"That's wonderful! Did he tell you anything?"

"He claims it's a mistake."

José Angel raised his eyes. "Those people don't make mistakes."

"Well, José Angel, it *has* to be a mistake." Vilma wriggled in her seat. "Felipe wouldn't—"

José Angel didn't wait for her to complete her sentence. "I just mean that the arrest wasn't a mistake. Could they have ulterior motives? Sure. But they don't arrest people like Felipe on a whim."

Serguey found the man's frankness refreshing.

"It's all speculation," Vilma said uneasily. "But we assure you, Serguey, that we'll take a public stance. Your father's not alone."

"I appreciate that. And if you find Mario, I'd also appreciate it if you let me know."

"We will."

Anabel reappeared and asked them if they wanted a glass of water before they left. José Angel said yes. Vilma commented on the apartment, saying the view was lovely. Serguey ushered them to the balcony, where José Angel drank his water as if it were hot tea. Serguey dove right into small talk, telling them how it was strange calling this neighborhood home, highlighting Gimenez's generosity. Vilma mentioned how proud Felipe was of his sons. Her diffident tenor betrayed her attempt as mediator: she was being cordial, saving face for her friend. She'd been to the house in Santos Suarez on several occasions.

"Your father and I have collaborated on many projects," she said.

"For as long as I can remember," Serguey said, "he's had people over at that place. He loves company."

Vilma smiled and stared out to the sea, permitting a few seconds to tick by. She turned to José Angel at length and said, "Are we ready to go?"

He handed the glass to Serguey. "Thank you."

"It was all the wife."

José Angel waddled like a penguin, searching for her, but there was no one down the hall. "Tell her 'thank you.'"

"I will."

Following convivial goodbyes, they began to head for the stairs.

"Is the elevator still broken?" Serguey asked them.

"There was a sign on it," José Angel said.

"Oh, I apologize."

"At my age," Vilma said, "I can use the exercise."

Serguey watched them leave quietly, their steps withdrawing farther and farther to the lower floors. He wondered why Vilma hadn't referred to the letter again. Maybe, as he'd believed, it was just a hollow, dissembling promise. She could always blame precarious circumstances for not following through. If she was on the fence about it, however, probing a little more—or even openly telling her how helpful such a document could be—might have improved the chances of it being drafted. But dashing down the stairs was a desperate move, and it was too early for desperation.

There was also the fact that, if indeed they wanted to help, how much could they actually accomplish? Felipe was not a popular television actor, a famed musician, an identifiable political figure. He was esteemed in a very particular circle—the performance arts world—his followers and colleagues all of scanty means. His shows attracted a very intellectually creative but politically disengaged crowd, people looking for a distraction, for emotional entertainment and stimulation. Many were students with artistic aspirations of their own. In Cuba, there were no patrons, no sponsors, no theater devotees with enough cache and influence to demand transparency in Felipe's case. That would require independent funds, the result of foreign capitalist enterprises. The country's communist government closely oversaw these kinds of people and entities. They forbade direct interaction between them and those who reached mass audiences, like theater directors. The government employed the majority of recognized artists in Cuba, and as the employer, they enforced and bent the rules at will. Express dissent and find yourself unwaged, forlorn. In a phone conversation with Serguey a few nights prior to the start of *Electra Garrigó*, Felipe had mentioned a speech by Eduardo Real, a prominent painter whose work had found its way to galleries and museums abroad, including New York City's Museum of Modern Art. Mr. Real, reading from a piece of notebook paper (his own manufactured touch?) said that Cuban artists should be willing to work for free, considering all the advantages and opportunities the country had provided for them.

"The nerve of some people," Felipe railed. "Put a couple of dollars in their pocket and a paid ticket to Europe, and they forget where they came from. Real's from the slums of Marianao. Now he wears designer hats, has dinner with foreign dignitaries, and thinks the rest of us should make art for the love of art."

Like every other sector of the Cuban workforce, artists were helpless. Best-case scenario, Felipe's colleagues would write their letter, and if fortune were so inclined, maybe it'd get some international press.

⁘⸎⁘

That night, Serguey checked in on Kiko. His friend was still waiting to hear from Claudia, but he sounded optimistic.

"I should get back to you in a day or two," he said.

Serguey gave him Mario's number and asked if he could do something with it. "I couldn't get the guy's address, though people keep saying he's gone."

Kiko chuckled. "I'd be, too, with so many people looking for me. I have a buddy who used to work for ETECSA. Maybe he can do something with the number. Just know that it might not go anywhere."

"I'll take whatever small thing he can give you," Serguey said sincerely.

A short while later, Victor called to announce he had an idea: they should go to the National Council for the Performing Arts.

"That's technically where Dad works," he said. "Maybe we can find Mario."

Serguey told him he'd already tried it to no avail, though he conveniently avoided the details. "Don't even think of showing your face there," he cautioned. "I mean it."

Anabel's mother also phoned. She had requested a meeting with the priest, and like Kiko, she was waiting on a response.

With hours of waiting ahead of him, Serguey was confronted with his own powerlessness. The role he could have in all of it—what he could bring to the table—the truth was that having a law degree in Cuba didn't mean much. After graduation, if you were top of your class, you were signed up to the National Organization of Collective Law Offices, pools of state-regulated attorneys. The salary was laughable, and the cases even more so. Clients were guilty until proven innocent. Political prisoners weren't afforded a lawyer of their own choosing, as he'd told Victor, their offenses so heinous and unpardonable, apparently, that they deserved no proper defense. In those cases, a handpicked attorney served as a stand-in, silent as statues during court proceedings, for the accused, whose sentences would only worsen if they dared speak on their own behalf. The press was controlled by that same state. So were the modes of mass communication. Protests against the government were prohibited, punishable by a good licking from a police baton, a follow-up thrashing at the police station, and an indelible stain on your civilian record. Get brave enough and you might win some prison time. Serguey had always known how the system was designed and assembled, how it was put into effect and to what ends. Not until his father's arrest had he been compelled to concede and confront its flaws, its irrationality.

Despite the shortcomings of practicing Cuban law, there was honorable repute associated with being a young lawyer graduating at the top of his class. No one in Havana wanted to be a prosecutor. Most of those who did accept these jobs quit after their two or three years of compulsory service, leaving the country's prosecuting pool eternally inexperienced. New graduates were herded into prosecuting offices year after year. Only the elite, like Serguey, got to join the much older ranks of lawyers, holding on to little victories and their clients' generosities. In this constant war versus disgruntled ex-classmates, as Serguey heard fellow lawyers call it, he found some fulfillment.

Right out of school, he had been assigned to minor cases: thieves, violence-prone alcoholics, black market food distributors. The penalties weren't too severe, not unless the accused already had an extensive record or said the wrong thing in court, pissing off the judge. In a handful of instances, Serguey had succeeded in obtaining a reduced sentence or as little as a fine. Occasionally, he won outright. But the outcome of his cases often depended on luck. The prosecutors were former students whose grades hadn't been high enough to land them a position as defense lawyers. Bitter and jaded, they feasted on their more privileged counterparts, the law disproportionately on their side. Judges were sometimes given preordained results to their cases, regardless of the evidence that was presented. Two men who had each killed a child, for instance, might receive entirely different punishments simply because their names had been inked on separate sections of the docket. To all of this Serguey had turned a blind eye, always racing ahead.

Throughout his years at the university, he'd noticed the blatant discrepancy between the students of modest means like himself and the offspring of high-ranking government officials, corporation managers, and state-sympathizing celebrities. The future of this favored group was bright, a direct line plugging them into the kinds of jobs Serguey and his poor peers couldn't realistically aspire to. Serguey witnessed many brilliant classmates drop out of school, disillusioned and outraged by the politically charged courses, at the narrow interpretations of communist law. A surprising number of them had desired to become attorneys inspired by movies and television shows: *A Time to Kill*, *Philadelphia*, *In the Name of the Father*, *A Few Good Men*, *Matlock*, *Law & Order*. But practicing Cuban law was so far removed from the ideal of truly representing and potentially saving your client, that it took a special kind of aspiration or necessity to keep one going. Serguey's main fuel had been his impassioned desire to achieve what to the advantaged students was a basic expectation. He had an irrational belief that his break would come if he just waited long enough, if he kept looking for it.

As it turned out, he didn't even have to.

During his last case, Gimenez had sat in the audience. He and Serguey's law school advisor were childhood friends. The advisor had highlighted Serguey as the perfect protégé, someone intelligent Gimenez could train and mold to his taste. Serguey's client—if he could be called that—had been charged for stealing cell phone minutes. The man had discovered a way to re-code the phone so that his allotted minutes automatically reappeared without having to pay ETECSA, the country's service provider. Allegedly, he had taught friends how to do the same. One of them, threatened with jail, gave him up.

Serguey was prepped by his own client. The man explained the ins and outs of cell phone trickery with such specificity that Serguey was able to pepper the prosecutor's lead witness and an ETECSA representative with technical questions. He got them to boggle, mumble, and say, "I don't know," "I'm not sure," "I'd have to verify that information." The fact that ETECSA didn't have concrete proof of misconduct forced the judge, who ostensibly hadn't been ordered to decide one way or the other, to dismiss the case.

Gimenez took Serguey to dinner that night: an exclusive Italian-style restaurant. Gimenez had a good rapport with the maître d' and the waiter, and he made a big show of it.

"Just bring my favorite," he told the waiter. He slit his eyes enough to suggest thoughtfulness. "I have a feeling he hasn't tried real Italian wine yet."

Serguey admitted, without much abashment, that he hadn't. He could count on one hand the people he knew who had ever tried imported wine.

Gimenez's argument for Serguey to switch careers, though unnecessary, was persuasive: a low stress desk job; tangible possibility to be stationed abroad, sometimes for years at a time; access to foreign goods. Not too far down the road, he could vie for his own car, maybe a beach house for a couple of weeks out of the year. Not to mention the numerous government and business connections he could make.

"Most of the kids who get in our doors are somebody's son or daughter or nephew," he said, pouring a tad more wine for himself than for Serguey. "And most of them are inept. From what I've seen and heard about you, they will all be choking on your dust in a couple of years."

Toward the end of the meal, Gimenez dabbed his lips with his napkin and folded it neatly beside his partially empty plate, whose leftovers he offered Serguey to take home when the waiter asked if they were finished. Serguey shrugged, and the waiter smiled.

"Don't be shy," the man said, palming the plate. "Even in a place like this people take leftovers all the time."

Gimenez stretched across the table and tapped Serguey's hand. "He's right."

At first, Serguey wondered if Gimenez was gay. He thought it natural to have such a suspicion. Gimenez's mannerisms were too refined. The absence of a wife and the way he studied Serguey seemed like clues to a much larger puzzle. It wasn't until he and Anabel attended a party at the home of the Ministry's Legal Director, as Gimenez's personal guests, that Serguey realized his new boss had a special infatuation for Anabel. Thankfully, he didn't flirt or hover around her. Instead he whispered in Serguey's ear, his breath a mix of alcohol and cologne, when another man engaged Anabel in conversation. It was as if Gimenez wished to vicariously feel the jealousy of a husband. Serguey wasn't proud of it—the husband letting his boss ogle at, or worse, manipulate his own relationship with his wife. But Anabel happily accepted her role. She even rebuked him when on the way home he complained about Gimenez's intrusions.

"These old men are used to getting their way," Anabel said. "As long as they don't touch or say anything offensive, we play our part."

Not long after, Gimenez tendered the apartment as a rent-free gift. It was at this stage that Serguey decided the doctor was just looking for company on his own terms, particularly after his sister deserted him. He wanted a human pet project, young people he could be proud of. Given the circumstances, Serguey was willing to oblige, since Anabel was too. In Cuba, one sold oneself out sooner or later, and it rarely was to achieve what Gimenez was offering.

All things considered, Felipe's ordeal had come too soon, too early in Serguey's career. Had it happened in five or ten years, he might have been more established, might have had sufficient independence and power to deal with the risks on his own. Serguey found it difficult not to see it as a kind of test, perhaps a punishment, especially now that he was at the mercy of strangers. Should Anabel have been more insulted by Gimenez's insidiousness? Should he have declined the job, the apartment? Should he have stayed closer to his father and brother, despite their differences? He needed something to snap him out of his stupor, to keep at bay the dread that comes from knowing that resisting the inescapable is to invite the tragic, and that the answer to some or all of these questions, whatever the end of Felipe's situation, might be "yes."

He was spared further brooding when Kiko phoned the next day with news of Claudia. She had agreed to meet on Saturday outside the popular Coppelia ice cream parlor. There would be enough people around for them to blend in, as well as enough of a buffer zone for a private talk.

"Be there on time," Kiko warned. "She's a stickler for punctuality."

According to him, Claudia was eager to help. She had already heard of Felipe's arrest and had been gathering information. As for Mario's number, his friend at ETECSA admitted that it might take a while longer to track it, if it was possible at all.

"But don't worry," Kiko said, the conviction in his pitch encouraging to Serguey. "We'll find that *hijo de puta*."

CHAPTER 12

On Friday, Victor turned up at the apartment at Anabel's request. Her face lit up when she saw him. Not a look of glee, exactly, but rather she seemed happy that he had accepted her invitation. Serguey shouldn't go alone to the meeting: that's how she broached it. Serguey didn't want to cause a scene based on flimsy suspicions or jealousy, so he chalked it up to just that—his wife wishing for him and his brother to work together. And the truth was he had grown accustomed to having Victor with him of late. If he were being honest, he could admit that he could've used Victor's help at the National Council for the Performing Arts.

"Where's Alida?" Victor asked, slumping on the couch with the same histrionic flair Alida seemed so fond of. "You guys kick her out?"

"She's with some of the actors," Serguey said.

"Thespians and their drama." Victor scratched his stomach. "Now, if you'll excuse me, I'm going to take a nap. I need my beauty sleep."

"Who sleeps at four in the afternoon?"

"The unemployed. Or most Cubans. You don't take *siestas*?"

"Never."

Victor yawned. "You won't make it to fifty."

A couple of hours later, Victor woke, his eyes bloodshot and his mouth a little swollen. Serguey stared at him from the balcony. He picked up an ice-filled glass that lay next to him and drank what was left. He waggled the glass, the ice clinking, as if it were an alarm clock.

Victor wiped his eyes and lips, and farted loudly.

"I heard that," Anabel said from the kitchen.

"Your husband's a pig!" Victor shouted. "What are you drinking, Coca-Cola?" he asked Serguey. Without letting him respond, he shouted, "Correction, Anabel. He's an imperialist pig!"

Serguey set the glass down and entered the living room. "Scream it louder, why don't you?"

Victor inhaled deeply and distended his mouth, as if to comply. Serguey cocked his fist playfully. His brother shielded himself and chuckled.

"My neighbors take themselves too seriously," Serguey said, sitting next to him.

"Your neighbors are communist sellouts."

"You mean like Anabel and me?"

"I don't blame you." Victor plucked a smooshed pack of cigarettes and a lighter from his pocket. "I like this place more than Dad's."

Serguey seized Victor's wrist. "Don't make it smell like Dad's."

"Come on, don't be a joyless asshole."

"I'm serious. We're keen on hygiene in this house." He wasn't ready to let go of the habits he and Anabel had developed in the apartment. The risk of losing it wasn't the same as giving it up.

Before Victor could unleash his next insult, Anabel called him from down the hall. He shoved the pack and lighter back into his pocket.

"The queen beckons."

"Don't forget that makes me the king."

"Like the one from *The Little Prince*." Victor stood and pretended to inspect his surroundings. "Where the hell is that mouse?"

Serguey scoffed. "I'll tell you where I'd like to shove it."

For the next half-hour, while Serguey read the paper, Anabel and Victor chatted in the kitchen. Victor was telling her, quite rowdily, stories about getting caught by the police, about business deals gone terribly wrong, about the absurdity of living a street life, the excitement and misery of it all. His statements were astute. Victor was capable of acuity. And in his typically suave demeanor, he managed to make himself out as both a victim and hero. In middle school, he used to come home with two or three bottles of perfume, a handful of flowers, and cookies or chocolate every Valentine's Day. Felipe called him Casanova, or Romeo, or Alain Delon. Serguey had gotten flowers once, from a teacher who was doling them out to everyone in class. Felipe always highlighted Serguey's intellect as the equalizer between the brothers. In a country where education had been prioritized as an emblem of the Revolution, intelligence was valued highest by society. Serguey was the boy with aptitude, the one who could be anything he wanted to be. Victor got the girls. This belief and its implications—the possible consequences of dealing with an irresistibly alluring young man—had accrued inside Serguey through the years like alcohol in blood, causing impaired judgment, provoking in him an inescapable, impulsive envy. Had this same state led him to misguidedly construe Alida's demeanor with him as attraction, perhaps even subtle seduction?

He dropped the newspaper and stole down the hall, slightly self-conscious but overcome with curiosity, halting a few paces from the entrance to the kitchen.

"We get on that Suzuki," Victor was saying, "and we can go anywhere we want to deliver the stuff. The way streets are designed in Havana, once you go into a neighborhood, the cops can't catch you if you're on a motorcycle. Even if all you have is a bicycle, in alleyways they have to chase you on foot. You start climbing stairs, I mean, it's easy to jump from roof to roof, hide inside a water tank."

Serguey thought of Raidel, of how long it took for the police to find him on the roof near the funeral home. He wondered if Victor remembered this detail, if it sparked up somewhere in his mind as he spoke.

"But we aren't criminals, you know," Victor continued. Serguey assumed Anabel had given him some sort of reproachful look. "We aren't hurting anybody."

"I don't know about that," Anabel said. From the lightness in her tone, Serguey could tell she was smiling. "Though I do see your point, I just don't think the risk is worth it."

Serguey stepped forward and peeked into the kitchen. Victor's hand was on Anabel's shoulder.

"With all due respect, madam," he said, his face slanting toward Anabel's, his mouth, from Serguey's viewpoint, turned toward her cheek, "if I lived here and had my brother's job, I'd be saying the same."

As he heard Anabel reply "point taken" with a gentle nod of her head and then add something—to Serguey's ears, not as assertively as she should have—about people still having to make a choice, one of the great paradoxes of Serguey's life surfaced in his mind: what he really wanted—and he would never admit it to another person, especially not his wife—wasn't to be the intelligent brother, the successful, righteous, privileged brother. He wanted to be the charming brother, the daring, brazen, spontaneous brother. What he wanted was what he didn't possess: Victor's bravado.

And there it was, in full display in his kitchen, with his own wife. He had always seen jealousy as a petty emotion, especially when he was the one experiencing it. But with Victor it felt ingrained, implacable.

Years prior, at Serguey and Anabel's engagement party, Victor had, after downing an irresponsible number of drinks, told Anabel through a repugnantly grinning mouth how his brother loved to watch other people get beat up, and how, if she ever needed her husband's help, he would probably stand on the sidelines before lifting a finger. Serguey had stood rigidly next to his brother, swallowing and sensing the flesh on his own face slowly flaming.

Anabel replied, resting her hand on Serguey's arm, that complex men have flaws, and that those flaws are often what makes them attractive. Simple, angry men, she said, are shallow and uninteresting.

"And you, Victor," she added, smiling gracefully to reduce the tartness of her statement, "you seem pretty transparent to me."

Serguey had fallen in love with his soon-to-be wife even more that day, but he had also been convinced that Victor was, at some level, in love with Anabel.

Now he heard her—the opposite of tartness in her voice—asking Victor to open the cupboard.

"I'm not used to women bossing me around," he joked, triggering an Alida-like giggle from Anabel. Perhaps this was, despite what she had told him at the wedding, what Anabel really noticed in Victor, why she always, Serguey believed, seemed so infatuated with his brother, no matter how much she tried to dissimulate it. He was not just the arresting idea of a culture—the one Serguey and Anabel had placed under an appealing lens—but he was the raw, vulgar, unabashed culture itself. He was a real Cuban, born and bred in the streets. Serguey wasn't even an intellectual or an artist, like his father. He was a government pawn, an office pet.

He returned to the living room, not as quietly as he should have, and sat down coolly, waiting for them. It wasn't long before they emerged from the hall holding three glasses. Victor was in front, Anabel close behind. She was grasping a bottle of rum by its neck. She flaunted it at Serguey.

"Did you really tell your brother we had no alcohol in the apartment?"

"Where did you get that?"

"Gimenez left a couple of bottles when we moved in, remember?"

Victor shook his head at Serguey. "What a selfish prick."

"I think a drink will help everyone relax," Anabel said. She removed the cap and asked Victor to hold each glass steady so she could pour the rum. Serguey was given a glass first.

"Let's have a toast," Victor said.

"What are we celebrating?" Serguey asked, getting up. "The fact that Dad's in prison, or that we can't get him out?"

Anabel's expression turned somber. "Everyone's worried. That doesn't mean we can't have a moment's peace."

Serguey gulped down a quarter of his rum. The wooden finish swamped his tongue, smooth and revitalizing. The robust, aged alcohol made his eyes water. "A moment's peace? You've been laughing and giggling for the past twenty minutes while my brother admitted to you that he's been breaking the law."

"I was just trying to help her unwind," Victor said.

Serguey walked to the edge of the living room, standing on the balcony's threshold. "I'm sure that's what you were trying to do." He swilled the rest of the rum, in prime Gimenez fashion. He elongated his neck and scratched his throat, as he had seen Victor do the night of the play, and guzzled the evening air through his mouth and nose.

Anabel laid the bottle on the center table. "Serguey, don't do this."

She said it piteously. It would've aggravated him less if she'd been demanding. But she was begging him not to make them uncomfortable, not to feed the elephant in the room. He walked toward them, seized the bottle, and served himself to the brim. "No, you're right," he said, raising his glass. "Let's drink, sing, and dance. Dad's fucked, anyway." He swallowed nearly half the rum in one shot.

"Here we go." Victor dropped his glass next to the bottle. "If I hadn't come, you wouldn't even know what's going on with Dad."

Victor was in good form, ready to spar. Serguey accepted the challenge. Here was his chance to be brazen, to fight back without reservation. There was too much unsettled between them, too much that had festered and deserved a confrontation. He and his brother needed it. "Ah, but you *did* come. Why was that? It's fun to brag about going around in a motorcycle selling god knows what, but not much fun when your brother's the one saving your skin."

"Are you listening to this?" Victor said to Anabel. "How do you put up with this fucking guy?"

"Forget the drinks," Anabel said. "Let's all calm down."

"No," Serguey said. His wife and brother were a united front against him. He was the villain, a part he hadn't played nearly enough. The rum made it easier to do, gave him voice. "Let my little brother tell us how he really feels." He glared at Victor. "It's gotta be eating you inside that you had to come to *me*."

"It is, actually." In the void of an implausible moment, Victor seemed equable, calculating. Serguey felt as if he were looking into a slightly skewed mirror: the features distorted but the essence the same. "You didn't do shit for your mother, who was killed in front of you," here Victor stooped his head for emphasis, "or for your little brother, who *you* were supposed to protect."

Serguey narrowed his eyes, telling himself it was the alcohol stinging them. He took the bottle and stared at its label—Havana Club, *Añejo Especial*—willing his mind to recalibrate. If he acknowledged the accusations, he'd break. What had festered, it seemed, was Serguey's conscience: it had been seized by a sense of remorse in grave need of release. In his inebriated tongue, he transformed into spite. Victor's controlled delivery, much like Serguey's public persona, had been a façade. He simply had to strip it.

Serguey offered the Havana Club to his brother. "Here, it'll make you feel better."

Victor braced the bottle by the lip, sprung to the balcony, and tossed it over the rail. Seconds later, as he stepped into the living room, the bottle burst on the street.

The satisfaction that Serguey should've experienced with the blast eluded him. No catharsis had come. "With his luck," he said, "he probably smashed someone's head." He pointed at Victor's face, which had sharpened into anger. "If you end up in jail, I'm not getting you out this time."

Victor clasped Serguey's neck. Serguey dropped his glass, spilling rum on the floor. Victor slipped as he pushed his brother. They staggered all the way to the sofa, Victor landing on top.

"Son of a bitch," he said, still clinging to Serguey.

Serguey pulled at his brother's wrist but couldn't shake him loose. Anabel shoved her body between the men and elbowed Victor. "Let him go!" she yelled. "Victor, stop!"

Victor released Serguey and took a step back.

"This is how he deals with everything," Serguey said, catching his breath. "Imagine if he were drunk!"

"You couldn't help Mom," Victor said, not with anger but with what appeared to be pangs of remorse. "You couldn't help me, and now you can't help Dad."

"Victor, go," Anabel said.

"You married a fucking coward, Anabel."

"Get the fuck out of my house!" she barked, signaling to the door.

Flustered, Victor wagged his head, mumbling on his way out, "Born a fucking coward."

"This is your fault," Anabel told Serguey.

"My fault?" he said. "Why don't you go with him, then?" He kicked the fallen glass, which had come to rest by his feet. It swiveled and sprayed the rest of the rum like a sprinkler.

Anabel went to retrieve the glass. "You have to go after him."

Serguey grabbed her arm. "Leave it. I'll get the glass."

She shook him off. "Go after Victor."

"But you just threw him out!"

"So he wouldn't hurt you."

Serguey laughed mockingly, hysterically.

Anabel cupped the glass in her hands. "Serguey, please go get your brother and end all this fighting. Do it for me. Do it for your father. Do it for your neighbors. But just fucking do it."

"You're complicit in this too."

She approached him and kneeled on the spilled rum. Her legs dragged the liquid like a floor squeegee. This, more than anything, made him profoundly ashamed.

"Yes, your lordship," she said. "We're all guilty in the eyes of the court. Now, can you get over yourself?"

He regretted it, the self-righteousness of it, as soon as he said it: "Why am I the one who always has to fix things?"

Anabel touched his thigh. "Because you're the older brother. That's how it works. I've been doing it with Alida all my life. And you're a fucking lawyer. You're supposed to fix things." She surveyed the entire living room floor. Parts of it beyond them were slicked with alcohol. "I'll take care of this mess you idiots made."

She hitched herself up, wiped her legs, and removed her shoes. Barefooted, she headed to the kitchen. Serguey loitered for a few seconds, swallowing his own hypocrisy, his own inadequacy, yielding to its acerbic taste.

He left the apartment and descended the stairs to the lobby and then to the street. Victor was crouched over the asphalt, closer to the opposite sidewalk, under the faint glimmer of a streetlamp. He was picking up shards from the broken bottle, accruing them in the palm of one hand. Serguey walked slowly, circumventing his brother so he could face him. Victor didn't look up. Serguey joined him, gathering wet pieces of glass himself.

"This is my mess," Victor said, avoiding eye contact.

Serguey stopped. He watched his brother make sure there were no big fragments left on the ground.

"Where's the closest pile of garbage?" Victor asked.

There was a big refuse depository around the corner. "Just drop them on the landing," Serguey said. "I'll take them upstairs."

They strode silently to the building's entrance and placed the shattered glass on the bottom step. Victor used his foot to mass the pieces against the wall. Then he squatted and lit up a cigarette. Serguey sat next to him, leaning on his elbows.

"Did I hurt you?" Victor said.

"Didn't even make a dent."

Victor nodded, blowing smoke through the side of his mouth. A scraggy man with a brush cut trotted by. A white T-shirt dangled from the back of his jean shorts like a tail. He was carrying a stuffed plastic bag under his arm.

"That one's up to no good," Victor said. "You can tell by the way he's running. I bet you he's not from this neighborhood."

His brother was looking to make peace. Serguey gazed up at a musky, monotonous sky. "Do you remember when we were kids, and we spoke to Toya for the first time?"

"When we tried to sneak into that party with Kiko?"

"Yeah, with the Santeros."

Victor flashed a muted smile. "I remember."

They'd gotten into the porch of the house, cloaked by shadows, pretending to be ninjas. Through a gap in the window, they could see people dressed in colorful garb—long dresses and headscarves—dancing in a circle around the living room. Two black men sat in a corner banging on drums. The twirling plumes of tobacco smoke and strange singing gave the scene a dreamlike quality. The women arched their shoulders and heads back, aiming their chests upward, then suddenly slouched their arms toward the floor and loosened up their necks, as if their bodies were possessed, sections of it about to be dislodged.

While the boys bunched by the window, taking turns with the best view, someone opened the front door. They became paralyzed. Serguey wanted to yell that they should run, but the woman—big-breasted and with strikingly round eyes—moved closer and blocked their escape.

"What's your name?" she asked Kiko.

"Carmelo."

"Go on home."

Kiko glanced at his friends, an apology written on his grimacing lips, and sprinted out of the porch.

The woman turned to Serguey and Victor. "You're the playwright's boys, aren't you?"

"Yes," Serguey said.

Every particle of her exhalation smelled like burnt grass and honey. Serguey was reminded of an amber-hued pomade that his grandfather Joaquin had owned and which Felipe stored in a nightstand drawer. Sometimes he and Victor would twist off the lid and dare each other to dip their noses in it.

She grabbed Victor's chin. "What's your name?"

"Victor."

"Do you know who I am?"

"Toya the Witch."

The woman raised her eyebrows and chuckled. "That's right, I'm Toya. But it's called *santera*, not *bruja*."

"How come you're not black?" Victor said.

Serguey couldn't believe what his brother had just asked. Victor later explained he thought that to be a Santero, one had to be black. Toya was light-skinned.

"Who says I'm not black?" was Toya's reply.

The brothers said nothing.

"Tell your father to get you an *Eleguá*, for protection." She leaned forward, her eyes darting between the boys, and said, "Now get out of here. This is no place for children."

That night, Serguey told his father what'd happened.

"Don't pay attention to Toya," Felipe said. "She's a nice woman, but Santería is not for us."

"What about grandpa's statues?" Serguey asked, referring to their obvious African themes.

"There's a difference between observing or exploring something in your work and actually living it. Santería is not for us."

Victor didn't remember his father saying such a thing. He believed Felipe not only liked Toya, but he venerated what she did. He took one last drag and snuffed his cigarette on the steps. "Toya's my spiritual advisor."

Serguey resisted a laugh. "You can't be serious."

"I even made Dad go see her once."

"Victor, you can't be serious. What did she tell him?"

"That he was hanging out with the wrong crowd."

Laughter overtook them both, a deep-rooted, wicked laugh—the kind that brothers can share at the expense of the world. Soon, however, they noticed the implicit misfortune in Toya's words, and their amusement simmered.

"Holy shit," Serguey said. "A spiritual advisor."

"It gets worse."

"What do you mean?"

"I want you to see her. I want us both to, actually. She doesn't talk about you and me. She knows it's a sore subject. But it's been in the back of my mind."

"You know I don't believe any of that stuff. I wouldn't even know how to react. You might get offended . . ."

Victor stared at him earnestly. "Do it for me."

Serguey took a deep breath, responsibility chopping away at his resistance. "Okay."

"You'll do it?"

"I'll do it."

"Good," Victor said. "I'll talk to her."

Serguey clutched his brother's shoulder. "Let's go in."

"Your wife cursed me out, remember?"

"She also asked me to get you. We can't have any more petty fights."

"You're telling me?"

"I'm telling myself."

Victor flicked the cigarette butt onto the grass. "I'm not trying to stir up shit between you and Anabel. I've always liked her, and I've always been kind of envious of you two. But I wouldn't mess with my brother's wife. And I didn't mean what I said about mom and—"

"I know you didn't," Serguey said. It had been a draining week; certainly a draining evening. He didn't have enough left in the tank for *that* conversation. He pursed his lips at the wall behind Victor, his eyes looking to the ground. "Don't forget the glass."

"I can't believe I wasted a Havana Club," Victor said, his weary smile riddled with remorse.

❧❧ ✴ ❧❧

Serguey couldn't sleep. His throat felt constricted, as if still in his brother's grasp. His limbs were sore. Victor was passed out in the guestroom, no doubt drooling copiously on the pillow, as he had done in his childhood. At one point, Felipe had taken him to see a psychologist, worried that, along with his wetting the bed, he might have a condition. Apparently he was just a deep sleeper, unaware of his bodily functions. Victor's conscience got so switched off he never remembered his dreams. Not one. Serguey wondered if his brother just didn't have any, his mind remaining vacant throughout the night.

Serguey's own dreams were vivid. It wasn't rare for him to remember the details. He had a recurring dream of a Spanish fortress by the water. Sometimes it was abandoned; sometimes it was a museum full of ancient statues. He'd gotten lost inside its corridors so frequently, he could map the entire structure if asked. He couldn't imagine what it was like to not have dreams, to not remember them. But such a thing couldn't be called an ailment. Victor's only condition was his irrepressible impetus. It came in bursts and then fizzled, leaving him a warm, approachable person. Serguey was more cerebral, his brain harder to switch off in favor of emotions.

Anabel lay beside him in silence. The lamp on the nightstand was still on. The sheets had scrunched and wrinkled beneath his body and were now coarse against his skin. Anabel turned on her side and stared at him.

"I'm sorry," he said.

"That's not what I want to hear."

He understood what she meant. "I'll speak with Victor again tomorrow. I'll fix this for good."

"Why do you dislike each other so much? No matter how different you are, what happened tonight's not normal. It's worse than animosity. It feels like resentment. What did he mean you couldn't help your mom or him?"

Serguey's body tightened. "I don't know."

"Yes, you do. What did he mean?"

His lips contorted. He began to cry. He resisted it at first, covering his mouth, but his sobs broke through. Anabel rested her head on his. Her own tears fell on his shoulder. They didn't do this often—cry together. Serguey's breath became hot and moist. He moaned and exhaled, as if trying to release the growing pressure in his chest. He swallowed hard to relax his throat.

And then he told her.

When he was fourteen and Victor eleven, Felipe sent them to their grandparents' house in San Antonio de las Vegas, a rural town twenty-five kilometers south of Havana. With the whole summer ahead of them, the boys decided to imitate peasant life, adopting the kinds of activities that were impossible to carry out in the city. They fished in a nearby river until the sun buried itself beyond green fields, the twilight birds and crickets serenading them as they trailed their way back to the house. They competed to see who could climb trees the fastest; they gathered avocados, guavas, and mangoes in burlap sacks and hid them inside their grandfather's storage room, a shack concealed at the heart of a wooded area; they learned how to feed the pigs and chickens that their grandmother, Estela, bred in her backyard.

Toward the end of their stay, the boys took to hunting with their grandfather's pellet rifle. Larido, a rough-skinned man who had moved to the countryside over two decades before, taught his grandsons how to aim steady and search for the fallen prey—mostly small birds like the black-plumed *toti*.

One afternoon, after they had shot at least thirty rounds and killed four birds, they opted for a different route home. The brothers loved to explore. They liked getting lost in the tangled branches of a thicket, slogging across a field of chest-high grass, swimming the width of the river in an area they hadn't traversed before. On this particular day, Victor asked to carry the birds. He hung them proudly from a rope tied at his waist. Their wobbly, upside-down heads smacked against his thighs as he walked.

The boys entered a clearing, and in the distance Serguey recognized the fence they usually skirted all the way to the house.

"I told you I have a good sense of direction," he told Victor.

As they continued on, they were startled by the sound of approaching voices. Three young peasants came into view. Two of the peasants were wearing straw hats; the one in the front, shorter and brawnier, had on a baseball cap. He squinted and said, "Hey, aren't you the boys staying with Larido and Elena?"

"Yes," Serguey said.

The peasant chuckled. "You've been hunting?"

"Got me four birds," Victor said, his jaw slanted high.

"Our grandma asked that we bring her something," Serguey added.

"What do you think, guys?" the peasant said to his buddies. "We could make a stew."

"We can give you a bird," Serguey said.

Victor shot him an angry look.

"Listen, city boy," the peasant said, "just pass me the damn *totis*."

Serguey went to untie the rope, but Victor swatted his hand away.

"I killed these birds," he said. "They're mine."

"The little one has balls." The peasant crept forward. "I thought all city boys were wimps."

"Victor," Serguey said, "just give them the *totis*."

"No." Victor aimed the rifle at the peasant, his voice and body shaking with rage. "They're mine."

The guys in straw hats raised their arms. "Take it easy, *enano*," one said.

"He's not going to shoot," the brawny peasant said, trying to grasp the barrel.

Victor pressed the trigger. It clicked. He was out of pellets.

The peasant grappled the gun from Victor's hands and threw it on the ground. "You're going to get it, *habanerito*!"

Victor swung twice and missed. The peasant dropped him with a well-timed punch to the chest.

His companions lunged forward, one of them toward Serguey, who stretched out his arms hopelessly, as if trying to keep an oncoming train at bay.

"Stop," he heard himself mutter.

The peasant cocked his fist. Serguey winced and tripped, falling on his own. The other peasant had Victor in a chokehold. Victor was screaming furiously. The brawny peasant punched him in the stomach repeatedly. Victor coughed and whimpered. As soon as he got a second wind, however, he kicked his assailant in the groin. The peasant grunted, incredulous of what'd just occurred. He hit Victor with a right hook to the face, and Victor went limp, though he was still conscious. The peasant yanked Victor's pants and underwear down and squeezed his genitals. He produced a knife, bringing the blade close to Victor's testicles. Victor squirmed, groaning with every breath. Serguey feared that his brother's fright would cause the blade to slice skin. The three bodies shambled backwards, the knife inches from its target. The straw-hatted peasant, perhaps worried like Serguey that the threat could become a gory accident, suddenly released his chokehold. The knife-wielding one had no choice but to let Victor go. Victor slumped to the floor, barely moving on the dry soil.

From ground level, his brother looked like a mangled assembly of limbs. The birds were now attached to him at the knees, their carcasses scattered like rocks around his feet. Victor reached for his belt, mindlessly, frantically attempting to pull up his pants. Their mother had died at the hands of a knife. It was unfair, Serguey thought, for life to have placed such a weapon in the peasant's hands, and for the rifle to have run out of pellets.

"What about him?" the leader asked the third peasant, who had been staring in confusion at a stiff Serguey.

"He's too scared."

"City boys are cowards." The brawny peasant cut the rope with the birds and flung it over his shoulder. "You tell Larido about this," he warned Serguey, "and we'll chop off the little one's balls and dump you in the river."

As soon as the peasants were out of the clearing, Serguey strode anxiously toward his brother. Victor was breathing heavily. There was blood and dirt on his cheeks and nose. Serguey grasped his arm and asked him if he was okay.

"Leave me," Victor said, his voice low and hoarse. He fixed his pants and massaged his stomach, groaning. Then he began heading for the river. Serguey grabbed the rifle and followed.

Without taking off his clothes, Victor submerged himself in the water, rinsed his face, and scaled his way back up the riverbank. "If grandma or grandpa asks," he said, "I slipped on the rocks."

Serguey nodded.

Grandma Estela inquired a few times if Victor needed to go to the doctor. He insisted that he was fine, that the bruises were only superficial. Serguey corroborated the "falling on the rocks" story but didn't say much else. Victor apologized for having wasted the pellets and not killing a single bird. His grandfather told him not to worry, but he forbade them from going to the rocky section of the river again. Grandma Estela gave Victor half an aspirin and let him skip dinner so he could get some sleep. Serguey volunteered to feed the pigs. As he dumped the *sancocho* on the trough, he wept, the squealing of the pigs drowning out his sobs.

Over a decade later, no one knew about the incident: not Felipe, not their grandparents, not any of Serguey's closest friends. Not a word about it had been exchanged between the brothers.

In the dim glow of the bedroom, Serguey cried again. Anabel held him like she would a child. He was exorcizing his own shortcomings, confessing his cowardice and shame, yet he found no relief. He appreciated the warmth of his wife's embrace, the patience with which she waited for his weeping to subside and his thoughts to regain order. But what was unraveling in his mind—the memories, the guilt—he no longer felt could be reined in. It terrified him.

Anabel told him, "You have to speak about it with your brother. He can't hold what happened against you."

Serguey stifled his sobs and numbly nodded.

She said, "You've more than made up for whatever you think you didn't do."

He returned to his side of the bed. "I've barely seen him and my Dad since I left the house."

"You know that isn't completely true. And it's not like they've gone out of their way to come visit you."

"They didn't want to intrude."

Anabel's sigh mimicked the steam-thickened fizz of a pressure cooker. "Really? After all these years criticizing them and telling me that it was better to keep some distance, you're going to make excuses for them? Getting Victor out of jail counts for something. You've gone to every single one of your Dad's plays. You pick up the phone when he calls. You don't have the best relationship in the world, but who the hell does?"

Serguey masked his face with his hands, containing a forceful sneeze. Anabel handed him a tissue. He cleared his nose, crumpled the tissue, and lobbed it in the vicinity of a small basket Anabel kept by the door. "I only got Victor out of jail because my dad asked me to. I didn't do it out of the goodness of my heart. I didn't even go see him when he was doing his military service."

She rotated on her side, her bent knees pointed at him. She pulled down the hem of her nightgown to cover herself. "That's because he explicitly said he didn't want visitors, and you were busy with your university workload. He knows that. We're not playing games here, Serguey. We're possibly giving up our future to help Felipe. I'll always be the first one to tell you to take care of family, but you owe your dad and your brother nothing."

It sounded soothing, neatly logical, but he couldn't accept it. "I'm sorry. That's not how I feel. That's why I got angry today."

She looked at him for a while, expecting him to append his statement. "You got angry because you were jealous of Victor. You two have this pent-up animosity, and you can't even talk about it like adults."

Serguey chuckled, twisting his mouth uneasily. "We're not very good at that in my family."

"Then you have to learn." She moved closer to him, letting him caress her legs. Her lotion-glazed skin persuaded the tip of his fingers to drift back and forth. "Alida and I always lay everything out. We fight, we make up. We know what we think and feel about each other. When we were little, she had this friend who came to play with her toys, this beautiful black boy who wore orthopedic boots. Alida had a crush on him, and one day, I started teasing her in front of him, so much that the boy never came back. Apparently, he got embarrassed. To this day she won't forgive me, but I've already told her I'm sorry. I feel really bad about it, and she understands it." Anabel's eyes followed his hand as it glided away from the bottom of her nightgown. "When she first said she wanted to do ballet, I mocked her, told her she had no grace. I took it back the minute I saw her dance in her first recital. All my envy couldn't compete with how proud I was. I still love seeing her on stage. But that's only because we've moved beyond the old stuff, the petty stuff. What happened with the peasants isn't petty, and what happened with your mom . . ."

Serguey retrieved his hand. "Victor and I didn't get the proper help, Anabel. We were never taught how to speak about it."

She looked at him, her face saturated with sorrowful sincerity. "You're going to have to do it yourselves, even if it's ugly. You can't let your pride get in the way." She smiled, her dimpled chin holding on to traces of sadness. "You Blancos love pride and pity. You can't live without it."

"I wish my mother would've been around a while longer." He scratched his own hands delicately, absentmindedly. "Maybe I'm remembering wrong, but I have this sensation that she was good at talking to me and Victor. I remember her saying that obsession was man's perdition, or something like that. I always thought she'd stolen that from Dad, but I'm not so sure. She said one had to care for everything and everyone, not just what attracted us the most." Serguey understood that Irene had left his father for a violent drunk—that she, like the Blancos, had been a hypocrite—but her decision to move in with Raidel was presently delegated in Serguey's psyche to the irreversibility of a mistake, nothing more.

In a mellifluous voice, Anabel asked, "How much have you and Victor talked about your mom since she died?"

"Neither one of us likes to bring it up. When we do by accident, we pretend it was an error, a slip of the tongue. I guess we figured this is how it's going to be, so we never questioned it." He could intuit her next inquiry. "Dad's the worst person to ask about her. He starts rambling about how hard it was for him, and it's excruciating. It's like we weren't there, only *he* was."

As Anabel began to reply, they heard a loud thud in the living room. Serguey motioned for her to stay silent. He wondered if he'd forgotten to shut the balcony door (the wind often knocked things around). He left the bed and scurried to the bedroom's entrance, listening for another sound. There were footsteps, maybe a grunt. He told himself it had to be Victor, unable to sleep, moseying in the dark to not give himself away. He turned the handle carefully, poked his head out, and felt a sudden, chilly draft on his face. The living room light was on. Victor was standing on the balcony, a shirtless figure in a booming breeze, smoking a cigarette. Serguey closed the bedroom door and returned to the bed.

"It's my brother," he said, getting under the covers. "We're not the only ones who can't sleep." Anabel curled up against his chest, waiting for him to continue. He couldn't. He simply whispered, "I get everything you said, but it's not that easy."

She lifted then tucked her head. "I know."

In a few minutes, she fell asleep. Serguey didn't hear Victor pass by the bedroom. No more dropped objects or human noises. He helped a drowsy Anabel accommodate her body the way she liked it: a hand nuzzled under her cheek, the other near her mouth. He lay on his back with his eyes closed, picturing himself feet up on the railing, sharing a smoke with his brother. That's what brothers should do, he thought as his mind inched toward impending sleep. They should see and feel themselves, in the inconspicuous plainness of a moment, luckier and bigger than all the world combined.

CHAPTER 13

Claudia requested that the brothers meet her at 8:30 a.m. in Coppelia Park. She would be wearing blue jeans and a gray T-shirt and carrying a backpack. The brothers hustled down La Rampa, the wind boosting them forward. Their gait was steady and synchronized. The air was already humid despite the early hour, but there was a temperance to the way the sun fell on the city, as if gently asking it to wake. At this time on a Saturday, Havana was predominantly asleep. Senior citizens traipsed about, tote bags at their shoulders. The occasional biker swished by, likely hoping to be the first in line at some vendor's food stand, if he could find one.

A small group of people had gathered outside the sprawling ice cream parlor at Coppelia Park. Gimenez had taken Serguey and Anabel here once as part of his courting process. He paid in CUC, the Cuban convertible peso, and just like a tourist he was allowed to skip Coppelia's infamous long lines. He was well acquainted with the workers, mainly because he tipped them well. He wanted to show Serguey that he was special, above the masses—and it worked. For years, long lines had been a flagrant testament of the communist state's failure: a sign of inefficiency that invariably brought out the worst in people. Serguey and Anabel hadn't been immune to them. At the bodegas, stores, post office, bus terminals—the lines were ubiquitous and mercilessly slow. Skipping them was as high a crime in Havana as anything else. People were berated and often beaten because of it. Possessing the means to skip a line without repercussions was a significant signifier of status, an indulgence enjoyed by few. To do it at Coppelia of all places, where the lines were—according to Gimenez—almost as tedious as the ones at the Eiffel Tower, was an impressive feat. Serguey and Anabel loved the experience, and they let Gimenez know as much.

Serguey's memories of Coppelia prior to that moment were of waiting in line with Felipe and Victor. The payoff tasted sweeter after such protracted anticipation, however. As you got closer to the entrance, people sat at their tables all around you, the aroma of chocolate, strawberry, almond, or mango wafting from their dripping fingers. Felipe liked to sit outside, encircled by trees and fresh air, and not inside what was called 'the tower,' a seemingly levitating, circular space deluged in natural light, with smaller, scrolling rooms partitioned by multi-colored glass panes, bedazzling to the brothers' eyes. Despite having to do as their father wished, Serguey loved the ice cream, especially being able to savor multiple flavors at once. Victor waited for his to turn into a syrupy concoction before dipping his *biscochos*, letting them soak to the marrow. Then he drank the rest of the ice cream like soup. On one of their visits, Felipe told them that an important scene in *Fresa y Chocolate* had been filmed there.

"It's the only Cuban movie to be nominated for an Oscar," he said.

Serguey remembered watching his father eating strawberry ice cream. He recalled the Coppelia scene from the movie quite well too: an awkward exchange between a straight young man and a gregarious homosexual, portrayed by acclaimed actor Jorge Perugorria. Felipe taught them the name. He also made them learn the directors: Tomas Gutierrez Alea and Juan Carlos Tabio. Gutierrez Alea, nicknamed Titon, had directed some of Cuba's best-known movies: *Death of a Bureaucrat*, *Memories of Underdevelopment*, *The Survivors*. Knowing names and titles, Felipe stressed, was a way to honor your country's cultural history.

Despite the pleasantness of his recollections, the truth was their trips to Coppelia had been sporadic at best. Felipe took them more often to the Ward ice cream parlor on Santa Catalina Avenue in El Cerro, which was closer to their house. The options there, when available, were chocolate, vanilla, and, on a lucky day, *mantecado*, but the quality was consistently poor. It wasn't rare to find chunks of insipid ice mixed in with the sugar-deficient flavor. Victor and Serguey beseeched their father, widening their eyes and tugging at his arms, to let them play baseball in the nearby Ciudad Deportiva, a public sports complex with more open fields than any child could hope for. It excited Serguey to hear the clink of an aluminum bat smacking a ball, the roar and gasps that followed. But Felipe disliked sports, especially baseball. He called it "the true opium of the masses." So the brothers ate their ice cream as they straggled the Ciudad Deportiva's massive outer fence, watching kids diving to catch a swerving ball in the outfield or cackling at a ridiculous strikeout swing.

The adult Serguey took inventory of the people outside Coppelia and noticed that there was no child among them. He looked at their faces, sifting for a woman his age, but didn't see anyone who might be Claudia.

He and Victor kept on.

Not far ahead, Victor discreetly pointed her out. She was on a bench, shaded by a thick-branched tree, reading a book: *The Collected Poems of Octavio Paz.* Her edition was identical to the one Felipe owned.

"*Hablar es pensar,*" Serguey said as a form of introduction.

Claudia closed her book. "I didn't know lawyers liked poetry."

"I wasn't quoting one of his poems."

"That's true." She buried the poetry collection in her backpack and made room for the brothers to sit.

Serguey took the spot nearest to her. A scent of roses with a hint of violet emanated from her hair, a smell he associated with mothers-in-law and grandmothers, not a woman in her twenties. She wasn't wearing makeup, not on her brown eyelids or lips. Her billowy T-shirt, which draped awkwardly over her skinny arms and torso, had *The Ramones* printed on it. Her hair, dyed red, was cut short, accentuating her winsomely rounded head. She had thin, child-like eyebrows, and freckles on her cheek just a tinge darker than her *mulata* complexion. Her vocal tone was deep and confident, as was her stare. A perpetual smile seemed to hover at the corners of her mouth. Everything about her felt like an odd mix. The book, the T-shirt, the flowery scent. Serguey figured it must be deliberate. A person in her position, antagonizing the government—or at the very least, doing her work in spite of it—had to remain elusive, hard to read.

"I'm a big fan of your father's work," she said. "I was at the last showing of *Electra Garrigó.*"

Serguey chuckled.

"What's so funny?"

"We were there too," Victor said. He was keeping watch.

"Then it's fate," Claudia said.

"I don't believe in fate," Serguey said. "But Kiko did say you could help us?"

"That depends."

"On what?"

"If you want to be helped."

"We do," Victor said.

"I have to be able to trust you," Claudia said, "and you have to trust me. Kiko vouches for you, so I agreed to meet you in person. I made an exception this time."

"We appreciate it," Serguey said.

Victor cleared his throat. A couple passed by, holding hands. The man, clad in brand new jeans and a pink polo shirt, was talking about buying a pair of Adidas shoes. The woman wasn't listening; she was screwing the back of her earring, smirking thoughtfully.

Once the couple was far enough away, Victor asked, "You sure this is the best place to do this?"

"Best way to know if someone's following you." Claudia looked beyond the brothers, perusing her view with poise, unsurprised by what she saw. "You can blend in. I come here often and know the regulars."

Victor gave an understated tip of his head. He seemed satisfied.

"I looked into your father's situation." Claudia's voice was tepid, unemotional. "He's not in trouble because of his work."

Serguey said, "What is it then?" The fact that he'd been anticipating precisely *this* didn't reduce his sense of dread. He waited for her reply, telling himself not to budge or swallow no matter what she had to say.

Her near-smile dissolved, her lips curling into a sympathetic frown. "He's been dealing with an international organization."

"Which one?"

"I still have to confirm that. I don't give names unless I'm one hundred percent sure." She paused, gauging how to proceed. "I . . . I think it's anti-government."

"You think?" Serguey sneered at her uncertainty. "What was he doing with them?"

Claudia dispatched her disapproval at the sneer by raising her shoulders. "Don't know yet," she said. "I've heard something about money, but again, I don't want to speculate. When I have something specific, I'll share it with you." She displaced her hair from the front of her face to behind her ear. "I do know that they've labeled him a mercenary, so the money rumor makes sense."

"A mercenary?" Victor said, baffled. He stopped keeping watch, engrossed by Claudia.

She puffed out her chest. "Technically, I'm a mercenary."

Serguey found the idea ludicrous, but he was aware that according to the Penal Code, if his father had been given money by an international organization which the government deemed an enemy of the state, he was automatically considered a mercenary. "Do they have proof that he accepted funds?"

"Again, I—"

"I get it." He wanted to appear civil and considerate, but to his own ears, he sounded curt. "You don't know yet."

"How are *you* a mercenary?" Victor asked Claudia, still perplexed.

She blinked at Serguey, seemingly ashamed of her limited information. Then she looked at Victor, who had sufficient judgment to inspect their surroundings once more.

"Have you read the article in *Granma* about independent journalists?" she said, her voice tamed, unrushed.

Victor hadn't. Serguey, though he believed he had, echoed his brother. It was best to let her explain.

"They accused independent bloggers and writers of accepting funds from US and European institutions that oppose the Cuban government." She twisted her lips mockingly. "Supposedly we're part of a new cyber offensive against our little island. That's what they called us: cyber-mercenaries and cyber-terrorists. The act of taking money automatically means you're being paid to undermine and attack State Security. We're inciting riots, as you can see." She swept her hand inconspicuously from left to right, covering the length of the block.

Though she was attempting to underplay her profession, Serguey thought it transparent that she was proud, daring in her delivery.

"What if the money my dad took was for his work?" Victor asked. "If he's not using it to—"

"It doesn't matter," Serguey said. "They won't make that distinction. If they believe he's colluding, that's what they'll argue, and they'll win."

"So the law's there to fuck people over."

"Welcome to my world." Serguey thought briefly of the countless occasions in which he'd gotten his brother out of trouble, how, if not for him, Victor could still be in prison.

"In my world," Claudia whispered, "I'm only granted press rights 'in accordance with the goals of a socialist society.'"

"What the fuck does that mean?" Victor whispered.

There was a pause, a moment's reflection for all of them. A middle-aged woman in a spaghetti strap blouse cast a sideways glance at them. She trudged along, her shorts unattractively wedged between her thighs, a splotch of sweat at the small of her back. A stagnant humidity had usurped the early morning breeze.

Claudia said, "Do you know any of your father's connections abroad?"

"No."

Victor attested the same.

"He seems to have a lot of friends. I've been contacting some people in Miami and Spain, and they replied almost immediately. They're already working to spread the word about his situation. I'd like to stay in touch with them, with your permission."

Like a doctor, she had saved the encouraging news for last.

"You have it," Serguey said.

She lifted the backpack to her knees. "It'd be useful if you and your brother can record a video or give me a signed statement I can share, something that can be circulated among TV and radio stations. That way it isn't just my word. Kiko can give you a hand with the video if you want."

"What should we say?"

"That's up to you."

Serguey pondered the idea. "We'll discuss it with Kiko."

"I'll post an entry on my blog about Felipe. It'll get reshared on Facebook and Twitter."

Her demeanor was inspiriting enough for him to believe her.

"I do want to request," she said, "that you please don't share my name with anyone. Everything between us has to be confidential. If somebody shows up at my door or they pick me off the street, I won't be able to do my job."

Serguey agreed.

"We'll be in touch through Kiko," she added. "Hopefully we can make a difference. It seems the wheels are already turning."

"Have you heard anything about Mario Rabasa?" Serguey said.

She creased her forehead. "Who's he?"

"My father's dramaturge. We think he's involved."

Claudia puckered her face and bit her bottom lip. "I'll find out about him, and I'll get you more details about the organization your dad's involved with."

"There's a cop," Victor said, shivering his legs. He nudged his chin toward the end of the street. Serguey saw how sweat had drenched his brother's collar, forming a small wet triangle down his chest.

"He's here to protect the tourists," Claudia said. "Don't worry about him."

"Thank you for everything," Serguey said.

"Don't thank me yet. Pleasure to meet you both."

Serguey offered his hand, but she didn't see it. As she walked away, he saw that she was tall, much taller than he expected from how she appeared sitting down. She moved with a certain languor in her step, unhurried. He and Victor waited a while, the air getting muggier by the minute.

"What did you think?" Victor said. "Can we trust her?"

"Do you trust Kiko?"

"Fair enough."

Serguey observed the police officer, gaunt in his baggy uniform. "We have to talk to Kiko about making the video."

"That's not going to go over well with those State Security assholes."

Serguey spurned the notion. "Want to grab some ice cream?"

They stood and began to walk in the direction from which they had come. Victor flapped his shirt.

"They won't open for another hour," he said, "and the line's already long."

"Do you have somewhere to be?" How many moments together might be left for him and Victor, Serguey wasn't sure. He was looking for pockets of normalcy, moments to unwind in between the grave task of helping their father. "Besides, I know how to skip the line."

"I have more of a craving for a *pan con croqueta*, but all right."

They ambled past the policeman on the corner. He was eyeing a blonde woman and her teenage daughter, who had a British flag printed on the back of her blouse. The officer wasn't staring at the flag, exactly. Victor elbowed Serguey and scratched his own head.

Distancing themselves from the man, he said, "That cop's spoiled. So much foreign ass to ogle at."

Serguey didn't answer his brother's comment. He had been paying attention to the deriding stares of those in line as he and Victor sauntered past them into the shade of the flying saucer-shaped Coppelia building.

Chapter 14

Following the ice cream breakfast, the brothers lingered by the curb outside Coppelia. The day was in a full bout of sultry heat. The tourists had left, but the cop was dutifully on the corner, the flecks of sweat on his shirt an archipelago of stains. Victor coordinated a ride home with a friend who was in the area. A quick phone call was all it took. While drinking his melted ice cream, he had boasted about using his sociable personality to strategically develop friendships all over Havana. This was consistent with his general philosophy: if you're going to need a lot of meat, become pals with the butcher. In a city filled with needs, Victor's little network—as he called it—was an enviable asset.

Serguey wanted to ask about the man on the motorcycle from the night of the play, about what had been in the bag. It'd been pestering him, making him concerned that his brother was dealing more dangerous merchandise: counterfeit money, drugs. But Serguey worried that he might come across as judgmental, as leery or fatherly—to which Victor had never responded well—so he left before Victor's ride showed up, since there was nothing else for them to deliberate. His brother had already told him that he was going to discuss filming the video with Kiko. Serguey replied that he needed a few days to draft a statement. He had to research what other political prisoners and their families had said, and for that, he would have to find a place other than his office to access the internet. All of this, however, was an elaborate excuse. He simply wanted the opportunity to meditate on what he should say, on the consequences of making such a statement. If Felipe had been charged as a mercenary for accepting foreign money, he and Victor could find themselves prosecuted under Law No. 88, the Gag Law that had been used to indict the Black Spring writers and journalists. Claudia's request to remain nameless, Serguey presumed, was directly related to those circumstances. If he recalled correctly, the law targeted those who intended to destabilize the country and subvert the Socialist State. Propagating information that criticized and undermined the government—especially in a video recording—certainly applied under the articles of the Gag Law.

What purpose would it serve if he and Victor got arrested? It would put the onus to save all of them on Anabel, and he couldn't do that to her.

She was on the phone when he arrived at the apartment. He presented a half-pint of vanilla ice cream, the paper cylinder container starting to cave in, and she waved it away. He placed it in the freezer, his eyes fogged by the lack of sunlight in the kitchen. He let the icy ventilation freshen his face, vanquishing the sweat from his pores with a tickling chill, before he returned to the living room and waited for Anabel to finish.

"Yes, we can do it tomorrow," he heard her say.

"Do what?" he mouthed to her.

"Tell him 'thank you,'" she said into the receiver and hung up. She looked up at him. "Father Linares will see us tomorrow."

He joined her on the couch. "Good."

"How was the meeting?"

He shared what Claudia had told them: about Felipe's possible associations, his friends abroad, the video. "I'm going to start writing something today, but ideally I want to do some research."

"We'll ask the priest," she said. "He might have some experience."

"That's not a bad idea. Hopefully we can trust him."

"My parents have known him for a decade."

"That's fair. I've only met Claudia once, and I think I trust her."

"Great." She lowered her gaze and twiddled her fingers. "Did you talk to your brother?"

"Not yet. It wasn't the right moment." He hooked his arm around his wife's neck and drew closer. "I was wrong yesterday, reproaching you and Victor. This whole thing's fucked, but it doesn't mean we need to suffer or be angry every second of the day. There'll be enough stress if things get worse."

She moved her hand along his jawline. It was cool, as refreshing as the freezer air. "You've always needed a few hits before getting off your stubborn streak."

"What's that supposed to mean?"

She ignored him, changing the subject. "So, you brought me ice cream?"

"Vanilla."

"I don't like vanilla."

"Exactly."

She punched his arm. "You don't like to lose, do you?"

"Anabel, if this couch were made of vanilla, there'd be none of it left. You've got like three different vanilla-scented creams in the dresser."

"One of them was a gift from Gimenez."

Serguey snorted. "Like my mother used to say: don't speak of the devil or he'll come knocking."

❦❦❦ ⁂ ❦❦❦

The next day, they went to his in-laws' house. Anabel's parents resided in Mantilla, on the southern edge of Havana. Serguey and Anabel had lived with them at the beginning of their marriage, back when the plan had been to find a place nearby with his father-in-law's help. Antonio had worked in construction for twenty-five years until an accident broke his leg in three places, leaving him with metal pins in his tibia and a permanent limp. He'd helped build the home in which he and his wife lived. The only thing he was more proud of than his house was his family—his daughters. He said this in a way that underscored both his love for them and how important his job had been to him. Like Claudia, he seemed remarkably proud of the way he'd made a living. He had belonged to a micro-brigade, a group of government-funded workers (many of them without prior experience and some with criminal records) who built apartment complexes and modest houses six days a week for low pay and the promise of a decent living space. Antonio put in twelve exemplary years— volunteer work on Sundays, no tardiness or missed workdays, immaculate attendance record at the Communist Party's labor meetings—before he secured his two-bedroom house.

Anabel's mother, Julia, received them at the door. She hugged Serguey and told him how sad she was that Felipe had been imprisoned. People like him, she said, shouldn't be treated that way.

Julia was a retired cafeteria attendant who sold homemade sweets like *panatela borracha* and *boniatillo* to the neighbors when she and Antonio were strapped for cash. Her culinary escapades, as she called them, were more to keep herself busy than to make a substantial income. Serguey had always seen his in-laws as simple, hardworking people. The venerable outcome of the Revolution: men and women who sacrificed to see their children go to school and become more worldly and ambitious. Family was their main priority. When Serguey and

Anabel moved into Gimenez's apartment, Serguey recommended to Antonio that he rent Anabel's room. Alida was already rooming at her ballet school.

"Get a little something under the table," he told his in-law. "After all you've done for the country, there's no harm in it."

Antonio was nearly offended, not because he didn't want to betray the government, but because he wanted to have the space available for his oldest daughter. To rent the room was to disown her, to deprive her of her birthright.

"God wants us to be selfless," Antonio said, "especially with family."

His in-laws had turned to religion after Antonio's accident.

Serguey had joshed to Anabel, "The painkillers didn't take, so he looked to *Jesucristo*."

Anabel had explained that her maternal grandmother had been a devout Catholic all her life, fervently so after Fidel began to exile priests and persecute the Church. Julia's transition had been easy, since her own mother was such a steadfast believer. Antonio's path was more difficult. He sank into depression following the accident, feeling crippled despite being able to walk. He wanted some relief, maybe an explanation, something to make sense of his misfortune. Sunday Mass at the San Cristobal Cathedral in Old Havana became the solution. The dedication he and Julia had previously shown to their daughters and their jobs they now gave to the Church. They were Father Linares's favorite parishioners.

"He doesn't fault us for having been Revolutionaries," Julia had divulged to Anabel. "He thinks our dedication is a sign of moral integrity and servitude, which God rewards."

Serguey displayed a pensive face whenever his in-laws spoke of religion, but he dared not open his mouth. He was afraid a Felipe-ism might escape him. Unsurprisingly, his father had raised him and Victor atheists.

"God's a great character," Felipe liked to say, "but to think he's real is to miss the whole point of the Bible. It's to miss the whole point of storytelling."

Growing up shaded by these views, Serguey naturally adopted them. Though he liked and cherished his in-laws, he saw them as creatures living in a world separate from his, from his own upbringing. Victor had occasionally fostered spiritual beliefs, but Serguey had been privy to his brother's cynicism, his pragmatism and atheistic lifestyle. Antonio and Julia were committed believers, their moral compass and view of life regulated by their religiousness, something Serguey wasn't accustomed to seeing. His in-laws' conversion, however—from secular revolutionaries to open Catholics—he respected and, to some extent, admired. It must take an exorbitant amount of faith, he'd always thought, to renounce the system in exchange for probable discrimination. Maybe this was why Anabel and Alida hadn't become religious themselves: in a communist state, piety got in the way of personal ambition.

Julia took them to the dining room. It shared its space with the kitchen, which consisted of a grease-crusted gas stove and a refrigerator with corroded blotches, like the bottom of an old car. At Julia's insistence, Antonio had promised to give the refrigerator a nice coating of paint. But getting hold of the adequate oil-based paint, he'd grumbled to Serguey, proved impossible, even with the construction connections he had left. Without telling Antonio, Serguey asked around at the Ministry. Unfortunately, the references he got led to dead ends. He was deeply disappointed, not just for being fettered by the shackling mark of a poor country—to have the means and not be able to get the goods—but because he believed the paint would've been a wonderful gift to give his in-laws.

The table had been set nicely with a floral print tablecloth, two trays of *croquetas*, and a set of handcrafted glasses.

"I have a pitcher of *mamey* shake in the fridge," Julia said excitedly. "The Father loves *mamey*."

"Who doesn't?" Serguey said.

Julia smiled. "I thought we could soften him up a little. Always worked on my uncle, and he was the sternest man you ever saw."

His in-laws had gone to surprising lengths, spending money on what was usually invested in important celebrations. Julia was wearing a dress that, in Serguey's mind, matched the tablecloth too well, but her pearl-imitation earrings were elegant, and the perfume she'd sprayed on, which he'd smelled when he kissed her hello, had a light but memorable touch. Antonio emerged from their bedroom donning a plaid suit jacket. As always, he wore the stoic, subjugated countenance of a man whose days had been painfully similar to each other. He struggled to slide his left arm into the jacket's sleeve, untucking his shirt in the process.

Anabel came to his rescue.

"What women put you through," he said, trying to shake Serguey's hand while his daughter stood between them, fussing with his attire. "I'm sorry about Felipe," he managed to add.

"We're not doing this for ourselves," Julia reminded her husband. "Do you still have to complain about your clothes?"

Before Antonio could respond, there was a knock at the door.

"He's early," Julia said. "Everyone, stay in the dining room. No need to crowd him all at once. We don't want to seem desperate."

"Mom's right," Anabel said.

"And leave that chair for him. I want him facing out to the yard, not the kitchen."

With the panes agape, the taped-over crack on the coarse glass of the dining room window wasn't as noticeable. Through the flat steel bars, which overlapped like an ambulance cross, large portions of green and blue could be seen hanging behind a power line. The black cable traversed the air above the fence, dividing Julia's home from a dusty alley. One's eyes could still reach the horizon, reducing the odds of the priest feeling cornered, as could happen if he were staring at the boxed-in shadows in the kitchen.

Serguey was expecting a tall, imposing figure. That's how he imagined all priests to be. Or perhaps it'd been the way Anabel had spoken about him, the reverence Antonio and Julia showed toward the man. Father Linares was, in fact, a short, chubby creature. His head was round at the sides and concave at the top, verging on complete baldness. His cheek was ruddy, which reminded Serguey of a set of Matryoshka dolls he'd seen as a child—a gift from Raidel to Irene. His skin was pale, his silver-rimmed glasses expensive. He seemed to be from another country. If there was a universal dictum in Cuba, it was that no one escaped the sun. It showed on your scalp, your toasted forearms, the crackling pores under your eyes. The Father might as well have been fresh off a plane from Europe or Canada.

Linares coddled Julia's hands as if they were delicate things, which Serguey also pictured all priests doing. He murmured some unintelligible words and proceeded to wave at everyone in the dining room. Serguey started to raise his hand, but he hesitated and brought it back down.

"Look at him," the Father said in a low, frothy voice. "Poor thing's rigid as a pole." He walked toward Serguey and patted him on the shoulder. "I'm not always this ceremonial. I figured you'd be nervous and wanted to break the ice."

Serguey was confused. "Thank you."

Julia said, "Why don't you sit down, and I'll serve the food and drinks?"

Everyone indulged her. Anabel showed Linares to his seat. The Father's manners, Serguey immediately noticed, felt organic and spontaneous. He drank the *batido de mamey* with gusto, spilling some on the tablecloth. He ate the *croquetas* using his fingers, as one is meant to eat them, joyfully beholding the remaining piece in his hand after every bite. Only when Julia offered him a wet hand towel did he clean himself. He spoke briefly with Antonio about needing his advice for the restoration of the ceiling above the sacristy. He repeatedly complimented Julia's culinary skills. He paid most of his attention to Anabel, asking about life in El Vedado, about her future plans, about Alida's burgeoning passion for theater.

Here, Father Linares found the perfect segue: he proclaimed his admiration for Felipe's work. He'd seen Felipe's production of *A Death in the Kremlin*, a satirical mystery set in communist Russia. He'd been in awe of the actors' energy and amazed by the sharpness of the language.

Serguey said, "My father likes his work to connect with a contemporary audience." Whether this was true, he didn't know. He was just trying to ingratiate himself with Linares.

"It shows," the Father said. "How was he when you saw him?"

"At the prison?"

The priest nodded.

"A bit roughed up but not too bad."

"I don't mean to upset anyone, but I need to ask these questions."

Julia began to collect the trays and smalls plates she had given them. "I'll clear the table. We can mosey out to the living room and leave you and Serguey alone."

"Oh, that's not necessary," the Father said.

"It really isn't," Serguey said. "We're all in confidence."

"Nonsense." Julia carted the plates and tray to the kitchen counter. "You'll feel more comfortable in private. Come on, Antonio."

Antonio flung his hands up in surrender. "She's the boss."

"I'd like for Anabel to stay," Serguey said.

She smiled in appreciation.

Father Linares waited for the family to settle in their respective places. He was a tactful man, experienced with people, unfazed by the nuances of a tense situation. Serguey stared at him. The ease and pleasantry he had demonstrated earlier had vanished, replaced by an expression of concern.

"Do you know why they went after Felipe?" Linares asked, his tone deeper, more heartfelt.

"I'm still trying to figure it out, if you can believe it."

"I can. These people play everything close to the vest."

Serguey sensed that the Father had done this before, or, at the very least, he had knowledge as to how the process worked. "I don't mean to be imprudent or insinuate anything," Serguey said.

Linares interrupted him: "Ask away."

Serguey parted his lips and sucked in air.

"I'd be curious and cautious too," Linares said. "Ask away."

"Have you done this before?" Serguey found it difficult to hold the man's serene gaze. "Helping a political prisoner, I mean," he nearly stuttered.

"Not personally, but I've assisted bishops who have. And it's not because I haven't wanted to, but this is the first time someone has come directly to me."

Serguey was emboldened by Linares's sincerity. "Why do it? Won't you get in trouble?"

The Father placed his arms Sphinx-like on the table, his puffed chest protruding over his belly. "The Church in Cuba has been in trouble since the Revolution. Forgive my haughtiness, but if anyone has endured the wrath and derision of communism, it's us. I'm sure they don't teach this at school, but the majority of priests, even protestant ministers, were forced to leave the country after the Revolution's triumph." Those who didn't, Linares went on to say, were persecuted, some accused of collaborating with the CIA and storing arms for a counter-revolutionary attack. The atheist ideas incorporated into the Cuban constitution established a secular population. Citizens who believed were afraid to baptize their children or congregate in protestant celebrations, so they hid their saints, as the saying went, in grandma's room. "From what Julia tells me," here he looked at Anabel for a moment, "your grandmother was one of the few who refused to do that and flaunted her beliefs. She must have been a brave woman."

Anabel smiled, humbly shaking her head in appreciation.

"I'm aware of what you're saying," Serguey said politely. The state's persecution of the Church wasn't news to him, but it seemed right to let the Father finish his speech. In a way, it felt like relief for them to say these things aloud, to find harbor in speaking without fear. It also meant Linares trusted him.

"It wasn't until the end of the Cold War," the priest continued, "that they removed the constitutional guidelines against the Church—which I'm sure you know well, as a lawyer. Finally," Linares made the word vibrate, looking sardonically at the ceiling, palms up as if in the presence of a Supreme Being, "we were allowed to join the Communist Party." He brought his hands and gaze back down. "But by then, our beliefs were, you know, tagged as retrograde and superstitious. Or they defamed us as scheming with the enemy. I must admit, things have changed over the past few years. Religious practices are easier to notice throughout the country. Any priest will tell you that." Linares stretched his lips into a perceptive smile. "I can visit my parishioners, as you can see."

Serguey monitored his tone to sound respectful. "I get all you've said." He made an effort to look directly into Linares's eyes. "But again, why help political prisoners? Why help my father?"

Linares seemed to appreciate Serguey's insistence. "Because we have the resources. Because we've already shouldered this, let's call it *mission*, when few others did. Because it's inhumane how these prisoners are treated. Because we're certain God would want us to help." The Father looked over his shoulder to where the kitchen transitioned into the living room, then leaned over the table and waited for Serguey and Anabel to do the same. "But most of all," his voice was little more than a breath, "because we've figured out that the boys in charge are willing to play ball."

When Serguey told Linares that he was satisfied with his reasons, the man proposed that they use Felipe's status to their advantage. The government would never admit his arrest as politically or ideologically motivated. They would paint Felipe's involvements, whatever they were, as a more tangible threat. "We need to put them on the defensive without being abrasive."

Serguey grew more confident that he could count on the Father. His use of "we" was telling. It seemed that he did, in fact, have resources at his disposal, maybe even from other members of the Church. Nonetheless, Serguey reminded himself, as he got ready to respond, that whatever Linares inquired, he shouldn't give up Claudia's name. "I can't confirm it, but I think they've pegged him a mercenary."

The Father's eyes coasted to the window, his voice reaching out to the blue strip of sky. "Mercenary, counterrevolutionary, terrorist, a threat to the safety and fabric of our socialist society, I've heard it all. I've seen them beat innocent women on the street. But I digress . . ."

Linares was referring to *Las Damas de Blanco*, the wives or female relatives of political prisoners. Every Sunday they marched silently toward mass, wearing white as a symbol of peace. They were often verbally and physically attacked by authorities dressed as civilians, inciting others to do the same.

"So how can *we* help Felipe?" Anabel asked.

"Our job," Linares carried on, "is not to fight the government or State Security head-on. We're not here to show them they're wrong. We don't have the authority. But we can do what we've done in the past."

"What's that?" Serguey said.

"Make an official plea."

"Ask for benevolence, for clemency," Anabel said.

"Exactly. Allow them to appear merciful." Linares prefaced his next declaration with a shrug. Rather than dismissive, it felt questioning, optimistic. "I hear the new boy in charge wants to make his own dent."

The "boy," Serguey thought, was Raul, the Party lapdog turned leader. For years it was presumed that his alcoholism and excessive fondness for young soldiers would keep him from permanently succeeding his older, more menacing and intelligent brother.

"Now," the priest said preemptively, his palms hovering over the tablecloth, "keep in mind there are no promises here. I'll discuss the situation with the Cardinal. If he deems it prudent, he'll be in touch with members of the Church in Spain and a few other organizations. With their support, he'll have the government's ear. From a political standpoint, and I'm just being bluntly honest here, Felipe is the ideal person to help, so you have that going for you. He's a public figure, a commemorated artist. In many people's eyes that makes him a representative of individual freedom. The Cardinal has been working tirelessly for the release of the Black Spring detainees, but few of them have the reputation Felipe has." Linares's hale expression transmuted into a candid confession: "Maybe your dad's the key to this whole thing."

"I hope he is," Serguey said, offering a confession of his own. He hadn't expected the Church to involve itself out of the goodness of its heart. His principal desire was to liberate his father from the government's volatile grip, whatever the method. If the Church was after a political victory or good press, so be it. Let Felipe be their banner.

The Father smiled reflectively. "In the meantime, I can write letters on Felipe's behalf, make public statements if necessary, all within the confines of what's allowed to us. If I can add a pebble to the scale in your favor, it might make a difference."

Serguey was brimming with renewed optimism. "We're immensely grateful."

Linares said, "You should be aware that if they release your dad, it'll probably be to another country. They won't allow him to remain here and return to work."

Serguey was suddenly silenced. He felt stunned and stupid, as if he should have known this. Exiling the opposition was common practice for the Cuban government, though it was always painted as a matter of choice for the accused.

Felipe had travelled, but Serguey couldn't remember an instance in which he had expressed interest in defecting.

"This is what they do," Linares said, perhaps intuiting Serguey's distress. "The best way to avoid bad press and not have to worry about their prisoners is to force them abroad. Unless . . ."

"Unless he agrees to work for them," Serguey said. Felipe wouldn't do it, he was sure.

"Something along those lines."

"Anywhere but prison," Anabel said.

"His career's pretty much over," Serguey said somberly.

The Father's eyes were grief-stricken. He hushed his voice to ensure that Antonio and Julia couldn't hear: "Great independent minds seldom survive in Cuba. We've lost so many to emigration and exile, it breaks one's heart."

Linares bid his goodbye as regally as he had his arrival. He thanked Julia emphatically for her food and drink. He called her generous and solicitous. He told Antonio to stop by the church on Friday.

"Father Brito will receive you," he said. "He's our renovation extraordinaire. He'll explain more about the ceiling."

To Anabel, he again dedicated the most time. He hugged her, blessed her, and assured her that she had the Lord's protection. He invited her to mass and teased that they had plenty of saints to choose from. He then shook Serguey's hand and blessed him too.

"I encourage you to have faith," the priest said. "Even if you don't believe in God."

Serguey guessed that his in-laws had blabbered about his atheism to Linares. "Is it that obvious?"

"God is an amorphous thing." Linares stacked his hands piously and delimited his voice so that it evoked a dignified, ritualistic timbre. "He takes many faces and shapes. All good men believe in something. It's just easier for people to give that something a name. In your case, you have no need to, and this takes the burden of faith away from your expression. It gives you a certain air of freedom."

Serguey wondered if he'd just been paid a snide compliment.

Linares seemed to recognize his confusion. "I don't judge. I listen, I accept, and I advise. My advice to you is to keep fighting for your dad. God will be pleased."

Serguey nodded.

"Have a safe drive," Julia said

"Sweltering sun out there." The Father put on his glasses. "But I have a sickly relative in El Cotorro."

Julia grimaced. "I'm sorry to hear."

"Nothing serious, but family's always first." He waited for Julia's polite smile, then sauntered toward his car.

She waited in turn until he drove off before she shut her door.

Serguey's in-laws failed to hide their interest in what the priest had said. They crowded him, Julia softly prodding him to take a seat. An air of anticipation was plastered on their faces.

He told them Linares had offered his full support, along with the Church's.

Antonio was discernibly content. "I better do a good job with that ceiling."

Julia clamped her hands together, less ceremoniously than Linares, and whispered a swift prayer. She invited Serguey and Anabel to stay for dinner. Serguey didn't wait for Anabel to give some sort of sign as to her inclination. He stood up and said yes.

"We'll walk around Mantilla tonight," Julia said, clutching her daughter's elbow. "Antonio definitely needs it."

Antonio removed his jacket and tossed it onto the backrest of a chair. "What are you saying, that I lie around here all day?" He smirked, reinforcing what everyone already knew: he was teasing.

Julia rolled her eyes. "I just don't want the bad leg to go stiff."

Antonio rotated his muscular shoulders, embracing his regained freedom of movement. "She really hits you where it hurts."

⁂

They began their stroll at 8:00 p.m., their stomachs stuffed with Julia's chickpea and pumpkin dish. A neighbor across the street, who was sitting on a rocking chair next to her husband on their porch, yelled that she could smell the chickpeas and was jealous. Julia told her she'd bring leftovers. The lady, whose name was Leonor, graciously declined.

"She has terrible rheumatoid arthritis," Julia intimated to Serguey as they walked on. "Her husband does most of the cooking, and let's just say practice hasn't made perfect."

"What about her daughter?" Anabel asked. "Yadira moved out?"

Julia was excited to share her fresh piece of gossip. "I thought I'd told you. She's been in Venezuela for three months. One of those medical missions to help Chavez."

They ambled down the street, Julia and Anabel chitchatting about other neighbors and distant relatives. Antonio droned on about Industriales' chances in the playoffs, about their pitching not being up to par. It allowed Serguey to decompress, to refocus. The sky in Mantilla was proud of its stars, displaying them with vitality. The wind cruised discontinuously, like greetings from friendly passersby. The smell of *sofrito* and *congrí* exuded from someone's open door. Serguey looked inside at what was a very small living room. A group of people, including two young men on the floor, had plates and clear glasses in their hands.

Julia caught him snooping.

"They used to sell food in those small birthday paper boxes," she said. "Rice, beans, fried plantains, *masitas de puerco*. When they got some corn, their tamales were to die for, but they only included a slice in each box. Sometimes when Antonio had a rough week at work, we'd treat ourselves."

"They don't sell anymore?" Serguey said.

Anabel was the one to respond: "The house was raided by the police once. The CDR people gave them up. The two young men you saw on the floor spent a month in jail for stealing ingredients from a warehouse."

"Now they just cook for themselves," Julia said.

Serguey thought for a moment about his next-door neighbor, Carmina, how she might be culpable of a niggling act of betrayal toward a fellow neighbor. People like her spoke with envy and suspicion fastened to their tongues. She was probably capable of going after *Las Damas de Blanco* if handed a baton.

Not wanting to spoil his night with theories, Serguey pushed these thoughts from his mind.

"I miss those little boxes," Antonio said.

Julia backslapped his arm. "Maybe you should get Leonor's husband to cook for you."

In the space of four blocks, the houses began to look increasingly more run down. Chain-link fences rose, as if germinating from the original concrete front yard walls, turning the homes into cages. The sidewalk gave way to overgrown weeds and littered soil, so they moved onto the street, skirting the curb. Not far ahead, a feisty mutt was sinking its teeth into a dusty bone, the crunch audible as they passed him. Serguey lagged behind the women, next to a limping Antonio. This was a true family, friendly and pleased to be together, in the most humdrum of walks. He had no complaints, except that for an instant, he wanted his brother to be with him. For a decade, they'd ducked each other's presence; they'd made a habit out of it. Now he missed Victor. He missed his family. He missed something that he wasn't sure had ever existed between them: the unalloyed enjoyment—the inherent need—of each other's company. He fondled the cell phone in his pocket, but he thought it rude to call Victor while surrounded by the others. He waited until his in-laws decided to go back to the house, where, in Anabel's old bedroom, he could have a minute to himself.

Victor had wasted no time in speaking with Kiko. That's the first thing he said, still looking to prove his worth to his older brother. Serguey realized a heart-to-heart conversation was not on the books, so he let him carry on. He had arranged for the two of them to stop by Kiko's apartment on Wednesday morning. The computer would be set up for the video. Serguey and Victor were to rehearse their statement, making it sound as natural as possible.

Serguey told him that it was a good idea, and that he would be spending Tuesday night at Felipe's house so they could prepare.

"Make it Tuesday afternoon," Victor said. "I need a lot of practice. I'm not good at reading stuff out loud."

"I'll prep you as if you were my witness at a trial." He hadn't escaped the desire to impress his brother.

Victor's response might have, at another time, piqued Serguey. Now it vitalized him: "Then we better win the fucking case."

CHAPTER 15

On Tuesday he headed to his father's as planned. He could rely on Anabel if there was news from Linares—she would call him at a moment's notice. He had meditated on whether they should go through with the video. It made him nervous, taking such a publicly flouting stance. Morally and practically speaking, it was the right approach, but if Linares's involvement turned out to be effective, rendering the video unnecessary, would the risk be worth it? He concluded that they needed to act on every front. The combination of the Church, Claudia's posts, and the video would have more impact than one thing alone.

Walking toward the house, Serguey saw his brother (from a distance, he seemed shirtless) standing on the front steps and hollering at a group of people. Serguey hurried, trying to make out individual words amidst the shouting as he got closer. On Victor's side, below the steps, another man was facing the crowd, wagging an object at them. Serguey still couldn't follow the dispute as he joined them, but it was now clear that Victor—clad solely in shorts, arms crossed, his muscular pectorals reddened from anger—and Norton's son, Yunior, were calling the group rats and cowards. Yunior was shaking a rolled-up newspaper as if trying to slice the air, standing sideways against the crowd like a fencer daring his opponent.

"You sons of bitches know exactly what you're doing," he was saying. "Keep pushing it and you're going to regret it."

"Look at this shit," Victor said to Serguey, tilting his head back at the porch.

In bright red, the word MERCENARIES had been written on the wall. Serguey turned to the group, recognizing the couple in charge of the CDR among them. The woman, whose body—awkwardly short, wide at the torso, legs so spindly she constantly seemed on the verge of toppling over—made Serguey think of Gregor Samsa. Her husband, his shirt tucked into a beltless pair of frayed pants, had a spiteful gleam in his eyes. Staring at them, an improbable question escaped Serguey's lips, "Where the fuck did they get the paint?"

"And the eggs," Victor said.

Serguey climbed the steps and looked into the porch. The dried up yolks had stained the lower parts of the wall in streaks. The shattered white shells lined the floor like tiny cracked skulls. It was as Felipe had said, what had taken place during the Mariel boatlift. The tactics hadn't changed. Perhaps it was just the sight of the smashed eggs, but Serguey thought he could smell their foulness.

"When did it happen?" he asked Victor, staring again at the crowd.

"Fuck if I know," Victor answered. "I went to see Kiko and came back to this. Yunior was waiting for me. He was passing by and saw it."

Yunior was smacking his newspaper on a tall man's shoulder. "You ain't even from around this neighborhood, *acere*. It's obvious you're a mole."

The man was wearing a blue *guayabera* with a pair of sneakers. His thick-veined forearms were muscular, his stance stoic like a soldier's.

Serguey vacillated, but he felt he had to ask his brother: "Have you done anything stupid?"

Victor's jaw protruded tautly like a growling dog's. "No, but I have to tell you, I'm really close." He shook his head, his eyes welling up with tears. "How I wish they would've tried while I was inside." He pointed at the group. "But I'm sure it was one of these motherfuckers."

The tall man had seized Yunior's paper and was yanking it. "Watch it, negro," he said. "Your granddaddy knew how to behave."

Yunior pulled the newspaper free and put it to the man's stomach like a knife. "I was his least favorite grandson, so that should give you some idea."

"Why don't you all get out of here," Serguey said.

The CDR woman, taking two quick, unstable steps forward, said, "That's what your family should do. No one wants you in this block!"

The small mob reacted with "That's right!" and, Serguey thought, quite unimaginatively, "Mercenaries!"

He leaned toward his brother. "How many of these people do you recognize?"

Victor aimed with his index and middle fingers. "Just the CDR assholes. I found a guy this morning on the side of the house. He had a clipboard, said they'd sent him to check something on the gas meter."

"Did you let him in?"

"Of course not. I chased that son of a bitch away."

In addition to the CDR couple, there were three men and two women in the crowd. It couldn't be a coincidence that, not being from this part of Santos Suarez, these people had magically gathered. This was a political performance, the strangers likely State Security pawns. Felipe was no longer their only target.

A strong chill rippled down Serguey's limbs.

Yunior turned to the brothers. "It's like a circus with these people." He approached Victor, looking up at him from the sidewalk. "How do you want to handle it? I haven't been in a good scrap in a while, and I'm itching for one, if you get what I'm saying."

Serguey placed his hand on Victor's chest. It was warm, throbbing. "That's what they want." He tapped his other hand against his own temple. "Use your head."

Victor released three short, loud breaths. "*Dale*, Yunior," he said. "Go home. We'll talk later."

"All right," Yunior said, no judgment in his voice. "I'll bring a bucket and sponge tonight, help you clean this fucking mess."

They bumped fists. Yunior directed the newspaper at the mob again, then traced his neck with it to mime beheading, and strode off.

The brothers began to walk up the stairs and past the gate onto the porch. Someone in the dispersing crowd shouted, "Felipe is a worm!" Serguey paced back to the gate, flipped his phone open, and moved it slowly over the group.

"Smile for the camera," he said.

The man Yunior had confronted said "hey" to the others, nodding for them to leave.

"Your phone has a camera?" Victor whispered.

Serguey shook his head. "But they don't know that."

They gazed at the door. Two splattered yolks had defaced the sections where the original paint was still holding.

"Did you count the eggs?" Serguey said. "Was it a full carton?"

Victor grabbed the knob despondently. "I don't think so. These idiots probably kept some for themselves."

Once inside, Serguey shut the door. "Thanks for sending your friend home."

"I would've fought them," Victor said, "but Yunior's newspaper wasn't hollow. He would've cut somebody's throat."

❦❧❦

Serguey sat in the living room, waiting for his brother to dress. According to Victor, Toya was expecting them. He didn't want the paint and egging incident to interfere. His line the previous night about needing extra time to prepare for the video had been a lie. Serguey felt disappointed at his brother's lack of faith that he could stick to his word, relying on a lie to force his hand. They would have time that night to prepare for the video, Victor had said. Serguey wasn't in the mood for a spiritual consultation, for the performance he'd have to put on, but there was no harm in indulging his brother, especially after the calm way in which he'd handled the mob situation. And the deeper Serguey got into helping his father, it seemed to him, the less willing he would be to meet with anyone who wasn't part of the ordeal. This was as a good a moment as any to see Toya.

Sitting on the sofa, he caught a glimpse of a cinder block by the front door, heaped sideways against the wall. He hadn't seen it during the house cleaning. It felt incongruous, not matching Felipe's taste.

Victor reappeared, fully clothed.

"What's up with the block?" Serguey asked.

"I use it to work out. I don't have a lot of space in my apartment, so I do it here."

"So this is your personal gym now?"

Victor sighed heavily. "Serguey, why do you give a shit?"

"You're right," he said, getting up.

"I'm sorry." Victor raked his scalp with his fingers. "I'm just stressed with all that's going on. I guess I have these people on my back now. I can't make a move. If this thing with Dad doesn't get solved quickly, I have to plan for the long haul."

Serguey had heard this phrase before: plan for the long haul. It derived from their maternal grandfather, Larido, whose black market predilections were now being replicated by Victor. Felipe had mentioned, when talking about Irene's family, how people shouldn't be fooled by Larido's reticent personality.

"He was up to a million different trades on any given day," Felipe had said one morning, not moving his eyes from whatever piece of writing had captivated his concentration, which meant he was being sincere. He put a lot more attention and effort into his lies.

Serguey had seen sacks piled up high in the countryside shack where they played as children, though he only witnessed Larido discussing business on one occasion. Two men had stood with his grandfather by the foot of his bed while Serguey played in the living room with a Rubik's Cube he'd brought from the city. One of the men's wet, uncombed hair seemed ironed onto his scalp. He wore muddy boots, a machete tucked into his belt. The other, better outfitted and with bloated eyes that reminded Serguey of a frog, was saying, "They've got me by the balls, Larido." The phrase had been permanently imprinted in Serguey's psyche. His grandfather didn't allow cursing in his home. Larido, however, said nothing about it to the amphibian-eyed man. He slipped an envelope inside the guy's shirt as if it were a mailbox, stabbed at it with his fingers, and said, "If you walk out of here with that, you're in."

As this was going on, Estela swung in her rocking chair by the front door, flapping her handheld fan below her neck and swatting at flies. She didn't reply when the men said their goodbyes and walked out of her front yard. In retrospect, the independence Serguey and Victor had been given to rove the countryside made sense if he put it in a certain context: their grandparents lived off illegal transactions and didn't want the children embroiled in them. Better to explore the fields and hunt than interact with their grandfather's business partners. Serguey made a mental note to ask Felipe about the intricacies of Larido's trades, what they entailed, and to also learn more about Joaquin, their paternal grandfather—about his defiance and prison sentence. The large bedroom photograph notwithstanding, Felipe only spoke of Joaquin as one would of a deity: the details scarce, the tributes abound. It was up to Serguey to dredge into the trenches of his past, something he'd avoided for what now seemed too long. A person should know their family's history, the untold secrets wrapped in one's genes. Larido's life could be a precedent for Victor's behavior. His black market involvements could confer reason to Victor's street-dealing tendencies, despite growing up in a house brimming with intellectuals and artists. Joaquin's journey might've been the genesis of another pattern, continued by Felipe, presently bequeathed on Serguey. Perhaps it was all in the blood, he and Victor prone to follow different strands.

Or maybe it was all in Victor, and Serguey took more after the women.

He stared at his brother, trying to capture Felipe's earnest tone when he'd spoken of their grandfather, and asked, "Do you need money?"

Victor found it hard to look at Serguey. "No, no. I'm doing fine. It's just I had some good deals in the works. The timing sucks."

Serguey placed his hands on his hips. The possibility that his brother would back out of fighting for Felipe was making his shoulders wilt. "Do you want to stay out of it?"

"No fucking way. I'm venting, that's all."

The certitude in Victor's voice reassured him. "So, are you going to take me to your spiritual advisor or what?"

Victor showed traces of a smile. "After today, she might be yours too."

"Let's get this over with," Serguey said, yanking his brother's neck.

Toya lived five blocks away, in the opposite direction of Kiko's apartment. Her home was buried deep inside a cluster of three ramshackle buildings. The one on the right had lost a large portion of its sidewall. It was now abutted by a huge blue canvas that, anchored by a row of leftover bricks, swelled and smacked in the wind. At the end of a long hall in the middle building, eggshells and chicken feathers were scattered on the ground. A pungent scent of tobacco and boiling meat emanated from an open window. Serguey peeked through the iron bars, but it was too dark to see. A sign hung from a nail on the door: bring an open heart.

"Do you think it's meant literally?" he said.

Victor wasn't amused. "The eggshells and feathers are for show. She charges some people for consultations. But the sign, she means."

Victor knocked, a light rap this time, and Toya opened.

"The turns life takes," she said and kissed Serguey. Then she directed something at Victor in Yoruba, planting her lips on his forehead. New lines had formed on her face, and she had lost a few pounds, but she still looked like the Toya Serguey remembered from his childhood and teenage years. She constantly rolled her blouse's long sleeves, as he'd often seen her do, though they kept sliding back to her wrists.

"Godmother," Victor said, "I hope you don't mind the company."

"She didn't know I was coming?" Serguey said.

"Of course I did," Toya said. "Your brother likes to be dramatic."

Serguey followed them into a small room immediately to their left. It felt like the miniature version of a regular-sized home: the ceiling too low, the walls too narrow, like a *barbacoa*—a kind of cramped attic built inside Havana homes to maximize living space.

"Let's do the reading first," Toya said. "We can banter over lunch." She looked at Victor. "I made your favorite."

"*Tortilla de papas?*"

"With a bit of cream cheese. Don't ask me where I got it."

Victor nudged his brother's arm. "These *santeros* got it all figured out."

Toya laughed a sad, ironic laugh. "We're the bourgeoisies of the Revolution."

"Looks like it," Serguey said. He was instantly concerned that his humor would be seen as tasteless.

Toya switched out her laughter for a haughty expression, making Serguey's concern all the more real. The contours of her eyeballs, he saw, mushed into a thin layer of gelatin as she compressed the skin around them. He'd never considered that the inside of an eye was susceptible to such visible aging.

"What do you think of *Santeria*?" she asked.

He would offend her if he joked again, he was sure. But insincerity would insult her equally. He caressed his mouth and chin with a downward motion that ended at his chest, concealing his Adam's apple as he swallowed.

She noticed his reluctance to respond. "Do you think us mentally ill, like the government used to?"

"Of course not."

Through a play his father had recommended, titled *The Light of Darker Days*, Serguey had learned that after the Revolution, Santeros were portrayed as people who spoke in strange languages and conducted violent rituals. Individuals like Toya were ostracized, turning *Santería* into an underground religion. In an awfully ironic decision, the supposed purge of racial discrimination in the island led to the prohibition of Afro-Cuban institutions. The government argued that it would be too divisive to officially recognize organizations dedicated to a religious culture that was mostly black. It was a blatant form of racism, but since more prominent faith-based traditions had fallen victim to the new regime's extreme brand of secularism, the plight of the *Santeros* went largely ignored. However, *the religion* persevered. It conserved its language and idiosyncrasies, and after the fall of the Soviet Union, when everything and everyone in Cuba became for sale, it wasn't rare to see flamboyantly clothed Afro-Cuban dancers and singers at a tourist-frequented plaza. Homes were adorned with altars of all sizes; ceremonies were carried out publicly; *Santería* believers attended Catholic mass on important dates, a barefaced embodiment of syncretism.

Santeros weren't the bourgeoisies of the Revolution. They were one of its staunchest survivors.

Toya silently accepted his "Of course not" just as he had accepted Victor's "No fucking way" earlier at the house. Her altar was straight ahead. Serguey recognized the more popular saints: *Oshun, Yemaya, Chango, Obatala, Babalu Aye*. He had seen similar renditions before. There was a painting on the wall—a reproduction of Wifredo Lam's *The Jungle*—and a framed image of Christ bleeding on the cross, the crown of thorns haloed around his wilting head.

Victor crouched on one knee before the altar, rang a bell that was on the floor, said, "I've arrived," and crossed himself.

Toya gestured at Serguey to do the same.

"Take off your shoes too," she said.

Victor was already in the process.

They sat on a mat facing each other. Toya grabbed half a coconut shell filled with *caracoles*. She positioned herself at equal distance from the brothers, her knee bones cracking as she lowered herself and looked at Serguey.

"I'm glad you're here for this. It was long overdue."

She threw the cowrie shells twelve times, each instance uttering a word whose meaning escaped Serguey: "Okana, Eyi Oko, Ogunda . . ."

He couldn't figure out whether it was really part of the ritual. Was she attempting to seduce him into believing? Toya said nothing specific, nothing he could make sense of until the end, when she gathered the shells and placed them back in the hollow coconut.

"How do you want this? The harsh truth or the spiritual version of it?"

"Shoot straight," Serguey said, skeptical.

She delayed her answer until he lifted his eyebrows. "Your path," she finally said, "has just taken a detour. Like a river forced to swerve in the direction of rougher waters. And your waters are about to get exceptionally rough. Much of what you have, you're going to lose. There's a debt to be paid, and it's your time to pay it. You're going to be tumbling near some big rocks. Whether you avoid them or smash against them will be up to you. And that's your ticket. You will have choices. You just won't know which one's right until long after you've made them."

Serguey's elbows were jammed into his thighs, his body tilted forward. He rocked slowly as a form of acknowledgement. Thanks for the abstractions and metaphors, he was really thinking.

Almost instantly, Toya said, "I know you don't believe any of this. Might as well be gibberish to you. But you're going to need protection, and you can get it through your brother. The saints are with him because he's earned it."

Where had they been, Serguey pondered, on every instance Victor was arrested?

"Now," Toya continued, "the last thing I'll share is that one of you will have to make a sacrifice. I can't tell who. The shells won't show me that. But it'll be a big one." She paused, staring at Serguey. In this light—private and unforgiving—she looked older. "Why did you come here today?"

This was the chance to speak his mind, and he would take it. "Can I be honest?"

"The saints will respect you for it."

"I just wanted to indulge my brother."

She leaned forward, her spine straight and inflexible like a tower crane. She took Serguey's hands just as Father Linares had taken Julia's. Her fingers were long, like twigs, and her skin felt chapped, like dry clay. "Your spirit and Victor's are like magnets that repel each other."

She stopped again to look at him, a knowing smile sprouting from her lips. The magnet metaphor was his. He couldn't recall if he'd used it in Victor's presence.

"How can we fight it?" Victor asked sincerely.

Toya's eyes stayed on Serguey. "Embrace the discrepancies. See the arguments as part of who you are. The saints fight all the time."

An unlicensed therapist, Serguey mused. A vague consultation wouldn't be enough to persuade him. "Do they ever figure out who's right?"

"It's not about who's right," she said. "Wisdom and intelligence are two different things. The simplest man could be the wisest."

"Can you do something for Serguey?" Victor asked. "Something to give him more protection?"

"Won't do any good. He's not open to it." Toya leaned to one side and began to laboriously stand. Serguey tightened his grasp on her hands and bounced up. He assisted her, making sure she didn't lose her balance as she got to her feet.

"He's kindhearted, though," she said. "Not as much as you, Victor, but kind-hearted nonetheless."

Serguey's face flushed, incapable of evading his embarrassment. He retracted his hands.

Toya turned to Victor, pushing up her sleeves. "He dislikes being compared to you. Really gets under his skin if he's not being celebrated as the better brother. Felipe didn't do him any favors by being vocal about his superior intellect."

It was obvious to Serguey that his brother had spilled his guts to Toya. He wondered if the meeting had been a set-up, a trick to berate him, to teach him a lesson. "Did you tell my father that when he visited you?"

"I told your father the truth, same as you. And he took it the same way." She tipped her head toward the wall behind the altar. "He did give me Lam's painting. That was nice."

"I didn't bring anything," Serguey said self-consciously. "Victor didn't tell me—"

"Not necessary."

Victor passed the cowrie shells to Toya. She put them away in the cabinet from which she'd retrieved them, a fusty, severely nicked piece of furniture whose contours were no longer sharp. "Offerings are nice for the saints if you believe." She grunted as she pushed the shells to the back of the shelf. "Otherwise you're mocking them. It's better this way. No gifts."

"Then Dad's gift must have offended them. I don't buy that he believes any of this."

"Serguey . . ." Victor said.

"At least he didn't give me a copy of *El Monte*." Toya simpered at her own joke. She approached the painting. "I love Lam's work. I saw this one as a child at my uncle's house. Your father had nothing but good intentions with it. He's always been full of good intentions. They just pour out better on the stage or with friends than with his family."

I won't argue that, Serguey thought.

Toya walked deliberately to the entrance of the small room, halting on the threshold and facing the brothers. Despite her restrained movements, she was restive. She'd arrived at an age when the body found itself at a tipping point, a battle between rapid decrepitude and mulish resistance. Toya was doing everything in her power to be resilient.

"You know, a few of Felipe's friends used to visit me for consultations."

Serguey couldn't discern if she was making small talk or implying something worthwhile. "Was Mario one of them?"

"No. Victor asked me about him too. We've been doing work on Mario, but he's hard to track down. The people who came were other acquaintances of your father. The majority showed up only once. I think they were embarrassed, because they always came really late. Your father kept sending them my way. Maybe it was for the experience, or research for their stories."

"She's exaggerating," Victor said. "It was only two or three guys."

"Serguey, I'm going to sound very intrusive." She nodded to herself. "I guess I've been sounding like that since you came in."

He held her gaze. "It's no problem."

"Don't begrudge Victor for today. I was the one who asked him to bring you. I thought it'd be good for him."

He stepped toward the window and glimpsed at the wall on the adjoining building. "I won't." The wall was stained with dark-green mold at a height which made it seem as though the area had outlasted a massive flood. As he now considered it, the interior of Toya's compact home had a humid dreariness, an aroma and aspect that he correlated with smeared wet charcoal. "I appreciate everything you told me. My brother believes in you, and I respect that."

"All right." She rubbed her palms together. "Let's have some food."

"Are you boiling some kind of meat?" Victor asked.

"That's for later." She massaged her stomach, grinning. "For the saints."

Serguey declined the potato and cream cheese omelet, blaming a hearty lunch Anabel had made. He was repelled by the intense odor of the simmering meat and the grungy appearance of Toya's skillet. A voice at the rear of his head murmured that he was wrong for feeling this way, that maybe it wasn't these things at all, but rather the conversation that had transpired. Victor took his omelet to go, perhaps aware, the way siblings can be, that Serguey wished to leave.

Toya walked with them to the sidewalk. She paused under the slender shade of a lamppost and, from the breast pocket of her blouse, subtracted a cigarette. Making a megaphone of his hands, a man blasted her name from the far end of the block. He was wearing flip-flops and tattered denim shorts, the hanging white threads like piñata strings. His hyperbolic strides reminded Serguey of an ostrich. Toya's broad smile, a cavity separating her teeth, was a sign of real elation. She kissed Victor's forehead, sending him and Serguey on their way with another burst of Yoruba before the man arrived.

CHAPTER 16

They were losing natural light, so Victor flicked on the porch lamp, showering the space in bright yellow. Yunior had been true to his word: he'd brought a bucket, which Victor filled with soaped water, a small can of paint remover, and two sponges. Serguey was given the job of cleaning the egg mess using a throwaway rag. He was surprised to see how little Yunior and Victor spoke as they scrubbed the paint off the wall. They toiled with care and precision, their arms tightening and expanding like unrelenting machines. Their bones, muscles, and veins seemed to pulsate in unison. Serguey snuck glances at Yunior—his nose and cheeks, and maybe the shape of his head, too, a reminder of Norton.

Though, under these circumstances, he should welcome the quiet, Serguey felt an increasing tension, as if every moment that passed without acknowledging Yunior's generosity would deter the man's willingness to help. The rolled-up newspaper jutted from his back pocket, bending in a way that refuted Victor's theory of a knife. It was this sight: the folded wad of paper, that made Serguey believe he should speak.

"I knew your grandfather," he said.

Yunior continued scrubbing the wall, and Serguey worried that he'd made a mistake, but to say nothing else didn't feel right. Victor hadn't looked at him, which was a good sign.

"My buddy Kiko and I used to get baseball scores from him."

"Yeah," Yunior said. "A lot of people knew my grandfather."

Serguey detected no reproach or annoyance. "I was sorry to hear he passed."

Yunior stopped working and scratched his face with the nook of his elbow. "He was old. Went out on his own terms. All that cigar smoking got to him."

Serguey had seen a cigar in Norton's mouth on some occasions, but it was not the first thing he associated with the old man.

"When I went to see him at the hospital," Yunior continued, "toward the end, he looked nothing like himself. My mother let me in the room for only a minute. He was wheezing bad. Fucking tubes sticking out of his nose." Yunior mimed the tubes with the hand holding the sponge, dripping soaked up paint on his shoes, but he didn't seem to mind. His pupils peered into the bucket near Serguey's feet. "He finally looked his age. Worse than his age, I'd say." Here he started cleaning again. "I ain't going out like that. I rather it'd be my liver or my heart than my lungs."

Victor took a glimpse at Serguey and pressed his lips. All right, he was saying, don't get him started.

They worked for another twenty minutes without stopping. They were covered in sweat, their heightened breaths combining to form a rhythmic flow. Serguey had spent too much time in offices. Despite feeling physically tired, there was something refreshing about manual labor, about seeing immediate results. Up-close, one could see faded smidgens of red, but overall they had done a good job. As they stood back and beheld the wall and door, Serguey had the sense that they'd reclaimed something, a restoration to the way things should be. Cleaning the apartment was a mere vanity act for him and Anabel, all for the sake of proper appearance. This was more than that. It was a refusal to submit. This home was theirs: fuck whoever had tried to deface it.

"You should paint the entire outside of the house," Yunior said. "I can get you what you need for it."

Maybe he had searched for his in-laws' refrigerator paint in the wrong places, Serguey thought.

"My dad has final say on that," Victor said.

"Maybe you can do it as a gift, for when he gets out."

Victor forced a chuckle. "Maybe." He shook Yunior's hand, neither men worried about the residue of paint and chemicals on their skin. "I'd buy you some *jama*, but my brother and I gotta get some stuff done for tomorrow."

Yunior bobbed his head appreciatively. "No worries. I got dinner waiting at home. Just don't forget about me, like you said the other day."

Serguey and Victor observed from the porch as Yunior dumped the soiled water on a plot of dirt a couple of houses down, dropped the sponges into the bucket, and walked with a slight hop in his step, the newspaper still drooping from his back pocket.

"His cousin got a job at a paint warehouse," Victor said. "If you need some, he can get you a good price."

"I thought you said he was a shit talker."

"He is, but usually not with me."

"You should've let him eat with us, then."

"I know, but he drinks a lot when he eats, and I'm running low on beer."

After dinner, the brothers read over Serguey's statement for the video. Serguey recurrently probed his brother's opinion—unsure as to what sounded too general, too confusing, too obtuse. To Victor, the whole thing was enormously harsh. He recommended that it be more emotionally descriptive, more relatable.

"You want people to be moved by it."

"Is that what Kiko told you?" an irritated Serguey asked.

"He might've mentioned it."

He made some edits, but he told Victor that he intended to come across as fairly provocative. He'd mulled it over, and tiptoeing around the situation would accomplish nothing. "I want people to know Dad's worth helping," he said, "that his family's on his side. Unless they release him, he won't get a chance to talk, so we have to do it for him."

By midnight they had the final draft of their testimony. Victor retired to his apartment while Serguey lay in his father's bed. The box spring creaked the same notes it had years before, when he and Victor pretended it was a boat lost in the middle of raging seas. Victor's feet had tangled once with the sheets, which they employed as sails, as he fell overboard. He'd split his lip upon hitting the floor.

Felipe said afterwards, "No more sails. Use imaginary oars."

Serguey imagined himself living in this house, sleeping nightly on this bed. He felt like a stranger. The sensation he experienced after cleaning the porch had receded, gone from him like a tide that leaves your feet trapped in the sand. He was stuck in the house, in this bed. The familiarity of the objects around him didn't purge his alienation. He thought of Toya's words, the one piece of advice he could in fact use—to embrace—and he tried doing just that. He gazed at the wall to the right of the bedroom door, at the sooty silhouette of a frame. The painting that used to hang there, a fine reproduction of Fidelio Ponce de Leon's *The Children*, had fascinated him without end. He'd been mesmerized by its texture, by the eerie semblance the image had to his dreams. He would stare at it sometimes, picturing the thick brushstrokes, one swooping stroke after another. His father told him that Fidelio had applied them dexterously, masterfully, forming dark layers, making it hauntingly alive with movement, the wind practically visible on the children's clothes.

Serguey had wanted to touch them, but Felipe forbade it, afraid he might ruin the painting.

"The man died prematurely of tuberculosis," his father reasoned. "He didn't go to Europe or study with any masters like his contemporaries. He did it his own way and ended up a misunderstood alcoholic. We must respect his work."

One day, seeing Serguey entranced yet again by it, Felipe approached from behind and hoisted him inches from the painting. From this viewpoint, the image was much more haunting. The expressions on the children's faces looked aghast and nightmarish. The brushstrokes could be easily traced, streaks that burrowed and swelled in miniscule detail.

"Softly," Felipe said. "Just once."

Serguey ran his juddering index finger across the bottom, where the painting seemed thickest. It felt smooth and dry.

Felipe lowered him and said, "It's a reproduction. Not the real thing. And don't dare tell Victor you touched it. He's already broken two of your grandfather's statues."

He was Felipe's favorite, Serguey had to admit. Victor had been more attached to Irene. Unfortunately, he had lost her before memory and cognizance could take hold. Maybe this was why Serguey was being punished. Life made sense that way. He'd been given the easier childhood, the easier adolescence, the easier beginning to adulthood—all an effective antidote to a dead mother and aloof father.

Victor lived inside an ever-present reminder that he was the least favored child.

There had been plenty of times when the only sound inside the house was Felipe's typewriter. Serguey remembered joking about it to Anabel—as though it were just an anecdotal detail—the first time they watched *The Shining* together. Did Felipe spend time at his typewriter now, or had the writing duties been passed on to Mario completely? Could Victor still hear his father through the wall from the adjacent apartment, the click-clack they had left behind as Irene led them from their home to Raidel's car?

Sinking deeper into his ruminations, his body feeling heavy on the bed, Serguey remembered Victor being hesitant to race inside the house for fear that Felipe might discipline him. Serguey pictured his little brother carefully pushing their bedroom door open, Felipe's hammering of the typewriter invading the room with its monotonous, nonsensical language. Victor would bend his front knee forward, the sole of his foot firmly planted on the floor. The other leg he stretched back, anchored on the toes, his heel in the air quivering twice their father's typing speed. He was like a runner eternally on the verge of sprinting. He stayed like that until Irene came to get him. She carried him in her arms as she cooked, her hair wrapped in a headscarf. She let him taste the food and laughed when he made a face. She let Serguey try things too, if he went to the kitchen, but Serguey had his homework, his Rubik's cube, his coloring books. It was Victor who needed his mother to keep him from running, to make him forget that he wanted to run in the first place.

After Irene's death, Victor took to racing inside the house. He no longer idled by the door, but rather shot out like a cannon at will, which led to the broken globe and shattered statues. Maybe he was rebelling against the previous restrictions, but it was more likely that, at his age, he was simply acting out. Felipe wasn't a violent man, not even an unreasonable man. He allowed Victor to run, as a father should a motherless child. He wasn't negligent, either. He punished Victor after he broke things, locking him in the bedroom, but always for less time than he would initially indicate.

To Serguey he gave tasks. The eldest son could be trusted with those. At Felipe's request, he'd scurry to the local bodega to buy a box of cigarettes, back when Serguey barely knew how to count. Serguey lingered on that box of cigarettes for a moment, seeing it clear as day next to his father's typewriter, surrounded by ash and fingerprint-smeared sheets of paper. When they were older, Victor stole a pack once (maybe it was more than once, but Serguey was only aware of this one instance) and sold it at half-price to a neighbor. Felipe checked the inside of their mouths and made them stick out their tongues.

"You ask, you don't steal," he said. "Stealing is cowardly unless it's out of necessity. Last time I checked, you don't need more than you already have."

That same night he took the boys out to the movies and bought them *pirulis*, thin caramel cones on a stick, while he bought himself another pack.

That'd been a good day.

At some juncture, Serguey concluded that his father's biggest flaw wasn't his narcissism, though it could, at its peak, feel unbearable. It was how he had chosen to deal with the family drama through his work and not with his sons. Felipe's obsession with theater aside, Serguey believed his father had been unable to emotionally navigate the slipstream of Irene's infidelity, of her death. It wasn't his narcissism that led him to bury his head in his art. It was fear, spawned by emotional deficiency. His response to the tragedy revealed a weak man, one unqualified to warmly nurture his own flesh and blood. When Irene made the decision to leave with Raidel, she had taken the boys. Her wishing to lead a different life did not exclude her children. Felipe, on the other hand, stayed at his typewriter. Later on, when he accepted the boys back, he turned to his directing, his artistic friends, his popular plays. Serguey and Victor were largely left alone, with Serguey, the favorite son, having the upper hand.

Many were the evenings when a babysitter watched over them. Mariela, a sixteen-year-old obsessed with acid-wash jeans, spent hours talking to her boyfriend on Felipe's landline or paging through his painting books. She let them watch the 9:00 p.m. *telenovela*, which put Victor to sleep and numbed Serguey's brain. Paquita, the elderly neighbor who had worked at a daycare before the Revolution, forced them to eat at the table and spend the rest of the night in their room. Whenever Victor's pent-up energy was too much to bear, he would scream uncontrollably, prompting the woman to give him a glass of orange juice, which Serguey knew was laced with a sleeping aid.

Serguey fixated on the outline of Ponce de Leon's painting, his eyelids getting heavy, his mind dimming like evening morphing into night. He wasn't like his father, he thought—so fervently that it made his head shake slightly on the pillow. He couldn't be like his father. He wished, more than he had in years, that his mother hadn't died, that for his brother's sake she were still in the house.

❦❦❦ ⁂ ❦❦❦

They made their way to Kiko's under an overcast sky. The air was cool, carrying with it a persistent spray of rainwater. The streets took on an ephemeral fresh smell—an earthy, almost floral scent—whenever it drizzled, as if the raindrops themselves had aromatic properties. Heavy precipitation, on the other hand, caused the gutters and sewers to flood, relocating garbage and a myriad of unsolicited, deplorable smells from one block to another. Not that the children minded. They turned puddles and the sturdy streams jetting from rooftop drains into their personal playground. A sprinkling shower, on the other hand, did nothing for them, not even excuse a school absence.

It was on a day just like this one, under a light rain, that Irene had taken Serguey and Victor to Raidel's house. This particular weather prompted Serguey to remember himself inside that car. But it was Victor who seemed most bothered by gloomy early mornings.

"Does Kiko think we're safer at this hour?" he said, shielding his eyes from the rain.

What was Victor's memory like? Did he not remember that morning—the water dripping from their mother's hair, the perturbing stillness inside the car—like he didn't remember his dreams?

Serguey said nothing. He could feel his own hair wet and laden.

"First Claudia and now him," Victor continued. "Can't we just meet over dinner or something?"

"We'll record the video holding a hot plate of rice and fried egg. That'll make a statement."

His brother waited a moment, then said, "What did you think of Toya?"

Without a second thought, he chose to be truthful. "I'm not into that stuff, Victor. I don't believe any of it. But she's a nice lady."

"I think I'm the one who'll have to sacrifice. She said one of us would have to."

"They all say that. It applies to anybody."

Victor didn't reply. After a moment, he said, "Thank you, anyway, for seeing her."

Serguey bumped his shoulder against his brother's as if they were marching in a crowd.

Kiko had coffee waiting for them. His computer monitor was opened to a video recording application. A slim microphone jutted from the base of the monitor. Kiko explained that the brothers had to sit close together, their mouths far enough from the mic to not create any feedback. He could remove some background noise and static afterwards, but the initial recording had to be as clean as possible. He had also shifted his furniture and removed a poster so that only a white wall could be seen behind them.

"Have you recorded yourself having sex?" Victor asked Kiko, slurping the last of his coffee.

Kiko chuckled and looked at Serguey. "Was your brother ever dropped on his head as a baby?"

Victor shrugged. "All I'm saying is that if you record yourself, maybe you won't have to listen to me through the wall anymore."

"Again with the listening to sex."

Serguey construed the lamentable timing of Victor's crass humor as his way to combat jitters. "He lacks imagination," he told Kiko. "He's going to beat that joke to death."

Victor said, "You better hope State Security never goes through this computer. They'll find some perverted shit."

Kiko seized the empty coffee cups from Serguey and Victor. He positioned the brothers in front of the monitor.

Victor studied his reflection. "I'm definitely the good-looking one."

"Let's get serious," Serguey said.

Victor breathed in and out. "Okay."

They needed four takes. Victor stumbled twice. He blamed it on Serguey's handwriting. His section described how Felipe had been arrested, how the house had been violently searched and Felipe's property confiscated or destroyed. "I'm not aware of any political involvement on my father's part," he read. "He's a good-natured, affable, and respected man. He has always behaved in a way consistent with the demands and expectations of the system." *Demands* and *system* had been Serguey's choice. It implied oppression, bedecked in the nobler tone of a family plea. Victor went on to give more details: "We have attempted to visit our father at Calderas, just to be forced out, rifles at our backs, and told to return in a few weeks. We have not been allowed to see or speak to him since." Serguey's idea for Victor's last words was to imply helplessness, to create suspense and let the viewers formulate their own opinions as to what might be happening to Felipe in prison. The diaspora would never give the government the benefit of the doubt. They'd immediately think, and rightfully so, abuse, torture.

Serguey spoke about his father's physical condition and his lack of access to a lawyer or proper medical treatment. He listed some of the plays Felipe had directed and the accolades he'd received. "A career encompassing over twenty years," he read, "serving his country as a model citizen. Now the authorities bank on his family's and colleagues' fears, on the government's unconditional control over mass media to keep both Cubans and the rest of the world blind and deaf to this injustice." Serguey criticized the treatment of prisoners he'd seen in the past, who'd been accused of politically related offenses. "The Cuban legal system," he concluded, "offers no rights to the detained. They're not allowed to choose or confer with their own lawyers. I am calling for my father's release, or at the very least, a fair, open trial. Those of you who are watching, we implore you to help in any way you can, and we beseech you to make others aware of the situation."

Kiko's pupils were aglow. "Claudia's going to love this," he said when the recording ended. "Don't get me wrong, you're going to get in a shitload of trouble, but this is gold."

"I brought it up last night," Victor said, "about the trouble, but he wouldn't listen."

Serguey was tired. Reading the statement and maintaining an earnest, staunch attitude throughout had necessitated copious amounts of strength. "We need to get as much attention as we can."

Kiko played back the short video. It clocked in at just over three minutes. The short length had a clandestine feel to it, an immediacy that rendered their appeals more urgent. The visual and audio quality was acceptably clear.

"We definitely have a winner," he said. "As a fellow Cuban, I applaud you. But as a friend, I should tell you that there are going to be repercussions. What you just said won't go away."

Serguey fluttered his eyelids. They felt as hefty as fronds. "How soon will you get the video to Claudia?"

"Tonight." Kiko inserted a flash drive into the computer's USB port. "If by some chance it gets damaged, we'll have to record it again. I'm deleting the file from my computer."

Serguey thanked his friend. Victor bobbed his head, blinking at the monitor.

"I'll let you know when Claudia has something new," Kiko said. "I have to go see my dad in Regla, so I'll meet with her on the way."

Serguey watched his friend drag the audio file into the flash drive folder. "How's your old man?"

"He's been having some trouble breathing at night. His doctor came by the house and told him he was fine. He gave him a prescription that's supposed to unclog his airway or something." Kiko glanced at Victor. "My mom gave the doctor half the pork leg, and it worked wonders. Now he's going to be checking in once a week."

Victor didn't wait for Serguey to ask. "I got Kiko's parents the *pernil* before all this. I've been staying put, I swear."

"He's telling the truth." Kiko body-checked Victor, wordlessly requesting that he move. The brothers stood, and Kiko sat in front of his computer, opening several folders on his desktop. "By the way, my buddy at ETECSA told me that Mario's number isn't disconnected. He's just been using calling cards with it, like we have. The account was blocked for a while, probably by State Security, to see if he got desperate."

"So we can call him?" Serguey said.

"Been trying since I woke up. Goes straight to automated voicemail, which is full."

"Can I at least text him?"

Kiko swiveled his chair toward Serguey. "They can track it, but yeah, you can try."

Serguey brought out his phone. He selected Mario's number and wrote call this number. He showed it to Victor and Kiko.

"Are you sure?" Victor said.

Serguey nodded, pressed *Send*, and deleted the message.

Kiko returned to his computer. "Now you two get out of here."

Kissing his friend's head, Victor said, "I love you, buddy."

The siren-like domain of the screen had instantaneously absorbed Kiko's attention. "Sure you do."

CHAPTER 17

It required some convincing, but Serguey ultimately accepted a proposal by his brother to spend the night somewhere out in El Vedado. The alternative—sitting at home with no plans—beset him with baleful anxiety. In a matter of days, it was as if every element comprising his personal and professional life had been loaded into a dump truck, its bed gradually tilting toward a precipitous release.

Victor, in his small bedroom, was jamming clothes into a backpack. "We could treat Anabel and Alida to some nice food and drinks. I know you're worried about what we just did." He seemed free from his own conscience, unafraid of what might happen. "Kiko's right," he continued, "that statement was ballsy. So let's do something that can make us forget for a bit. Maybe I'll get you drunk."

"We shouldn't be spending money." Serguey paced tensely around his brother's bed. As they'd returned to the house, a prickling sensation had infiltrated his skin. His joints ached, a thumping emanating from within his bones. Despite being damp from the rain, his neck and face felt hot. He looked at his reflection in Victor's mirror to see if red blotches had materialized on them. "I'm going to lose my job, and we don't know if we're going to need—"

"Don't worry about money." Victor zipped the backpack closed. "I have friends in low places. I can get us stuff for free. You've been getting me out of jail, right? Let me repay you, show you why I've been to jail in the first place."

"I know why you've been to jail, Victor. I've seen your record."

"In theory." His brother showed a wry smile. "I want you to see it in practice."

They strode away from the house under a gray sky. Though the rain had stopped, its vestiges remained, scooped up from the glazed pavement by a misty wind. How small the neighborhood seemed when soaked and tamped under the mantle of low, dark clouds, like the chamber of an ancient underground city. Even in the anonymity of their walk to the bus stop, Serguey felt singled out from the crowd, differentiated by the video they had just recorded. He was reminded of a classmate in his seventh grade civics course. After their teacher made a rhetorical claim lauding the economic achievements of the Revolution, the boy did the unthinkable: he raised his hand and said that his grandfather had told him there'd been more food and clothes before Fidel took power. His imprudence prompted a venomous stare from the teacher, and Serguey got the sense, when the boy was instructed to stay after class, that punishment awaited him.

As they waited for the bus, he found that the open air alleviated his apprehension, prodding him to consider the positives. The people he had neglected were coming through for him. It was such a curious thing, how life worked, why people like Toya were prone to believe in spiritual truisms and the magical weavings of human interaction. The irony of one's life, the balance and unbalance, the circles that seemed to close when one least expected it: there had to be an order to it all. And yet Serguey preferred it as he always saw it: chaotic and surprising, no otherworldly explanation necessary. To impose harmonious form or mystical sense on life was to be naïve, to diverge from the rational pragmatism that had built and still sustained the world.

He and Victor stood quietly, watching cars and bicycles go by, glad to be in each other's company. This moment, for instance, begged for no elevated meaning, no spiritual reasoning. The heart of the matter—if one disrobed it to its fundamental truth—was that Serguey felt afraid. The words he had spoken in the recording weren't an act of bravery; they were an act of desperation, a reckless attempt at honoring his father. What tempered his fear was having his brother next to him. He had debated whether to remove Victor from the video altogether, take the fall himself, but the unity demonstrated by their side-by-side image would have a greater effect. The night before and that morning, he'd been unmistakably sure. Now, as they clambered into the predictably crowded bus, he realized he had also needed Victor as a source of strength, of camaraderie, to validate the fantasy that it would be harder for State Security to persecute them both.

Anabel and Alida weren't at the apartment when they got there. Anabel had replied to a text from Serguey prior to leaving Victor's place, assuring him that she would be home. He called her, an eruption of concern crawling toward his hand as he held the phone to his ear.

"Come on," he whispered with each ring in the garroting dusk of his bedroom.

She answered on the fifth ring and told him they were taking a walk. She sounded nervous, but when he referred to it—to the jiggling notes in her voice—she swore to him that she was fine, that they'd be back soon. She asked about the video.

"It went great," he said matter-of-factly, but he preferred not to discuss the details on the phone. "Victor and I are going to have some lunch and take a siesta. He's finally convinced me it'll do me some good."

She promised to keep quiet once she and Alida returned.

✤✦✶✥✦✶✤

He woke late in the afternoon. Victor was already chatting with the women in the living room. His brother and Anabel were on the couch. Through his bleary eyes he could see their feet, rigid and sallow like marionettes, parallel to each other. Alida was on the floor, legs crossed. Her buttocks protruded from the bottom of her arched back, a picture of sensual elegance. He lurched toward the group.

"How are you, Sleeping Beauty?" Victor said when he saw him.

Anabel bounded from the sofa and kissed him. "Your brother was telling me about the video."

Alida looked up at him. "Sounds like you went all in." There was a demure aura to her expression, the source of which Serguey couldn't place.

He yawned into his hand. "We did what was right."

Anabel leaned her head on his shoulder but withheld most of its weight. An act of solidarity, and at times, he knew, an advent of bad news. She said, "I had something important to discuss, but I didn't want to wake you."

Serguey appraised the group, sensing that he'd been the topic of conversation. "You should have."

"Do you want to sit?" she asked him.

"Here." Victor pounded the sofa with his hand, then went to the balcony, brought in a chair, and offered it to Alida.

"I'm fine down here." She bit one of her nails and stared uneasily at the floor.

Victor took the chair for himself. He wasn't as tense as the women, but his actions were carefully contained, as if he were walking down the aisle of a packed, speeding train. Serguey and Anabel rested their bodies on the sofa cushions. She interlaced her fingers with his, keeping their hands perched on his leg, another act of solidarity.

"Gimenez called," she said, her countenance glumly expectant. He smiled, the faux contrivance of the wounded, the defeated. He'd become such an expert on contrivances, they were now reflexive. "He wants to see you tomorrow," she added, perhaps wishing to avoid confusion. "He says it's about your contract."

A lugubrious silence overtook the room. Everyone was waiting on him. Serguey inspected Anabel's eyes. Had she cried? Had the walk with Alida been to mourn the probable loss of his job, to grouse about Gimenez, to seriously reflect on her situation, on the perils of a rocky future with Serguey Blanco?

"How did he sound?" Serguey said.

"I asked him outright. He says you're not fired but that it's urgent he sees you tomorrow."

Serguey couldn't mask his disappointment. Whatever Gimenez had to say, it wouldn't be good news. "I knew this was coming," he said softly. In essence, he was nothing more than a glorified errand boy; that's what he'd been to Gimenez from the start. And what had he gotten in exchange? A loaned apartment, a job, the promise of a trip: a terminated contract would nullify all of it. What human connection did he and his mentor have? Some runny paella in a plastic container, that'd been Gimenez's attempt at providing comfort. That, and the assurance that he'd call, the one thing for which Serguey could be grateful in the long run, if he chose to see it that way.

"I'm sorry," Victor said.

"Me too," Alida said. Her empathy was sincere, which made it nearly unbearable.

"He's not fired yet," Anabel said, kneading his fingers.

Serguey kept his pulse and breathing steady. The video, Gimenez, Claudia, Linares, his father: everything conspired to break the quaking foundation of his calm. "All right, no moping," he said, launching outward what he wanted to tell himself. "Victor's taking us out tonight. Let's shower and get ready."

"What do you mean?" Anabel said.

He used on her the same logic his brother had used on him. Panicking and scrambling would achieve nothing.

"With all that's going on, I need a fucking drink."

Anabel was apprehensive, and he could understand why. The last time, there had been a fight, spilled alcohol, and a broken bottle.

Alida, however, supported the plan. It was three against one, and Anabel wasn't disposed to be the contrarian, not in front of the others.

He pulled her hands to him, not so much an appeal as it was an exhibition of dignity. "The problems will be there tomorrow," he said plainly. "I'll deal with it then."

In the beat of a breath, she nodded, a subtle pinching of his fingers her sign of agreement. He knew instantly that he'd succeeded in eluding the issue—the possible loss of his job and apartment—and the decision-driven conversation he and Anabel needed to have. He'd succeeded in delaying it, but only for a while.

For one night, he would see his own passivity as a victory.

The group left the building by sundown. Serguey wore a glossy gray shirt—the color the sky had been that morning—with folded sleeves and dark-navy pants. He refused to try a pair of jeans Victor claimed would fit him just right. Victor had brought them in his backpack to try a new look on his brother, but Serguey wouldn't budge. His preference for certain clothes, he explained, wasn't a mere pretense for the people at the Ministry. For better or worse, his taste had settled on a more mature look. Anabel picked one of her cocktail dresses, this time green with an oval opening between her shoulder blades. Alida wore a red blouse with short transparent sleeves and a ruffle mini-skirt, making herself look even younger. Victor, proud of his body, wore a tight purple T-shirt with an unrecognizable logo and slim-style jeans. He put on an inordinate amount of hair gel. The women teased him the minute they saw him exit the bathroom, his hair shining like a polished granite countertop.

"I don't think I've ever seen hair sparkle like that," Alida said.

Victor was undeterred, saying his hair was a gift. "The kind that must be shared."

They hailed a taxi on Twenty-Third Avenue, a 1950s Chevy that was missing the rear door panels. Victor asked the shabby-looking driver to take them to El Capitolio and proposed extra cash so he wouldn't pick up anyone else. The man snatched the bills, stashing them in his pocket, his face unchanged in the rearview mirror. Taxis were a shared mode of transportation in Havana, fitting as many commuters as possible on every pre-determined trip. With bench seats on virtually every old vehicle, it wasn't uncommon for six or seven people to cram inside one.

The car sputtered its way to Fraternity Park, bustling at this time of day. Evening began to take hold of the city as they got off the taxi and rambled down Paseo de Martí. The diagonally parked cars in the middle of the avenue served as the center of a raring, desperate desire to attract tourists. Competing rates, cash exchanges, genial shouting matches between cleanly dressed drivers, questions in garbled Spanish: the Malecon, Museo Revolucion, bueno restaurant. They left El Capitolio and its gigantic white cupola behind, passing by the old Palace of the Galician Centre, renamed the Cultural Complex of Garcia Lorca's Great Theater. It hosted Alicia Alonso's renowned Cuban National Ballet Company. Grand titles and labels were ubiquitous in Cuba, a way to proclaim prestige when the dignity of a decent plate of food might escape you. The palace itself was one of Havana's most striking buildings, an unmistakable illustration of Neo-Baroque architecture, beautifully balanced with marble statues, decorative balconies, and high-rising columns. As a whole, it looked elegant and lavish, a renovated remnant of a city whose grandeur and glory now relied on its resistance against becoming rubble.

"Such sad memories," Alida said, hugging Anabel as they walked.

Serguey recalled that Alida had once practiced her craft inside those walls. She'd been an aspiring ballerina, a member of Alicia Alonso's school. She attended seminars and workshops with famous dancers, seeing up-close—no doubt wide-eyed and eager—an auspicious future for herself. Yet, with the snap of an ankle, it had vanished. Serguey could see his own struggle in Alida's, though hers had undoubtedly been more painful. Life was a cycle repeating itself, camouflaging its recurrence behind individuality, behind the idea that our paths are unique.

The sisters moved together, hands at each other's hips. They bore sardonic, layered smiles as they listened to Victor brag, half in whispers, about selling stolen old editions and mediocre Cuban art to tourists on this very boulevard. He got the idea from one of Felipe's friends, a young painter and sculptor. The man had sold an abstract watercolor painting to a French couple for thirty-five dollars.

"To them, that's nothing," Victor said to the women.

"Is that so?" Alida said.

"The trick," Victor said, "is to let the license inspectors in on the deal. People have to make money somehow, right? The problem is the government wants the money being spent in their hotels and restaurants, not the black market."

"Why don't you just get a license?" Anabel asked.

"They'll suck you dry that way. Better to pay the inspectors on the side. Much cheaper."

As Serguey's preoccupations hummed like an engine inside a calm exterior, Victor seemed unflappable in his own skin. He'd appeared concerned prior to making the video, but after the fact he had reverted to his natural state. He had gelled and combed his hair back, his distinct eyebrows highlighting his face. He'd gotten them from Felipe. Serguey's were much thinner, less conspicuous.

He had inherited Irene's. But there were similarities: the brown eyes, their narrow jawlines, their slack noses. The same comparison applied to Anabel and Alida. There were slight differences between them—in size, skin color, the thickness of their lips—but they were indisputably sisters.

Alida's head hung slightly tilted toward Anabel's chest, her cheek rested at the top of her sister's breasts. The smirks were still embossed on their faces, but their bodies were huddled as if the ground beneath their feet was unsafe. Alida looked like the protected child, Anabel the valiant mother. Serguey found Anabel's strength alluring. Her composed demeanor had been intimidating in the beginning, when they were teenagers. Even then he saw her as a woman, not a girl. He hadn't seen himself a man until years later, when he attained his law degree and began signing and stamping official documents—and for the first time, receiving a salary—during his year of mandatory social service.

Questions about the future were inescapable now. He couldn't fault Anabel if she had them. Was he supposed to get by on personality alone, on pretentions and under-the-table deals? Here lied another irony: Cuba was a country sustained by the black market. Government status didn't really apply at the neighborhood level. One had to learn to socialize, mingle with strangers, fall in love with the young girl from your block, go to the movies and create your own History of Film quasi-manifesto. One had to pick up respectable hobbies and read books on any subject. How else could you join the retired men on a park bench and hold your own at debating or at chess? That was *real* prestige: to be hailed the best chess player in your neighborhood, to be nicknamed "The Killer Russian" despite not knowing a word beyond *tovarish*, because of your shoddy but unbeatable imitations of Kasparov and Karpov on the board. Or maybe you could become an artist, like Felipe, and feel part of something larger, more esoteric. A rich tradition of expression and suffering and ecstasy. Serguey didn't believe in the human soul, but if he were to, no doubt art would be the best way to satisfy it. It required you to be intellectually and emotionally sensitive to the human condition. If he had allowed himself to be this person, he would've spat at Gimenez the first time they met.

"Why so quiet?" he heard Victor say. "Always brooding about something."

"Brooding," Serguey said. "That's a big word."

They kept on down Paseo del Prado, Havana's first paved street. It divided the Centro Habana and Habana Vieja municipalities. Under their feet was a wide, diamond-shaped strip of sidewalk, flanked by weathered marble benches, black streetlamps, and the occasional tree. They passed theaters, cinemas, and hotels—old European-style mansions now caked with dust and fading paint jobs, the result of appropriation by the government. As they approached the sea, the occasional renovated building rose on one side, mirrored on the other by a pile of debris or scaffolding enclosing a brittle wall. Night had fallen almost completely. The air from the sea began to reach them. It carried a subtle scent of salt and refuse. Across the mouth of the harbor, the dazzling lights of El Morro fortress beamed in a yellowish hue, aimed ominously at the fortified walls and the lighthouse, reflecting back in streaks over the ridged motions of the waves.

They stepped beyond Lover's Park and, further to the right, the monumental statue of Dominican-born general Maximo Gomez. The illustrious Ten Year's War and War of Independence's main strategist, depicted on horseback, was propped on a dozen columns, in turn supported by a series of sculptures narrating some of his heroics. Serguey had been brought here on an elementary school field trip. Across from the park, he got to see El Castillo de la Punta. Together with El Morro, the Spanish built it to protect the entrance to the harbor. He also got to see the entrance to El Tunel de la Habana. The tunnel left the biggest impression on him when his teacher, a sweet lady serendipitously named Dulce, indicated that the road dipped below the harbor and continued all the way underwater until it emerged behind El Morro. Serguey marveled at the ability of a man-made structure to withstand so much weight, his excitement amplified by the possibility that it could drown at any moment.

A couple of years later, Felipe took him and Victor to El Morro. Serguey was already in secondary school. He could now remember flickering lights rolling by as the bus sped inside the tunnel, the echoing rumbles and swooshes of adjacent cars. He kept thinking about the sea above him, about the tunnel caving in and tons of water engulfing vehicle after vehicle.

From El Morro, Felipe and the boys beheld the sprawling splendor that was Havana. The Malecon promenade curved away from them, graceful as a fine blade. Regardless of the physical desolation of so many neglected buildings, taken as a whole, Havana inspired awe. Felipe had described it once as an expansive cluster of varied architecture, unified by a lingering colonial aesthetic. At its core, the misery was so abundant, he said, so overwhelming, that it transformed itself into something evocative and beautiful. A young Serguey had understood what his father meant, but he was more captivated by something else: the vibrant blue of the water; the music of the waves lapping at the rocks below the fortress like a bristle broom gently sweeping; the air emboldened by the height and open spaces. His senses were acutely stirred.

It put him in a meditative trance as he observed Havana. He didn't think of history, the Revolution, martyrs—what was inculcated at school. It was as if he were suddenly capable of simplifying everything, as if he were maturing in a moment's spell, finding himself able to do what only grown men or women could: willfully fall in love with his country.

As the group prepared to cross First Avenue, Serguey considered asking Victor if he recalled the trip to El Morro, but he decided against it. With the women present, Victor was bound to boast about something inconsequential, or worse, make fun of Serguey somehow.

"Let's wait by El Malecon," Victor said. "My buddy should be calling me soon."

"Where exactly are we going?" Alida asked.

"A restaurant, just a few blocks away. It's called Casa Fina."

"Are we allowed in there?" Anabel said. She and Serguey had walked by it before, though they had never seen the interior.

Victor shook his head. "Tourists only. We have to pretend to be Spanish."

"Have you looked at your jeans?" Anabel said. "Who's going to believe you're from Madrid or Barcelona?"

"I'm kidding," Victor said. "One of the servers and the manager owe me one. I took the rap for a deal that went bad."

"What kind of deal?" Anabel said.

"Stealing meat from the restaurant and selling it to some contacts I have. We got caught, and I basically claimed I was the only one stealing. They acted like heroes for catching me, and they got to keep their jobs. So tonight I'm cashing in on their debt. They're going to give us a corner table, food on the house, drinks on me."

"You shouldn't be spending that money," Serguey said. "Didn't you tell me you were worried about your prospects?"

"I was just complaining. I got some money stashed away, don't worry. A crook like me plans for the future. I'm not shortsighted."

They arrived at the seaside promenade, and Alida hopped backwards onto the wall. Serguey buttressed Anabel's elbow to help her sit. Below them, a wave crashed on the rocks with a thunderous, guzzling sound, foam and droplets leaping like fireworks over their heads. The seawater sprayed the group as it plummeted. Serguey tried making himself into a canopy, but it was too late.

"We should move over," he said, shaking water from his hair.

"Such a gentleman," Victor said.

"You should learn from him," Alida said, hopping down from the wall.

"Too bad for you, he's already taken," Victor said.

Alida struck his shoulder. "You're such an asshole."

They moved along the promenade, swerving around a few puddles and settling on a dry spot about twenty meters from where the wave had crashed.

"Alida's always had a crush on Serguey," Anabel told Victor.

Serguey held his breath. His wife had never uttered such a thing, not even in jest.

This time Alida punched her sister. "Et tu, Brute?"

"Ah, so it's true!" Victor said.

Serguey had sensed a sort of affinity from Alida, perhaps as far as a modest attraction, but he hadn't considered it a full-on crush. This revelation made his sexual dream analogous to mortal sin, a conclusive betrayal of his wife's trust.

On the verge of blushing, Anabel committed to her disclosure, a tinge of social artistry in the tapering progression of her words: "She's always been jealous of me. When Serguey and I got married, she told me I was very lucky, but she said it while looking at Serguey. Right away I knew."

"Damn, Serguey," Victor said. "Leave some women for the rest of us!"

Serguey hoped that in the dim twilight his reaction wouldn't show. He could feel his cheeks blazing. His eyes stared in shock.

"There's nothing wrong with liking a person," Alida said, herself blushing. "If there's something I've learned from theater, it's to be in touch with my emotions."

"Thank you," Serguey said, finally able to breathe. "I appreciate the honesty. We're all adults here."

"Well, to be *honest*," Anabel said, "if you ever get too close to her, I'll chop off your balls."

Victor laughed, the sound strident in Serguey's ears. He felt a surge of anxiety behind his own uneasy grin. He gazed at the water, spectral and soundless except for the occasional wave brushing along the seawall. The sun had vanished to their left. In the distance he could see sparks of lightning glinting like a camera flash. Soon they were all looking out at the darkness. A gust of wind buffeted them, and Alida's mini-skirt flapped and billowed enough to expose part of her underwear. She quickly shoved the skirt down.

"Happens to the best of us," Victor said.

Alida held on to the hem of her skirt as the wind died down. "That's funny. When's the last time you showed your butt in public?"

Serguey cast a sideway glance at Anabel. The Alida dream, his fantasies, they've been splattered on his face like a cake, the frosting of his humiliation still dripping from what he thought had to be a dumbfounded expression. Anabel took a deep breath, and he zoomed in on her lips, struggling to deduce, in the span of a second, what she was about to say. The rush of excitement from her delighted manipulation of the conversation had disappeared. She was now gloating within a curtain of introspection that unnerved him further.

"Victor, what did you want to be when you were a child?"

He hadn't expected this.

Victor was quiet for a while. "Can't really remember."

"A medieval warrior," Serguey said, happy to shunt the talk down another road. "When he was eight, he took a piece of cardboard and cut a big circle to make a shield. He used markers to draw a lion. Then he glued a handle wide enough that he could stick his arm through it. One of Dad's friends, I don't remember if he was a sculptor or just a stagehand . . ." Serguey looked at his brother. "He made a wooden sword for you, remember?"

"Camilo," Victor said. "He was a prop master."

"Right! Anyway, you walked around riding a palm tree leaf like a horse, calling yourself Richard the Lionheart, after hearing it in some movie."

The memory seemed to filter from Victor's mind to his eyes, which glimmered more endearingly than he would've conceded. "I think it was a TV series."

Serguey turned his attention to the women. "Whenever Dad talked about Richard III—you know, Shakespeare's play—Victor thought he was talking about the same guy."

"So your little brother was always a fighter," Anabel said. They were all facing each other now.

Serguey said, "He broke a couple of things in the house with that sword."

"I always wanted to be a ballerina," Alida said. "We watched Alicia Alonso on television when I was a kid, and I fell in love with her. She was so stunning and gracious."

"She did have a talent for it," Anabel admitted of her sister. "I couldn't dance to a slow ballad, never got the steps right, but Alida learned the difficult ballet techniques so easily."

"What did you want to be, Anabel?" Victor said.

"A veterinarian," Alida said. "She dissected lizards in our backyard."

Serguey was embarrassed. He'd never heard Anabel's lizard dissecting story. They must have had a conversation about these topics before, while sitting on the shore of some beach or in bed. His mind raced, searching for the most accurate guess as to what *he* thought Anabel had wanted to be.

"Yes," she said, lifting her chin proudly, "a veterinarian. Even when I met Serguey, I was kind of interested, but then I saw that the practical part of the studies was too far outside Havana. It would've been a hassle going everyday, and for what, to end up working with emaciated cows? There are dogs and cats all over the streets here in the city, and no one cares."

"You could've studied biology," Serguey said, irked that she hadn't told him any of this, and that—more inexcusably—he conceivably hadn't asked.

"I figured being a teacher was better."

"School's a waste," Victor said.

"Says the convict," Alida said.

"Actually, I've never been convicted. I have my brother to thank for that."

Serguey was anticipating irony, but what he detected in Victor was smugness.

"How were you able to get him off?" Alida asked with sincere curiosity. "Hasn't he been arrested a lot?"

"It hasn't been that many times." Serguey browsed their surroundings, making certain no one was near enough to spy. "It was a combination of things. My dad was friends with the sector chief; Gimenez knew one of the police captains in our area; Victor usually got caught mostly on suspicion of intent to sell but never in the act. He was smart enough for that. And there was never a reliable witness. They can still convict you if they want, but if you know the law well, you can scare the officers into releasing a suspect. They don't want to fuck up and have their names end up on an official complaint or a blog. You'd be surprised how many officers are afraid of being mentioned in an internet post or independent article somewhere. Some of those guys want to leave the country. It doesn't look good if they can find out you were screwing people over. But if you're the accused and your case gets to trial, that's when you're fucked, because then it comes down to the judges. If they want to hang you, make an example out of you, they'll hang you. Look at Dad, there's no lawyer who can help him, not through legal channels. Some lawyers take advantage. They make people pay whatever they got, whatever their families can send them from abroad, knowing they're not going to win. They sell hope." Serguey stopped. He'd gotten carried away. He sensed it in his expanding chest, his accelerated breathing.

Anabel shot Victor a look. "What were you saying about school being a waste?"

Victor chuckled. "All I'm saying is, no matter what you study, you're going to either hit a ceiling or get fucked. Salaries are shit. Doctors and architects can make more cleaning hotels. You can't travel unless you get some lucky work assignment. This country has nothing to offer."

"That's not true," Serguey said instinctively, though an absence of total confidence snagged at his statement.

Victor became animated, struggling to keep his gesticulations ringed inside an invisible boundary. "What are our prospects, Serguey?" He took a step forward. "Tell me, where are we going to be when we're forty, fifty? And who's to blame? You, me, the system? The people across the water," he extended his index finger with the impetus of someone at the helm of a ship sighting land, "they aren't as fucked as we are."

Victor's phone rang. He composed himself, looking at the screen longer than he had to, and answered. It was his friend. Their table was almost ready.

"Sorry about my little rant," he said, flipping the phone shut. "It's my hunger talking."

"It's all right," Alida said, cascading her fingers over his elbow. "I think I'm starting to warm up to you."

The restaurant was a handful of blocks to the west, on San Lazaro Avenue. They walked past slick awnings and patio-style tables on the sidewalk. The muffled notes of classic Cuban singers crooned behind a few walls. Exoticism and antiquity—the biggest exports after cheap sex, tobacco, and rum—were being sold to tourists. Victor's friend was standing at the end of the street. He was dressed in black, his shirt tucked in. As they got closer, Serguey smelled a hint of seafood. He noticed the man's bald head was slathered in sweat. The restaurant's exterior was unassuming except for a couple of freshly painted wrought iron windows. A car drove by, and Victor's friend waited an instant before speaking.

"Hello, everyone," he said with hushed agitation. "I have to take you in through the back."

They skirted the building down a narrow alleyway and stepped into the sound of clattering pots, spoons hitting plates, and wine glasses clinking like the gentle tap of a mallet on a xylophone. There was no music playing, just the hum of a dozen-throated conversations.

Serguey heard the man whisper to Victor, "The binds you put me in."

Their table was in the rear corner, near the kitchen. It felt cramped, a forced addition to the space. Serguey didn't dare complain: the farther they were from the rest of the patrons, the better.

"Did you tell them the rules?" the man asked Victor.

"They know, they know."

No, we don't, Serguey wanted to say. Not exactly.

The man bared a spurious smile. "I'll be back with your menus."

Victor explained that they were not to use the bathroom unless it was an emergency. They couldn't speak with any patrons or get obnoxiously loud. Serguey was well aware, as was every Cuban, of the government-imposed apartheid when it came to tourists, something he saw Gimenez circumvent again and again. That was one of the biggest perks of working at the Ministry: dealing with foreign people was part of your job description.

"We're each getting a two-course meal, with two desserts to share," Victor added proudly. "I'm buying a couple of bottles of wine to go along with the food."

Anabel's eyes livened, discouraging Serguey from babbling another remark about the money.

It didn't take long for the awkwardness of the situation to pass. The wine, which was served quickly, worked as a distraction, as did the appetizers. Anabel and Alida were given a pair of round croquettes with a diminutive side salad. Serguey and Victor got a modest assortment of imported hams and cheeses, which they split with the women. They found the food delectable. Alida said she couldn't remember the last time she'd eaten anything of such quality. Her ballerina and actress stipends barely covered government-sanctioned groceries.

The group drank their wine and chattered again about their childhoods, what they'd do if they didn't have to worry about money, about what restaurants might be like in other countries. Alida said the lead actress in *Electra Garrigó*, who'd been to several countries in Europe and South America, claimed that Spain and Italy had the best food.

"I really want to go to Madrid," Anabel said.

"Paris for me," said Alida wistfully. "The Eiffel Tower, Notre Dame. Did anyone read the book by Victor Hugo?" She was asking everyone and no one.

"What about you, Serguey?" Victor asked, finishing his first glass. "Where would you go?"

"Egypt," he said. "The pyramids. Or maybe China, to see the Great Wall."

"Your wife wants to go to Spain, and you'd take her to China?"

Serguey released the empty glass and wiped his hands sloppily on his napkin. "You asked where *I* would want to go."

"I'd go to China," Anabel said, stealing Serguey's hand.

"California for me," said Victor, his lips and teeth daubed with red wine. "Beaches, surfing, movies."

"And they got palm trees over there too," Alida said. She involuntarily banged her elbow on the table. Serguey suspected she was already a little inebriated.

They dug into the main course like ravenous children. They remained quiet, exchanging nods and slight moans of gratification until the plates were wiped clean. This was a Cuban condition, the inconsolable longing for food. Dismally staring at white rice and fried egg—the epitome of the "not again!" food in the country—was by now a tradition. Eating the same food over and over had a defeating effect. Nothing ridded a person—especially a capable, educated person—of optimism like the perpetual image of the same plain plate of food. Going to fine restaurants wasn't part of the culture. One could acquire so much with the money spent on a two-hour meal that the experience just wasn't worth it for most.

Although he didn't tell the others, Serguey thought of Felipe, of the dinner he owed his father. He envisaged him sitting among them, vaunting about some artistic achievement. He'd raise the tips of his fingers to his chest, drop his head to one side, and conclude with, "Not that I deserve it." Or maybe he would've told humiliating stories about Victor waking in a pool of urine and staunchly claiming it wasn't his, or Serguey running into the house in a fit of panic, holding up his limp right wrist because he'd been "stung by a fly."

Serguey could share embarrassing stories about his father, too. One morning, he'd found Felipe collapsed on the living room floor. Serguey asked him if he was sick. His father told him he'd gotten drunk the night before because he was depressed. Everyone had been celebrating one of his colleague's first plays, which Felipe considered a real success. Out of petty jealousy, he had consumed too much alcohol.

"I'll get over it," he told Serguey, pulling himself up by gripping the center table. "I'll spend the day writing, and I'll feel better." He limped his way to the bathroom and slurred from the door, "Jealousy is one of man's most effective sources of inspiration."

Everyone devoured the dessert, crème brûlée and a slice of chocolate cake, before Serguey could regret waving off the bite that Anabel offered him.

He turned to Victor and said, "Thank you for this. I needed it. I needed to see you all happy."

Victor traced a circle with his spoon. "We all needed it." He released the spoon, hoisted his glass, and said, "To Dad."

They followed Victor's lead, each lifting their glass, and gulped down the last of the wine. Victor's friend approached them and asked if they were finished.

"Are we going out the back door?" Victor said sarcastically.

"I'm sorry if I've seemed rude tonight," his friend said, addressing the group. "Very busy."

Anabel flattened the tablecloth along the edge of the table. "We understand."

The man blinked. Victor slipped a bill into his pants' right pocket, and he vanished into the kitchen.

They filed out of the restaurant, peeking at the adjoining tables. The lighting was too dim to discern anything specific. Anabel almost tripped on someone's seat. Serguey prevented it just in time, clamping his wife's shoulders and whispering to her neck, "You'll start an international incident."

They decided to amble down El Malecon, let the wine wear off. Alida again leaned on her sister, more for stability than sisterly warmth. The wind was still blowing in from the sea. Pockets of people had situated themselves along the promenade wall. Far past El Morro lighthouse, two glowing ships appeared like eyes leering over the horizon.

Victor listed toward Serguey and said, "How do you think the old man's holding up?"

"It's bullshit they won't let us see him." Serguey was emboldened by the alcohol in his blood. "If I had any balls, I'd be standing with a sign in front of the State Security building every day. Sending letters to Fidel and Raul, telling them to go fuck themselves."

Victor clicked his tongue. "You'd get arrested, and then what? Who'd be out here trying to get him out? Me? I'd probably do something stupid and get locked up with you. We're doing the smart thing, Serguey. The *right* thing. What have protests accomplished in this country?"

"No way!" the brothers heard Anabel shout. They were startled, thinking it'd been directed at them. She was glaring at Alida. "We already discussed this. You're not going anywhere."

Alida scowled back at her sister.

"So she can't make her own decision?" Serguey chimed in, no longer confused.

"Thank you!" Alida said. She distanced herself from Anabel with a slight stagger and crossed her arms.

"You can't keep doing things on a whim," Anabel said, ignoring Serguey.

"I'm not a child," Alida said. "I didn't do ballet or theater on a whim. I have talent and I'm dedicated. I can't do anything with it here."

Victor flapped his arms as if trying to put out a fire. "Ladies, we should maybe wait until we're at the apartment to have this conversation."

"Stay out of it, Victor," Anabel said. She turned to Alida. "Mom and Dad won't allow it."

"They don't have to. I'm a grown woman."

"She's right," Serguey said. The alcohol, it seemed, had completely unshackled him.

Anabel spoke through clenched teeth: "You want to leave with her?"

"I'm sure this is what I want to do," Alida said. She thrust her chest out and boldly revealed: "I already have some contacts in Miami."

Victor swiveled his head up and down the promenade. "You won't if you keep announcing it to the world."

Serguey pushed him softly, advising him not to get involved. There was a selfish, enjoyable indulgence in being the only one wedged in between the women's argument.

"Contacts?" Anabel said. "Is that what you've actually been doing with your theater friends? Planning and scheming?"

"I'll just stop a taxi," Victor said to himself. He stood on the fringe of the sidewalk, arm out at any and all approaching headlights.

Serguey said, "Anabel, there's nothing you can do. Let her."

She stuck her index finger into his chest. "You're a piece of crap, you know that? A fucking weasel of a man."

Alida said, "I knew you'd do this."

"I'm talking to my husband," Anabel said slowly.

Serguey said, "You'll wake up tomorrow and see that she's right."

Anabel angled her face toward him, the residue of perfume and flavored alcohol whirling into his nostrils. "Maybe you'll wake up tomorrow and see your bags packed."

"And maybe you'll move in with Victor," he replied, "the love of your life."

She frowned with such vigor that her features nearly mutated her into another person. "Oh, fuck *you.*"

"It's not fun when it's thrown back at you, is it?" His enjoyment was beginning to wither. He'd become spiteful, admitting to himself that Anabel's mocking of Alida's crush had bothered him a phase or two beyond embarrassment. "I can make threats too, you know," he said as a form of defense, though not a good one by his standards.

She stared at him, the warping of her lips showing her to be more hurt than malicious.

"You people have been watching too many damn soap operas," Victor said, successfully hailing a car.

Upset with himself and looking for some kind of punishment, Serguey was disappointed that Victor had ignored the last exchange. Was he maturing or merely loath to grabbing his brother's neck in front of both women?

As they reluctantly got into the taxi, Victor murmured, "I can't believe I'm the voice of reason in this family."

CHAPTER 18

They climbed out of the taxi in front of Serguey and Anabel's building. A fetid silence, like smothering fumes, had accompanied them inside the car. Victor paid the driver, and the man drove away slowly. Serguey lingered on the sidewalk, observing the women, gauging whether the argument was over. Alida was approaching Anabel, extending her hand discreetly, seeking reprieve. The screeching wail of skidding tires, like the prelude to some thunderous and horrific accident, shook Serguey's attention away from them. A bronze-colored Lada came to a halt where the taxi had been. A compact cloud of burnt rubber rose above the doors, through which two plainclothes men exited and flashed their credentials so briefly that Serguey wasn't able to make them out. One of the men, the shorter one, grabbed Serguey's sleeves and pushed him against the building. The other man, tall and portly, said to Victor, "You know the drill." Victor shrugged and stood against the wall, arms up and legs spread.

"What's going on?" Anabel said, turning back, Alida at her side. "Who are you?"

"State Security," the shorter man said, searching Serguey. "Stay out of it or we'll arrest you too." He removed Serguey's wallet and cell phone and dropped them in his shirt pocket.

The first thing that flashed through Serguey's mind was the moment in which he had deleted the text he'd sent to Mario. The second was from moments earlier in the taxi, when he'd verified Mario had yet to respond. The third was the consolation that, if the authorities were to keep his phone, he could ask Kiko for the dramaturge's number.

The man gruffly ran his hands up Serguey's inner thigh and thrust them into his testicles. Serguey flinched, briefly losing his ability to breathe as his knees trembled and pleated. Right under the nape, the man bundled a fistful of

Serguey's shirt, and, as if clamped by the jaws of a bigger animal, Serguey was yanked back to an erect position.

"Getting soft on me?" the man whispered jeeringly just above Serguey's earlobe.

"It's all right," Serguey said to Anabel, his heart pounding but his voice serene. "Take Alida into the apartment."

"You can't do this!" Anabel shouted.

Lights began to flicker on above them. The balconies, Serguey knew, were about to become theater seats.

"Is that one clean?" the short man asked the fat one while putting handcuffs on Serguey.

His buddy was doing the same with Victor. "Yeah, he's clean."

"All right, let's go."

"Where are you taking us?" Serguey asked loudly. "What's your name?" The man lifted Serguey's arms by the handcuffs. Serguey felt a straining pain in his shoulders and elbows. He started to resist, buying time. It worked. People were now standing on their balconies. Serguey could hear them mumbling. He looked up and said, "This is the country we live in! This is injustice! This is abuse!"

Anabel rushed toward the short man as he dragged Serguey to the car. "Comrade," she said, entreating him this time, "they haven't done anything."

The man didn't respond.

Serguey said, "Anabel, it's all right. Stay with Alida."

"This is nothing," Victor said. He was being hauled around the rear of the car. "I'll watch over him, Anabel. This is nothing."

"What's your name?" she asked the man. "Show me your badge again. I have a right to know who you are."

Serguey was already inside the Lada, the door slammed shut. He could barely hear the voices outside. He saw the man raise his finger to Anabel's face. He heard the word "arrest" again. The man also pointed at Alida, who was now sitting on the building steps, crying.

"I have a right to know," Anabel was saying, her voice muffled and frantic. The man walked away.

Victor was shoved into Serguey until they were both uncomfortably jammed against the door. The fat man sat next to Victor. The short one took the passenger seat. A third man, small-headed and crumple-faced, was the driver.

"Go," the short man said, securing his door.

As the car raced out of the neighborhood, Serguey said, "Officer, what's your name? We have a right to know who's arresting us."

"The name's Silvio. Memorize it because we're going to become friends."

"Rodriguez?" Victor said, sneering. "Like the communist singer?"

The driver chuckled, though his companion wasn't amused.

Victor looked at the paunchy man next to him. "Who are you supposed to be? Pablito Milanes?"

"I'm a lawyer," Serguey said, a despairing attempt at his own brand of intimidation.

"And I'm the law," Silvio said. "Now be quiet, or I'll send Pablito back to pick up your ladies."

The brothers were transported to a police station in La Lisa, fifteen kilometers from the apartment. Serguey figured the officers wanted to make it difficult for their family to find them. They were led to a windowless room with three chairs and a table. The bare-bulb floor lamp in the corner reminded Serguey of nighttime construction. Their grandfather, Larido, had once spent an entire summer evening erecting a short wall for a friend of Estela's. He and Victor had assisted him under an incandescent canopy of light bulbs, their bodies dowsed in brackish sweat, as their grandfather shoveled mortar from a bucket and smeared it on bricks, stacking them up with a level.

In this room, Serguey felt the same heat, saw the same kind of shadows.

They waited for a half hour, handcuffed. Serguey told Victor to say nothing and keep the goofing to a minimum.

"For all we know, there's a microphone somewhere in here," he said.

"I really need to pee," Victor said, as if the fact rendered him weaker, susceptible.

Serguey struggled not to think about the metal of the handcuffs, digging and cutting his wrist bones. His fingers were going numb, and he, too, needed to use the bathroom. The adrenaline rush had subsided; their pulses had dropped. It made him feel naked under the bareness of the light bulb, the stuffy silence of the room.

It was Montalvo who finally entered. He had on olive green military pants and a red polo shirt, the sleeves wrapped tightly around his chiseled biceps. With no flag or halo to speak of—no visual theatrics to distract them—Serguey feared on this occasion Montalvo really meant business.

"What happened to Silvio?" Victor said.

Serguey thought it smart, showing Montalvo that he had numbers on his side, that by himself, he wasn't as menacing.

"He hasn't gone far," Montalvo said dismissively. He stared at Serguey. "So, how was the lobster?"

"What lobster?"

"The one you ate tonight."

"They didn't have any," Victor said.

"Don't," Serguey told his brother. One taunt had been enough.

Montalvo leaned on the table. "Let me see if I understand: your father's in prison, and you two take your women to celebrate at a tourist restaurant?"

The brothers didn't reply.

"I thought you'd be out at Calderas with signs, yelling at some TV camera, demanding his freedom, claiming his innocence. Or dragging those mercenary journalists to Section Twenty-One to get more information."

Victor chortled, Serguey presumed at the word "mercenary."

Montalvo didn't acknowledge him. "But you haven't," he said. "Well, to be fair, when this one here," he gestured at Victor, "showed up at the prison after your mutual visit, he left with his tail between his legs. So I wondered, have they seen the light? Are they disavowing their counterrevolutionary father?"

Serguey repelled the urge to scowl at his brother. Victor hadn't disclosed his second visit to Calderas. Then again, he couldn't reprimand him. Serguey himself had withheld the scrap with Parra at the National Council for the Performing Arts.

Montalvo stood and walked past the brothers to the end of the room. Serguey stared over his shoulder, not wanting to lose sight of him. Victor drooped his neck and squinted. Maybe the onset of a headache.

"So, what I'd like to know," the ex-colonel said, "is what you've been up to."

Again the brothers declined to speak.

"I haven't seen any official documentation stating that you've distanced yourselves from Felipe Blanco, so I'm going to give you the opportunity." The door opened and Silvio came in, a premeditated entrance. He had two folders pinned under his right arm. He placed them side-by-side on the table, revealing a typed and stamped statement in each one. Then he proceeded to remove the brother's handcuffs.

Serguey felt relieved, capable. "What do you want?"

"Sign those." Montalvo pointed at the gaping folders. "Proof that you're cooperating and will tell us what we need to know. In exchange, we'll show your father some leniency."

Serguey took the statement and read it.

"What kind of leniency?" Victor said.

Serguey put out his hand and shook his head at his brother. "Don't fall for it."

He turned to Montalvo. "You give me something in writing that says my father will be released, then we can talk."

"You're getting greedy. You sign those, *then* we can talk."

"This is an indirect admission of my father's guilt. You're going to have to do better than that. I already told you people that I'm a lawyer."

Montalvo ordered Silvio to take the folders and leave the room. He stood between the brothers and moored his hands on their shoulders. "Your father has been in contact with individuals who are members of international organizations. The mere act of letting them in his house is sufficient to convict him as an enemy of the state."

"You have proof of this?" Serguey said. "Photographs, witnesses, a confession?"

Montalvo squeezed Serguey's shoulder, his grip strong, controlled. It made Serguey shudder.

"You're jumping in front of the wagon. Besides, proof will always be on the side of justice."

Serguey didn't care for vaguely crafted maxims. "I don't know what that means."

"It means they don't need proof." Victor blended a smile and a sneer.

Montalvo made an umbrella of his fingers, pressing them against his chest. "*I* didn't say that." He sat on the table and commanded the brothers to tell him about their own involvement. "I know that *you* know your father's friends. I also know that you've been talking to independent journalists, those fucking rats. They make shit up online so that people will send them money. It's really just another form of prostitution. *Gineteras intelectuales.*"

"We haven't spoken with anybody," Serguey said.

"And you haven't recorded a video either, right?"

The air coagulated in Serguey's lungs. Was it possible that Claudia had already posted the video? Should he cop to it? Had Montalvo actually seen it himself or simply heard about it? He was tired of the ex-colonel's posturing. "We've done nothing that we regret."

Montalvo stepped toward him and clipped a pen into the single-breast pocket of his shirt. "If you want a normal future in Cuba, you'll use that pen. On my mother's grave, I swear," he raised his right hand, "no harassment, no black stain record. I don't want you to work for us. Just sign the documents, and we can all move on."

"Take your pen," Serguey said groggily. "We're not signing."

"There's no gray area here. You're with us, and we help you. You're against us, and we fuck you, literally."

Victor began to fall asleep (or was he pretending?). Montalvo slapped him, the flat, whipping sound bouncing off the peeling walls. He jabbed his fingers into Victor's jaw and said, "You like prison, don't you?"

Victor snorted forcefully, like a horse after a long sprint.

Montalvo released him. "We have enough to throw you in any prison we want and let you rot there before you even see a judge."

The slap had triggered Serguey's heartbeat into overdrive. The bare light bulb was now a source of excruciating heat. "You can't do that," he managed to say. "It's unconstitutional. I'll get someone to publish a list of your violations. I'll make sure your name's front and center."

Montalvo touched Serguey's forehead with his own. "Who?" He began to apply pressure—a furious ram establishing dominance. "Who's going to publish it?"

The ex-colonel's breath, husky and bitter, made Serguey want to hurl. He averted his eyes and blinked repeatedly.

Montalvo's voice turned rancorous, filled with aggravation. "We're going to expedite your father's trial. Then we're sending him to Cienfuegos. You'll see him every three months. He'll probably die of dysentery. Have you heard how dissident prisoners are doing? We granted one medical leave after the Church begged for clemency. The guy was spitting blood and shitting his pants. Felipe won't last as long."

"He has the right to see a lawyer," Serguey said.

"What I'll let him see is a priest, to give him his last rites."

Did Montalvo know about the Church's involvement too? Serguey laughed unintentionally, out of fatigue. "I have nothing more to say. If you're not charging us, you'll have to release us in forty-eight hours."

Montalvo's neck and armpits were soggy with sweat. He went to the door and banged on it. Silvio and Pablito entered, another prepared appearance.

"Season them up a little bit," he told them. "Don't touch the face, no lasting marks. If they fight back, call a couple of more officers. Tie them down if you have to. Then throw them in the cell with the two guys who stabbed that drunk at the party. Tell them there's a pack of cigarettes for them if they give these idiots here a sleepless night." Montalvo looked at the brothers. "See you tomorrow."

Serguey and Victor were thrown to the corner of the room. Silvio and Pablito shouted for them to drop to the floor, then kicked them, again and again, in the ribs and stomach. Serguey wilted under the blows. Tired of the beating, Victor made as if to stand, but Serguey pulled his brother's forearm, pleading that he not fight back. Victor protested as he lay down and shielded his lower torso with his elbows. After a few seconds, dark spots began to appear in Serguey's blurry vision; it hurt to suck in air. They took hit after hit bunched together, their shoulders touching, without saying a word. Along with the kicks, Silvio and Pablito would yell "Son of a bitch!" or "You dissident queers!" They were looking to bait them, to get them to retaliate.

The brothers never did.

Eventually the officers hauled them by their collars into a cell. The men Montalvo had mentioned were standing by the entrance. The brothers sat on the floor, leaning their heads back against the wall. They were grunting and sighing, hoping to remove some of the pain with each exhalation.

"I think I have a broken rib," Serguey whispered.

"Where?"

Gingerly, Serguey lifted his shirt. Victor massaged his brother's ribcage, and he winced.

"It's not broken," Victor said. "It's just sore. And get ready, 'cause tomorrow it's going to hurt more. That's why they did this. We're lucky they didn't use batons. Those suckers leave nasty welts."

"Look at these *maricones*," one of the detainees said. He was short and sinewy, wearing a white tank top and jean shorts. As he smiled, he revealed a missing tooth on the left side of his mouth. His companion was taller and thicker, not as muscular, and by the look of his droopy eyes and protruding lower lip, possibly slow-witted. He was also wearing a tank top, reddish stretch marks radiating from his armpits. When he'd heard about prisoners, Serguey had hoped for plants, State Security disguised as criminals. These men were the real thing. As he looked at them, he became acutely aware of a festering stench, like vomit—a mix of beer and rotten meat—that seemed to have infused every centimeter of the cell.

"Where are they taking you?" Victor asked the men. "Eastern Combine? Villa Marista? Whatever you were doing out in the streets, you can forget it. You're going to be selling your asses for cigarettes now."

"Watch your mouth," the toothless one said.

"I don't know what they told you," Victor said, "but if you fuck with me or my brother, I know some people inside who will slice your dick off. Ever heard of Melao?"

"Yeah, I've heard of Melao."

Victor bent his knees with a grunt. "He's my second cousin."

The man chortled. "Just don't fall asleep."

"What are you in for?" Serguey asked. "I'm a lawyer."

"We shanked a guy," the bigger one said, miming a stabbing motion.

"Allegedly," said the other.

"Weren't you at a party?" Victor said.

The toothless one was taken aback by Victor's detail. "So what?"

Victor scoffed. "By the look of you two, probably half the crowd saw you do it."

The bigger one treaded slothfully toward the brothers.

Serguey stood. "Take it easy." He took off his shirt and offered it.

Victor sprung up and snatched the shirt. He pressed it against Serguey's chest. "Don't give them anything."

"Tell me what happened," Serguey said. "Maybe I can help."

The toothless one smacked his large companion on the shoulder twice and shook his head. They leaned against the wall opposite the brothers.

"Just don't fall asleep," he repeated.

Throughout the night, whenever Serguey or Victor dozed off, the toothless man would yell "Hey!" and clap. Serguey found it exasperating, but the discomfort and ache in his stomach, chest, and ribs was growing with each hour, and he was in no mood for another beating. Victor didn't seem to be either. He remained immobile for the most part, holding the men's gazes.

Deep into the night, he decided to ask them, "Don't you sleep?"

"They gave us a little something before you were brought in here."

Serguey figured they meant drugs.

At one point, Victor asked Serguey to watch his back as he relieved himself in the corner of the cell. Sitting down again, he said, "Lighting here's pretty bad, but I don't think I had blood in my piss. That's always good news."

Serguey was alarmed. "You've had blood in your piss before?"

"I was at this party, and Special Brigades showed up. They came rushing out of a van. I think it was some kind of raid. I tumbled over a cement block trying to get away, and one of the officers hit me with a club. I don't react well to those things, so when I tried to get up to fight him, he kicked me with those huge boots they wear. Got me right in the kidney."

"Why didn't you tell me? I would've filed a complaint."

"What for? I didn't have any witnesses. Besides, you fuck with those Special Brigades guys, they'll come after you worse than these State Security pricks."

"Was it a red beret?" the toothless man asked.

"Yeah," Victor said.

"I took down a black beret once. Broke his nose."

"Good for you."

The man said nothing else. He and his companion continued keeping watch, hour after hour, ensuring that Serguey and Victor didn't fall asleep.

Early in the morning, as sunrays percolated through a window opposite the cell, a uniformed police officer came for them. He led them back to the interrogation room. As he walked, Serguey felt that every part of his body except the bottom of his feet contained some measure of pain. He had spent the past few hours fretting about Anabel, about the terrible fantasies that might be tormenting her. If only he could call her, tell her in his clearest voice that he was fine.

Montalvo was already inside, wearing the same outfit from the previous night. The brothers took their respective seats without being told, their quiet acceptance a form of resistance. Without the support of a wall, Serguey's head felt cumbersome, as if on the verge of unhinging itself from his neck. His mouth was desiccated, his mind drowsy. The lack of sleep, the repetition in the location and Montalvo's clothes, made the entire time at the station seem like a bad dream.

Victor stretched his legs and said, "So what is it, Serguey, twenty-four hours more to go?" He yawned determinedly, pretending to welcome his exhaustion.

"You boys sore?" Montalvo asked.

"I'm taking this to court," Serguey said, his voice garbled like a drunk's.

Montalvo reached behind him and produced one of the folders. He was giving it another shot. He leafed through it aimlessly. "You go fill out your paperwork, make your phone calls, quote the penal code. In fifty years, people like you have never won." He closed the file and smacked it against his leg like a drummer counting off a slow, heavy rock song. "That's why it's just a matter of time before you see it from our point of view. Now, let's get you some coffee." He looked at the door and called for Silvio.

The man walked in with a plastic thermos and two cups. Their timing, Serguey had to admit, was impeccable.

"Have some," Montalvo said to the brothers, pouring the steaming coffee into the cups. "Just for kicks, I'm going to ask you again: what do you know about you father's political involvements?"

Serguey shook his head, rejecting the coffee. It was a dodgy move: how much fuel he had left in the tank without a shot of caffeine was hard to say.

Montalvo placed Serguey's cup at his side. Wraiths of steam danced upward, escaping beautifully, mournfully from the mouth of the open thermos.

Victor accepted his coffee and drank half of it. "Tastes like shit," he said to Silvio. He drank the rest insolently and squinted at the bottom of the cup. "I bet the wife has to make it for you at home."

Montalvo laughed. "His coffee does taste like shit. I make my own."

"We know nothing," Serguey said curtly, addressing the ex-colonel's question about Felipe's involvements.

"All right." Montalvo set the folder back on the table. "But you should know that you're running out of friends. Your former boss, Roberto Gimenez—a nice guy, by the way—has been really cooperative."

Gimenez had no substantial information. But Montalvo's bait was too tempting. What exactly had he shared? "Gimenez is human garbage," Serguey said, refusing to ask outright. It was too early to believe that his mentor had sold him out (there was still a possibility that his wanting to meet this very morning had been to warn his protégé), but Serguey wasn't exactly in a forgiving mood.

"That's open to interpretation," Montalvo said. "He claims you've been acting suspiciously around work. He recommended that we go through your computer, maybe have a word or two with your wife. You two are inseparable, he says."

"The computer's clean." Serguey swallowed laboriously, though he wasn't lying. "We'll see about that."

"I'll volunteer it. It belongs to the Ministry, so you can have at it with a hammer."

"No need. Our guys are already looking."

They'd been inside the apartment, Serguey surmised. Had they been waiting for Anabel and Alida? Were the women being held in another room?

Victor said, "If you touch Anabel or Alida," he presented his coffee cup like a tiny baseball, "I'm going to smash your face."

Montalvo grabbed the thermos and took a couple of steps forward. "The fun never ends with you." He clinched Victor's wrist with his free hand and commanded him to let go the empty cup. Victor stared daringly at him before obeying. The cup bounced on the floor but didn't break. Looking into Victor's eyes, the ex-colonel poured coffee on his knee. Victor shouted in pain and vaulted backwards, tripping briefly over his toppling chair.

Serguey jumped up and said, "He's trying to trap you, Victor. Don't hit him."

"Was it really that hot?" Montalvo said.

Victor refused to touch his own knee. His tightened fists shook with rippling ire.

The ex-colonel dropped the thermos, part of the rim shattering off upon impact. The sound, like Montalvo's slap the previous night, ricocheted across the sealed room. He seized the files from the table. "Relax, Victor. I'm a gentleman with the ladies. Gimenez already warned me that Anabel's feisty, so I'll go out of my way to take it easy on her."

Victor looked imploringly at Serguey. He was asking for permission to assail the ex-colonel. His groans were beginning to end in weary whimpers. A persistent tremor had overtaken his limbs.

Serguey's eyes were so dry they couldn't conjure up tears. "Gimenez is a desperate old man."

Montalvo paced toward Serguey and tapped the folders on his head. Again his ammoniac exhales curdled Serguey's stomach.

"Our favorite kind of witness."

"Where's Anabel?" Serguey asked angrily. "Did you bring her here?"

Montalvo ambled to the door. "If she hasn't left you, she should be at the apartment."

Serguey targeted his attention at the files, which swayed precariously between the tips of Montalvo's fingers. "What about my father?"

"The pen I put in your pocket," the colonel said, "keep it as a souvenir. Silvio will drive you home. I can't wait to get my hands on that video I keep hearing about. If it's as good as I expect, I might just ship you both to Oriente. Anabel's going to have to get a new husband. As for your daddy . . ." Montalvo dislodged the papers from the folders and tore them with ease. The pieces fell like floating leaves by his boots. "Look at your calendar. When it's been a month since your last visit, go see him at Calderas, that's if you're still free and he's still there. You turn up before then, I'm locking you up for public disturbance. You can read all about it in the penal code."

CHAPTER 19

The jarring drive on Havana's divoted roads didn't keep Victor from passing out. His head skidded against the window like a wiper. He had folded up his pant leg to let the burnt skin breathe. The wound was a deep red, with tinges of a brownish hue, but not big in size. The hair hadn't been singed, which Serguey saw as a good sign. He couldn't tell how much pain his brother was in, he looked so placid in his sleep. He began to watch the houses and people outside the window, mesmerized by the variations in shapes and colors, unable to process or hold on to any particular detail. He hadn't noticed it before, but a rank smell levitated like vapor from the floor mats of the car. The engine sounded like a tumbling bag of tin cans. He was reminded of a saying he'd heard as a child: "*La bejumina hace mas ruido de lo que camina*," a reference to a small motorcycle whose engine noise was far greater than its speed. Each time the driver switched gears, a grating noise crept through the bottom of the vehicle. The Soviet-era Lada was as much a Cuban symbol as the flag. Its abysmal quality was the center of countless Cuban jokes, but at least it wasn't a packed bus or the sizzling bed of a truck in an infernal summer.

The scraps of thoughts in Serguey's weary mind didn't relate to the last twelve hours but to what lay ahead. He was finally re-joining the masses—with a sullied record to boot. The kind of stain that made him a pariah, an infectious disease in the paranoid, protective consciousness of the people. The massive exodus of Cubans made more sense now. It had been easy to ignore it standing on his balcony with a romantic view of the sea. Now he was looking at himself in that sea, unable to get past the turbid waves, like a rafter, sand-laden water plugging his lungs, able to gasp long enough to retain the illusion that he was actually making progress.

The car began to weave its way into El Vedado. How much longer would he call this neighborhood home? He should be selfless, he knew, and worry only about his father. But it was *he* sitting in this car, Victor next to him, the likelihood of State Security harassment hovering like a black cloud. Any breeze now would feel like the prologue to a storm. Threats weren't empty when you were locked behind bars, kicked, mocked, and proven what you'd long believed: that your knowledge of the law only secured you an ironic downfall. As the vehicle turned into Serguey's block, he grasped, quite consciously, that he now had one job—get his father and brother out of the country, any way he could.

"See you soon," were the only words Silvio said after barking for him and Victor to exit the Lada.

Victor ruffled his hair as the car rumbled out of view. He threw an arm around Serguey, reclining the bulk of his weight on him. "What a night."

Serguey's gait turned labored, as if someone were completely perched on his shoulders. "How's the leg?"

"Just need to put an ice pack on it."

"We should take pictures of the bruises." Serguey took a glimpse at the elevator sign, coveting with all his heart to tear it down. He and Victor waddled like two drunks up the stairs. "We have to document what happened."

There was no disagreement or resistance in Victor's pendulous expression.

Anabel hugged them by hurling the breadth of her arms as if she were enveloping them with a blanket. She kept blinking, crinkling her pale nose, like she'd developed a twitch. No one had been at the apartment when she and Alida entered. No one had come to speak with them. She'd sent Alida to her parents', and since Serguey had given her Kiko's number, she called him for advice. With his help, she'd scribbled a list of places where they might have taken Serguey and Victor. In a decision that angered Serguey, she had also contacted Gimenez.

"Your husband should do a better job of communicating with the authorities," Gimenez said. "I'm guessing he's finding this out right about now."

Serguey wasn't surprised or disappointed. Men like his boss survived by washing their hands of people and things. What angered Serguey was how Anabel could think, at this stage, that Gimenez should be a source of help.

Anabel rubbed her eyes with the heel of her hands. "I was desperate," she confessed, her voice feeble, fragmented.

He circled his fingers around her forearms and removed her guard. "We have to get used to the fact that we can't depend on him anymore. He basically gave me up."

"What do you mean?"

"He talked to State Security, told them I'd been acting suspiciously at work. He even tried to get you involved. He went for the jugular, Anabel."

She was suddenly untroubled. Maybe, like him, she was unsurprised and just needed evidence of Gimenez's lack of loyalty before she truly gave up hope. She told Serguey how relieved she was that he and Victor were okay, but—and here she seemed to reconnect with her distraught self—his laptop and digital camera were missing. The officers had been in the apartment before the arrest.

"They might've wired the place," Victor said.

"I looked everywhere," Anabel said haggardly. "I couldn't find anything."

Another search through the apartment came up empty. Serguey wasn't worried about the computer since it contained no compromising information. But without the camera, they had no way of photographing the contusions on their bodies. It did worry him that the officers had been able to access his home so easily. There was no sign of forced entry, nothing damaged or evidently out of place. He began to play a few scenarios in his head, but he found his thoughts disorganized, incoherent. He decided it was best for all of them to put food in their stomachs and get some sleep.

Anabel prepared tea, which Victor accepted without any snide commentary, and boiled some potatoes to mash. Victor made it through half his plate before stumbling to the guest room. Anabel handed him an antibiotic cream to apply to the burn, which had begun to blister. Serguey slurped the last of his tea in a haze and would later not even recall heading to his bed.

He woke close to 5:00 p.m. While he showered, he saw that his bruises had started to dissipate—it was hard to tell where they began and ended. The muscles beneath the skin were tender. So were his ribs. He found it excruciating to wash his legs, the pain concentrating on his lower abdomen. He let the water slither down the back of his neck and soak his naked, frail limbs, ridding him of soap and leaving him with a sleek texture glued to his body hair. He would have to take an aspirin if he wanted to avoid a headache. As he drenched his face under the shower, he suddenly became certain of how Silvio and Pablito had gotten into the apartment. The week he and Anabel had moved in, they exchanged spare keys with Carmina. The woman was a stickler for following rules, a vestige of an older generation who saw the promises of the Revolution devolve into prevalent poverty and social restrictions, and who nonetheless decided to carry on with their civic duties. How else was she to give meaning to her life, to prop herself up onto a higher moral ground? She was a guardian of the Revolution, clipping feathers to the bone before any subversive or opposition group could grow wings. She had let the officers in. Serguey was willing to bet his own pound of flesh on it. And she'd enjoyed it too, faking concern, saying Serguey and Anabel were nice people, but that, to be frank, lately they were acting strangely. She had been asked—not asked, entrusted—to keep a watchful eye and report what she saw. She was a valuable asset, a street level troop, a cog without which the Revolution couldn't grind ahead. And there was, in all probability, an incentive: during the next neighborhood allotment of electronics, she would be at the top of the recipient list.

During his childhood and teenage years, he and Victor had learned to divide their neighbors into two groups: those who could get their hands on what they considered rare merchandise—video game consoles; color televisions; Sony, Sanyo, or Panasonic stereo systems; brand new freezers or blenders—through family abroad or black market deals, and those who depended on the government for breadcrumbs: a Chinese Panda TV; a second-rate multi-speed fan; a bicycle; a refurbished, decade-old refrigerator or washing machine. These items were usually given out immediately after Cuba had received a cargo ship worth of donations from China or Mexico. Only one or two people per neighborhood were selected to receive them, if that many. More recently, the government had implemented a rent-to-own plan to provide air conditioners, water heaters, rice cookers—which had previously been as rare as laptop computers—to the masses. People paid monthly quotas to keep these items. Retirees like Carmina could only afford them if they received money from overseas. In her case, government allotments were a welcomed price. A microwave was worth someone going to jail.

Serguey put on a pair of khaki shorts and a white T-shirt and headed over to his neighbor's. Water was still dribbling from his hair. His ears felt clogged. He knocked several times to indicate urgency. Carmina opened the door with a look of apprehension on her wrinkled face.

"My keys," Serguey said tersely, handing Carmina hers. "I need them back." He could hear a pressure cooker hissing in the background. The smell of boiling beans pervaded Carmina's living room. Now that he thought about it, her entire home reeked of old age.

"What happened?" she asked. "You know, a couple of officers—"

Serguey cut her off. "I need the keys. Now."

She dithered a moment, then took her own keys and nudged the door shut. Her shuffling steps returned a minute later. She stretched out her hand, the keys dangling from her swollen, pockmarked fingers.

"You and Anabel haven't fulfilled your duties . . ." she started to say.

"Scratch us off your list. We're moving out of here soon."

He didn't give her a chance to retort, to snoop, to lecture. He marched into his own apartment and slammed the door. He wanted her to feel confused, and if he was lucky, scared. The idea of Carmina standing inside his home while State Security dug through his things—probably itching to scour through the rooms like a curious rat herself—it incensed him. The audacity and impudence of it, the sense of entitlement one had to have to do away with someone else's privacy like that. The warped communist notion that all must be shared equally, that private property was somehow a mark of greed and moral corruption, had given the people a carte blanche to meddle, to question what you were hiding behind closed doors. Spies, moles, informants, they'd been bred right out of the populace. The senior citizen who offered everyone coffee, the university student who sometimes tossed a baseball around with the kids, your uncle's best friend, who'd driven your family to the beach—they could all turn on you in a heartbeat. Some might go out of their way if they were looking to score points, to obtain the government's commendations and rewards for weeding out counterrevolutionaries.

Carmina wasn't an exception. She was part of a bigger malady.

Victor picked up his belongings and told Serguey and Anabel that he was going back to the house. He had to let Kiko know things were fine and warn him about State Security for his own sake. Anabel told him to keep the antibiotic cream. Victor made Serguey promise that he wouldn't give up, that their father's release was still the final goal.

"I just want to be sure they didn't soften you up too much," he said.

"He's stronger than you think," Anabel said.

The brothers agreed that as soon as there was word from Claudia, they would meet with her. They just had to be more cautious.

"And we need new phones," Serguey said.

Victor agreed. "I'll see what I can do."

Early in the evening, Serguey and Anabel sat at the dinner table, staring at a warm plate of chicken and rice soup and one-a-day bodega-allocated bread. Anabel thought it best for him not to eat anything too solid until the stomach and rib pain was gone, in case there was some internal damage. She suggested going to a clinic or maybe the family doctor in their neighborhood, but Serguey snubbed the idea. Reluctantly, she asked him if he wished to file a report. It was good to have a record of the incident, in case he needed to plead his case later.

He told her in a hushed but dogged voice that he'd already considered it, but he'd resolved not to seek assistance from the system. The government could easily manipulate the procedures available to him. They wouldn't keep him from being harassed or immured, not if they really intended to fuck with him. Anabel responded that he should at least issue a statement through Claudia about the beating and overnight incarceration.

"Your dad's no longer the only target," she said.

The understatement of the year, he thought, but it would've been unfair to point this out when he hadn't told her about the house being defaced, when he'd been so cruel to her about Victor just before getting into the taxi the previous night. Serguey split his crumbling bread to dip it in the soup. "I'll speak with her about it."

"There's something else we need to discuss."

He bit into the sodden piece of bread. As he swallowed, his sore belly contracted, but he felt he could eat the whole thing. "What is it?"

Anabel ran her spoon slowly across her plate, the rice and chicken swirling in tiny vortexes. "We're running out of food. The freezer's almost empty. I was able to get a few things at the bodega today, but it wasn't much. Now that we won't have Gimenez's help, I'm not sure what we're going to do."

"I'll figure something out."

"I was thinking maybe I could ask my dad."

Serguey shook his head, making a flippant sound with his throat, as his mouth was full of bread.

She raised her tone. "He has contacts in Mantilla and here in the city through the Church, and we have a little money saved."

Serguey swallowed again with a frown. "Out of the question."

Anabel sighed and dropped her spoon. "Serguey, don't fight me on this. You have other things to worry about."

He wiped his mouth. "I knew we shouldn't have gone to that restaurant last night. That money Victor spent, we could be using right now."

"It was your idea."

"Technically, it was Victor's."

"So it was his. What does it matter?"

He leaned back in his chair and caressed his stomach, reflecting for a moment. "All of this is going to keep getting worse. I'm not sure we're prepared to handle it."

"We're not alone. We're going to be all right, mistakes and all."

He looked at her repentantly. He loved how she could forgive him, though he knew that a discussion about the previous night was eventually going to happen; it had to happen. He loved how she always convinced him that the two of them, as a unit, were enough.

"How's the soup?" she asked.

"The soup's fine," he said. "It's the stale bread that's killing me."

✥✥✥ ❋ ✥✥✥

That afternoon Anabel spoke to her father. Serguey was glad to see her focus on these simpler but no less important things. For his part, he decided to not see Gimenez, not on this day. If Montalvo had been honest about Gimenez's disposition, there was not much left for Serguey to salvage. His firing was inevitable, as was losing the apartment, and it seemed to him that meeting with his now ex-mentor would only serve to expedite the process. Let Gimenez do the work, he thought. Let him be the one to come and throw us out.

Serguey wanted to speak with Anabel about the post-restaurant argument. He really did. But if they were to plunge into another argument, he might detonate, go berserk like his brother. He might say something he couldn't take back. They drifted inside the apartment like an old couple, sighing their way through dinner, and were only jolted back to mindfulness when Victor called in the evening.

Claudia wanted to meet in two days, he said. As before, she preferred to do it early in the morning, though in this occasion she had picked El Malecon, near The National Hotel. Serguey recommended for Victor to join him on the way to her. The apartment had become too compromised. He didn't want to fall down a rabbit hole of paranoia, but it was difficult to ignore their recent incident. No need for State Security to have them cooped up in the same place they'd been detained.

Serguey recognized that the stifling sensation he had begun to experience—the fear that stepping outside his building put him at risk—was perhaps the most effective method the authorities could use against him. There were only two ways to get rid of that sensation: collaborate with Montalvo or leave the island.

But he thought of these things only transitorily. He had less grand but more pressing matters to tackle. His father-in-law had given Anabel a few contacts in the city where they could procure food at a reasonable price. They spent the next twenty-four hours rushing all over the city. Cooking oil and soap they could still afford at the dollar stores, but not for much longer. Buying rice, beans, plantains, tomatoes, avocados, coffee, and meat dug considerably into their modest savings. The latter, which after the Special Period had been the hardest to find, they bought in San Miguel del Padron from a man who was missing part of his arm. The stitching job on his stump looked like the *morcilla* he'd hidden in the shack behind his home. He told Serguey and Anabel that in another life he'd been a butcher, deft with knives and hooks. Serguey sensed a shade of sarcasm in the man's voice, but he didn't laugh, in case he was wrong. The man went on to claim that his greatest achievement had been in carpentry: he'd given the exterior of the shack the appearance of an outhouse to evade suspicion. It was a delicate balance, Serguey thought, attracting reliable customers and fooling the Carminas of the world.

To his relief, the meat inside the rusted freezer was clean and smelled fairly fresh. Since Anabel's father vouched for each one of his contacts, they bought a few chicken leg quarters, a cut of beef, and a dozen eggs, which the man assured them were less than a week old.

Back home, Serguey advised Anabel to exhaust their ration booklet at the bodega. On the weeks when Gimenez had gifted them food or led them in the direction of someone who could, they hadn't taken full advantage of the booklet. They hadn't even gotten their share for a needy neighbor or for Alida. Victor, in contrast, had gifted Kiko's parents a *pernil*. Now he and Anabel had to scrape and hoard. Perhaps this was what spiritual people, like Toya, referred to as karma.

When visiting Antonio's contacts, he had to be particularly careful. Acquiring food from proscribed vendors was a crime against the state. The authorities could exploit any misstep, any evidence of wrongdoing—such as purchasing illegal meat—to throw him in jail. Thus, he appreciated the small things, such as the vendors being unaware of his father's political prisoner status, a fact that would surely cause them to refuse him service. If he and Anabel couldn't fend for themselves, they would become a burden upon her family. Dividing whatever they could would put a strain on their relationship, not to mention the amount of pressure they would all have to get food. That was the fate waiting to befall them: the grinding, daily quest for lunch and dinner. How would he look Antonio and Julia in their eyes? How would he face Anabel each morning with the feeling that he was a failure?

It occurred to Serguey that, in all honesty, it was no simple achievement for the government to sell the people on communism when their stomachs were growling. It took a special kind of hypocrisy and abuse of power to get away with it.

Together, they drafted a budget. The numbers looked grim, so they debated the possibility of asking Victor for help. Serguey told Anabel he'd speak to his brother after the meeting with Claudia, to gauge how much he could rely on the contacts and vendors he knew. For all his redeeming attributes, and despite his expert bragging, Victor hadn't been the smartest of delinquents.

CHAPTER 20

The colossal Hotel Nacional sat on a rocky hill, within eyeshot of the sea. Nearly a year ago, on a Sunday afternoon, Serguey had accompanied Gimenez to a café inside the hotel, a rendezvous with a mid-level Italian diplomat. He recalled the diplomat speaking so fast even some of the Spanish-sounding words got lost in translation. The man breathed heavily every few sentences. His belt and tie looked as if they were choking his sagging belly and wattle of a neck. Serguey recalled, quite fondly, not having to pay for a pastrami and cheese sandwich and a Cuban Corona beer. He laughed at a lot of bad jokes during a dessert from which he did not partake, out of respect. He recalled Gimenez being proposed an all-expenses paid business trip to Rome in exchange for a free stay at a Varadero beach resort for the diplomat's family on his following visit.

The hotel's history was fascinating. Fidel had dismantled its popular casino in 1960, and later he and Che Guevara had settled their headquarters there during the missile crisis. Prior to that, celebrities such as Frank Sinatra, Rocky Marciano, Buster Keaton, and Ernest Hemingway were among its most famous guests. Singer Nat King Cole, who'd been commissioned to perform a concert at Tropicana, wasn't allowed to stay at the hotel because of the color of his skin. A bust and jukebox had been built on site, in his honor, as a symbol of Cuba's racial tolerance post-Revolution. Serguey reckoned that in the post-Soviet world, Nat King Cole would've been permitted to pick the most extravagant room not because racial prejudice had been eradicated but because he would've brought something the Cuban government coveted more than integrity or equality: American dollars.

The bus Victor had taken arrived on schedule. He had brought with him an extra cell phone and a new calling card for Serguey. As they walked down Twenty-Third Avenue toward the seaside promenade, Serguey spoke to him briefly about the importance of remaining watchful. They couldn't be responsible for getting Claudia arrested. They scrutinized their surroundings—slow-moving cars, people loitering on the steps of some building for no apparent reason, pedestrians on the opposite sidewalk heading in the same direction they were. A sidelong glance, a pause to tie a shoe, these things had taken on a more portentous meaning. The mustached man on the bench with a row of brown-tipped avocados at his feet, he was no longer a private seller. On another day, he simply might've been trying to take advantage of an avocado shortage in the city. But today the odds that he was an informant had increased. It would explain his extortionate prices and mediocre produce.

Claudia was sitting on the promenade wall, listening to music from what had to be an MP3 player. The wind ruffled her hair, pressing it over her right ear toward her face. She'd propped the backpack against her hip, secured by her elbow. Even in her nonchalant presentation, she seemed vigilant. She'd already seen the brothers moving toward her, yet she hadn't reacted. She swayed her head slowly as if to the music. Serguey took it as a sign that it was safe to approach her. She removed one earphone while he and Victor sat next to her. Serguey gazed over Claudia's shoulder across the water. El Faro del Morro, which a few nights before had been so close and majestically illuminated, rose like a small white syringe in the distance.

"Nice place you've picked," Victor said. "Whenever I wanted to hook up with a tourist, I'd come here."

Claudia avoided eye contact. "I use the internet in the hotel to post things online."

"They let you?" Serguey asked.

"As long as I pay and don't bother anyone."

"How much do they charge?"

"It doesn't take me long. I come prepared. Everything written and saved on a flash drive."

Serguey took her sincerity and openness as a vote of confidence, though he was still curious about Claudia's source of income. Browsing the internet was not only rigorously restricted and supervised, but it was also costly, some might say unaffordable. A clever way for the regime to claim accessibility when, in truth, the vast majority of Cubans got their information by word-of-mouth, the government-run nightly news, and the cesspool communist propaganda that were the national newspapers. Serguey recalled a recent debate on the Round Table television show, in which the five men in the panel had spent the whole hour discussing the economic situation in Cyprus. That's what was considered a germane topic: the financial and commercial unraveling of a small Mediterranean nation most Cubans hadn't heard about.

"It's gotta be hard, what you do," he said to Claudia, coalescing deference and a cautious brand of curiosity. "An activist with little access to the outside world."

"I'm a journalist," she replied. "And like I said, I have my ways. You'd be surprised how much information you can circulate with a CD or flash drive." Claudia's eyes followed a police car as it drove east, away from the hotel. "But yes," she continued, "it's hard. Cuba's the country in the Western Hemisphere with the least internet access. I'm guessing at the Ministry you could sneak in here and there."

Serguey chuckled. "I was too low in the food chain for that. Most of the computers I could get to were programmed to only access national databases."

Claudia gave no response. She seemed to still be leering at the cop car.

Based on her demeanor, he thought it best to end the small talk. "So, did you get the video?"

She removed the earphones completely and shoved them into her backpack. "I did. Really brazen stuff."

"That was all Serguey," Victor said.

"It's been shown on TV stations in Miami and Madrid," Claudia said. "It's also been shared on several websites. The headlines spread like wildfire." She mimed a flashing news screen: "*Respected Cuban Theater Director Imprisoned by Cuban Government; Political Persecution of the Arts.* I think that not knowing exactly why your father was detained actually worked in our favor. People are speculating. The story's taking on a life of its own."

"Good." Serguey envisioned himself being shown on television and computer screens, and he sensed a certain disquieting lightness—as if he hadn't been that person, as if the Serguey who recorded the video was a separate entity that had subsequently found a way out of his skin.

A shiny, vintage yellow Pontiac convertible skirted the hotel and curved in the same direction as the police cruiser. The stylishly gleaming vehicle sped down El Malecon, anachronous to its stony, granular, ramshackle backdrop. A tourist family of three—wearing sunglasses and dangling arms out the door— was being driven by a paunchy, brown-skinned man. Mother and daughter were sitting in the back, holding on to their floppy hats with their free hand. Miniature Cuban and Canadian flags, like cut-up streamers, flailed just above the rearview mirrors. This early in the morning, they were probably on their way to Santa Maria or Varadero Beach.

Claudia followed the Pontiac until it blended into distant traffic. "People outside the island aren't blind to what's happening here. They see what we write and share, often in real time."

Serguey looked back at the hotel. "Too bad it isn't the same here."

"Have you heard of Twitter?"

He had, but he wasn't sure what it was exactly or how it worked.

She made a small screen out of her left hand, pointing at it with the other. "You can post these short messages for the people who follow you. Supposedly, you need the internet, but you can send a message from your phone with your password, and the message posts to your account. You can do it through phone calls too. They cost a dollar, and you can't read the responses to your post, but you can let people know what's happening right away."

Serguey was impressed, though he appreciated Claudia's explanation solely in theory. Impulsively, he said, "I don't think we can hope for real change until Cubans here can see and interact with all of that information." This was as sweeping and specific a statement, sans the video, as he'd ever made about his own country. He felt secure enough in his words to stare at Claudia and absorb a pinch of emancipation from her agreement.

"That's the next challenge," she said. "Here, the government can stay mum if they want. They can scare people into believing that their best friend is a traitor, or a theater director a dissident."

Serguey nodded, narrowing his eyes. "I do wish more people would stand up for my dad."

"Some of your father's colleagues published a letter," she said spiritedly. "I was going to print it for you, but I didn't get a chance."

"Really?" Serguey felt a flutter of delight. He hadn't expected this. "A couple of them came by my place after my dad got arrested. I wasn't sure if I could trust them." It was uplifting to have his suspicions disproved. Perhaps there was more humanity and mettle in his father's circle than there'd been in Parra and his peers at the National Council for the Performing Arts.

"Well, all I can say is not everyone's willing to expose their skin like that."

Serguey realized that Claudia was very skilled at layering her information, stacking it like building blocks.

"The letter has been released on a few independent news sites abroad," she said. "They're not talking about it here for obvious reasons, but it's out there."

"Have you gotten any responses to the video?" Victor asked.

Claudia planted her palms on the seawall's jagged concrete. "I've gotten some interview requests. I can put you in touch with people, if you want."

"If you think it'll make a difference," Serguey said.

She canted forward and smiled at him. "Actually, what I'm trying to say is that you can afford to see how what we've done plays out. Your father's connections will count for something. If you do the interviews, State Security might go after you too."

"They already did."

Claudia's eyes widened.

Victor said, "We got detained and beat up pretty good."

With a slight torsion of her lips, she stammered into a whisper: "What did they say?"

"That our dad was involved with an international organization." There was brash skepticism in the tone of Victor's response. He seemed to be questioning why she didn't have this information herself.

She was unruffled by his challenge. "Liberty Now."

Serguey blurted out, surprised, "How did you know?"

She took a deep breath, as if gathering strength to reply. This was her final building block, though it seemed like it could undo what the meeting had thus far accomplished: give Serguey substantial reason to hope. "I heard they funded some of Felipe's plays in exchange for contacts, but that he wasn't directly involved with them. That's why I wanted to meet again, and well, to tell you about the video and the letter."

"What contacts?" Victor asked, his inflection like a rising tremor. He wanted no more compartmentalized details.

She fidgeted with the zipper sliders of her backpack. Victor had put her on the defensive, but Serguey's interest in her answer dwarfed his urge to intervene.

"People willing to make public statements," she said tenaciously, her chest suddenly swelling, "to write articles about the current situation in the arts. The kind of inside stuff that can give the Minister of Culture and Raul headaches."

"Yes, but how do you know about Liberty Now?" Serguey said.

"I have sources."

He could see in her reserved, indefatigable expression that she wouldn't tender any more specifics.

"Liberty Now's pretty passive compared to other organizations," she added, "but I guess State Security doesn't want to take any chances."

"So you were right," Victor said. "Dad just accepted some money for his plays, and that's why they're fucking with him. That's why he's a mercenary."

The tide behind Claudia had retreated below the rocks. Mangled cartons and bent cans floated and bobbed in the confining space of a puddle. Serguey had witnessed both old men and children with hem-ripped shorts straddle the coastline, emptying cans and bottles of saltwater and hoarding them inside a bag. Would it all have been different if he and Victor had grown up in another neighborhood, with another father? Would this have been their playground?

"I've seen them go after people for a lot less," Claudia said. "Sometimes they want to send a message. Sometimes they want to break up links, or land a bigger fish. When the Pope visited in '98, they scooped up the opposition and kept them in jail until the Pope left. People have gone to prison for owning the wrong books. All the bloggers I know have been arrested multiple times. Things don't have to make sense. It's all about not loosening their grip on the rope too much."

"Have you heard anything about a trial?" Serguey asked, afraid of the answer.

"Not yet."

"If there's a trial, then I'd definitely like to do the interviews."

"That's fine. Just keep in mind that by now, they must know I've been reporting on Felipe's situation. If there's going to be a trial, they might pick me up until it's all over. That way I can't report what's happening."

It should have been obvious, but he hadn't consciously thought about the magnitude of what Claudia was risking. He waited a moment, then tried to infuse enough honesty into his look to make sure she wasn't offended at his question: "Could someone else do it?"

"If I get detained, it'll become news, believe me. My friends will know it's in relation to your father's case."

"They might arrest *us* again," Victor said.

"If they're asking you guys questions, it means they don't have what they want. That might not be good for you, but it could be good for Felipe."

"They don't have enough proof," Serguey said. "I could tell right away."

Claudia nodded slowly. "I'm sorry that they beat you."

Victor slapped Serguey on the shoulder. "He took it like a champ."

Never a missed opportunity, Serguey thought, for his brother to show off. "Can you find out more about what happened between Liberty Now and my dad?"

"Not without getting in some serious trouble." She hooked her arms inside the straps of the backpack, wearing it like a vest. "Think of me more as a reporter than an investigative journalist. In your case, I made an exception because of our mutual friend."

"I didn't mean to pressure you or imply—"

She shook her head dismissively. "It's fine. Have you located Mario? The police haven't."

"Not yet," Victor said, his lips warping as if he were chewing something bitter.

"If you get to him before they do, maybe he can tell you more. That's if he hasn't left the country."

Serguey fetched a button-sized rock from a crevice on the seawall and chucked it at the water, watching it sink. "He probably has."

Claudia enfolded the bulging bag as if it were an extension of her abdomen. She looked to Serguey like a student from his high school days. Why such a young person could imperil her own safety for the sake of sharing information was a mystery to him. He wondered if she'd lost someone, if a relative or friend had been incarcerated. Motives were never transparent, not in Cuba, especially for those who took a vehement position for or against the government. In this instance, Serguey had trusted her blindly because he trusted Kiko. As he examined her words and demeanor—the narrow sample of interaction they'd had— he was left with the impression that she was someone who'd found her calling. Her aptitude matched her work. She could be a voice for newer generations, even if those generations had no idea who she was. She would always be more popular outside of Cuba, where people were allowed to freely read her reports, to access what was absent inside the island: newspapers and magazines with varying agendas and points of view. The available literature, as she'd pointed out, had been regulated for decades.

Serguey pondered how his father—an intellectual and sensible man—had not only lived with these truths but been affected by them in his core. If Serguey himself had been an artist, a creator, how would he have dealt with censorship and ideological incongruences from a government bent on squashing anyone at the first sign of dissent? Would he have joined in some kind of fight? Would he have spoken out and accepted contributions from Liberty Now? He would never know. He was not Felipe. But he was here speaking with Claudia, intent—now more than ever—on locating Mario. He'd been arrested and assaulted. He was a story, a piece of evidence, just like his father, in the condemnation of the state.

"I'll comb through the requests for interviews," Claudia said. "If any seem worth doing, I'll let you know. In the meantime, I'll try to get concrete information on your father's status abroad and keep an ear out for a response from the government."

Serguey expressed his gratitude.

Claudia dismissed it with an understated flapping of her hair. "If you find Mario, let Kiko know. It's better if we continue to communicate through him."

"You don't exist," Serguey said.

She smiled and kissed him on the cheek. Victor turned toward her, and she kissed him too. "See you, boys," she said, not bothering to attach the backpack more comfortably on her body. She hurried across the avenue toward the entrance to the hotel.

☙❧

It sounded like the frantic, discordant tapping of *timbales*. Ringing bicycle bells and the indistinct cacophony of human shouts convoyed the rambunctious music. Though he had no reason to think it, the first association Serguey's mind made was riots, protests, unrest. But the metallic *rat-tin-tan* was approaching at an alarming speed. It couldn't be on foot. Suddenly, a small, peculiar parade materialized. A red Jawa motorcycle led the procession. A balding man with a waist pack fastened to his belt stood on the motorcycle's sidecar. He was snapping photographs of the scene behind him, his knees buoyed on the sidecar's backrest. A few meters from the vehicle, just out of the smoke's reach, a black man dressed in a white suit commandeered a bicycle, the handlebars shaking in spurts. He wore a matching headscarf, a bulk of exquisite dreadlocks jutting from its arrowhead-folded rear. A resplendently attractive woman in a modest wedding dress sat on the carrier. Her legs were on the same side, the bottom of her dress draped over one arm so that it wouldn't jam the spokes. Numerous strings flung like appendages from the carrier to the ground, dragging a loud assortment of sundry-colored cans. Four additional cyclists encircled the cans, ringing their bells and waving at those who stopped to watch the curious celebration.

"Only in Cuba," Victor said, grinning.

Though Serguey doubted his brother was right, the picture did seem surreal, exclusively Cuban somehow, more genuine than tourists riding around in vintage vehicles.

The festivity took a few minutes to recede from their gaze toward the water. Victor stopped at a greasy cart to get a pizza. The vendor's sign read: *queso y jamón — $7*. The words *y Jamón* had been crossed out. The brothers were in on the ruse. The vendor never had ham; he just wanted to give the illusion that sometimes he did. Victor folded his pizza—a round, spongy, rim-charred breading with bubbling cheese that solidified too quickly—and presented it to Serguey.

"No, thanks," he said. It was nothing like the one carried by the boy who'd banged into Alida the night of the play, the kind Gimenez would have treated him and Anabel to.

As they returned to the apartment, they spoke about Serguey and Anabel's food situation. Victor was more than happy to help in any way he could. He revealed how much money he'd saved with the same swagger he disclosed other details of his life. The amount impressed Serguey. For every time his brother had been detained, it seemed, he'd gotten away plenty with bigger deals. A clever delinquent after all.

"I'm giving the money to Anabel," Victor said. "It's not that I don't trust you, but if I had a wife, I'd give it to her."

His brother also convinced him that his contacts were reliable. His arrests were the result of excessive ambition, he said, always wanting to make an extra buck. The people he'd been involved with were trustworthy.

Victor bit into his pizza with childish abandon. Like the wedding procession, Serguey found this sight—an insolent, rakish, fickle young man with pizza sauce slobbered on his chin—a truer representation of Havana than what was sold to the world. He put out his hand with a knowing frown.

"Have at it," his brother said, giving him what remained of the pizza.

⁂

At home, they found the living room and kitchen empty. Serguey searched for a note from Anabel but didn't find one. Then he realized the bedroom door was closed. Anabel was sitting against the headboard, her nose chafed, her eyes flaring with the red-tinged glow of a recent cry. Serguey felt a manic pulse at the base of his throat, irrationally believing that Anabel's condition was somehow related to Alida. He signaled for Victor, who was standing by the entrance to the bedroom, to go down the hall, to the balcony.

He sat by his wife's feet, afraid to ask her the obvious.

"I'm never trusting anyone again," she said, her voice fracturing, yet subtly charged with rage. "We can't be this fucking stupid. We can't."

Now he had to ask. "What happened?"

"Gimenez left ten minutes ago."

"He was here?"

"It's like he knows when you leave."

A surge of anger rose up in Serguey. "What did he do?"

She sniffed and dabbed her nostrils with a handkerchief. "He charged in here and called me a 'weasel.' He said it was all my fault because I'd manipulated you, that I'd taken advantage of him to get a house and a cushy life. He said I was the worst kind of woman, and that we had seventy-two hours to leave the apartment or he'll come with the police. I swear on my own mother, Serguey, I wanted to break that Chinese vase he left us on his head."

Serguey slid toward her, his breathing intensifying. "I'm sorry."

"He said that if you were a real man and we had any self-respect, we would've left this place already, and that with your dad and your brother, it was a miracle you weren't in prison. I told him to get the fuck out of *my* house. The son of a bitch smiled and said, 'There's a misconception.' I told him that I could tell why his sister had left him, why he didn't have a wife. He didn't like it, because he walked right out, saying you can find him at the Ministry."

Even as his head started to cloud and his body jumped from the bed, part of him understood that this situation had been coming; they had stretched it well past its sustainable point. Gimenez was holding all the cards.

Serguey grabbed Anabel's keys and his own.

"Let that asshole have it," she urged him on.

"Where are you going?" Victor said from the balcony when he saw him at the front door.

"I'll be back soon," Serguey said. "Stay with her, please."

He didn't give his brother a chance to respond. The instant he locked the door, he saw Carmina open hers. Her face was squashed into a scowl.

"Serguey, we need to speak," she said, blocking the corridor.

"Fuck off, Carmina." He squeezed past her.

"I'm going to report you!" she said, wagging her finger.

He paused on the top step, his right hand clinching the rail. "You know what you are?" He started to approach her. "You're a rat, feeding on the crumbs they throw your way. You ever wonder why your family only comes to see you once a year? Why your oldest son left on a raft without telling you and never called you again? Oh yeah, I know about that."

Carmina struggled to remain stoic. "You know nothing of my son!"

"Do you think you're the only one who snoops around? If you want to report me, go ahead. Keep track of your little numbers, of the neighborhood watch, of who's coming in and out of the building, and keep hoping to get a rice cooker out of it. Because that's what your life is worth. The government you so devotedly serve made you a bottom-feeder, and you gladly accepted the role."

She arched her chest and head toward him, her mouth tensed, the bottom frame of her eyes overloaded with tears. "What about you? Don't you work for the Ministry? Didn't you sell out like everyone else?"

The evidence of his own hypocrisy didn't deter him. "You aren't fooling anyone, Carmina. We all know who you really are, you old, bitter bitch."

"Coward! Counterrevolutionary! Traitor!"

Her screams, reverberating and chasing him down the stairs, sounded to him like a glorious, symphonic march.

Chapter 21

He made a pit stop at a corner café, two blocks from his apartment building. He had passed by it every day on his way to the Ministry. He never stopped for a coffee on account of the old men standing by the service window—a permanent fixture at the place. He had been tempted by their conversations, which consisted mostly of baseball games from the previous night or news of European soccer. But he had timed his eight-block trek to the office within a five-minute window, which didn't leave much for banter, and nothing could make a Cuban man late for something like discussing sports.

As for coffee, Anabel usually had it ready by the time he came out of the bathroom.

Today, however, there was no hurry. Serguey didn't want to appear distraught, to give Gimenez the pleasure of witnessing his explosive anger—his desperation—at the Ministry, a place where Gimenez's minions could protect him from an unhinged, vindictive protégé. At the bottom of the contract he'd signed upon being hired, in laughably small letters, he'd read a statement similar to the one included in legally binding documents between employees and socialist companies: "It is prohibited to criticize or contradict company directors or the country's leaders." How glad he was to have been freed, if only symbolically, of such nonsense.

He ordered a cup and eavesdropped on the old men. Two of them were arguing Pelé's and Maradona's all-time ranking.

"Who got more World Cups than Pelé?" one of the men asked defiantly. "Fifty-eight, sixty-two, and seventy." As he uttered each year, he repeatedly looped his right arm over his left and opened his hand, as if showing a card from a deck. "The only reason he didn't win in sixty-six is that they kicked him into oblivion.

In the game against Portugal, the Portuguese got away with a red card. Pelé was out there limping all game like a lame chicken."

"Why didn't they take him out?" asked a bald man sitting on a milk crate.

"Wasn't allowed back then. Nowadays you get a bruise, they take you out on a stretcher."

"I'd have to say Maradona," Serguey said. "Best goal in World Cup history, and no one can pass like he did."

"What do you know, young man?" the Pelé advocate said. "Were you even alive when Maradona was playing?"

Serguey took a sip of coffee. It burned the tip of his lip. He pretended it hadn't. "I saw him get robbed in Italy."

"How old were you then?"

"Old enough to remember."

"You mean against Germany? Argentina didn't get robbed. Besides, Maradona spent half his playing life doing drugs."

"Not sure that's true," the bald man balked.

Serguey drank the coffee in one gulp, the heat overtaking the taste as it washed over his tongue and down his throat. He placed the cup on the service counter and said, "It doesn't matter, anyway. When Lionel Messi is done, he's going to be the best ever."

His comment drew a raucous response from the men. They flung their hands in the air, wobbled their heads, and cackled. The one sitting on the milk crate jumped up and shouted, "That's what I've been telling you! That boy's a speed demon, ball attached to his feet!"

"He's in Barcelona," the other said. "Talk to me when he transfers to Real Madrid."

Serguey contemplated if this would be his future: milling around with other retired men, disputing inane anecdotes and facts, pitting them against each other for the sake of entertainment and puerile pride. They were still going at it as he crossed the street into the next block. He'd been seeking a distraction, something different, trivial. He wanted his mind clear in order to face Gimenez. If not the conversation, the coffee had certainly done it. His tongue felt swollen and tender. He kept breathing through his mouth, hoping his thoughts wouldn't stray back to what awaited him at the Ministry. He watched the familiar streets and buildings. When he turned onto Linea, he concentrated on the sound of transient cars. He had wished at one point that the trip to Sweden could yield a vehicle for himself after he and Anabel had returned. The Ministry could have assigned him one. Even if he'd had to share it, he would have been more than pleased. He could have taken Anabel and Alida to the beach himself. He could have picked up his father and Victor and taken them out to lunch.

Though these things now seemed less important, there was a dreadful feeling in relinquishing the opportunity for such future rewards. There had been a cost for doing the right thing, and it had been high.

He turned left on Avenida de los Presidentes and marched past the Ministry's Protocol Building on Fifth Avenue. To his right, he could see the cul-de-sac split by a receptionist's stall, culminating at the rear in a heavily guarded fence. Here, through that fence, Fidel and his advisers usually entered the complex. Minutes later, he arrived at the five-story Main Building on Third Avenue. He tapped his employee card at the door to gain access and was surprised to find that it still worked. Gimenez probably wanted him to return it in person. He saluted the receptionist and noticed that the base of the front desk had been polished: the Cuban flag, coat of arms, and the Ministry of Foreign Affairs plaque were starkly reflected on its golden surface. He rode an elevator to the third floor, which housed specialists and assistant directors to the Chief Legal Executive. He veered left at the end of a long hall and bypassed Gimenez's secretary, Leticia, with a nod and a "good morning." He knocked on the door to Gimenez's office, rapping his knuckles below his boss's name and title.

"Gimenez is in a meeting," Leticia said, her pleasant tone an indication that she was unaware of the situation. She had chased after him just to be polite. A pair of blue hair clips bit into her close-cropped hair. Serguey considered complimenting her on them, but she'd never fall for it. "I'm not supposed to tell you this," she continued, "but I think they're discussing the first round of embassy assignments."

She was either really unaware or proficiently merciless. "Where is he exactly?"

"Conference room upstairs. Should be done soon."

"Can I wait in here?"

Leticia opened the door. "Go right ahead."

Serguey sat staring at Gimenez's desk, at the crystal paperweight, the Polynesian statue (or was it Peruvian?), the adjustable lamp. He knew that in the second drawer from the bottom, next to a stack of letters clutched by rubber bands, was a brown case garnished by a red-laced bow—a gift from a woman whose story Gimenez hadn't divulged in detail. Inside that case was a silver-trimmed, black fountain pen. Gimenez planned to sign his contract as Chief Legal Executive with that pen, when his long-desired promotion was finally bestowed on him. He had saved a bottle of Scotch and assured his staff that he wouldn't forget about them. Serguey wondered about the woman. Was she from another country? Had Gimenez made her up? Were the letters from her? And why a pen? As he pondered these questions, he almost smiled to himself, conceding that mystique was an important element in Gimenez's game.

Outside, the purple-speckled windows of the Administrative and International Relations Building glinted in the sun. Serguey could see how a person beholding the world each and every day from this place could lose perspective. How the leather chairs, the computer monitors, the glass exterior, and the insinuation of freedom carried by the breeze from El Malecon could unleash an interminable bout of delusion.

"What few want to admit is that men in suits make the world go 'round," Gimenez had said once. "How do you think we've been able to keep this whole communist mess afloat?"

"Men in suits?" Serguey had numbly answered.

"Communism, capitalism, they're just titles. The trick for us, of course, is to sell what we have a little bit more adamantly, especially to ourselves. In this country, what you say is a huge part of what you are. You say the right things long enough, you might get to do what others can't."

"You're saying we have to be hypocrites."

"Not hypocrites. Realists. There's a difference."

Serguey didn't care for semantics. He didn't care for the morality of it, either. That's what the apartment and the prospect of travel were for—to do away with moral questions. "Satisfied stomach, satisfied heart" was the common expression. His own father's life work was about morality, about dissatisfaction. One went to prison for that.

He did have to disagree with Gimenez on one thing: what you say is what you are. Felipe hadn't said the wrong things, not publically, and he was still taken in. Serguey himself had played by the rules for so long. He'd been on the cusp of substantial rewards, and yet here he was, unable to salvage that future.

He heard the door handle turn behind him. Gimenez stepped in and squeezed his shoulder.

"I figured you'd be here by now."

Serguey watched him take a seat at the desk.

"You want something to drink?" Gimenez asked, almost compelling Serguey to laugh. He took out a bottle of cognac, just like the one at his home, and two glasses from the bottom drawer. Serguey knew about those too, and the cigar box at the back of the drawer.

"No. I—"

"I'm going to level with you." Gimenez poured the drink into both glasses. "You want to know why I betrayed you, why you're fired, why I'm kicking you out of the apartment, if I work for State Security." He gently pushed one glass to the edge of his desk. "You want honesty, and that's what I'm going to give you. I'm not State Security, though yes, I spoke with them and told them you'd been aloof, acting a little strange. I had to."

"You had to."

"As for your being fired, I tried making a case for you. I really did."

Serguey stared at his glass. "I don't care."

Gimenez undid the top button of his shirt and drank his cognac. "You were here on a contract. You were not a permanent part of the staff. That was a tenuous position to begin with."

Serguey chuckled and scornfully bobbled his head.

"You were here because I brought you in," Gimenez continued, "because I was trying to give you an opportunity to show these people what you could do."

"And I was grateful."

"I know you were, but that's not the point." Gimenez poured more cognac for himself and raised the bottom of the bottle toward Serguey's glass, encouraging him to drink. Serguey didn't move. "The boys on the fifth floor told the boys upstairs about your father. They asked me to terminate your contract. They said you're not worth the risk." Gimenez took a sip and stared at Serguey.

Serguey took his glass and cradled it in his hands. "What did you tell them?"

There was tension in the veins of Gimenez's forehead, in the flaps of skin pulling at his jaw as he elevated his chin. "What would you have told them if you were in my position?"

"Definitely not what you did."

"I told them that you were willing to sign a letter denouncing your father as a counterrevolutionary, stating that you also have nothing to do with your brother. Then, you were going to have a meeting with the director and personally share your story with him. There would've been a couple of State Security agents present to record it. They might've tailed you for a few days, just to make sure you were not meeting with anyone. Think of it as a vetting process."

"And if I didn't do those things?"

"State Security would have a field day with you."

"They already did."

His boss dumped more alcohol into his own glass, stalling. "I'm sorry to hear that. I really am."

"Why didn't you tell me the letter was an option?"

"Would you have done it?"

Serguey drank his cognac. It burned his already sensitive throat.

"I couldn't attach my name to yours. Put yourself in my position. Even now, by letting you walk in here, I'm blindly trusting that you have nothing to do with your old man's problems."

Serguey extended his arm toward Gimenez, spilling some alcohol. "Maybe you're wearing a wire."

"No. I'm just trusting that you're the same person I brought in here the first day. Had you played your cards right, you might've gotten an assignment in a year. That's if they had found your story convincing. It wouldn't have been Sweden, but you could've gotten there. To the Serguey *I* know, this whole thing should've been nothing but a hiccup, a stepping stone. But they say you dug deep for your father. Your name became marred, and in that case so could mine."

"God forbid."

"Listen kid, I love you and Anabel, but I've worked my ass off to get to where I am. If you were going to fuck me over, you should've told me, because I promise you that I can fuck you right back."

"Like you did your previous protégés? You've already done that. Montalvo sends his regards, by the way. Anabel too."

Gimenez grabbed the armrests of his chair. "You're being childish, Serguey. And I won't apologize for what I told Anabel. Don't mistake my generosity for weakness. You weren't in this for the long haul. You got sentimental on me."

"Sentimental?"

"With your mind and personality, you could've gone far."

Serguey slammed his glass on the desk. "It's my family we're talking about!"

"Your father's in theater, right? Ever read the Greeks? Shakespeare? Family means shit. They always ruin you."

"This from the man who said he'd gotten here because of family."

"Because of my family *name*. I might've left that out. Who knows, maybe you got your father's artistic spirit. Maybe his rebellious nature runs through your veins. That's what State Security was worried about."

Serguey considered seizing the glass, flinging it the way Victor had thrown the bottle from the balcony. Instead, he stood calmly and walked to the window.

From this viewpoint, the city was largely neat and charming, with traces of modernity: painted concrete, rows of giant flagpoles, shiny glass windows. The snow globe effect, as someone had described the life of the Cuban bourgeoisie, a life that'd been proclaimed as extinct. To Serguey, it was clearer than ever that the world was nothing more than a tug of war between classes, the deprived being allowed insignificant victories—the false sense that unity, hard work, and integrity could counteract the political and economic systems of an oppressing force. This game had been going on not for decades but for ages. Not just in Cuba but everywhere. It'd been going on between him and Gimenez.

"I never wanted this," he said.

Gimenez's unbuttoned shirt exposed the white hem of a tank top. His ironed pants fell straight to his smart shoes. He was collected, orderly, with just a touch of informality. But the lines converging on his mouth—exposing a lifetime without sufficient laughter, without sufficient love—they didn't lie. The wry smile, the protruding belly, the strange neatness of his person, devoid of a woman's presence and energy, of children: Gimenez was a lonely man. For a second, Serguey found himself gazing at his own father, at a parallel world in which Felipe was an experienced prosecutor and Assistant Legal Director at the Ministry of Foreign Relations. A man dedicated to his work, his vision, his personal goals. Serguey found himself gazing at the driven men he'd adamantly believed he should become.

"I wanted none of this," he said again.

Gimenez edged his chair toward him. "It won't bring you peace of mind, lying to yourself like that."

"I don't know. I feel unburdened. It takes a lot out of a man to be two-faced."

Gimenez wet his lips with his drink, then sucked them against his teeth. "All the worries you have, I don't. The petty musings and preoccupations of the lesser man, one could say. The only way you'll travel outside this country now is to leave it for good. Me? I've seen a lot of the world. I've dined in fine restaurants, driven nice cars, met exotic women." He paused, took a deliberate sip, and raised his glass. "And this is as warm a companion as any."

"That's all fleeting," Serguey said, "all distractions. When your head hits the pillow, that's what counts."

"If you want to be a philosopher, go ahead. If you want to believe that this is all a fantasy, that we take none of it when we die, that it's unfulfilling and superficial, be my guest. If you want to believe I'm unhappy because it softens the blow, I won't stop you. But the moment you walk out that door, you don't know where you're going to wake up tomorrow. You're a suspected dissident, the son of a political prisoner. Your life here's over. Meanwhile, I'll still be drinking my cognac."

The words slid off Serguey like warm water. The old man was hurt, wounded enough to become acerbic. There was pleasure for Serguey in this paltry battle of "who's got it better?"

"They let you off the hook upstairs?" he asked tauntingly. "Because I have to tell you, if I made you look bad in any way, if I made them question your recruiting skills, that would make my day."

Gimenez twisted the corner of his mouth into a gawky smile. "They took me off the Stockholm assignment. That hurt a little. I had to sign a statement denouncing you. Like I told Anabel, you have seventy-two hours to leave my apartment, so we can sever all connections."

"Okay, so I'm a stain on your record. Not enough retribution for having me and my brother physically abused, but I'll take it."

Gimenez scoffed. "*You* got yourself and your brother physically abused. As for me," he showed the number with his fingers, "three months of travel restrictions. After that, I'm going to Peru. Just need to clear an advisory board evaluation. I've never been to Lima, so I'm looking forward to it. By this time next year, I'll be back in Europe. Where do you think your father will be? What about you and Anabel? Your lowlife brother?"

"Anabel and I will be rid of you, so that's a start." Serguey fished the keys and employee card from his pocket and lobbed them at Gimenez, who failed to catch them. "State Security is going to interrogate me again. They're still looking for names. I think yours is as good as any."

"They'll never believe you."

"It'll get them thinking."

"Ah Serguey, you have no idea who I am."

"You're a man with no empathy, a hypocrite."

"I'm a survivor."

Serguey remained equable as he spoke. "You're a hyena to the lions. When this whole system crumbles, and it will, you'll be dragged through the streets with most of your friends. There are plenty of people out there itching to get their hands on you. But until then, I'm going to be that fishbone you can't get out from between your teeth, deep enough in your gum to drive you crazy."

"I picked you for your guts, Serguey. Turns out you were weak. Don't forget I was a prosecutor. Empty threats don't scare me."

Serguey distanced himself from the window. "Anabel was right. It's easy to see why your sister left."

Gimenez pouted his lips. "She let her husband ruin her life, like you're doing with Anabel. You two should take whatever you need from the apartment. God knows you can use it more than me."

"That was your mistake from the beginning. We didn't need you. We used you. We took advantage. You wanted to adopt two young people, so we played the role. Anabel always found you repugnant."

Gimenez forced a laugh.

"You're a relic," Serguey continued, "a limp-dicked geezer. No one will remember you or put flowers on your tombstone. If you're okay with that, then you're the weakest man I've ever known."

Gimenez stirred his glass and glared at Serguey. "I think it's time you get out of my office."

Serguey didn't move. "When I was a kid, my dad used to sit around with his friends and make fun of people like you. You were a punch line to them."

"And where are they now?" Gimenez put his glass down and stood. "Where the fuck is your father now?"

"You're a lawyer, Roberto, which in this country really means you're a clerk, an ass-kisser. Like I pretended to be for you. You whore yourself to those fat Italian diplomats like a *jinetera*."

Gimenez's face flushed. He stepped to the door and opened it. "Seventy-two hours."

Serguey took his time. "You should check on the apartment tonight if you don't want to lose your stuff. We have no way to lock the place, and the next door neighbor is the curious type."

He walked out of the office, bypassing everyone in his way. Though he hadn't sensed any friction or unease when he had walked in, he now felt like an outcast, a thing to be derided and omitted. No one, he realized, would miss him. What exactly had been his function? What could he say he'd really accomplished during his time here? Leticia didn't call after him. Neither did the other assistants. He had no allies at the Ministry, no compatriots in his struggle. They were probably glad—and if they didn't yet know about his situation, they would be—that Gimenez's mutt had been whipped and banished.

He glanced at the Ministry's logo before he reached the doors and felt sick, a stranger in his own clothes. Once outside, he untucked his shirt like a child leaving school. He wanted the sun to comfort him, the air to give him a modicum of freedom. As he made to cross the street, a silver VW with tinted windows pulled out of the Ministry parking lot and rolled by. A pallid arm extended from the backseat and ditched a cigarette butt in Serguey's general direction. It skidded on the asphalt and rebounded off the curb, close to his feet. He construed it as an act of aggression, though he had no idea who was inside the car. He quickened his pace, as if he could catch up to the vehicle, and began to head home faster than he'd come to the office.

The old men were still outside the café. This time they were debating Kasparov and Karpov.

"What about Bobby Fisher?" Serguey heard the bald man on the milk crate ask.

He kept on, shallow bursts of breath fueling his hurried steps. It wasn't panic gripping his lungs. It was impulse, a bucking will, as if the burning of his muscles would actually lead him somewhere. He hustled under the intermittent shade of banyan trees, their sinewy tentacles excavating like snakes into dry ground. Moving swathes of sunlight shocked his eyes like a flashing projector. In El Vedado, nature prevailed more audaciously than in the gritty entrails of the city. Here, trees canopied your daily commute, brown-spined roots allowed you to keep your feet dry after a puddling rain. At the most impressive homes, clipped bushes served as front yard decoration—a barrier between the fortune inside and the outside world.

Serguey had strolled by here many times. The houses and buildings, for all their patchy decline, were often brought to life by upkeep and size. A few modern residences battled for attention with their ornate window grates, an effective combination of protection and elegance. Some had a resplendent color, it didn't matter which—blue, yellow, pink—accentuating the baroque columns fringing the entrances. He and Anabel made a game out of imagining who lived in these impressive homes. She preferred to think that it was people like them: young, determined, lucky. Serguey believed them to be of higher standing, amply experienced, years of proper work and enviable connections boosting them forward. A number of these houses bore an arrow-shaped sign next to the door, specifying that they accommodated tourists willing to conduct cash-only transactions. As he raced by them now, he wanted to mock himself. How selective their minds had been. He'd seen rowdy children in the streets, running in packs after egging a porch. He'd seen stray dogs, splotchy and starved, neck-deep in garbage cans, growling and gnawing at each other over ant-coated bones. He'd heard the old men with nothing but coffee in their stomachs debate who and what was best in the world, a world none of them would ever get to experience. El Vedado was not impervious to poverty. As Victor had said, it'd gotten bad everywhere. But this neighborhood offered glimpses of something more, something desirable, and that's what they chose to see, to imagine. Serguey realized that the stories in this neighborhood didn't belong to him, just as he hadn't really been a part of the Ministry. Maybe it was better that way, better for Anabel and him to have made up the stories. They could easily undo them now, disown them at a moment's exhale.

CHAPTER 22

Anabel was sitting at the kitchen table with Victor. From the living room, Serguey perceived smidgens of a conversation about Anabel's parents, something to do with their respect for privacy. He suspected that she was making a case to Victor for Serguey and her to move to her folks' home. She had no clue that he had come ready to propose the same plan, with a small caveat.

He gave her a peck on the cheek and settled next to her. By the nearly empty glasses of water in front of them, he could tell they'd had lunch.

"Your food's on the stove," Anabel said. "Victor prepared it, so brace yourself."

This was precisely why he'd married her. She had no proclivity for drama. The way she had taken care of Alida and remained even-keeled with Gimenez—through his cunning advances and offenses—Serguey could do nothing but admire her. But he needed to rid himself of his former boss's specter, like removing the bandage to a mending wound. He shared with them what he had told the old man. He underscored *limp-dicked geezer*, *relic*, and *clerk*. He was proud of the bullets he'd fired.

"You should've let me go with you," Victor said.

Anabel batted her eyes dismissively. "You don't mess with Gimenez that way. And definitely not at the Ministry."

"It's over," Serguey said. "We're done with him."

She waited for him to eat his food—an onion omelet with homemade French fries—before she dove into her proposition: they could move in with her parents, taking over her old room. They could try finding a job through the Church once Felipe's ordeal was over. "Something low-key," she said, "to avoid the authorities." She assured him that her parents would welcome their presence.

There was also the possibility of finding some kind of an occupation in the countryside, since Mantilla was not far from Mayabeque.

"I can find you some contacts out there," Victor said.

"We'll have to see," Serguey said.

His grandparents had been peasants. Maybe he had retained some of it in him; maybe he could make it work, build a new life for them. He would have to speak to Victor about the regrettable incident the day they had gone hunting for birds, as Anabel had advocated. He couldn't return to a place marred by such bad memories. It would be like inheriting Raidel's house, the site of his mother's death. Even Felipe's house, as he'd told Victor, was no longer his home.

He pressed his thumb on the tines of his fork, catapulting the handle like a see-saw. The metal clanked on his plate. "I told Gimenez we'd be out of here today."

Anabel smiled, her relief palpable. "Victor, you're helping us pack."

Victor flexed his arm. "I don't do any heavy lifting."

"You're in luck," she said. "The furniture is Roberto's."

They spent the early part of the afternoon cramming their possessions into travel cases they'd inherited from Anabel's grandparents and two large back-packs Serguey had been given at work. Victor kept checking with Anabel what belonged to Gimenez. The furniture, television, refrigerator, DVD player, most of the ornaments and decorations around the house, the silverware—it was all his. Victor insinuated that she should take a few things. It felt embarrassing to Serguey. How tragi-comical it must've been to his brother, seeing to what extent they'd been living someone else's life. Everything had been a charade, a loan, a favor from a contemptible man. Whatever possessions Victor could claim, they were truly his own. There was pride in that for a person.

Anabel combed through the apartment, looking for anything of theirs that might be left behind. They would not return, regardless of what might be lost. Victor lugged the travel cases and backpacks to the living room, piling them up to get an idea of how much they had to carry. Serguey perused his work papers—the ones State Security hadn't seized—shredding anything that could be used against him later. His briefcase, which he'd bought right out of law school, felt awfully light when he was finished. His palms had grown accustomed to the undulating shape of the handle, which fit him like a knuckleduster. He'd heard the click of the latches day after day. These rituals had provided him with a sense of grandeur, of importance. In truth, he'd been a kid playing house.

As children, whenever he and Victor pretended to be adults, Serguey was always a superior to his brother: a bodega manager and his employee, a surgeon and his assistant. Serguey had memorized military rankings to make sure Victor was always beneath him. He even learned the difference between Brigade and

Division General. But those games didn't last long. Victor grew bored quickly. He didn't enjoy fantasizing about being older as much as Serguey did. He was perfectly content with marbles and spinning tops. If he *had* to be an adult, he preferred games involving guns or swords. On the day they'd gone hunting, Victor was the one shooting the birds. Serguey just gave directions as to when and where to shoot.

As he disposed of all the torn papers, a loud banging at the front door stopped him. He impulsively shoved the papers to the bottom of the trash and slipped the briefcase under the bed. He rushed down the hall, overwhelmed with the sensation that he would no longer be able to hear a knock without expecting the worst.

Victor asked, "Who is it?"

The muffled voice outside the door said, "Alida."

Victor turned the lock, and she shambled in, dropping a hefty canvas bag by his feet. Her lips formed two small bubbles, like a child holding her breath, stifling tears. She bypassed Victor and clung to her sister's neck.

"I can't take this!"

Anabel grabbed Alida's elbows and tried, as gently as she could, to move her sister back. She cradled Alida's chin and said, "What happened?"

Alida sighed, avoiding Anabel's inquisitive eyes. "They came to the apartment and went through everything." She made as if to weep, but with the intractable aplomb of an actress, she summoned up the strength to continue. "They interrogated me and Dosiel. They said they'd already talked to the other actors in the play and demanded to know where Mario was. We kept saying we had no idea, but they wouldn't leave us alone. They asked what we knew about Felipe, if we knew we'd been working with a counterrevolutionary. We denied everything, but they didn't care. They threatened Dosiel with prison, told him that *negros* belong in the Eastern Combine or Oriente."

"What did these guys look like?" Victor asked.

Alida stammered, "I . . . I don't know. They looked like civilians."

"Was one of them fat?" Victor insisted.

She narrowed her eyes in an effort to recollect. "Maybe."

Serguey approached Alida but looked at Victor. He brought his index finger to his mouth, warning him to say no more.

"Don't worry," he said to Alida. "They're just trying to rattle you."

She corralled his body in her arms, the top of her hair brushing his Adam's apple. "What am I going to do? I can't sleep knowing they can show up any time they want."

He wanted to tell her that he empathized. He glanced at Anabel, whose grim expression he couldn't exactly read. "I think you two should go to your parents' house."

Anabel crumpled her eyebrows. "You're not coming?"

Serguey discharged himself from Alida's grasp. She went to her sister, nesting her head on Anabel's shoulder.

"I can't leave Victor by himself," he said. "Not now."

Victor said, "Are you joking?"

"These people are putting an all out offensive. If we split up and you get arrested, what then?"

"And what if they take you both?" Anabel said.

"We can watch each other's back," Serguey said. "I fucked up with my dad. I'm not doing it with my brother."

Victor remained silent. Tears fogged his eyes, his face enveloped by an implausible susceptibility. He swallowed before he spoke. "Serguey, I appreciate—"

"There's no debate," he interrupted. "I don't know if it's the best decision, but it's the right decision." He told Anabel that he wanted to be there for her and Alida, but he and Victor had to finish what they'd started. "You'll be fine with your family. Let State Security worry about me and my brother, with you and Alida out of the picture."

"Why can't we all stick together?" Alida said. It was evident in her spirited voice that she'd come with her own agenda. Before she could present it to the others, it was already disintegrating.

Anabel's face was still grim, still indecipherable. "Okay," she said, her voice a wisp of smoke. She wasn't accepting defeat, simply demonstrating loath agreement. "I can handle myself. Let's get everything out of here."

Serguey kissed her forehead, grasping at her hands. She tendered no reaction.

"Good thing you came," Victor said to Alida. "We have a lot of stuff to take."

She didn't care for Victor's crack at humor, but after a nudge from her sister she began listening to his instructions as to what she should carry.

Serguey walked assiduously to the far end of the apartment. He scanned every room, recording one final mental image of the place. There was no atmosphere of solitude or incongruity, as one often senses in emptied homes. Instead, it felt too familiar. He wanted to be repulsed, besieged by a compulsion to leave. At the very least, he wanted to be indifferent. But he could see in Anabel's eyes that it pained her to lose the apartment, that there maybe was an entrenched feeling of entitlement simmering in her. She had cleaned and cooked and fought and slept and fucked in this place. She had dreamed in it. She had been motivated and patient. Serguey revered her willingness to give it all up for the sake of his family's well-being, but it broke his heart to snatch away what for a while they called theirs, and which in Cuba they would surely not regain.

He thought of a few things to say, but nothing seemed to suffice, so he chose to take this final walk as a silent, ceremonious act.

Anabel shattered his presumptions when she said, "I understand your wanting to stay with Victor."

Perhaps she hadn't been paying attention to the apartment after all. Her pain was associated with a different kind of loss.

"If I don't follow through," he said, aware of what he had asked of her, "if I don't stick it out with Victor to the end, I'm going to regret it, like you've told me."

"I know."

This time she took his hand, and they returned to the living room together.

"This one's impervious to tragedy," Alida said to them, pointing at Victor, halfheartedly attempting a joke of her own.

The group departed from the apartment burdened by the weight of the various bags, cases, and backpacks. As they passed Carmina's front door, Serguey stopped and yelled, "We're going to miss you, Carmina!"

Almost immediately he heard a scuttling, then a faint thump, then more scuttling, like a mouse behind a wall. She still didn't dare open her door. The sound of their laden steps ebbing lower and lower was proof enough for her final report to the authorities.

They trudged out of the building to nearby Linea Avenue. They waited for one of Victor's friends, whom he had called the moment Serguey and Anabel agreed to leave the apartment. The man, nicknamed Carlitin, packed his delivery minivan with the couple's belongings. Anabel sat on Serguey's lap in the passenger seat. Alida and Victor rode in the back.

Carlitin spent the trip to Mantilla gushing about how he'd gotten away with using the minivan, which belonged to a state-sanctioned bakery, for personal errands and a side business he'd recently arranged.

"No more running around in my uncle's motorcycle," he said happily, as if everyone in the car could appreciate precisely what this meant.

Serguey stared at Carlitin—assuming him to be the mysterious man in the

Suzuki from the night of the play—and saw no mystery in his features. He was a hustler like his brother, using all the tools at his disposal.

The business, Carlitin explained, consisted of erasing boxes of bread and pastries from the books and selling them to independent restaurants, the *paladares*. His manager at the bakery was in on it, so he felt buoyant about the whole enterprise. The quality of the food was exceptional, Carlitin assured them as he would a potential customer, since the bakery delivered mainly to pre-approved tourist locations. As they neared Mantilla, he made a pitch to Victor, gloating that they were looking to expand the delivery routes.

Victor laughed off the proposal. "I'm too hot," he said. "I'm like a spark on a dynamite fuse: you set me on the wrong course, shit will blow up."

After arriving at their destination, Victor took Carlitin aside for a short chat. The two men slapped hands and bumped shoulders, animatedly nodding their heads. Carlitin began to drive off a half-minute later, saying "Good luck!" out of his window.

Prior to entering Antonio and Julia's house, the group agreed to behave as naturally as possible. The conversation was aimed at Alida, whose hands were now shaking. Victor's effort to lighten the mood at the apartment hadn't worked, not for long. She kept gnawing her nails as if playing a harmonica. Serguey asked her to say nothing specific about her experience with State Security. There was no reason to worry her parents more than necessary. She waggled her head a tad too enthusiastically for him to trust her.

Julia seemed disconcerted when she opened the door. She struggled to smile and said, "But . . . what is this?"

Anabel hugged her. "We're setting up camp."

Julia craned her neck to catch a better glimpse of the bags. "All of you?"

"They told me the food's good here," Victor said.

Julia looked at Anabel, pitifully confused.

"This is Victor," Serguey said. "My rude younger brother."

Victor gave the woman a kiss. "I was my parents' favorite, so you can understand why I'm so spoiled."

Julia laughed nervously. "Look at this one," she gestured at Alida, "spoiled with the best of them."

Alida's mellow reply was, "Hey, Mami."

They filed inside, the hefty bags forcing them to stand far apart in what was a narrow living room space. Serguey saw that poor Julia didn't know quite how to react to this abrupt siege. Her eyes darted from person to person, not sure whom to address, what to say. Serguey looked across from him at the woven three-chair back settee, the seats sunken and frayed like an inverted hat. He didn't feel confident asking everyone to sit. Antonio's chair was out of the question. Standing stiffly between the TV and the round center table, on which stood a green vase teeming with sunflowers—Julia's favorite—Serguey was confronted by the reality that invading his in-laws' household made them not only irrevocably complicit but collateral damage of his homeless misfortune.

Anabel's and Alida's *Quinceañera* portraits presided over them from the wall, perched high on either side of their bedroom door. The contours of the photographs had a dreamlike, bluish hue. The sisters' features doddered between childhood and womanhood, marking their history in this place, their attachment to those who, day after day, looked at their images with fond remembrance. He and Victor were intruders, desperate men whose roots belonged elsewhere. Out of deference, they refrained from speaking until one of the women did.

Julia finally placed her hand on Alida's neck, then her forehead. "What's going on with you? Do you have a fever?"

"She's fine," Anabel said. "We'll tell you more in a bit. Where's Dad?"

Julia was happy to change the conversation. "Limping his way through town. He's been complaining that his legs are cramping, so he wanted to stretch. He's probably arguing and cursing with the *bodeguero* about last night's game."

"I don't think I've ever heard Antonio curse," Serguey said, his stab at allaying the mood.

Julia shrugged. "Baseball does that to him. He confesses it on Sundays."

Victor said, "If I ever had to confess to a priest, I don't think he'd stay in the booth."

"It's called a confessional," Alida said, her eyelids drooping from apparent exhaustion.

Julia squeezed Victor's shoulder. "What a bragger. You should be more modest, like your brother."

Serguey raised his eyebrows and dipped his head toward Victor. Don't say anything stupid, he was trying to communicate.

Victor smiled broadly at Julia. "Yes, I should."

She told them they could put the bags in Anabel and Alida's bedroom. Serguey was taken aback by the tidiness. The piles of clothes he'd seen in previous visits were gone. The foldable closet door was shut all the way, no boxes spilling from it. White-and-green patterned crochet blankets covered the grooved and slightly slanted twin beds. Had Julia suspected they'd be returning? She began telling stories about the sisters fighting over the same toys, about Anabel hiding under the bed to clutch her sister's ankle while barking.

"I don't know how many times this poor angel came crying to me," she said of Alida, "terrified that there was a vicious dog under the bed."

"Wow, Anabel," Victor said. "You have an evil streak in you."

"She's as harmless as a little hamster," a lilting voice said.

The group turned in unison to the room's entrance. Antonio stood with a haughty grin and set gaze so undeviating that it appeared mortared on his face.

"We didn't hear you come in," Julia said.

"The next door neighbor told me he saw the youngins, so I slipped in through the back door. I wanted to see if an old limping man could still sneak up on people."

Anabel and Alida each snuggled under their father's arms. Antonio stared at Victor. "Who's this, Alida's boyfriend?"

"No," Victor said. "She won't accept my advances."

"Good for her." Antonio shook Alida gently. "I raised her right."

Serguey said, "Antonio, I think we should go to the dining room and have a talk."

His in-law's grin thinned into a pained smile. "We should."

Antonio and Julia had been expecting things to develop just as they had. They intuited that State Security would get involved beyond Felipe's case, badgering family members and friends. Antonio revealed that he'd spoken again with Father Linares. The priest warned him that even he and his wife might get a visit from the authorities.

"The good news," Antonio said, pulling up his afflicted leg and folding it over the other, "is that Felipe's situation has gotten traction abroad."

"The Father told you this?" Anabel asked.

"He said not to get your hopes up too much, because in the end it'll be up to the government. But whatever can be done, it's being done. They're in talks already. Father Linares has faith that a resolution might be near."

"I appreciate it," Serguey said. He regretted not having asked Claudia if she'd heard about the Church's participation. To believe that the wheels were in motion while being unable to actually witness it required—Serguey thought ironically of himself—more faith than Linares could ever claim to have.

They arranged for Anabel and Alida to stay. Julia said that if they all needed to move in permanently, including Victor, they could make it work. She insisted that the brothers stay for dinner.

"When life's going badly," she said, "it's best to cherish every second with loved ones. God rewards unity in times of plight."

The brothers couldn't find it in themselves to reject her invitation. It was especially difficult for Victor, who had caused an impression on Julia. She mostly directed her attention to him when she spoke, and she blushed when he told her she had a beautiful, caring family, which no doubt had to be because of her. She'd never reacted to Serguey's praises in quite the same way.

⚜ ⚜ ⚜

The sun had splayed purple-tinted rays behind a series of clouds above the horizon. Serguey, Anabel, Victor, and Alida were sitting on mangy wicker chairs in the backyard, engulfed by the darkening air of twilight. Julia was toiling in the kitchen after having refused any help. Antonio was taking a lengthy shower. It was moderately quiet here, near the edge of Mantilla. A child's overwrought screams during a game of marbles, a dog woofing and chasing after a cyclist— these were the only sounds reaching them. Antonio and Julia's next-door neighbors had owned chickens at some point. The birds occasionally stole under the fence and scoured for worms in Julia's yard. She didn't mind except for the droppings. Antonio had strategically positioned cinderblocks along the fence, deterring the chickens from passing. Eventually the birds disappeared, and now that Serguey thought of it, he'd never asked his in-laws what'd become of them.

He was happy to see Victor reclined, his eyes bolted, his legs extended and crossed at the ankles. His brother, almost supine, emitted the kind of serenity only the overly confident or utterly naïve possess. He had a switch, as if he ran on batteries, and at this instant he was recharging. Anabel had cupped Serguey's hand in hers. Alida was transfixed by the horizon—perhaps a look she hoped to one day replicate in her plays—inviting an audience into her inner world, while a part of her remained elusive. Felipe had selected her for obvious reasons. The story on Alida's face, although fascinating, wasn't complete. It made it that much more enticing.

Anabel didn't have as broad a range of emotions mapped on her countenance. What she did have was the kind of grit Serguey often lacked. And he found splendor and comfort in her fortitude. He cuddled his wife's hand and smiled to himself. She nodded slightly, not looking at him. He began concocting something to say, but Alida beat him to the punch.

"I'm more sure than ever that I'm leaving." Her eyes were wide open, as if daring the sun.

Anabel released Serguey's hand. "Don't start again."

"She's right to feel that way," Victor said. He spewed the words so delightfully, they seemed to have been bursting in his mouth like ripened fruit.

"Victor, go back to sleep," Anabel told him, a drop of venom in hers.

"We all know you like to be the master puppeteer behind the scenes."

"What the hell is that supposed to mean?"

Victor sat up straight. Serguey had a hunch that it'd go downhill from here.

"It means you like telling my brother and your sister what to do. If Alida wants to leave, let her. She's an adult. I'm out there on the streets every day, and let me tell you something, there's nothing out there for her. With my dad's problems, she's tainted. Sorry, Alida, but it's true. What happened today with State Security won't go away. Do you think she'll be able to rehearse and do shows with that on her conscience? Do you think the people she works with will just ignore that?"

"Lower your voice," Serguey said.

"What do *you* know?" Anabel said to Victor, shifting her body toward him. "You're in no position to give advice or opinions."

"Then how come you were telling me back at the apartment that you wished Serguey could be more like me?"

Anabel's features became infected with the same venom that'd been in her voice. She stared dolefully at Serguey. "That's not what I said."

Victor said, "You like manipulating people, Anabel. It's the truth."

"What's wrong with you?" Serguey asked his brother, though the real question in his mind was, what had happened during lunch while he'd been at Gimenez's?

"Nothing, I just hate it when one of you two tries to be condescending or dismissive with one of us. We may be younger, but we're not stupid. We know what we want."

"He's right," Alida said. She'd found a stronger ally, someone she could identify with. "Victor and I are emotional people, but that doesn't mean we're immature or irresponsible."

"You think he's a responsible person?" Anabel said.

"Who got us here today, huh? Who took us to the restaurant the other night?"

"We're *all* mature," Serguey said, maintaining a composed tone and spreading his arms. "We're all capable of making our own decisions. It's just instinctive for an older brother or sister to be protective, same as parents. It's a weird fucking dynamic, but we have to learn to navigate through it. If we start fighting now, then everything goes to shit. And that's the real truth. We want to act mature? We focus on what needs to be done and deal with ourselves later. There'll be plenty of time to sit around and blame each other, and that's if we're lucky. So let's relax, enjoy the food that Julia's preparing, do what we have to do, and we can talk about leaving or staying or who is what later."

"You would've made a great judge," Victor said.

Serguey glared at him. "You can be *such* an asshole."

They avoided conversation over a supper of rice, red beans, chicken thighs, and tomato salad. The scheduled blackout hit right on the dot, as Antonio liked to say, mocking the government's efficiency at ruining dinnertime. He positioned two kerosene lamps and a few candles around the table. Everyone's face, partially eclipsed, bore a devious aura. They spoke only to praise Julia's cooking. Antonio talked about how his daughters would be safe as long as he had a say in it. He went out of his way to thank Serguey and Victor for taking care of them.

"They're the ones who take care of us," Victor said, which made Anabel frown and Julia beam.

Anabel ordered a grouchy Alida to help their mother with the dishes, then led Serguey to her bedroom as Victor immersed himself in small talk with Antonio. She didn't bother to bring a light, as if the darkness of the room gave them more privacy.

"I didn't tell your brother that I hoped you could be more like him."

"It's fine." He paused, struggling to make out her features. He desperately hoped that no irreparable fracture was erupting between them. "It's always been awkward between the three of us, and maybe that's how it'll always be."

She looked down and tapped her feet. "I feel like crap."

"Me too. All this tension brings out the worst in people."

Anabel kissed him. He held her close, beseeching his mind to always remember how warm she felt against his chest.

"You make sure to call me at least once a day," she said. "If I don't hear from you for more than forty-eight hours, I'm going to assume you were arrested."

He concurred. "We'll be careful. Try to go with your parents to church on Sunday, maybe speak with Linares. We need to figure out where my dad's situation is headed, if we need to prepare for a long battle."

"Of course."

"And don't fight with your sister. Let her decide what she wants. It's not like she can leave tomorrow."

She sighed. "I can't promise anything."

"I'll take that. And no playacting as a dog under the bed."

That extracted a tender laugh out of her, which he also entreated himself to remember.

The brothers chose to take public transportation back to Santos Suarez, even if it meant not getting home for a few hours. Victor didn't want to call in any more favors in case they required them in the future. Serguey carried a cumbrous backpack with enough clothes for a handful of days. They rode on the bed of a truck, which for ten pesos took you into the city. They were bounded by a collection of swarthy, anguished faces, looking under the starless sky and frigid wind like an artist's rendition of the dead. The truck swayed and rattled, pitting bodies against jagged metal. It stopped every few kilometers, loading the bed with an interminable number of commuters, cramming the brothers within arm's reach of the cab roof.

Straining his words versus the noise and drastic quaking, Victor attempted to speak about what he'd said in the backyard, specifically about Anabel. Serguey shut him down.

"Save it for another time," he said during a stop. "Call Kiko and see if we can drop by tomorrow. I need him to give me Mario's number. And I don't want us to rely so much on Claudia. I want to see for myself what people are saying on the internet about Dad, and if any of what she said is actually true."

"So now you don't trust her?"

"It's not that. We have to be proactive. We got nothing else to lose at this point."

Victor's eyes wandered with purpose, as if seeking his own reflection. "Just the way I like it."

That night, the incongruity Serguey had experienced sleeping in his father's bed gradually dissipated. Anabel's absence made the mattress feel colder, gratuitously spacious, but otherwise he felt recognition of something regained, akin to what he'd undergone while cleaning the front of the house. Fidelio Ponce de León's absent painting watched him from the wall (he could still picture it clearly). The heft of Joaquin's photograph, also absent, hung above his head like a ghost but didn't unsettle him. Maybe if he concentrated, he could hear Irene's voice somewhere in another room. This was, after all, his childhood home. After his former boss's treachery, it was best to see the apartment as a suite at some remote hotel. Such a perspective softened the loss. If he and

Victor were to lose the house—if this were yet another price to pay for helping Felipe—Serguey would have to add it to his bag of burdens. Tonight, however, he wanted nothing beyond being enveloped by the singularity of a familiar sensation. He slept well, dreaming of Victor and Kiko working the fields at a youth labor camp. Serguey repeatedly told Victor to go home, that he was too young to be there, but Victor refused, saying he was going to sell all the tomatoes they could pick.

CHAPTER 23

Serguey woke with a warm sensation on his torso, right beneath the ribs: his skin had been exposed to sunlight breaking in through the window. He shuffled to the opposite end of the bed, cloaking his body in the much cooler shade. As he tried dozing off, he heard Victor's voice somewhere outside the bedroom. He extricated himself from slumber, arching his neck and concentrating on the words his brother was speaking. Someone replied, but he couldn't tell who it was. He scurried off the bed, rushing to put on his pants.

Victor burst into the room. "Serguey, wake up . . ."

Serguey stared at him, one pant leg in. His eyes were still brittle, his vision hazy. Morning drool stuck like filament to his mouth. Victor was shirtless, wearing only briefs.

"Who the hell's out there?" Serguey asked.

"It's Mario."

"Mario's here?"

"No, at Toya's. She came to get us."

Serguey wiped his lips and eyes. His limp ankle and foot, pinioned inside the pant leg, required a full transition into alertness to be wriggled free. "Is he alone?"

Victor was already slipping out the door. "Come on, just get ready."

As he washed his face and brushed his teeth, Serguey considered whether it was his text message that had done the trick. Or had Kiko found a way to reach the dramaturge? He tried to focus on what he should ask Mario. When a wanted man shows up at your door, his motives are what you most covet to know. Serguey could ask leading questions, then some "yes or no" ones, maybe catch him in a lie, force him to reveal something he hadn't planned. When caught lying, people went one of two ways: they poured out their hearts in search of relief or fumbled to cover it up, burying themselves in the type of hole where an attorney could sink them deeper.

The brothers walked simultaneously into the living room. Toya was sitting on the sofa, her head shrouded in a white cloth that corresponded with her dress. She stood and kissed Serguey.

"Am I glad you're here," she said. She slapped the bony palm of her right hand against Victor's robust pectorals. "I don't want any trouble at my house, you understand?"

"Serguey will do the talking."

She went for the front door ahead of them. The meeting would be on her terms. "Last week the shells told me I'd get an unexpected visitor," she said. "I thought it was going to be my cousin Estrella, the one with the goiter. She hasn't come by in two years. Then this lanky gay man shows up this morning. Good thing I'm an early riser."

"I thought you knew Mario," Victor said.

"I do. That doesn't mean I'm happy to see him."

Serguey remained vigilant on the way to Toya's, surveying the streets and porches and nooks between houses. He saw no one out of the ordinary, no strange cars. They entered the hallway to Toya's home, and he felt a bolt of fretfulness, like sudden nausea, at what Mario would have to say. He made sure to walk in front of Victor, to keep him at bay in case he snapped.

Toya stepped in and motioned the brothers to do the same. "He's in the consultation room."

Mario was standing at the far end. He was wearing gray shorts and a light blue polo shirt. His neck and forehead were sunbaked, as were his forearms. His moustache had vanished. He looked nothing like the white-suited man Serguey had met after the play. Maybe that was the point.

"So, where have you been hiding?" Victor said.

"Everybody take a seat," Toya said. She paced to the back corner of the musty room and hauled two barstools for the brothers. Serguey leaned his body on his. Victor sat with his feet braced together on the foot holder, his knees spread. His arms clamped the small space of stool in front of his crotch. His chest was heaving silently as he stared with his head sloped toward Mario. He looked like an ape creeping toward the verge of an attack—right at that instant when the animal stiffens, its gaze giving the impression of cognition, of consciously deciding when and how to strike.

Mario sank slowly into a wooden chair. The tall, stylish man Serguey had met at Mella Theater now bore the appearance and demeanor of a repentant recluse.

"The sun is the only thing that's kept me sane these past few weeks," he said, bobbing his head almost imperceptibly.

"How much sun do you think my father's getting?" Victor said.

"All right," Serguey said. "Let him speak."

Victor straightened up. "Okay. Talk."

Mario looked at them like a man beholding his executioners. "I'm the reason your father's in prison."

Victor's legs quivered. "Oh, man." He glanced at Serguey, his throat vibrating with anger.

"If it's going to be like this," Toya said, "go outside and let your brother handle it." She addressed Mario. "When I was a child, my mother had to hide the knives in the house whenever her brother came over. He was a violent drunk and took it out on whoever was around. This one here," she touched Victor's nape, "has a bigger heart but the same type of blood."

"He loves his father," Mario said. "I deserve his hatred."

"Did you rat him out?" Serguey asked.

Mario exhaled as if expulsing cigarette smoke. "I didn't. The only reason I'm not in prison with Felipe is that I wasn't home when they came for me. They'd been working my partner for a while, asking about my whereabouts and schedule. He pretended to help them, but he always tipped me off and gave them misleading information. I had no idea they were looking into Felipe too."

"That's a lie," Victor said.

Toya shushed him, then said a prayer in Yoruba. Victor bit his lip. He was more a rabid dog than an ape now.

"You're right," Mario said, crossing his wrists over a raised knee. He was regaining his spruced mannerism, his confidence. "Maybe deep inside I suspected something. But I always thought his name would keep him out of trouble. Plus, Felipe was never involved in anything against the government. He was mostly in it for his plays."

Serguey mounted his stool. "Start at the beginning and tell us what the fuck you're talking about."

"I'm sorry." Mario scraped his hands like block planes on his thighs. "You'd think a writer could be more articulate." He laughed awkwardly. "It hasn't been easy, you know. Felipe's my best friend."

"Were you two involved with Liberty Now?" Serguey asked. He was tilling the field for a specific conversation, rid of tangents or delays.

Mario sighed again. "Yes, I'm—was—one of their main contacts here. They've been funding some of Felipe's projects in exchange for information. It was actually a division of Liberty Now, a small group of exiled artists."

"What kind of information?"

"Other contacts. People in the arts with an influential position who aren't happy with the status quo."

"Like who?"

"Film directors, actors, musicians." The dramaturge relaxed his shoulders. "The idea was to have them leak out evidence of oppression and lack of financial support in the arts. You know, about the bureaucracy, the politics of it. They'd already gotten a few people to write up accounts of their experiences using pseudonyms." A studious stare embellished Mario's vision. "I believe their real goal was to write up a kind of manifesto for Cuban artists."

To Serguey, it sounded too intellectually motivated, even for Felipe. "So my dad was involved purely for the money?"

"Do you want the long or short explanation?"

"I just want to know the truth."

Mario flattened the hair on his arm and picked at an invisible sleeve. "Felipe wrote an essay about the separation of government and the arts when he was younger."

"I'm aware."

He stopped fiddling. He had heard the answer he was looking for. "A lot of people respect your father because, back then, he pointed out what others were afraid to do: that communism tries to control everything." Mario seemed to get briefly lost in reverie. "With his expressive personality, there's a certain mystique that people are attracted to. I certainly was." He cleared his throat and added, "Felipe knows a lot of artists. He's been around long enough to also know who hates the system and who's a brown-nose, and he's very good at motivating people."

Serguey nodded, indicating he followed.

Mario allowed for a moment of silence to fall over the room. "In truth," he said, and here Serguey prepared to dissect the dramaturge's words in real time, "the bigger goal was to attract international attention to the arts, hopefully get the government to accept more collaboration with foreign institutions."

It was no state secret that after the Special Period, the emphasis on punitive censorship had been gradually supplanted by economic strife of historic proportions. Ideology took a back seat to practical needs, and artists—Serguey was aware through the occasional complaint from his father—were no exception. Since the government saw the island as a pressure cooker for which they must always find ways to let off steam, Serguey speculated that perhaps Liberty Now wished to take advantage by increasing the pressure on the artistic front, getting the government to loosen up the valve.

"You wanted more resources," he said.

"The financial support we get is a joke," Mario said. "Your dad was a direct victim of this. How else could we change that? The government won't do anything unless they have an urgent reason."

Victor said, "Or they can just lock you up."

"You know . . ." Mario dallied the complete cycle of a breath, looking at the saints in Toya's altar. A soggy cigar stub had been left in the center of a boat-shaped ashtray, encircled by several candles. Wax had collected at their bases like hardened lava. Black shot glasses decorated by stenciled white skeletons lay at the saints' feet. "What's happened to Felipe could be a good thing in the long run."

Victor skewed his body forward enough for the hind legs of his stool to momentarily levitate. "Are you serious?"

Mario squirmed in his chair. "A letter was published recently, asking for his release. Do you know who wrote it?"

"We do," Serguey said.

"Activists and artists are speaking up. If he's not released soon, there will be protests, especially with all the interest in his situation."

"And yet you ran at the first sign of trouble," Victor said. "Last time I checked, you haven't accomplished shit. Fidel and Raul are still doing whatever the fuck they please."

Mario bowed and shook his head. He was consigning himself to his potholed logic. "You're missing the point, Victor. Liberty Now's not a full-on political organization. No one's calling for Fidel's or Raul's head."

The sun had progressed toward an angle that caused rectangular shafts to shine on Mario's right cheek and side of his forehead, like an oddly arranged spotlight. The granular shadows that engulfed the rest of his figure made Serguey think of German Expressionist films.

"People like Felipe and me," Mario continued, the quiet music in his voice like a confession, his breath propelling minute grains of dust, discernable in the sunlight, into squally swirls, "we're the backbone of the cultural image that Cuba sells to the world. We're enabling this regime, and for what? For a title? For the opportunity to present at bigger venues?" He elevated his jaw, as if experiencing a surge of wounded pride. "We go home and count our pennies. We swamp our noses in mediocrity and are supposed to smile when we get a certificate or a short trip abroad. There are plenty of Cuban artists and writers with big ideas, with the talent to do special things, who don't have the means. But then they have to sit in an interview and tiptoe around the challenges they face, ignore the leaking roof in their house or the watery plate of *chicharos* they eat four times a week, and bloviate about how much creative freedom Cuba's regime gives them. And it's not just artists; it's journalists too. I'm friends with plenty of them who get paid shit for their articles, which have to meet a certain criteria, and then those articles get sold to magazines and newspapers around the world, and who do you think keeps all the revenue? Why do you think there are so many independent journalists now?"

Serguey wondered if the autonomy that Claudia had achieved paralleled that which his father and Mario had been after. Claudia could afford to loiter at a hotel lobby, paying their high internet-access rates with a foreigner's account, the one-dollar Twitter posts, proliferating news that contradicted the Cuban government's propaganda. Someone had to subsidize her work; chances were it wasn't someone inside the country. That kind of internal influence would not go unchecked. How the money got into her hands without being intercepted, how she was allowed to roam the streets of Havana and Felipe wasn't, remained a question for another day.

"The work you do still has an impact," Serguey said. He was looking, through flattery, to wrest details out of Mario. "I'm sure my dad believes that." Then he provoked: "How many people did you expect to support you, anyway?"

Mario smiled knowingly, his whole countenance now suffused in sunlight. "More than you'd imagine."

"Bullshit," Victor said with a patronizing scowl.

Mario glanced at him, then aimed his eyes again at Serguey. "And you're right, your father does believe in his work. That's why he initially didn't commit to participate in what Liberty Now wanted to do. He simply gave them advice and pointed them in the right direction. He only met with the members I brought to him, the ones who could offer funds. Since the government shut down places like the Spanish Cultural Department, we've really struggled to finance our plays. Liberty Now was part of the solution."

"You said *initially*," Serguey pointed out. "What did he do differently afterward?"

"He offered to write some things himself. He wanted to get more involved, so he went to see some members who'd already been tagged by the government. Maybe they were being shadowed, I'm not sure." Mario went on to note that it was best to avoid specific names. A few members were still inside the country, afraid to show up at the airport. Plans had already been put in motion for them to leave the country another way. These members, he said, had not only agreed to lend Mario a hand but had been keeping him informed of Felipe's status as news trickled in from abroad.

"What's the word on him?" Serguey said.

Sweat had begun to bubble on the stubbled shadow of Mario's missing mustache. "Last I heard, the government is dealing with Spain to get him out. I don't know if it's just a rumor, but it sounds probable. I'm sure they're asking for something in exchange; they always do. If Felipe's released, they'll treat him as a dissident, so he might not be able to come back, at least not for a few years."

Victor scratched his neck, inclining his chin in Serguey's direction. "I don't get why Dad would get involved with these people. If he needed money, he could've come to me."

"It's not that simple," Serguey said.

"You might not remember it, Victor," the dramaturge said, "but your father was very politically opinionated early in his career. And then there's your grandfather, the internment camp. Felipe doesn't talk about it, but you don't just forget that."

"What are you implying," Victor replied, "that he turned into a coward?"

"Not at all." Mario retreated in his chair, a block of sunlight descending onto his lap. "But it's almost impossible to be open about your political views and do what we do for a living. There has to be a perception that your beliefs align with the government's. Your father had to make a choice, and given his talent, I think he made the right one."

"You're saying he sold out."

"He compromised. I did too."

Serguey didn't feel equipped to speak. He'd done as much compromising as anyone in Cuba.

"Do you know Felipe's two biggest regrets?" Mario paused, gauging whether it was safe to proceed. He was delving into personal territory. Serguey looked at him expectantly. "Not being a more attentive father, and sacrificing his ideology in public."

Victor said, "You don't know my father better than I do."

Though Serguey disagreed, he decided not to contradict his brother. It was clear that Victor felt vulnerable and still on the brink of violence.

"Can these people from Liberty Now do anything to help?" Serguey asked Mario. "Can they deny that my dad had anything to do with them?"

"They won't," Toya said. Her sudden interpolation bore the cachet and ascendancy of a judge. "That's why he's here, looking to absolve himself."

"I wouldn't dare ask for absolution," Mario said.

She smiled with half her mouth. "Is that what you've been telling yourself?" She pointed at the saints. "They know otherwise."

Mario spoke to Serguey as if he were the sole ally left in the room. "Your father has a great chance of getting out. The government has released political prisoners in the past in exchange for concessions."

"We've been speaking with someone who's engaged in those things," Serguey said.

Mario narrowed his eyes. "Who?"

"Don't you dare tell him," Victor said.

"Of course not."

"You should be careful who you speak to," Mario said. "You never know who works for the state."

"Do you work for the state?" Victor said.

"No." He looked at the barred window. "If they got their hands on me, I wouldn't last a week."

"But my dad will be just fine, right?"

Serguey said, "They've been harassing everybody involved with *Electra Garrigó*. Even the actors."

Mario took a long breath. "God." He scuffed his sweat-patched face, as if trying to wake himself from a bad dream. "Those poor kids."

"Were any of them in this whole Liberty Now project?"

"No. Your father cares about them. We both do. We love them."

"Just not enough to think of the consequences."

Mario nodded, not in agreement, but in defiance. "Nothing worth doing's completely safe. Felipe was aware of the dangers. It's unfortunate that others have to pay."

"Like my dad paying for what you did," Victor said.

"I accept that." Mario's eyes misted with tears. He drilled his teeth into his lips, a congruent mixture of remorse and rage. "Whatever Felipe has had to go through, I'll have to live with for the rest of my life. I'm not proud of how everything turned out. I'm not proud of hiding." He tapped his knees together and breathed into his hands, recouping his composure.

Serguey pitied him. It was ludicrous to make him solely responsible for Felipe's misfortune. His father was a methodical, intelligent person. Not easy to fool, to set up. "Do you know if anyone else has been arrested?"

"As far as I've been told, only Felipe. I'm guessing he's been questioned about other people."

"I bet you he has," Victor said. "Beaten too."

"Don't speculate," Toya said. "You start fantasizing about the wrong things, and there's no stopping you."

"He's not speculating," Serguey said.

"Have you heard of Colonel Montalvo?" Victor asked Mario.

He hadn't.

"My brother and I got a good licking from his guys."

The tears dropped from Mario's eyes. He gazed at the saints again, slowly gasping, fighting to contain any sound that might attempt to flee him. Serguey was struck by the notion that his father would never display such blunt contrition.

"Are you buying this?" Victor turned to Serguey.

"He's being sincere," Toya said gently.

Serguey replied, in an augmented whisper, "Mario," and waited for the dramaturge to regard him. "Why exactly did you want to see us?"

"I . . ." His voice was hoarse and choppy. He swallowed hard.

"I'll make you some coffee," Toya said. She tugged at the sleeves of her white dress and left the room.

"Mostly, I came to apologize," Mario said. "I'm hoping I'll get to do the same with Felipe in person."

Victor said, "He's allowed visitors this Sunday."

"Are you leaving the country?" Serguey asked. There was something in Mario's confessional act that reeked of finality, of oncoming change.

"Yes. On a boat."

"When?"

"Ten days' time. That's the other reason I came. I asked the people who are behind it to give me extra spots. They said they could only do two, for you and your brother."

Victor laughed brusquely. "We're not going anywhere with you."

"You should think about it. I have faith that Felipe will be sent abroad."

"You think I'm going anywhere without my wife?" Serguey said.

Mario's eyelids fell. "I can't guarantee space for your family because of the cost."

The whoosh of a gas burner just switched on travelled from the kitchen to the consultation room. There was a clatter, like marbles smacking together, and a metallic sliding sound. Then the subtle scent of ground coffee. Somewhere in the building's corridor, closer to the street, a bucket of water had been dumped, a stubborn door had been forced shut. The neighbors were starting to wake. Mario was indifferent, his face showing an air of liberation, of unwarranted good fortune, like someone who's come out unscathed from a spiraling car.

"The offer will be standing until the minute the boat leaves. It's the only thing I can do to atone." Mario dug into one of his pockets and produced a folded piece of paper. "This is a phone number where you can reach me. I've been staying at my cousin's house outside Batabanó. He has a big backyard with no street view. I've been holed up there, losing my mind."

Serguey accepted the paper. "Victor, would you give us a moment alone?"

"You said we'd do this together."

"I'm asking for a moment. Go help Toya with the coffee."

Victor hopped off his stool and brought his index finger near Serguey's nose. "Don't get soft on me now." Begrudgingly, he headed to the kitchen.

Serguey stood and locked his eyes with Mario's. "So my father's in prison because he took funds for his plays?"

"That's how the authorities will broadcast it. They'll say it was illegal. He was getting money from the wrong people."

"Why didn't he ask my brother?"

"What father wants their child to bankroll them, especially someone as proud as Felipe? Do you know the cost for props, building a set, costumes? I don't know what business Victor is involved in, but I doubt he could afford all of it. And like I told you, Felipe wanted to get more politically involved. I feel responsible. I was the one who introduced him to them."

"You *should* feel responsible. Why the hell did you get him mixed up in all this?"

"I got caught up in the idea of bringing about some change, whatever that might be. I can't stand this regime, Serguey. I really can't. Part of me is glad I get to leave. I'd like to think that some part of your father feels that way too."

Serguey scoffed. "That seems to be a lot of people's solution."

Mario rose from his chair, mooring himself on the armrests, which creaked and groaned like stretched or twisted leather. "The youth in this country could care less about change. In a way, your father and I didn't for many years."

Serguey stepped away, allowing the dramaturge to claim his own space. He stared at Lam's painting, at the slim, elongated figures resembling sugar cane stocks. The contours of his own face seemed imprinted as a ghostly image behind Lam's vibrant colors.

Mario paced toward the middle of the room. "But if not us, then who?" he said. "The washed-up guys with piles of accolades and cushy positions? The young ones who go to New York and Amsterdam and Quito and come back brimming with pride, who believe that worshipping Severo Sarduy is a form of rebellion or autonomy?"

Sarduy, an openly homosexual author who emigrated to France and despised Castro's regime, had been condemned and censured for years in Cuba. Serguey knew his name but hadn't read any of his work.

Mario carried on: "The starving artist life isn't for everyone, especially when you have to compromise how you express your views. There are so many artists in exile who would've loved to build and finish their careers here. There are people in prison for having the wrong books in their house, and we carry on like it's normal, like it didn't happen."

"I sympathize," Serguey said, "but I—"

"You took a different road. Your father always respected that."

Mario's head, darker in the spectrum of the painting, overlapped Serguey's, a breach of space that unsettled him. He removed himself from the image, walking past the stools to the door. "Did he?"

"He's really proud, of both you and Victor, even if you don't have much in common with him. He says that's his failure. He shut you out. I can't imagine what it'd be like for me to have children . . ." Mario adopted a pensive expression. "The damage I could do to them."

Serguey saw Toya and Victor walking down the hall, his brother carrying a tray with small coffee cups.

"This is the best coffee you all have had in a while," Toya said.

Serguey grabbed two cups and extended one to Mario. Victor laid the tray on his stool.

"Five minutes," Toya said.

Serguey blew on his coffee and dipped his top lip into it, unsure of her meaning.

"Thank you," Mario said. "My ride's almost here."

"Your cousin?" Serguey said.

"You should seriously consider leaving with me. You'll have a better chance of reuniting with your father." As soon as he emptied his cup, Mario said to Toya, "This *is* some good coffee."

Serguey watched him for a moment. "Did you get my text?"

"I tried calling you back, but no one answered. I called the other number that'd been trying to reach me, and your friend responded. I knew it was risky," here he looked at the brothers, "but I had to see you both."

"Don't call that number again," Serguey said. "State Security has it."

Mario nodded. Toya took the cup from him, and he was gone, his lanky, elegant gait momentarily reappearing through the window, his shadow gliding across the room.

Victor glowered at it and said, "Can you believe him?"

Serguey flailed the piece of paper with Mario's number. "You should really think about this."

"You're out of your mind. Is that what you were discussing? I think we should turn him in, trade him for Dad's release."

"We can't do that. There's no guarantee they'll let Dad go. And that's his best friend."

"You think he's a friend?"

Serguey placed his cup on the tray. "Let's go wake Kiko."

"Yes, go bother your friend," Toya said. She ambled to the front door, which Mario had left ajar, and opened it wide. A rush of light dyed the nondescript walls. She fetched a broom, shuffled her feet back toward the consultation room, and started sweeping. "And tell these people you're dealing with that this isn't a meetinghouse. I don't want them bringing their negative energy here."

❦❧

Kiko was already up. His uncombed hair was littered with tangles, but he was alert and spry and in a suspiciously good mood. As the brothers strode into his living room, they noticed the orange light of a lamp in the far corner, casting a cozy glow on the otherwise dim space. The windows were closed, the air imbued with the scent of lilac. The bouncing, mutating balls in Kiko's computer screen saver seemed like a pair of cat eyes hopping back and forth in the dark. An elusive guitar melody echoed above them.

Victor asked him if he had a girl over.

"No, no," Kiko said.

"What's with the romantic atmosphere?"

"Residuals from last night. That's Amaury Gutierrez playing. His last album's wonderful."

Victor walked to the fridge. "No beer!" he bellowed, his head blocked by the open door.

"Your brother's an alcoholic," Kiko said to Serguey.

Serguey sat on the couch, Kiko across from him on the armchair. Just like Toya's home, Kiko's shuttered room was murky, submersed in the specter of collusion, of ill-fated intimacy. Victor was still fumbling around in the refrigerator, foraging for an escape, a distraction. The meeting with Mario had drained a lot from him.

"Thanks for getting us Mario," Serguey said.

Kiko perked up his eyes. "He came to see you?"

"We met at Toya's."

"Good! I wasn't sure he'd do it. I told him we had ways of finding out where he was, just to scare him a little."

"It worked."

Kiko seemed proud that he'd made a difference. He swung his thumb over his shoulder toward the kitchen. "How did this one behave?"

"How often do you talk to Claudia?" Serguey said. He wasn't interested in banter, not today.

His friend was rattled by the question. He plucked outer strands of his hair and stammered, "It, uh, it depends."

"What I mean is, does she usually initiate contact, or do you?"

"We both do."

Serguey detected in Kiko, in the absence of confusion in his eyes, that he could drill straight to the core of the matter. "I'd just like to be clear about my dad's status. I feel like I'm relying on assumptions, not on facts."

"It's difficult." Kiko draped the entirety of his body like a discarded piece of clothing on his seat. "Concrete information is hard to come by. Nothing's really official unless they announce it, and even then . . ." He gyrated his fingers into the air, parodying the embroidered narrative the government usually dispensed.

"I understand, but Claudia's the only person who has more immediate access to that kind of information. The uncertainty's starting to get to me."

"Do you want me to open the shades?" Kiko asked, as if the orange dimness were smothering Serguey.

"I'm fine."

Kiko jerked his body into an upright stance. "Listen, the information that reaches Claudia is definitely solid. I can press her a bit, but I'm not sure it'll yield what you want."

"Victor and I are going to see my old man this Sunday. I want to have an idea what to tell him and what to ask him."

Kiko nodded, his silhouette half-aglow and half-shadowed. "I'll get you something by then."

Serguey was done tactfully dancing around his request. "Can you get me on a computer with an internet connection to see for myself?"

Kiko bent forward and slapped the inside of Serguey's knee. "You should've opened with that. It might cost some money, though."

"That won't be a problem," Victor said, returning to the living room empty-handed.

"Okay. I can find you something."

"You need to open the windows," Victor said. "People are going to get the wrong idea. Or are you getting paranoid about State Security?"

Kiko inhaled and caressed his inflated belly. "They have nothing on me."

Victor sat on the arm of his friend's chair. "And I did behave with Mario. I mean, it wasn't easy." He went on to share—in his own mocking tenor and with carefully selected emphases—what the dramaturge had said. He accentuated how cowardly Mario had acted, how laughable Liberty Now's plans were, how outrageous it was for Mario to offer him and Serguey a spot on the boat. He said nothing of Felipe.

"Mario believes that my dad's going to be released," Serguey said. "Because of the international attention."

"Well," Kiko said, "about a year ago, a couple of journalists who'd spent decades in Cienfuegos were put on house arrest. The government sold it as an act of compassion, but it was really because pictures of these guys in putrid cells showed up on international news channels. I don't think with Felipe it has to get to that point. The government can't get away with abuse as much as it used to." He stopped and turned to Victor. "And what Mario offered is not a bad idea."

"You mean leaving with him?"

"We're always messing around, Victor, but you're a mistake away from being locked up. And now that State Security's involved, you're holding on by a thread. As your friend, I'm telling you that you should consider it. You have to be pragmatic."

Serguey said, "We should have a serious talk after we see Dad."

Victor chuckled, squelching his anger. "What the fuck is it with you guys?"

Kiko shoved him off the armchair and got up. "Be smart and listen to your brother." He stood on his toes, arms strained toward the ceiling, and shook like an animal shedding the last of its old skin. "Now, let's find you some internet in this dead zone of a country."

CHAPTER 24

Serguey was astonished to see his father's name in a myriad of places: blogs, online newspapers, forums, Twitter. Claudia had invested her time and money intelligently and without moderation. Questioning her finances or how she got away with her work was suddenly a source of compunction for Serguey. She had delivered what she had pledged. That was all the validation a person in her position should need. There were articles condemning the Cuban government, calling the arrest an appalling injustice. He also came across the letter written by Felipe's colleagues. It was largely apolitical, respectfully demanding more transparency in the case, and painting Felipe as an artistic beacon and ethical man. It contained the same civil, staid tone Felipe had employed in his essays reproaching Socialist Realism. Serguey realized he'd missed an opportunity to ask Mario about those who'd written the letter, but like Claudia, their actions were enough. He assumed, in any case, that the names at the bottom were not compromised. They might not even know about Liberty Now—their display of solidarity an earnest attempt to stand by a friend. A couple of pieces detailed Felipe's career. One quoted the infamous essays, which, as far as Serguey knew, were only available in their original limited printing. How on earth they'd gotten access to them, he couldn't begin to fathom.

The most recent posts spoke about dialogue between Cuba's and Spain's governments, supposedly mediated by the Catholic Church. Discussions had already taken place regarding prisoners from the infamous Black Spring. Felipe's arrest had poured fuel over the fire, as Linares had projected. The writing, from what Serguey could interpret, bore a heartening tone. But what exactly it all meant was impossible to know. The state could be as irrational as a spoiled teenager, unhampered by contradictions or petulant impulses. Ultimately, it was encouraging news to see that Claudia and Mario hadn't misled him: Felipe had support, lots of it. Cuba was no longer as isolated, its people not as silenced as they'd been in past decades.

The brothers showed Kiko their appreciation by treating him to lunch. Kiko had taken them to an internet café whose manager he knew well. He'd met the man while he was a university student, spending hours in line to get his projects done at this location. As anticipated, the tab had been pricey. The manager could forgo asking for I.D., to preserve their anonymity, but he couldn't justify missing funds. Kiko assured Serguey he'd been saving for more than a rainy day and volunteered to pay half.

"Another contribution to the cause," he labeled it.

They ate at a paladar, a house-set, family-owned restaurant whose ludicrously French name—*La Fête*—had been printed on a chalkboard and mounted on an easel by the gated entryway. The seating consisted of wooden chairs decorated in colorful wrapping paper. A mushrooming canvas canopy sheltered the dining area from the sun. Under it, a Spanish translation of the restaurant's name—La Fiesta—hung in individually fluttering letters. Through a square hatch with a miniature serving counter, Serguey could see a female cook, large-breasted and with very short hair, inside the house. She was strenuously stirring the contents of what he imagined had to be a cauldron. On their table, the sewn ridges of the plastic-enveloped menus had started to unstitch. Serguey picked at them while Kiko ordered the roast pork with *congris*. The brothers chose a chicken sandwich with a side of *mariquitas*, the lowest-priced meal available. The waiter, a dapper middle-aged man, opened a round of beers with a primly twist and poured them as if from a wine bottle.

Kiko began to talk about the rough patch he'd hit with his mother. She had developed the habit of calling him every morning to vent about Kiko's father and how capricious the heart attack had made him. Serguey felt a pang of guilt. His friend—devoted, trustworthy, unselfish—was opening up about his family issues, and all Serguey could think—maddeningly aware that he must soon overcome this sensation if he wanted to restore a reciprocal relationship—was how distant he'd been. Serguey listened intently to his friend. As a reply, he shared how frustrated he felt every time Felipe pretended to not need assistance, to the point that he couldn't avoid wondering if Felipe only refused their—Serguey's and Victor's—help.

"You've never seen someone so proud," he said. "It takes a lot out of you trying to risk yourself for someone like that."

Kiko shrugged meaningfully. "He's your father."

His friend understood, and Serguey appreciated it deeply, but it felt good complaining to a person other than Anabel. "Even so."

Victor didn't contribute to the conversation. His parents, Serguey decided, weren't anywhere near his favorite topic of conversation. How much had he revealed to Toya? She wasn't the type of person who would betray Victor's trust, so asking her was useless. But Serguey now feared that, eventually, his brother could wind up as aloof as their father, as absent as their mother. He envied how candidly Kiko spoke of his own parents, and wished that he and Victor could do the same about theirs.

As they drank their beers and later said goodbyes, Serguey's thoughts drifted until they landed, with heightened urgency, on whether emigrating to the United States was the smartest move Victor could make. He doubted that a change in locale would lead Victor on the right track. In all likelihood, he wouldn't have his older brother by his side: Serguey himself was deeply torn as to whether he should leave, or if Anabel would be willing.

In the following days, he made a few attempts at discussing Mario's proposition with Victor. His brother grumbled each time, disregarding Serguey's insinuations and hastening out of the room as if compelled by some unfinished chore. Serguey centered his energy on checking in with Anabel twice a day. He gave her progress reports, and in exchange, she vented about her sister.

"Alida's still obsessed with going to Florida," she said with a prolonged breath. Her voice, amplified by the receiver, seemed both urgent and defeated. One of the actors in the play, she elaborated, had paid her sister a visit and crowed about an aunt in Tampa who'd agreed to get him out. "My parents overheard the conversation, which led to a late-night family debate. I can't believe they sided with her."

"What do you mean?" He was grappling for an approving reason, something to justify Victor leaving the country.

"They gave her the green light. They think she's too talented to stay here."

This didn't help him, though he was happy for Alida. Talent couldn't be Victor's motive.

"I'm also worried about them," she said.

"Your parents?"

Anabel explained that although they liked to put up a resilient front, she could see they were frail. "It's like they're constantly tired but don't want to show it. Dad is always falling asleep, and he makes this weird noise, like it hurts him to breathe. He forgets things too, but Mom covers for him. When I catch her resting and offer help, she pretends she doesn't need it, but I can see that she's frazzled. She coughs a lot at night. Alida mentioned that she was sick a few times last year but that she doesn't like to tell anyone."

Serguey wasn't sure what to respond. He had sensed fragility in their gait during the post-dinner walk in Mantilla. To mention it now, however, would validate or worsen Anabel's worries, so he waited for her to continue.

"I guess you'd have to live with them to notice," she said. "But I'm getting worried. They've aged, Serguey. I know that seems obvious, but I guess what I'm trying to say is that they seem brittle."

"Well, they're not alone. They have you guys."

"Alida doesn't even seem to care."

"You have to give your sister a break," he said, more as advice than reproof.

Anabel let a few seconds pass before saying he was right. She began to talk about how, although she and Serguey had grown accustomed to their own space, maybe moving in permanently with her parents wouldn't be too bad. It would remove the trouble of having to somehow find a new place, which without Gimenez was nearly impossible.

Anabel's comment about Gimenez demoralized him a little. His former mentor's name in his ear rang of guilt. He wasn't sure from the subtle shadings in Anabel's voice, however, if she, like him, saw moving in with her parents as a significant sacrifice—and a direct side effect of his failure.

"I'm so sorry," he told her.

"Stop." Her voice was no longer a breath but more of a moan. "None of this is your fault."

He couldn't dodge his regret, for putting them in their current position. "I was supposed to make our lives better."

"You're doing right by your family. You won't lose me because of that."

What would he lose her for? Victor? Her parents? There was so much to say, so much he didn't know. He owed so many conversations to her, to his brother, his father. He owed them confessions, apologies, reassurances. He could draw encouragement from his own sincerity, from a vulnerability he'd managed to stifle for years. He could draw even more so from theirs. But if these conversations led to arguments, accusations, denials, they could lacerate his poise, nullifying the momentum he'd been able to build. Yet, there was a persistent sensation needling him: their personal lives had become like baggage aboard a ship, and the longer the trip took, the harder it became to leave the contents untouched. Avoidance had splintered his ties to his father and brother. It could do the same with his wife. He needed to confront the knotty truths sooner rather than later, no matter how much strength or sanity what had taken place and still lies ahead might extract from him.

"I'm sorry for bringing up this thing about my parents," she said. "We can talk about it later."

The "later" hit him like cool seawater in a gentle wind. If he *were* to lose Anabel, he'd never recapture the implicitness they so naturally shared, not with anyone else.

He promised her that he would return on Sunday, after he and Victor visited Felipe at Calderas. She replied that she should have news from Father Linares by then. Everyone was depositing their two cents into the coffer.

"I miss you," she added, as if nothing else mattered, as if everything else were implicit.

He couldn't abstain from apologizing again.

❧❧❧ ⁂ ❧❧❧

At 7:30 a.m. on Sunday, he opened his eyes to the sundry sounds of rain pelting concrete, tin, and bushes outside the window. It was a steady, insistent shower, awash with a harmonious rhythm. No lightning or wind. The brothers had breakfast, *a café con leche* and some toast, without saying much. This had been the theme of Serguey's stay. Victor's aversion to talking about the future, about the possibility of leaving Cuba, made Serguey fear bringing up the past. He hadn't fulfilled his promise to Anabel to discuss the peasants' attack in the woods, how they had dealt—or not dealt—with it. The uncertainty of what they would say, of what each of them remembered, seemed to strangle the words before Serguey could speak them. And where should he begin? What could he admit to his brother that would provoke an earnest response? How should he express feelings that might not make sense until after they've been uttered, questioned, and scrutinized? What assurance did he have that their ordeals could be openly debated without a permanent fracture, that either of them would be able to heal?

He exempted himself by rationalizing that if his brother started the conversation, he could trust its outcome more.

Victor complained about the weather, grousing that it might ruin whatever pair of shoes he might put on.

"You can go wearing flip-flops," Serguey said, dipping his toast.

His brother was nervous. Perhaps what Kiko told him about hanging by a thread had gotten to him. Maybe this had been the source of his caginess and evasion. They were now going back into the lion's den. Montalvo and his men might be waiting. Felipe's release, if it was imminent, might come only at a price. Serguey had spent a portion of the previous night going over several scenarios. He concluded that neither he nor Victor could prevent any actions taken by the authorities, so they needed to carry on, charging bulls at the mercy of the matador's benevolence. Whatever saints Victor worshipped, Serguey hoped he'd prayed to them.

The rain continued. So did Victor's silence as they rode the buses to Calderas. The partially flooded streets made it a longer journey than it would normally have been. For the latter part of the trip, they skipped around puddles and feculent accumulations of trash that seemed to have been excreted by the prison, as if the complex itself were an organism. A feeling of predisposition began to overwhelm Serguey. He and Victor loved their father; they had proved as much to themselves. But he fretted that Felipe's egotism could make them feel as though their efforts had been in vain, that he'd cling to a creed of self-reliance and dismissals.

The throbbing of an engine was getting closer, and the brothers were forced to abandon the middle of the street where it was less inundated. They jumped to the sodden edge of the road and waited for a van to roll by. Its windows were fogged, unyielding to Serguey's penetrating glance. As they resumed their walk, he was assailed by a sudden awareness: if this was the last encounter they'd have in Cuba, he wanted it to be a restoration of their relationships, a return to the roles of father and sons in the emotional sense. He wanted something from Felipe that his current circumstances might not afford him the luxury of giving: honesty.

At the prison, they encountered no resistance. The mere mention of their father's name got them through the front desk security check rather expeditiously. They were led down the same corridor to the same room in which they had previously met Felipe, though, this time, Yenier, the guard who'd been with them, was nowhere to be found. Neither was Montalvo. The brothers sat in the room and were told to wait.

Moments later, Serguey was relieved not just to see his father but to realize, as a guard bolted the door from the outside, that they were being allowed some privacy.

"Okay, so I was wrong," Felipe said with a labored shrug, halting Serguey's and Victor's approach. "So I wasn't out by the end of the week."

"You son of a bitch," Victor said, his voice steeped in compassion.

They embraced their father. Felipe buried his face in his sons' entwined arms. Serguey attempted to step back after a moment, but Victor held on firmly, so Serguey surrendered to his brother's wish. His father's nose and mouth felt warm in the nook of his elbow. When they finally released each other, it was evident that Felipe was weeping.

Serguey scrutinized him. He was clean-shaven, devoid of scars. His plush hair had been trimmed to the skull. His fingers twitched, as if involuntarily playing a piano. The month in prison hadn't been as calamitous as Serguey had expected. There was no alarming pallor, no attenuated body, no signs of rapid decay. The haircut gave Felipe a hardboiled look, inharmonious with his personality.

"I'm not much of a crier," he said, wiping his tears.

"I don't think I've ever seen you cry," Serguey said.

They took their seats. Felipe snuffled and brushed his eyes. Victor appeared enraptured by his own relief that their father was fine.

"You're looking better," Serguey said.

Felipe raked his thorny scalp. "About a week ago, they gave me a spa treatment. They said the hair had to go because of lice. They even had Montalvo's personal barber spruce me up this morning."

"Did they hurt you again after the pepper spray?"

Victor put a stop to the conversation with a hand gesture, then swept the other hand across the underside of the table.

"I don't think there's a wire," Felipe said. He looked at Serguey. "They interrogated me and slapped me around a few times. The first couple of days after you saw me, they had a prisoner take my food, making a scene out of it. But it never got worse than that."

"I don't think you've lost any weight," Victor said.

This wasn't true, but Serguey appreciated the spirit of Victor's assessment, so he stayed quiet.

"They've been bringing me better food," Felipe said.

Serguey said, "It's like they're grooming you." He hoped it hadn't come across as a reproach. He meant it as an invitation for his father to be frank.

Felipe lifted his hands but not his wrists, as if they were cuffed to the table. "They haven't said it, but I suspect I'm on my way out."

Victor banged his fist on the table and grinned, a premature celebration in Serguey's view.

"Why do you think so?" he asked.

"They transferred me to a cleaner cell and have been letting me outside when all the other prisoners are gone. Montalvo even had a guard take me to his office for a smoke."

"Did you tell him what he wanted to know?"

"What's the difference?" Victor said to Serguey, suddenly disturbed.

"Some of what's gone on in here, I'm not proud of," Felipe said solemnly. "At first I didn't want to accept the idea that I'd have to leave the country. But I think I'm ready. I was about to delve into the tail end of my career. Maybe now I can do the kind of work they're accusing me of." He looked at his sons with inklings of a smirk. "Or maybe I'll just work at a bookstore in Madrid, if that's where they send me. One of those really old shops with the spiral staircases and the smell of damp wood."

"Dad," Victor said, "don't start sounding fucking senile."

Felipe seemed rapt by his daydream. "Maybe you two could work with me."

Victor grimaced and shook his head at Serguey. "Have you ever seen him like this?

Serguey shrugged.

"Prison really broke you, *Viejo*," Victor said.

Serguey found his brother's disappointment endearing. Their father's mawkishness was a farce, the sort of trait a director would give a character. His smirk had been haughty and premeditated: the practical aspects of his future Felipe had already worked out.

Serguey dragged his chair closer to his father and whispered, "We talked to Mario."

Felipe refocused his attention on his sons. "What did he say?"

"He's leaving. He invited us to go with him."

"You should do it. We could all reunite!"

"What about the house?" Victor said.

Their father sighed a lungful of air. He seemed to shrink in his own skin. "Let them have it."

"We can't just give it up!"

"The house was never really ours. In this country, nothing is." Felipe's pupils contracted as he reclined back, recoiling further into himself. "I know how they treat family members of accused dissenters. Did I ever tell you about Cabrera Infante?"

Serguey was familiar with the story. One of Cuba's best writers, Guillermo Cabrera Infante had supported the Revolution and worked as director of the Film Institute and editor of a communist magazine. But then his brother made a documentary about Havana's decadent nightlife, which didn't sit well with Fidel because it showed the kinds of behaviors El Comandante was trying to eradicate in the new Cuba. As logic went for these things under the communist regime, Cabrera Infante was banned from publishing due to his brother's mistake.

"He was our Joyce," Felipe said, "and they forced him into exile."

"What about grandpa's things?" Serguey said, resisting his father's digression. "Did they tell you what they did with them?"

Felipe pretended to gaze out of a nonexistent window. "We're not getting them back." He leveled his gaze on Serguey. "Would Anabel go with you?"

Serguey squinted and blinked, trying to rein in his frustration. His father was once again shirking a painful conversation. "We haven't discussed it."

"How is she? How's Alida?"

"They're back at their parents'." He hesitated, then said, "State Security went after Alida, and Gimenez and I had a falling out."

Felipe closed his eyes and nodded. "I'm sorry."

A series of trotting steps reverberated just outside the room. Serguey heard what he identified as Montalvo's voice, howling, "Where did they put him? No, I don't care about that. Where did they put him?"

They all looked to the door, Serguey's heart beating faster. They waited until the sounds subsided and eventually died out, somewhere far-off in the building, before trusting that they wouldn't be interrupted.

"It's fine," Serguey said, alluding to his father's expression of guilt. "Alida understands this isn't your fault."

"It's somebody's fault."

"Mario said he was sorry too. He's convinced that you're going to be released."

"He's a coward," Victor said. "How could you trust him?"

Felipe aimed his finger curtly at Victor. "Mario's not a coward. There'll come a time in your life when compromising decisions won't be as black-and-white as they seem when you're young. Now you feel untouchable because there's always tomorrow. For Mario and me, that window's shrinking. No one's trying to be a hero. It's too late for that. We're just not built for prison."

"Who is?" Serguey said.

"The man who took my food, he's been here eleven years. He doesn't seem to mind it. There's a curious enjoyment in his face, like a child who gets punished for torturing lizards and is right back at it the next day. He doesn't know what else to do. The second time he snatched my plate, I made him fight for it. He spilled the food on the floor, then slammed me against the wall. I think I made his day."

"You didn't eat?" Serguey said.

"I've subsisted days on end with nothing but cigarettes and rum, especially when I was writing plays." Felipe twirled his index finger and raised his eyes, as if something were drilling into his brain. "You get lost in the writing."

Victor said, "I thought about bringing you cigarettes, but these assholes would confiscate them."

Felipe squeezed Victor's arm. "That's okay. What I've missed most is talking to other artists. Chatting with Montalvo wasn't the same. He's not intellectually bright. But one's own head isn't a fun place without stimulation, so I appreciated being able to discuss theater."

Serguey chuckled. "With Montalvo?"

"He did his best."

"Well, it *is* your favorite topic."

"That's a good dig. I deserve it. Can I be honest though, without getting too sentimental?" The curtains had gone up, and Felipe had walked on stage. "Do you know what's kept me calm in here?"

Serguey held off as long as he could before asking, "What?"

"Your mother."

Victor's head sunk meekly, hopelessly. Even he knew what was coming. "Dad, don't do this now."

"In another life, we would've had a wonderful marriage."

"You don't get another life," Serguey said, bringing his index finger down on the table. "You get this one. And mom isn't here anymore." He signaled at himself and Victor. "We are."

"Right after that asshole killed her," Felipe continued, "I seriously considered ending it all. That was another period when I didn't eat for days. I drank a lot. I wanted to go to the trial and stab him. I know," here he cracked a smile replete with agony, "how very Greek of me. When you and Victor were brought back, I realized I had to straighten myself out. But instead of relying on you two, I plunged into my work, surrounded myself with friends. Eventually it became a habit. You boys were there, in the periphery, but I could never bring myself to pause and really see you. I just kept going."

Victor's ears burned red as irons in a fire. His lips were pursed with an accretion of ire and sorrow. Serguey beheld his large frame as if he were staring at his gaunt little brother, the boy who'd crushed the butts of his father's cigarettes with his bare feet so he could wake Serguey with the stench from his soles. Serguey wondered whether Felipe knew that Victor had done such things, whether they were part of the memories he had of their childhood. Irene would've known. She would've remembered. Serguey also wondered whether his father had noticed that Victor had never, not once, spoken his mother's name after she'd been killed.

"*You* were suicidal?" Serguey said. "*You* were a wreck?"

Felipe swallowed. His mouth quivered, but he composed himself quickly. "I'm not good at this."

"But you're very good at talking about yourself."

"Serguey," Victor said. "Forget it."

Serguey puffed his chest, prideful and hurt, disappointed that his fears and predisposition had been confirmed. "I'm happy that you're going to be released, and I don't fault you for what's happened. But the past, our childhood, our mom, that's my and Victor's world. It's *our* territory. You chose not to be in it, to keep us in your periphery, like you said. One confession of guilt isn't going to do away with it."

"You're right."

"And to do it here, in this place." Serguey braided his fingers together and wrenched them as he would a rope, the tension creeping to his teeth. "Do you know how much Victor and I have had to put aside—to avoid talking about—in order to do what we've done out there for you?"

Felipe overlapped his arms on top of his stomach, as if repressing the onset of a stomachache. "Montalvo told me about your arrest. He said only one Blanco will slip through his fingers."

"Serguey," Victor repeated, "forget it."

The noises outside reappeared, this time as a congregation, bottling the silence inside the room. The voices were hollow and gulping, like water slopping out of an overflowing bucket, slithering away from the door. Serguey kept his attention on his father. Felipe was deflecting, hoping to steer the course of the conversation elsewhere. Maybe it was part of the witticism—his ability to seamlessly deflect—that made him a favorite among his friends. For the past few weeks, he'd been generating demons with whatever he had divulged to Montalvo. His own sons were now an inescapable extension of his actions, the type of collateral damage one mourns for a lifetime. Serguey had to believe that, despite everything, his father was capable of that type of regret.

Victor directed his hands at Felipe while looking pleadingly at Serguey. "We might not see him again."

His brother was right: in many ways, this meeting could be a farewell. He quietly skipped a handful of seconds, avoiding his father's gaze until he spoke. "I don't know what Montalvo told you, but you're an international phenomenon."

It took a moment to register, but Felipe couldn't resist his own sense of importance. His lips began to shape a smile, which he swiftly suppressed, and murmured, "I'm some phenomenon, all right."

Serguey tried lugging him away from the shame he'd experienced, provoked by Serguey's berating. "Some theater people wrote a letter demanding your release."

Felipe gave a slight nod. "I bet I can tell you exactly who was involved. Vilma and José Angel."

"I met them in person. They came by the apartment to show their support."

Felipe extended his arms across the table, his fingertips forming an arrow. "I *am* grateful, Serguey, to both of you."

Victor grasped his father's hand. Felipe remained patient until Serguey did the same.

"I'm going to demand that my family be permitted to leave with me," he said.

"Don't get cocky," Victor said. "If you fuck up your release, I won't forgive you."

"You take what they give you," Serguey said. "We'll figure out the rest."

Felipe cuddled their fingers. "I'm proud of you."

Somewhere in the complex, a scream prowled through the halls like an aftershock. It reached the room with the urgency of a siren. Footsteps rushed again in an unidentifiable direction. Serguey dreaded that their visit might be arriving at its end. He leaned forward and asked, "Will they come after Mario?"

Felipe shook his head unconvincingly. "I believe we'll all be reunited again somehow. Maybe then we'll be able to fix things."

"Are you going to be okay if they send you to Spain?" Serguey asked, anxious that they hadn't dedicated a suitable amount of time to the logistics of imminent exile.

His fear materialized when a guard opened the door and barged in.

"Time's up."

"So quickly?" Victor protested.

"Time's up," the man repeated, as if these were the only words he'd ever pronounced. He clutched Felipe's shoulder.

"Stick together," their father said, standing. "Whatever happens, you stick together."

As he was hauled out of the room, Serguey was glad to see Victor hold his temper. In Calderas, they would never have a say.

❦❧❦

They plodded away from the complex under a light rain. A fraction of sunlight had perforated the clouds somewhere behind them, making the wet surface of the street iridescent, like a mirage. They refused to open their umbrellas. Victor's shoes were caked by a mixture of mud and sand. The umbrellas hung at their sides, beads gliding like quicksilver down the folded canopies toward the metal tips. They didn't speak until after they had taken the first bus back into the city. They stuck around a state-managed cafeteria for lunch. The name, Las Alegrias, was painted in jovial cursive on a dirty wall behind a crummy counter. They settled on *pan con croqueta* and mango juice, Victor's treat. As they ate, the aproned server, perched on a high chair next to the register, ran a nail file between her fingers like a violin bow. At the opposite end of the counter, a man with cratered skin and a red Levi's T-shirt gaped at the sparse menu on the wall, next to a picture of Che Guevara smoking a cigar.

"Do you think the old man ratted people out?" Victor asked Serguey.

"Does it matter?" Serguey's sandwich bread was so dry, it disintegrated onto his paper plate. The *croqueta* stuck to the ceiling of his mouth with every bite. "Are these made with chicken or glue?" he told the server.

She rolled her eyes at him. "Honey, the prices here are in Cuban pesos."

Serguey didn't respond. He had been probing for a distraction. It pained him to see Victor ashamed of their father, especially since they had been in a comparable situation and had stayed quiet. He swallowed his juice as if it could intoxicate him—as if it could drown Calderas and his own childhood from his mind—and spoke no more of Felipe.

The man at the end of the counter gave up on the menu choices. He whistled at a child who was tracking a lizard in a knot of naked bushes, and they both walked past the brothers. As soon as Victor looked ready to go, Serguey told him that it was best to part ways. He was going to Mantilla to spend the night with Anabel and find out what Father Linares had said. He warned Victor that he was to stay at the house until they had unqualified confirmation of Felipe's release. Victor didn't argue. He peered at the bushes where the boy had been playing and sullenly nodded at his brother's decision.

Chapter 25

When Serguey arrived at his in-laws', it took him the span of a single moment to detect that they'd been waiting for him. The entire family was in the living room, carefully arranged so that he could sit across from them. Julia's cheeks were flushed (was it from simmering excitement, or was she as sickly as Anabel had made her sound?), a smile contained by her compressed lips. Antonio was composed, but the muscles in his face betrayed his ebullience. Alida wasn't hiding her smile, though hers was evanescent, purely out of solidarity. A bit of anguish lingered in the halo of her expression.

"The Catholic Church can be criticized for many things," Antonio said, as if reciting lines from a script, "but when everyone's looking the other way, pretending that the people in charge are doing a commendable job, they're in the trenches aiding the victims."

Anabel flumped her head. "Thank you for the cryptic message, Dad." She turned to Serguey, who eased himself onto the chair left for him. "Father Linares said he's sure Felipe will be released. Cardinal Morales served as mediator. It's just a matter of days now."

If the cardinal—the only person with his status on the island—had been involved, Serguey could trust the information. The man's reputation in Cuba was spotless.

"How did your father look?" Julia asked, a veil of concern passing over her face.

Serguey raised his eyebrows. "Better than I expected."

"They know he's on his way out," Antonio said. "It's all about perception for these people."

Anabel stepped around the table and gave Serguey a kiss. The family performance had concluded. "How's he holding up?" she asked.

"I think he's accepted his fate."

"Still, it must be hard," Julia said.

Anabel said, "Hopefully this means you and Victor won't be harassed."

"Yes, everything will be peachy now," Alida said, folding her arms.

"You're not the sun, Alida," Anabel said, her furious voice above Serguey's head like a loudspeaker. "Not everything revolves around you."

Julia displayed an embarrassed grin to Serguey. "It's been like this since you left."

"They're my babies," Antonio said dotingly. "My pedantic, oil and vinegar babies."

"I doubt they'll leave us alone that easily," Serguey said. "But we'll deal with things as they come." He skated his palms over the tablecloth, trying to suggest that he wished for a reprieve. More specifically, he was asking to be briefly excluded from their family drama.

Antonio said, "You're welcome to stay with us as long as you and Anabel need."

"It's like everyone wants to live in a fantasy," Alida said, her frustration growing. She looked at Serguey. "Half the block won't talk to my parents now. They found out what happened with Felipe and that you moved here, and they're treating them like lepers."

She wasn't blaming him, but he could tell that she didn't want to be walking on eggshells. She wanted the truth to be treated without a gullible, cheery lens.

"You're exaggerating," Antonio said. "The more recalcitrant neighbors don't speak to us because we go to church."

Alida climbed off her chair and began to walk out of the room. "It's gotten worse and you know it."

"She's still blathering about leaving," Anabel said to Serguey when her sister was gone.

He didn't reply. He needed to cool off, reboot his mind. "Could I take a shower?" he asked Julia.

The family dispersed, giving Serguey the space he hoped for. He cleaned up, shaved using one of Antonio's razors, and put on fresh clothes.

Closer to dinnertime, he and Anabel sat in the yard, watching the sunset as they had done before. It hadn't rained in Mantilla. The air was moist, but the ground and trees were dry, the leaves nimble in their zany flapping, like a blundering attempt at a glitzy dance. Alida was taking a nap. According to Anabel, she'd been taking pills and sleeping a lot.

"I'm starting to worry," she confessed.

"Once my old man's out," Serguey said half in jest, "I might start taking pills too." He then told her about his exchange with Felipe. He regretted chiding him, given the circumstances. He'd seen that Victor wanted them to behave like a functional family again.

"It's easier for Victor and your dad," Anabel replied. "Whatever differences there might be, they live together. They know how to be near each other. You're the last to the party."

"But that's on me."

She stared at him, piqued. "If you're going to blame yourself, then there's no point. You know it's more complicated than that."

"It's just difficult to process all this stuff with everything that's going on."

"Give it time. You and Victor are getting along. That's a start."

It was more than a start, and this he could cling to—the small victories and achievements. Modest progress. This was what most Cubans clung to, anyway: tiny glimmers of improvement as fuel for hope.

"How are your parents?" he asked her.

She shrugged, her shoulders remaining elevated. "They were happy today."

He looked at her, aware that she could feel his probing gaze.

Her shoulders sank, her eyes turning toward his. "They're also stressed. What Alida said about the neighbors is true. There's tension there."

Another "I'm sorry" would have been too selfish. So would have been telling her about the house's defacement, about his conversations with Carmina.

"We'll help them," he said with a nod, accentuating his solidarity. "Your parents won't have to be alone."

She smiled, the subdued melancholy that'd been fixed to her face since their argument slowly subsiding. She had grasped what he meant: regardless of what might happen, they would be together. In their years as a couple, they had never discussed deserting Cuba. In a country where thousands risked their lives on homemade rafts, where people married foreigners or Cubans who had become American citizens just to escape their poverty and bleak futures, not discussing the possibility of migrating was a clear sign of their intentions. Whatever her reasons—family, fear of change, faith that they could get by in Cuba—Serguey knew that she didn't want to leave. He wasn't going to pressure her, to persuade her to change her mind. His own decision to leave depended on one single thing—his wife. He was staying because he loved her. Of this, he was surer than anything.

As the afternoon transitioned into evening, hefty clouds began to line the horizon, glazed in a red tint akin to nebulae. Serguey heard chickens clucking in the adjacent yard. Perhaps the neighbor had bought a new batch. Antonio's cinder blocks were there, clogging the holes beneath the fence. One rarely saw live chickens in the city, though it was possible. Serguey associated them with rural life, with his grandparents. His grandmother was an expert at breaking their necks. Two quick twists were all it took. He wouldn't be able to do such a thing. Victor was the one who'd picked up the birds' limp, spastic bodies and tethered them to his waist. Serguey could hurt someone with the knitting of words: irony, insinuations, accusations. Felipe had passed these skills on to him like DNA. But wringing necks was Victor's business. Same with Montalvo and Gimenez. People like them persevered. People like Serguey starved, faded. And to think that, at one point, he had pictured himself dining with Anabel in Stockholm, showered by velvety snow.

Antonio spent dinner singing Father Linares's and the Church's praises. He beamed as he explained how letters and phone calls were made on Felipe's behalf. Alida ate dinner alone in the yard, under the lambent light of a bulb Antonio had wired up above the door. Serguey asked Anabel whether they should talk to her, keep her company. Anabel told him that she'd just shut them out. It was best to let her come to them. Anabel was using the same logic he had used with Victor at the house, so when he found himself privately disagreeing with her, he didn't bring it up. He told her that she was probably right.

At exactly 10:00 p.m., Kiko called. He sounded edgy, though he had good news. A source had informed Claudia that Felipe was indeed being flown to Madrid as early as Tuesday. Kiko said he didn't want to discuss any details over the phone but that Serguey could meet him and Claudia at his place the next morning.

"The back and forth must be killing you," he said, "but you'd do me a solid if you came."

Serguey exhaled away from the receiver. "I'll be there. Victor too?"

"He already knows. Scoop him up on your way here."

Anabel wasn't happy with the plan. If his friend were really worried, it made more sense for him to speak with Serguey over the phone.

"I can't turn my back on the people who've helped me. Kiko won't set me up." He said this without looking at her, a physical exclusion that dissuaded her from pressing the issue.

Close to midnight, the Industriales vs. Villa Clara baseball game Antonio had been watching was in the thirteenth inning, tied at five runs apiece. Serguey and Anabel decided to turn in. Antonio had fallen asleep in his rocking chair, unperturbed by the television's glare. Julia told them that she would take care of waking and dragging him to their bedroom.

"It's a routine for us," she said.

Anabel wouldn't have it. She helped her mother carry Antonio like an injured, incoherent soldier to the room.

Alida was already deep in slumber in her bed. Serguey and Anabel removed their clothes except for their underwear and slipped under the covers. A tall, rust-spotted fan stood by the bedroom door, rattling and warbling as it spun. Serguey couldn't see well in the darkness, but he felt Anabel's hand crawling down his arm, then his pelvis, and finally grabbing his penis. He kissed her slowly, digging his fingers into the curving slope of her ass. They locked their bodies, and he murmured into her ear, asking if it was prudent with Alida in the same room.

"The pills," Anabel said. "A train horn won't wake her."

That disarmed him. Serguey began pleasuring his wife, her moans not as quiet as he expected. After a while, she pulled him on top. The bed creaked, but the sounds they made merged with the fan's. Serguey timed his deeper thrusts to match the fan's movement at its loudest, when it turned away from them. He concentrated on his wife—her tightening thighs, her breasts rubbing against his ribs. As he sensed the end was near, he slouched forward. Anabel bit his earlobe, and he couldn't restrain himself. She ran her palms over his sweat-lacquered back as he lay on her, knee-buckled and out of breath. He kissed her neck and nibbled on it until she shrieked.

They took turns going to the bathroom, flicking the light on only after they'd closed the door. No one in the house noticed, especially Alida, who proved she was asleep by mumbling something incoherent about ballet. He hadn't thought of her. He hadn't imagined her face or body. Toward the end, he forgot that she was a few steps away, shrouded in a mound of shadows. None of this absolved him from his previous dream, but it undeniably lightened his shame.

❦❦❦

The next morning, Antonio worked out a ride for Serguey to Calzada 10 de Octubre and Santa Catalina. Serguey began to walk the rest of the way, nearly two kilometers, under a clear sky. Students had already nestled into their class-rooms, listening to their first period teachers. Adults were headed to work with coffee-fueled steps. Serguey passed his middle school, which, unlike others, had been repaired and painted. He resolved taking the same route he had as a teenager. He strode by the bus stop where he and Kiko had bought *cucuruchos de mani* from the toothless man with the camouflage fanny pack. A few people were cloistered under the roof, their faces made grim by the inflexible slitting of their eyes.

A quarter of an hour later, as he neared the house, he noticed a man standing in the corner. An open newspaper concealed his profile. He was leaning against the column of an abandoned, boarded up bodega. He appeared to have a black cell phone case attached to his belt, which for an instant Serguey confused with a holster.

As he planted his feet on the front steps of the house, Serguey glanced back at the man and saw him fold the paper while staring in his direction. He knocked with deliberate vigor. Victor opened the door, already dressed. Serguey kept him from exiting.

"Check out the guy to my left," he said, "by the bodega."

Nonchalantly, Victor crossed the width of the porch to the veranda and scanned the block. "If there was a guy, he's gone. You're not getting paranoid on me like Kiko, are you?"

"Maybe I'm seeing things."

He wasn't. The brothers began to walk away from the house, and three men in civilian clothing emerged from behind the columns. Soon they had changed sidewalks, trailing Serguey and Victor some thirty meters behind.

"We're going to have to lose them," Victor said, barely moving his lips.

"What do you mean?" Serguey whispered, his heart racing.

At the end of the block, Victor shoved Serguey to the left instead of going straight. He waited with his back against the wall of the corner building and gestured for Serguey to do the same. They could hear the men hastening their steps. Victor intercepted them the minute he saw their bodies.

"What the fuck do you want?"

One of the men reached for his lower back and retrieved a club. Victor latched on to it, their tussling becoming a tug-of-war. Another man grabbed Victor from behind. The three-headed mass scuffled toward the middle of the street, as if dragged by an invisible force. The third man ordered Serguey to remain close to the wall, a hand at his hip over what turned out to be a small pistol. Serguey watched the man's fingers begin to grip the gun. A vision of the other two holding Victor while this one aimed the pistol at him played somewhere in Serguey's mind.

When the guy finally unholstered the weapon, he pointed it at Serguey, almost absentmindedly, as if aware that the older brother didn't pose a physical threat. His face stayed turned toward Victor and the men, the sharpness in his eyes reinforcing Serguey's fear that this wouldn't end well. A suffusing ache swirled about in his gut, a painfully enlarging contraction he had experienced before, when his body froze and he became a useless spectator. Serguey resisted it with a scream as he kicked the man in the groin, out of sheer terror. A delayed response followed the hit, during which Serguey, holding his breath, could see the man's eyes rolling up and momentarily disappearing behind the eyelids. He ultimately dropped to the ground, grunting like a dizzy, wounded animal. The pistol fell from his hand, and Serguey punted it down the sidewalk, not wanting to get his prints anywhere near it. Emboldened by the effectiveness of his actions, he rushed to the curb and gripped a large rock, the size of a softball. He got closer to the downed man, who was beginning to stand, and sensing his own body expanding—getting taller and broader—he threw the rock at the man's head. The man fell forward, yelling "*Ay!*" as the rock ricocheted back to Serguey's feet. He writhed on the sidewalk, plugging his head as if trying to keep his brain from spilling out. Serguey picked up the rock again and ran to the street. Victor was on the ground, struggling with his two assailants. Serguey kicked the man on top, his shinbone clobbering the nose. He launched the rock as the man jerked backwards, striking him below the ribs. The man hunched over, heaving in pain.

Victor twisted his body and found himself mounting the last man. He jammed his knee on the man's right wrist, compelling him to release the club. Victor took it and struck the man repeatedly on the head and ears until his arms went limp.

"That one's got a gun!" Serguey yelled.

Victor looked around in confusion. "What?"

The previously armed man was crawling, more intent on covering the blood dripping down his forehead than retrieving the pistol. Victor tossed the club and shouted at Serguey to run. They sprinted toward Kiko's, Serguey a few steps behind. His legs were heavy, his feet impacting and retreating from the pavement as if on wet sand. Neighbors tracked their getaway with alarmed faces, but no one intervened. Serguey had the sensation that someone was right at his heels, that he'd be seized at any second, causing him to tumble on the sidewalk as his brother's leaping feet melted into a distant, sun-scarred haze.

They stopped at the base of Kiko's stairs, audibly catching their raspy breaths. No one had pursued them.

"What happened?"

The brothers glanced up and saw their friend leaning over the railing.

"Fucking State Security," Victor said.

Kiko looked down the street. "Come on, hurry in."

The pain in Serguey's gut returned as they went up the stairs.

Inside the apartment, they assessed the damage. Victor was bleeding from his right eyebrow and elbow. He had a bruise splashed across his neck. The second officer, he said, had tried to choke him. Serguey had a thin gash on his right index finger from throwing the jagged rock, but not much else. His shinbone and ankle were starting to hurt from the kick, but he refused to complain about it. Kiko got them bandages, some ice and a rag for Victor's eyebrow, which was swelling rapidly, and a glass of iced water.

"You did good," Victor told Serguey, patting him on the back. "You did really good."

Serguey downplayed the fact that he was on the verge of panic. It was as if his innards wanted to gush out of his skin. His hands and knees were trembling, so he kept pacing around the living room. "I'm not sure we did the right thing."

"They were coming to hurt us," Victor said. "You saw how fast that one guy went for his club." He looked at Kiko and let out an anguished chuckle. "One of them had a gun."

"A gun?" Kiko said. "Then it's really serious. I think they're onto us."

"What do you mean?" Serguey said.

"Claudia was supposed to meet with us here. She called about a half hour ago and said that the police had detained her. They searched her bag, put her in the back of the cruiser. They threatened to confiscate her computer and phone."

Serguey gazed worryingly at the window shutters, which were ajar. "This is it."

"They asked her a lot of questions about where she was going," Kiko said.

Victor groaned, kneading his elbow. "Did she say anything about us?"

"No. She's been detained before. She's not afraid." Kiko, maybe prompted by Serguey's implicit insistence, cranked the knob that closed the shutters and turned on the living room lights. "But I think State Security must have some idea that we know each other. Coming after all of you the same morning? That shit has to be coordinated."

Serguey hurried to the door, verifying that Kiko had locked it. "Maybe Montalvo finally saw the video and knows who sent it out."

"Why was Claudia coming to meet us?" Victor said.

"She wanted to give you the information about Felipe in person. She's worked hard on that."

"You should go to her."

"She's fine now. They released her." Kiko stood halfway between the brothers, unsure as to whom he should address. "I didn't want you to come to an empty apartment. I mean, look at you guys. Good thing I stayed."

"I think we're fucked," Serguey said. He momentarily considered whether it was possible for Kiko and Claudia to be colluding, whether Felipe's release was a lie. The wrong information could've been fed to the Church. Maybe Montalvo really wanted *all* the Blancos in prison. But there were so many arguments, so much evidence against this that, even in his panic, Serguey rejected it. He chose instead to have absolute faith in his friend.

"Whatever we decide to do," Victor said, "we have to act fast."

It took several breaths for Serguey to say, "What information did Claudia have about Dad?" He didn't want to leave the apartment without knowing.

Kiko spun completely toward him. "He's being flown out on Tuesday, like I told you. Apparently, one of Spain's ministers was already here for a scheduled visit, and the Church met with him. This minister has been dealing with the political prisoners situation for months. Claudia thinks that's what expedited Felipe's case."

The information went along the lines of what Father Linares had told Antonio, though the minister hadn't been mentioned. In the throes of their current circumstances, this was as much corroboration as Serguey could get.

"So the old man's getting out," Victor said. "What the fuck do *we* do next?"

The question rendered Serguey mute. He was shackled by a multitude of scenarios, which, under normal conditions, would demand lengthy mediation and careful planning. Under their present circumstances, he didn't have the luxury of time.

"Is the Mario option still available?" Kiko said.

"I'm not going with that guy," Victor said.

"Actually, we have to," Serguey said. He walked toward his brother. "We can't hide forever, not in this goddamn country."

A pall of terror Serguey had never seen—not even when the peasant wielded the knife—deformed Victor's features. "I'm not leaving."

"Do you think Montalvo's going to let it slide?" Serguey had to magnify his brother's fear. If attrition was the only way to soften Victor, he had to entrust himself to it. "We *have* to leave. We're going to rot in prison if we don't. We just assaulted three State Security officers."

Victor said nothing. He stared at Serguey, perplexed.

"When's Mario leaving?" Kiko asked.

"I think it's Thursday or Friday." Serguey stepped back to the door. All the hypotheticals and what ifs had come down to a singular speck of time. Hesitation was as daunting an enemy as the authorities. "We have to hide until then. We need to do what he did, go out to the countryside, away from fucking civilization. I just don't know where we can go."

Victor spoke with a resigned inflection, as if he'd had the answer all along. "You remember the shack where we used to play as kids, the one by grandma and grandpa's house?"

"That's got to be torn down by now."

"It's still there."

Victor sat with desolate abandon on Kiko's chair. Quite saddened, Serguey could see that his brother's resignation, and perhaps the fight, had sapped his usual strength.

"Dad and I visited last year," Victor said. "Some nostalgic trip he wanted to take. He said he was working on some play and wanted to reconnect with mom's family's past or some shit. I think he called you about it, but you were busy with your new job."

"I don't remember."

"It doesn't matter. I rented a car and drove him, out of curiosity. The shack looks abandoned, but it's there. We can make it work for a few days. The river's nearby. Lots of trees around. Everyone in that area takes the main trail, so there's little chance they'll pass by the shack."

"Who do we know that can drive us there?" Serguey said.

Kiko raised his hand. "I'll borrow a car. Give me fifteen minutes."

"We'll need to stop by the house and then Mantilla," Serguey said. "We'll have to make sure it's safe."

"The house's too hot," Kiko said. He looked at Victor. "Do you have anything there you *have* to pick up?"

"I need some clothes. Serguey's won't fit. Yours won't either."

"I got some stuff a cousin of mine brought me from *el Yuma*." Kiko ran to his bedroom, his voice resonating back to the brothers: "He's a big guy, so the clothes should fit you fine."

"Don't you have anything you absolutely need to take with you?" Serguey asked his brother. "If we leave, it'll be for good."

Kiko returned with a bulgy bag.

Committed to the plan, Victor rose from the chair and said, "My valuable stuff's with Yunior. After what happened with the house, I knew I could trust him. And I didn't want State Security to barge in again and suck me dry. Kiko has been holding my money."

Kiko handed him a plastic-swaddled stack of bills. "Way ahead of you."

Victor shoved the money inside the bag. "Yunior knows to sell the stuff if he doesn't hear from me for more than a week. He's supposed to get in touch with you once when he sells it."

The brothers sat in the living room while Kiko ventured out. Serguey watched the door and window, thinking about what to tell Anabel, praying that he would get a chance to see her.

After a few minutes of silence, Victor said, "Dad should've let you play baseball, the way you threw that rock."

"Victor," Serguey said, "I'm really scared."

His brother nodded. "I am too. But you can't let it get to you. You have to be yourself until the end."

It seemed so simple yet unachievable, like trying to snatch a full moon out of the sky from your bedroom window as a child. Fear was a familiar emotion to Serguey, almost a default setting in cases like this one. He had to rely on Victor and Kiko, feed off their pragmatism and audaciousness, however feigned they might be.

Kiko was true to his word. He came back with a refurbished Lada. "My friend says we can trust the engine and transmission. He's under the impression I'm going to the airport to pick up a relative and drop them off in Centro Habana, so we have to move quickly."

Beyond the building, the State Security men were nowhere in sight. They descended the stairs in a rush and were relieved to pull out of Kiko's block with no police cruiser in tow.

On their way to Mantilla, Serguey called Mario's number. The dramaturge answered after the first ring but didn't speak. Serguey identified himself before Mario, with a drop of excitement, told him how glad he was that they'd contacted him. The boat was scheduled for Thursday at 4:00 a.m. near Marhondo.

"My cousin has all the details worked out," Mario said. "I'm really happy that you and Victor have decided to join me."

With Victor's assistance, Serguey gave Mario directions to the main road closest to the shack. Mario jotted down the information and insisted that they needed to be at that spot at precisely 1:00 a.m., or he and his cousin would drive off.

"I'll be discarding my phone before then," Mario said. "I recommend you do the same."

Serguey assured him that he and Victor would be there, but he said nothing about the phones. He did tell Mario about Felipe's impending release.

"I've heard," Mario replied. "But it's great to have it confirmed."

Then he hung up.

"I won't say any more about it," Victor said, "but it sickens me that we have to depend on that guy."

Serguey and Kiko disregarded the comment. They concentrated on the road, on the vehicles behind them, the people bustling on the sidewalks. The buildings abutting Calzada 10 de Octubre were more derelict than in other areas of Havana. Entire blocks bore the appearance of slums, rubble-speckled and gray. Exposed brick showed like crooked grins on the side of every house, bodega, pharmacy, cafeteria. The lampposts—pared and splintered—doddered up in every direction, connecting a web of abraded power lines that, at certain intersections, looked like old tram cables. A peeling sign rose from a rooftop: *patria muerte.* Homeland or death. Later, a fading mural with Che Guevara's famous words: *¡hasta la victoria siempre!*

Until victory, always. It was a narrative, everywhere you went, allusions to an epic battle versus a larger evil. These maxims were sheared from the reality of Cuban life, from the beauty and indigence of daily existence. They lacked genuine emotion. The phrases were ostentatious and hyperbolic, saturated with irony of all ironies: if there had been an actual war, the crumbling city proved Cuba had obviously lost.

What these banners and sayings failed to capture was what Serguey had witnessed in recent weeks, contained within the world to which he had reconnected: the bare splendor of personal survival; the decency and selflessness of those betrayed or forgotten by the system; the contagiously defiant will to spend your day clawing and scratching in exchange for crumbs and scraps. As traffic intensified, the smell of smoke and gasoline flooded the car. Serguey inhaled it with pleasure, with the feeling that his senses were being infused with his brother's Cuba, his in-laws' Cuba, Toya's and Mario's and Claudia's. He raised his head as he observed his surroundings. The government had no idea what true victory was: to live in the heart of this rotting, wondrous city and still be able to proudly look anyone in the eye.

Kiko swerved onto Calzada de Managua, and the environment suddenly became rural. Not many tourists jaunted to this part of the city: trash heaped on one street corner, the cloying smell of rotting mangoes or pineapples on another. At Serguey's request, Kiko drove around his in-laws' neighborhood, but they saw nothing suspicious. They agreed that it was best to risk only one of them getting arrested, so Kiko parked the car a couple of blocks away from Antonio and Julia's home. Serguey disembarked cautiously. His ankle, having rested and cooled off, had become inflamed. His shinbone hurt whenever he took a step, forcing him to hobble toward the house.

Julia greeted him. She hollered at Anabel the instant she saw his limp.

The women led him to Antonio's armchair. Anabel taped his ankle while Julia held a bag of ice against the lower part of his leg. As they tended to him, Serguey described—plainly and succinctly—the altercation with State Security. Antonio and Alida listened attentively from the sofa. In Serguey's line of sight, the tip of their chins dipped behind a fresh batch of sunflowers Julia had deposited in the center table vase.

"We have to hide out in the country for a couple of days," Serguey said.

"Why don't you stay here?" Julia said. "That way, if anything happens, we'll know."

Serguey's mind careened down a mental tunnel of images: the portraits of Anabel and Alida scattered on the floor, the glass cracked, the photographs emblazoned with boot prints; Julia's sunflowers tramped on, the vase obliterated into shards; Antonio being heaved out to the street while the neighbors watched, snickering at his misfortune, his bad leg succumbing to the officers' savagery. The family would be talked about for weeks on end, falling prey to ridicule and verbal assaults. His in-laws' association with the Church could be used against them. Prison time wasn't beyond the realm of possibility.

He smiled at Julia, indebted to her generosity. "We need to go off the radar. They're going to be looking in all the expected places."

"We'll give you some things to take with you," Antonio said resolutely.

Serguey nodded. "I'd appreciate it." He looked at his in-laws, appealing to them with his eyes. "May I please have a moment with Anabel and Alida? The guys are parked nearby, and I'm kind of in a hurry."

Julia hesitated, glancing at her husband. "Yes, of course."

"Come on, *Vieja*," Antonio said. "Let's get some things for them."

Alida took her mother's place. "Here, I'll hold the ice."

Once his in-laws had left the room, Serguey said, "Mario offered for Victor and me to leave with him on a boat. What went down today, it was bad. It'll come back to us. I can try to convince Mario to let us all go, but I'm not sure he'll be able to make it work."

"I'm not going," Anabel said flatly, without looking up. She adjusted the tape as best she could.

Alida leaned into her ear. "Are you crazy? This is our chance!"

"I'm not abandoning Mom and Dad."

Alida reminded her sister that they had both been living away from home, and their parents had managed quite well. "We can send them money and medicine. Eventually we'll come visit, file an invitation letter so they can go see us. Maybe they'll want to stay over there too."

"They won't," Anabel said, her father's stanch tenor pulsating in her own voice. "You should go, Serguey. Be with your brother and your Dad. We can work it out."

"Alida, you're going to take my spot," he said.

Alida's eyes lit up. The ice bag slipped from her hands.

"Oh, no," Anabel said, glaring sadly at him. "You can't do that to me."

He stared back. "It's her choice, just like we get to make ours."

Anabel's hands stopped pulling at the tape. She said weakly, "I know I'm being selfish. I don't want you to get hurt. And I don't want to lose Alida. I just . . . I can't go. My parents, coming back here, I've seen how fragile they are. If something happens and no one's around, I won't forgive myself. If the police come . . ." She made as if to cry, seemingly out of frustration, but she choked back her sobs.

Alida hooked an arm gently around her sister.

"I understand," Serguey said. He had put his wife and her family in danger for his father's sake. He couldn't condemn Anabel for caring about Antonio and Julia. He emphasized to Alida that she needed to be ready on Wednesday after 11:00 p.m. Kiko would pick her up and take her to the departing point. "All the specifics should be figured out by then," he told her. He also warned her about the possibility that they'd get caught and arrested, the possibility that the people driving the boat could decline the switch.

"Think of it as a long shot," he said. "The disappointment won't be as bad if the plan falls through."

"Thank you," Alida mouthed, squeezing his knee.

"What about Victor?" Anabel asked, simulating composure. "How is he going to take it?"

"He'll think I'm going with him. I have to make sure he gets on that boat. It's not fair, but—"

"You have to save him from himself," she said in agreement. Her nose and cheeks were gaining color. She was still on the verge of sobbing.

"I wish it could be different," Serguey said, "but I can't afford to second-guess myself. I have to give him a chance. Heck, I'm not even sure Mario will hold his end of the bargain." After a short pause, he put his hands on Alida's, complaining that the ice was actually starting to hurt him.

She accurately interpreted that he wished to be alone with his wife. Alida thanked him again and went to the kitchen, disgorging the ice onto the sink.

"Your ankle should be fine," Anabel said. She hacked the tape off with her teeth.

He cradled her chin in his fingers. She still didn't want to look up.

"I know I'm failing you by not going," she said. "I don't want you to end up in prison. I mean it when I say you should go. We can figure things out."

He waited a moment. "Leaving without you isn't an option."

She raised her eyes. "Serguey, I'm sorry."

"If they arrest me, you'll have to make the trips to wherever they send me."

They were both silently crying. Anabel straightened up and wiped her tears, knowing their time alone would be short. Serguey did the same. They kissed—short, determined kisses—until they heard voices approaching the living room.

"Here," Julia said, giving Serguey a bag. "There's food, some aspirin for the pain, newspaper squares to use as toilet paper, knives and forks, matches, and a flashlight."

Antonio had another bag. "Some bed sheets and a mosquito net. Out there, those suckers will murder you. We're running low on soap, but there's a bar there too."

"It's too much," Serguey said.

"Nonsense," Julia said. "Don't tell anybody, but we get things through church donations. We're first on Father Linares's list."

"When God tenders you something, you take it," Antonio said.

Serguey shook his hand as sturdily as he could.

Anabel walked into the bedroom and brought him a backpack filled with clothes.

"You return to us safe and sound, you hear?" Julia said. She embraced Serguey. Alida followed suit.

Anabel went with him to the door. Her eyes were again brimful with tears. "You listen to me," she said, "you make sure Victor and my sister leave safely, and then you haul your ass over here, you hear me? You promise me that, Serguey."

"I promise."

"Everyone's doing their part, and we've all pretended to be strong and that nothing has really changed, but now it's going to be just you and me. It's all I have."

"It's all I have too."

Tears trickled down her cheekbones. "Then you come here the moment it's over."

"I will."

He hugged her. Her arms came up behind his back, her hands clamping on to his shoulders. Then she stepped back. Anabel was not one for dawdling. Decisions had been made, and now the outcomes had to be played out.

"They're waiting," she said.

Serguey left the home, the bags flanking him weighty as cannonballs, his body tilted to the right. The sun felt hot on his neck. Everyone he saw on his way to the car looked dubious: the old lady sweeping her porch, the young man with a purple Hilfiger T-shirt, smoking and scratching his sideburns. Serguey hastened his pace despite the obstinate pain in his ankle.

Victor and Kiko grumbled about the heat when he arrived, though they were pleased to see the bags.

"We're going to make a little pit stop on the way," Victor said. "I got a contact in Managua where we can get food."

Kiko looked into the rearview mirror and put the car in gear.

CHAPTER 26

The contact in Managua was able to offer only half a pound of beans, a few ears of corn, and black-spotted tomatoes that were a day from spoiling. Kiko insisted that there was no time to wander in search of better provisions, so they purchased the lot and continued on. Deeper into the countryside, suburbs were replaced by plowed parcels of red earth, wind-combed grass like a horse's mane, lines of barbed wire fences, cows roving and idling behind them. Broad portions of sky were suddenly visible above a quaint blanket of green. Kiko maneuvered around the occasional ox-drawn wagon or bicycle-riding peasant until, in a half-hour, they reached San Antonio de las Vegas and its soil-dusted streets. They sped through the town's main road past a bodega, a block of houses with large front yards that dipped below the road, and a cruddy barn-like building that was a storm away from collapsing. They climbed a hill and steered left at the summit. Following Victor's indications, Kiko led the car on a deserted gravel path for a kilometer before the brothers got off.

"You should turn off your phones," Kiko said. "Save the battery."

A dusty, whispering air patted Serguey's face as he jumped out. The gravel path curved out of view some hundred meters ahead, beyond it a flat expanse of vegetation. He powered off his cell, as Victor was already doing.

He walked to his brother's side and said, "I need to ask Kiko a favor in private."

Victor pocketed his phone. "You can kiss him goodbye in front of me."

"I'm serious."

Victor turned to Kiko and hugged him, vigorously slapping his back. "I'll send you some food, you bony bastard."

From where he stood, Serguey could see Kiko smiling, a smile that served to quell the melancholy frown fizzing underneath. Kiko had no idea that he would get another opportunity to bid his friend farewell.

"You better not mess around over there," he said. "Make your money the right way."

Victor grabbed Kiko's slouched shoulders. "Clean slate. Plus I'll have Serguey to watch over me, right?"

Serguey was already retrieving the bags from the car. "Right."

Victor took the two biggest bags from his brother. He dangled them from his shoulders, cupping their strained bottoms. He began to walk into a narrow recess in a wall of overgrown grass, which appeared to swallow him, the crown of his head barely rising above the blades.

"He's going to miss me," Kiko said to Serguey.

"And me," Serguey said.

Kiko leaned his head forward, his eyes opening in astonishment. Serguey shared his plan to pick up Alida, to have her take his place. He didn't give many specifics as to the reason: with his friend, he didn't have to. Kiko understood Serguey's dilemma, though he was disappointed that he'd risk staying in Cuba.

Serguey sighed dejectedly. "Anabel won't leave her parents, and I can't leave her."

"I respect that. The reason I broke up with the Mexican girl your brother mentioned is my parents. I can't leave them either. My old man is in rough shape." Kiko agreed that it was best to keep Victor in the dark. "If you tell him, he'll refuse to go, out of pure stubbornness."

Serguey would text Kiko the night of the trip from Mario's car to give him the exact location. Mario had already told him it was in Marhondo.

"I know the area," Kiko said. He assured Serguey that he'd deliver.

Serguey told him to thank Claudia again. "It's a shame she couldn't meet us."

Kiko looked over his shoulder at the rocky path, tracing his return to the main road. "Now I have to go deal with that, see how it plays out." He took a glimpse at his watch and said he needed to rush to the city. They shook hands, and his friend got into the car. Serguey watched the wheels grind the gravel, kicking up dust. The exhaust pipe spluttered copious amounts of smoke as the vehicle distanced itself from him.

He carried the remaining bags and his backpack, catching up with his brother in forty meters. Victor had trekked into the thick vegetation keeping the bags close to his knees, winding and sliding to prevent them from being slashed open.

"What was that back there?" he asked without looking at Serguey.

"Just something about Anabel."

"I didn't want to ask you about her in front of Kiko. I guess I should've. How did she take it?" Victor pushed an oversized branch with his hip as if it were a turnstile.

Serguey struggled to remain balanced. His bum ankle anchored him frailly on the rough terrain. "She knows this is a unique situation."

"Serguey, cut the bullshit."

He needed to commit to the lie more emphatically, more believably. He needed to give the illusion of tacit understanding between him and Anabel. "She's disappointed," he said, pausing for effect. The sound of crushed twigs and brushed-against leaves accompanied his steps. "I promised her I'd get her out. I'm sure she's mad at me, and probably at you too, but she trusts me."

"We'll get her out. Alida too. Anabel's not the type of woman who'll betray you. She's patient."

"Like Penelope."

"I'd love to say you're exaggerating," Victor grunted and ducked under a bough, "but this is a fucking odyssey."

They lumbered on, their bags scraping tree trunks and wedging between the narrow spaces in the foliage. They skirted the clearing where the encounter with the peasants had occurred. Serguey glanced at it twice, thinking the area more congested than he recalled it. Victor didn't bother to look, and Serguey wondered if he had forgotten the place. Had it been erased from his brother's consciousness like his unremembered dreams? Quietly, he continued on, recognizing the path to the shack from this point. He anticipated coming across a fallen trunk, the top shaved so flatly that it served as a bridge when rain pulped the soil into mud. Soon they hopped over the makeshift bridge, a lot smaller than Serguey remembered it. The shack's shoddy shape became visible to their right. The thatched roof was slanted, one side beginning to cave. The unwieldy branches from neighboring trees rested obliquely on it. A series of rocks still remained leading up to the entrance—a walkway their grandfather had set up to combat the trapping sludge. The wooden walls looked sturdy and damp. The window was shut, though one could see a narrow vertical breach created by the uneven size of the panes.

Inside, the air was riddled with a mossy stench. The shadows seemed thick with humid dust. Various cavities burrowed between the baseboard and the ground, ideal shelters for snakes and scorpions.

"We should've gotten some repellent," Serguey said.

Victor dropped the bags in the middle of the shack. "The mosquito nets will be enough." He went to the window and opened it. One of the panes fell off completely. "I guess we should've brought a hammer and nails too."

Serguey put down his bags and backpack by the door. "We need some palm leaves to use as a mattress."

"Man, this was our fort." Victor stood on his toes and stretched one arm, his fingers grazing one of the horizontal beams below the concave roof. When they were children, a tarp had been laid over the beams to ensure water didn't reach whatever merchandise Larido was storing. Sacks full of rice and potatoes had been stacked along the walls, giving the interior the fort-like appearance Victor was referencing.

"Damn!" Serguey said, slapping his own thigh.

"What?" Victor attempted to sit on the windowsill, but his head hit the top frame, causing him to jerk forward.

"We forgot to bring water." He stared at Victor wide-eyed, stunned that they'd forgotten something so essential.

Victor scratched his scalp, massaging away the pain. "We better hope the river's clean. Otherwise, we'll have to go into town."

Serguey rummaged through the bags his in-laws had given him. He was relieved to find two tin cups and a cooking pot. They ventured out and gleaned as many feathered palm leaves as they could, arranging them along the floor of the shack like two beds. They amassed dry twigs and a few small rocks for a bonfire and snatched guavas and Spanish limes off nearby trees, nuzzling the fruits in the shawl-like basket formed by their sleeve-tied T-shirts. Their last trip was to the river, two hundred meters way. The water looked clear. There were no animal carcasses or signs of chemical contamination from a turbine, so they filled the glasses, pot, and two emptied-out cans. Returning to the shack, Serguey noticed that his ankle had loosened somewhat, the pain kept at bay by Anabel's tape job. He still had to drag his foot, however, so he couldn't avoid tailing his brother everywhere they went.

As night fell upon them, they got the bonfire going below the window outside the shack. They boiled beans in the pot, sliced up a few tomatoes, and warmed up charred chicken drums that Julia had wrapped in tinfoil. They ate with gusto in the faint glow of the flames. They decided to save one can with water and the fruits for the next morning. Serguey switched on the kerosene lamp and hung it from a hook by the door, dimly illuminating the interior of the shack. They put out the fire with their shoes and used the flashlight to properly set up the mosquito nets. They conserved their energy for what needed to be done, refraining from speaking much while they carried out these tasks. Serguey felt drained by the time he blew out the lamp and they settled themselves inside the netting, using clean T-shirts as pillows. Even with the palm leaves, the floor was sharp and toothed, digging into his back. The night air was wet and brisk. Beyond the shack's walls, the countryside remained awake with chirping and hooting and the disquieting sound of snapping branches. Closer to Serguey, mosquitoes buzzed in the blurred spaces just outside his net.

"Whoever wakes up first has to wake the other," Victor said.

"Okay," Serguey said absentmindedly.

He listened for approaching voices as he lay beneath the sheets Julia had provided. He worried about the scenarios he might contemplate now that his thoughts were unhinged by the twilight of sleep. He was putting his brother ahead of everything. The sacrifice Toya had talked about seemed imminent, thirsting to manifest itself. The consequences of returning to the city might involve a fate worse than Felipe's, and yet, despite the anxiety and fear, his commitment to save his younger brother felt born out of his true self. It was a decision made not just out of responsibility, out of his guilt for owing Victor support, protection, even the simple act of company. It was a decision made out of profound empathy, familial devotion, and fraternal love. He was being selfless because he couldn't do anything else, and it comforted him that he was capable of it.

He did worry about what Anabel might be thinking, about the future of his marriage to a woman for whom, because of the legal issues he'd be facing, he was now a problem. What he had imagined could happen to his in-laws—the trampled flowers, the broken portraits, Antonio's humiliation—might be transpiring at this very hour. And this, perhaps, troubled him most of all: the collateral damage of his actions. It was one thing for him to go to prison, another for Anabel and family to suffer as a result. But what choices did he have? He was plunging all the way, as Anabel herself had urged him to. He was doing it intuitively, decidedly, as if nothing else made sense. Would she see it this way? If she or her own parents became victims of this month-long nightmare, would she really be willing to understand, to absolve him of blame?

Though he wished to, he didn't get the opportunity to delve deeper into her possible state of mind: he fell asleep after a few conscious breaths, physically drained to the point of surrender.

※❀⊰❀ ❀⊱❀※

It was Victor who opened his eyes first.

Serguey heard him returning to the shack. His movements were sluggish. He yawned and stood groggily, observing his makeshift bed, unsure of what to do.

"You were supposed to wake me," Serguey said, releasing his arms and legs from the grip of the sheets. A stiff ache clenched his muscles.

"You want me to hold your hand while you take a piss?"

Serguey hobbled out of his netting like a corpse from a crypt. He squinted and rubbed his eyes, fixating his vision just under Victor's armpit. "What happened to you?"

Victor gave him a bewildered look.

Serguey walked toward his brother. "The side of your body. It's all red."

Victor lifted his arm and examined the area, pulling the skin toward his stomach. "Oh, shit."

"Does it itch?"

Victor passed his hand over the irritated surface. "Not really. Looks like a rash. Must be the humidity."

"We have to wash up."

"I'm used to showering before going to bed. I can't tell you how uncomfortable I feel right now."

"Well, clean your hands before you eat breakfast."

Serguey decided to leave the shack as it was. Victor extracted a plastic bag from the bundle of clothes Kiko had given him. His money was stuffed neatly inside it. He perched the bag on one of the beams and looked at it from different angles, to verify that it was properly hidden. If a person were to come by, he said, they would be able to tell someone was staying there, but at least they wouldn't take the money.

Serguey followed his own advice and, after taking a piss, rinsed his hands with dewdrops. Victor tossed him a guava, and he dug his teeth into it, snapping off a chunk. They shared the remaining water, grabbed the bar of soap, and headed for the river.

They chose an area bounded by narrow-limbed trees, where the water was deep. The bank was covered in mud, the river bottom mantled by swaying algae. The clearer sections of the stream, pocked with smooth rocks, were too shallow and open, visible from a distance. Here, they had their own private bath, albeit murky. They hung their clean clothes from branches, stripped down to their underwear, and stepped into the cool water. The soft soil twirled and surged around their feet and knees. The algae grazed and tangled their legs, releasing them once they pushed off into the middle of the river, where they could glide more freely.

Serguey had taught Victor how to swim in this very body of water. It hadn't taken long. Victor was brave and strong, his strokes coordinated enough to allow him to quickly grow confident. He'd looked less gracious, like a frog, as he tried to remain in one spot, his skinny arms and legs frenziedly keeping him afloat. His chin had remained just above the surface as he laughed in delight, thrilled by the result of his effort: he had learned how not to drown.

As the years passed, Victor became the better swimmer, though he never acquired Serguey's ability to dive with grace. The handful of times Felipe took them to the Social Circles in Miramar—pre-Revolution yacht clubs and private seaside spas that were pillaged and then opened to the public—Serguey had put his innate diving skills in full display. The shoreline was studded with sea urchins and the remnants of broken-down docks, but the water was deep enough to jump into. Other children tried imitating Serguey as he leaned off a ledge—eyes closed, arms stretched as if on a cross—and flew like an arrow into the sea. Diving excited him more than swimming, which he found tiresome and monotonous. There was no moment of silence like the few seconds prior to plunging.

Here, in this mud-blanketed river, he had no choice: he had to wade and swim. He was in Victor's territory.

After a quarter of an hour of splashing and Victor practicing his backstroke, they washed with the soap. They rinsed their bodies and propped themselves onto a series of weaving roots that sank like deformed fingers into the river. Their heels and toes still touched the water. Serguey removed the tape, which had wicked the pale skin around his ankle. There was no more swelling. Sunlight reached the brothers in drifting blotches, mimicking the oscillation of the leaves above them.

"We should've come to this place more often," Victor said.

"Very relaxing," Serguey concurred. There was rejuvenation, a revitalizing of the senses by the calm way in which every element—air, water, soil—seemed to cohabit and give way to the other.

"I've been to pools at some hotels. But I mostly end up checking out the tourists." Victor was allergic to sentimentality, even his own.

"You can't compare a hotel to this," Serguey said. "This is nature."

"You're right." Victor roiled the river's plated surface with his soles. "Those tourists weren't bad to look at, though."

Serguey laughed, defeated by his brother's persistence. "You know, I think I've always resented that."

"What?"

"How no matter what's happening, you can turn everything into a joke. I really envy it."

Victor turned his head pensively to the side, a ribbon of sunlight spreading to his cheek. From Serguey's point of view, he looked a lot like their mother. "It gets me in trouble."

"Yeah, but in some ways it keeps you more honest. Sometimes I get so wrapped up in my posturing, I start to get mad at myself. It's not healthy. You feel like an old man."

A flock of birds entered their frame of vision. They flew from right to left, their pattern synchronized. Victor made a rifle with his hands and fired. Serguey watched the birds moving away, fluid dots in the sky.

"How I wish we hadn't run out of pellets," he said.

It took a moment for Victor to reply. "Me too."

"I'm sorry I didn't do more." He rushed the words, like yanking out a splinter.

Victor chuckled. "You kind of did nothing."

Serguey spoke slower this time. "You're right. I was a coward."

"We were kids. I got over it."

"I wish I could say the same."

Victor removed his feet from the water and dug them into the soaked soil of the bank. "When I got older, I realized we were just wired differently. I think we bring that with us from birth, like it's in our DNA. We can't control it."

Serguey frowned his smile. His brother was giving him his own version of forgiveness.

"I don't resent you for what happened with the peasants," Victor continued. "Those assholes are probably eating mud and fucking mares as we speak."

"We didn't talk the same way after that," Serguey said, hoping his brother would meet his eyes. "It's like we became angry at each other."

Victor seized a clump of muck and threw it into the river. "I dated this girl once who was studying to be a psychologist. Really nice ass, too. She got me to talk about our childhood and shit. To indulge her, I told her some of our traumatic experiences—she loved that word, 'traumatic'—and she said that I was probably angry at you before the incident with the peasants."

"Why did she think that?"

Victor looked at him. "Because of what happened with Mom."

"How so?"

"You know, about how you froze, same as you did with the peasants."

"I froze?" Serguey's heart was thudding.

Victor shrunk his shoulders empathetically. "You were standing by the bed, crying and shaking. I lunged at Raidel, that fucking scum, and he cut me."

"I thought you got cut by accident, when he was running out of the house."

"Maybe it was by accident, but it happened when I went at him."

Serguey was overtaken by a smothering panic. How could he not remember? He recalled the blood, his mother's body bent on the floor, her mouth gasping. He recalled the sound of his and Victor's crying, the neighbors bolting into the house, enfolding him and Victor in towels. He recalled uniformed police officers walking to and fro, the lights of an ambulance as they were taken away. Altogether, it was a jumbled assortment of images, an almost surreal montage. He and Victor had met with the psychologist following their mother's death, but he couldn't recollect a single word spoken in those sessions.

His voice began to break. "I honestly don't remember . . ."

Victor shrugged more emphatically. "We were kids. There was nothing either of us could've done anyway. It was meant to happen. At least we had Dad."

Serguey stared at Victor through blurry eyes. Victor smacked his brother's chest with the back of his hand.

"Don't break on me now," he said. "Who the hell knows if what I remember is what actually happened?"

"We've never really talked about Mom."

"It's a sore subject for Dad. And I wasn't sure how you felt about it, so I figured I'd just keep it to myself. But I think about her a lot."

"At least that piece of shit Raidel died in prison."

Victor put on a smirk. "Fucking pneumonia."

"I thought it was a lung abscess."

"Who cares? I hope he choked on his own blood."

Serguey was unable to speak for a while. The brothers sat together, their skin dry and their heads warm, taking in the view of green and brown and blue. An intermittent breeze flitted over and rippled the water, forming scale-like outlines. Leaves rustled. A frog leapt into the river. Serguey wanted to apologize again, but he kept swallowing instead.

"My ass is really starting to hurt," Victor eventually said. "These branches need a cushion."

They threw on the clean clothes, folded the dirty ones, and sauntered back to the shack. After a short nap, they returned to the river for some water, ate fruits and bread for lunch, and again amassed twigs for a bonfire.

During dinner—beans and boiled potatoes—they reminisced about their mother, now more comfortable with the subject. Victor talked about how he often fell asleep in her bed, nuzzled against her neck, Serguey about how she sat them on the bedroom floor and fed them from the same plate, alternating spoonfuls and making airplane sounds.

"It was the only way she could get you to eat," he said to his brother. "You used to make a huge mess."

There'd been joy in her face during those moments. There'd been joy for all of them. At the very least, Serguey figured, he and Victor had been good companions to their mother.

As they prepared to fall asleep in the pitch-dark of the shack, Serguey dissected the conversations they'd just had. It had been curative to hear Victor forgive him—or maybe not forgive him, exactly—but refuse to assign him blame. Serguey pulled the hem of his sheets to combat the chill of the night air. His breathing quaked his body like a mild convulsion. There was some rage in him still, perhaps more than was in Victor. There was regret, abhorrence at his own cowardice. Victor's version of their mother's death, of how they had each reacted, fit into the narrative of their respective lives. He needed to tell his brother what he felt. He needed to confess more than to receive forgiveness. But there was also great relief to be found in fighting off the State Security scum the day before. Relief in sensing that he might not freeze again in the future, that Victor could count on him to lunge like a rabid animal when required. They had also opened a trustworthy channel of communication. The possibility of confession without ridicule or indictment was now real, as was the possibility of forgiveness in a new light: two adult brothers who genuinely knew each other's remorse, each other's pain. Victor hadn't uttered the words "I forgive you," but he had offered absolution. He had shown himself capable of grasping the complicated truths behind one boy's inaction. Serguey had to respond in kind, embrace his brother's understanding as a pardon. Life had afforded him the chance to come through for Victor, and he hadn't wasted it. And what was this if not its own form of confession? What was it if not a genuine attempt at atonement?

In the shack's silence, the slightest of sounds became exponentially amplified. Victor's snoring, like the snort of a lazy hog, made Serguey think of torpor—a renouncing to the primal need for rest. If he had believed in the human spirit as a presence, he could've said that it was leaving him, that the rote flowing of his blood was more independent from his consciousness than ever before. It had been a good day, but it could bear no more. All they could do was rest.

The following morning Victor seemed jittery. He wasn't adept at waiting, not when there was something significant in store for him. He begged Serguey to take a stroll, maybe skirt the riverbank away from the town, under the claim that they had to "take it all in." This could be the last time they saw this part of Cuba. Serguey indulged him, despite thinking the idea might be too risky. The last thing he wanted was to bump into someone who could report them to local authorities. They might confuse them for livestock thieves or escaped convicts.

They walked for a couple of kilometers. Serguey's mind was lulled by the steady sound of grass lapping at his knees, his legs grazing the stalks and narrow leaves. He saw palm trees and *yagruma* strewn around them. In his first visit to the United States after 1959, Fidel had told the Americans that the Revolution was *"mas verde que las palmas."* Greener than the palm trees, not red like communism.

Nothing was greener than this, Serguey thought.

Larido had built the shack in this area for a reason. There was nothing but unkempt country—a sanctuary for the subversive. Just prior to a bend in the river, they found another portion of deep water to swim in. Serguey stayed by the bank, his elbows partially buried in mud, his outstretched feet floating in the soft current. He asked Victor to keep the splashing to a minimum. A block of low clouds coasted in a mild wind. Serguey wondered whether Felipe had already arrived in Spain. He fretted that if either Mario or Kiko told them he hadn't, Victor would refuse to go to Miami. It was bad enough having to convince him to get on the boat without him. He hoped that Alida would be the wild card, that her being there would force Victor to commit.

Serguey thought also about what was in store for his father. At Felipe's age, starting over was a colossal task. It didn't matter how many friends might be waiting for him. Serguey suspected that, at a certain point in life, one begins to feel as though there's nothing new to experience. The external world changes, but who you are holds too much weight. Your habits, what you've accomplished, your errors and successes, what you've taken from the particular external world you've always known, they feel like the entirety of existence. None of it can be effaced, replaced by the promise of a fresh beginning, not after fifty years. Life in another country, with all its challenges and perks, wouldn't be a sort of rebirth or transition for his father. It'd be a perpetual reminder that he was no longer home.

In the end—and in this, Serguey found solace—a melancholy existence was better than decaying in prison. And Felipe, the great theater director, had a penchant for playing whatever part he was assigned in all its glory, extracting whatever gratification he could out of it. He'd find a way to get by.

In the afternoon, they slept through a transient rain. The sky had cleared by the time they awoke. As they folded the mosquito nets and bundled them inside the bags, Victor asked Serguey how he planned to get the stuff back to Julia and Antonio.

"We'll figure something out," he said. "Maybe drop them off somewhere they can pick it up, or give it to Mario's cousin."

"I think the cousin's leaving too."

"We'll figure something out," he repeated. He signaled at the zip lock bag on the wooden beam and added, "Don't forget your money."

They made only small talk during dinner, eating the last of their rations and laughing at anecdotes. Victor reminisced about his illegal activities as if they were little triumphs in the face of absurdity. His tales contained familiar elements: crooked cops, nosy neighbors, idiotic business partners. Victor's most shameful moment, he admitted, was letting a skinny, needle-marked woman with two missing fingers give him a hand job in an Old Havana slum. She did it in exchange for a pair of oversized sandals he'd bragged to friends he could use as payment.

"It was fucking disturbing," he said, Serguey joining in his brother's laughter. "I took so long to finish. I still have nightmares about it."

Serguey hiccupped his way back to composure. "Why didn't you ask her to use the other hand?"

Victor scraped the grainy coating of beans from the walls of the cooking pot, shaking his head. "She kept saying she was a leftie."

Serguey's stories felt horrifyingly boring: Gimenez and his upper staff making "fat wife" jokes, dissing a foreign dignitary because he had bad taste in prostitutes, satirizing the laws of other countries for being restrictive. Victor found the stories fascinating. He asked about the kinds of meals these men ate, the beach houses they shared, the countries they traveled to.

"You gave up a good life," he said with a serious expression.

"It was never real," Serguey said. "Just the prospect of a life."

"Still, I know guys who'd kill for a shot at it."

"The shit you have to put up with, it's not worth it."

"Everyone has to put up with some kind of shit." Victor cobbled the last of the beans into a spoonful and said through a full mouth, "I would've put up with that asshole Gimenez if he'd given me a house in El Vedado."

They kept each other awake through the early night, the bonfire crackling between them. Now all they had to do was wait, so they talked, hoping to distract one another, pretending to be in a vacuum where leisure superseded anything, just as they had done at the tourist restaurant. The ground was drenched from the rain. The smell of doused wood intermingled with that of burnt twigs. Serguey pondered whether Victor was right, if this would be the last time they would see the Cuban countryside, Victor voyaging to another country, Serguey shipped off to prison. Serguey realized that there were factors he hadn't considered. Would he ever get to meet Victor's children? Would his brother, like Felipe, not be allowed to visit the island? The probability of their return would only increase if the communist government fell, or if it decided to pardon political prisoners and exiles.

"An unlikely scenario," his father would've said.

As the hours vanished, Serguey struggled to focus on the conversation. He began to dread, more specifically, what could be waiting for him in Havana. With Victor and Felipe out of Cuba, he'd be the one remaining to face Montalvo. The former colonel would not be happy that two Blancos had slipped through his fingers. What would Victor make of Toya's prediction? Serguey refused to believe in Santería, but he couldn't deny how spirituality was a fitting mask for coincidences, how it was best to have meaning than to accept you were randomly screwed. He had not only derided his brother's creed, but he was usurping his belief, his wish to be the martyr. He had done the same to his father at the prison. Maybe all the Blancos had a proclivity for martyrdom, after all: the fallen heroes in their own story.

At 11:00 p.m., they used Julia's flashlight to illuminate their way back to the gravel path. They followed it to the main road and stood, flashlight turned off, anxiously watching for any oncoming headlights. Mario's cousin would make only one pass, driving very slowly. Serguey was supposed to identify the car and call to it somehow. A truck roared in the opposite direction. Smaller vehicles whizzed by toward Havana. In the dull glimmer of the moon, he and Victor might as well have been two wooden posts. The road became absolutely dark beyond a few meters, except for the remote, static glow of houses. Then a soft rumble echoed, and two headlights appeared in the distance. They were inching closer, stopping at intervals. Serguey flicked on the flashlight and shook it. The car sped toward them. A voice emerged from the passenger seat:

"Get in," it said. "We have to hurry."

Chapter 27

Mario confirmed that Felipe had left the country. Serguey bottled up his breath in his lungs and stared at the ceiling. Whatever happened on this night, it wouldn't be for nothing. Felipe had been released under an extra-penal license, which Serguey knew meant that the charges weren't dropped. He could be arrested at any time on Cuban soil. In other words, his father's exile was permanent.

"He landed in Madrid this morning," Mario said. "I imagine he's being interviewed by TV channels and newspapers."

Serguey probed the credibility of the dramaturge's assured tone: "Do you think he's that big of a deal?"

"There's a strong Cuban artists community in Spain. He'll be fine."

Serguey noticed that Mario was wearing the same polo T-shirt he had worn at Toya's. His shorts were different, smaller, perhaps in preparation for the trip across the straits. He realized that Victor hadn't considered the possible conditions on the boat. He was wearing jeans and a red T-shirt. Not the most comfortable or inconspicuous outfit. They hadn't considered how long the trip might take, how long he'd be exposed to the sun.

"Do you know if my dad plans to end up in Miami?"

Mario tossed his head in a halfhearted glance. "It's too soon to tell. But I don't doubt it." He refrained from explaining himself.

The sound of the engine crescendoed as the driver—a squat, muscular man—sank his foot on the accelerator. Though Mario hadn't introduced him, Serguey assumed he was the famous cousin. He had a military haircut and pockmarked face. He was wearing sweatpants and a long-sleeve workout T-shirt, which in this sultry weather seemed odd to Serguey.

The man took a longer route, past San Antonio de los Baños and Guanajay, on the way to Marhondo. Serguey suspected it was to avoid getting close to the city. Outside the car, there was nothing but the billowing silhouettes of trees and the occasional cluster of homes when they traversed a town. A vigorous breeze blew endlessly against the vehicle, whistling as it entered through the windows. There were no romantic views of Havana, no recognizable neighborhoods to educe a symbolic, maudlin goodbye. With each fleeting minute, the darkness became unsettlingly repetitious. The city was farther and farther away. Without budging from his position, Serguey inquired about the exact place they were going, making him sound, he knew, apprehensive and distrustful.

Mario's cousin, in a matter-of-fact voice that tempered his palpable arrogance, described the roads he'd be taking. He took pride in showing how familiar he was with the area, in the niftiness of his strategy. He had picked a location not as concealed as others but was less patrolled. It was unquestionable from his accent that he'd grown up in Pinar del Rio, but his familiarity with Marhondo hinted that he could be from there. Regardless, his haughtiness worked in Serguey's favor. Had the directions been difficult or unclear, he would've had to confess to the Alida swap sooner than he intended. He let a handful of seconds pass, then turned on his phone and texted Kiko.

"What are you doing?" Mario's cousin said, glaring at Serguey's reflection on the rearview mirror.

He instinctively jammed the phone between him and the door. "I was texting my wife."

"Your phone should be off."

"Can't a guy say goodbye?" Victor said.

"How do I know he's not texting the police?"

Victor grabbed the driver's headrest and leveraged himself forward. "Call my brother a snitch again and see what happens."

"It's all right." Mario gripped his cousin's shoulder, and Victor retreated. "Serguey, just make it quick."

Serguey lifted his phone, the text already sent, so they could see the screen going dark.

As they ascended the incline into Marhondo, Mario perked up his head and stared beyond the windshield. The streetlamps were far apart, a rate of one per block by Serguey's estimate. A few minutes ticked by, and they took a winding road away from the town's center toward what Serguey surmised was the water. The sidewalks disappeared, as they did in Mantilla, dark grass now leading into every tin-roofed home. Occasionally, a line of clothes floundered in the drying wind with eerie, non-human movements under the nearest streetlight.

"Is that all you're bringing with you?" Mario asked the brothers.

They looked between their own feet and studied the bags.

"This is all we got," Victor said.

"I apologize for the obvious questions." Mario wiggled lazily in his seat. "I'm a bit nervous. I'm not used to doing this kind of thing."

The driver said loudly, "The guys who're coming have been doing this for a while." He checked the rearview mirror on his door and shifted the wheel ever so slightly.

"So, are you the cousin?" Victor said.

"You could say that."

Serguey observed the man's hands, his knuckles coated in calluses, as they rattled along with the car. "You're going with us?" he asked.

"No." The man narrowed his eyes, puzzled by the question. "Otherwise someone else would be driving."

"You can give him Antonio and Julia's stuff," Victor whispered to Serguey, and he nodded coolly.

Everyone was quiet as Mario's cousin veered into a series of off-road trails, wide enough for a single vehicle or tractor. His maneuvering seemed to match the directions he'd spewed earlier, but Serguey couldn't be sure. He prayed that Kiko was close enough to meet them at a moment's call. Directions of unmarked streets were always ambiguous, especially when followed in the dead of night. They bounced their way into the middle of a thicket whose surroundings looked like gnarled mangroves. To their right, there was a parked car. It was difficult to discern, but Serguey thought it was a 1950s Chevy.

Mario's cousin shut off the engine and headlights.

"Who the fuck is that?" he said, reaching under his seat. Serguey could make out a machete's handle.

Mario jerked his head. "No one else's supposed to be here."

"Should I peel back?" the cousin said. He cut his eyes at the brothers. "Did these motherfuckers set us up?"

"It's Kiko." Serguey reached for the door and swung it open. "He's a friend."

"Kiko?" Victor said, exiting on his side. "What the fuck is he doing here?"

Kiko emerged from the Chevy. Alida did the same from the passenger side. Serguey walked over and embraced him, then his sister-in-law.

"How's Anabel?" he asked her.

Alida had on a sweater. She tunneled her hands inside the opposite sleeves, forming a straitjacket. "She's worried about me, but she trusts you're coming home."

"Are you holding up okay?"

She leapt briefly on her toes. "I'm ready."

He smiled. He could tell she meant it. "Get your things."

Doors slammed behind him. Footsteps were moving closer.

"Serguey," Mario said, "the arrangement was for you and your brother. We can't bring any more people unless we pay extra. And even then—"

"I'm not going." Serguey pointed at Alida. "She is."

"Oh, dear," Mario murmured. He hadn't recognized her.

"This is really fucked up," Mario's cousin said. He folded his arms like a bodyguard watching a door, waiting for someone to address him. The machete dangled from his belt.

"It's fine," Serguey said, moving toward Victor. His brother was staring at Kiko's car, his features warped into a scowl.

"I can't be responsible for someone other than you two," Mario said to Serguey. "Does her family even know she's here?"

"They do," Alida said, stretching her neck from the opposite end of the vehicle, where she'd been retrieving her belongings.

"Really fucked up," Mario's cousin repeated.

Mario clutched Serguey's shirt just below the shoulder. "This is going to complicate things. Felipe—"

Serguey clasped Mario's wrist and brought his mouth centimeters from the dramaturge's ear. "You owe us. You wanted to be a man of action? Here's your chance. You're taking her."

The cousin sidled behind Mario, giving Serguey what in the gritty darkness became a hostile gaze. Mario stepped back and bumped into his cousin. Regaining his stability, he cleared his throat and showed his hands in surrender. "You're right," he said ruefully. "I'm sorry." He turned to his cousin. "Can we do the switch?"

The cousin held off as long as he could. He did a panoramic scan of the clearing. Then he nodded. "The boat guys only know the head count."

Mario hastened around the front of the Chevy and gave Alida a kiss. He seemed out of breath for an instant. "You're doing the right thing," he told her. He retraced his steps while holding hands with her; this, in Serguey's view, was a convincing gesture of commitment.

Alida was wearing a backpack and carrying a medium-sized plastic bag, the handles looped tightly on her left wrist.

"Is that all?" Serguey asked her.

She slid her thumb under the strap of her backpack. "Yes."

"Where do we have to wait?" Serguey asked Mario's cousin.

The man poked his head away from the group. "It's about three hundred meters."

A gust of wind swept over the thicket. It stirred the hair on Serguey's arms and neck. His nostrils caught the scent of the sea, as if they'd been standing on a cliff and were just now taking note. Above them, the sky was florescent, an eruption of stars.

"Lead the way," he said to the cousin.

"Is this a joke?" Victor said. He looked at Kiko, mumbling something inelegible.

Serguey stood in front of his brother. "You *have* to go."

"Fucking traitor," Victor said slowly, painfully.

Serguey's throat tightened. He could sense tears bubbling in his eyes. "This isn't about me and you," he said. "I can't leave Anabel, and you have to respect that."

His brother's heartbroken voice sounded shrill in Serguey's ears. "You set me up."

Serguey thought of them standing outside Raidel's car, Victor tugging at his arm. "You wouldn't have come otherwise." He tapped his index and middle fingers on Victor's chest, as Larido had done to the frog-faced man years ago. "This can't all have been for nothing."

Victor sighed deeply, silently, curving his head to one side and looking at the grass-spotted ground.

Serguey seized the opportunity—a crack of serenity in Victor's demeanor—and walked toward Kiko. "I'll be back soon," he whispered. "Say goodbye to my brother."

Kiko took Serguey's place. "Hey." He was asking Victor to raise his head. "This isn't easy for anybody."

"There's no time for second-guessing," Mario urged.

Victor gave himself a moment before hugging Kiko. His voice was muddled with harrowing acquiescence: "Goddamn it."

Kiko returned to the Chevy, coughing away his own tears.

Alida let go of Mario's hand and took Victor's. Serguey smiled gratefully at her.

Mario's cousin was plucking a military style canvas bag and a long rope from the trunk of his car. He informed the group that they needed to form a line, tied by the rope, since they couldn't use a flashlight.

"Can't risk being seen by the coastguard," he said.

Once they were all fastened, they filed into the mangroves. The tugging of the rope and sopping terrain made it a strenuous journey. Entangled, serrated branches barraged their bodies with the implacability so typical of nature. Whenever someone groaned or whined, Mario's cousin shushed them. After the first hundred meters, they understood they had to suck it up and get through it. Soon they could hear the sea gulping and swooshing, but in the impenetrable darkness, it was impossible to determine how close they were. The land beneath their feet became completely solid. Mario's cousin ordered them to untie themselves and remain quiet in a crouched position. They laid the rope on the ground and waited like a row of patient ducklings.

Twenty minutes later, Serguey's legs were cramping, nearly numb. The salty scent of the ocean, whipped about by the surf, dried his mouth and made his nose burn. Fearing that he might at some point have to sit, he kept shifting his weight from one half of his body to the other, often matching the rhythmic music of the waves.

Out of nowhere, Mario whispered, "These mosquitoes are killing me."

His cousin muttered, "Florida's full of mosquitoes too."

Serguey could hear Victor scoffing behind him, his anger and disappointment fermenting again.

Finally, his brother said, "You should've trusted me to know from the beginning."

Serguey refused to acknowledge him. He wanted to dodge conversation, any chance that either of them might waver. But a refusal to speak had been their undoing, and how safe or perilous a trip lay ahead for his brother, he could only guess. "I should have," he said as a form of apology.

Victor allowed a breeze to graze the compact ground beneath their stooped bodies before saying, "I still think Toya was talking about me."

Serguey smiled, relieved at his brother's acceptance. He was spared a reply when a dinghy abruptly materialized—as if out of a fog—and glided sideways toward the shore. He'd pictured a yacht of some kind, though, in hindsight, it didn't make sense for such a large vessel to pick up only three people.

"When I say go, you go," Mario's cousin said. He tiptoed over the rocks in anticipation of the boat.

Serguey felt a gentle pull from behind. He recognized the touch, from his balcony, from the night Alida had confessed she wanted to leave. When he didn't react, her hands bypassed his shoulder and yanked his chin. She kissed him briefly on the lips, then breathed the words into his eyes: "Take care of my sister."

"I will," he said.

"Let's go!" Mario's cousin said. He grabbed Mario's canvas bag and hurled it onto the boat. Mario hopped clumsily over the gunwale. The man who'd been piloting the dinghy, his features shadowed like an apparition, steadied him as he landed. Alida went next, not needing assistance.

"I won't forgive you for this," Victor said, his tone, the endearing glimmer in his eyes, his faint smile all signifying the contrary. He threw his arms around Serguey.

As soon as Victor released him, Serguey clamped his brother's collarbone. It was solid as a steel rod. "You take care of Alida."

"I take care of her, and you get the kiss."

"Hurry it up," Mario's cousin said.

Victor offered Serguey the keys to their father's house. Serguey took them, clinging to Victor's fingers. There was sturdiness in the tips of his brother's hand, in their hands being joined together—a complementing vigor he now was petrified of losing. Victor let go, and Serguey clamped the keys, stabbing himself with the toothed metal to keep from shaking. Victor walked away, slinging his bag on board. As he stepped in, the boat sank momentarily and took on water. Neither the cousin nor the shadowed man seemed perturbed. Victor stood next to Alida, looking back at Serguey. Mario's cousin pushed off with his right foot, and the man on the dinghy took hold of the oars. Serguey watched as Victor, Alida, and Mario lowered themselves. The man steered the boat out of what Serguey could now see was an inlet, a semi-circular stage under the stars. Eventually the figures all disappeared into a dark mass where the sea, vegetation, and sky seamlessly blended in the distance.

Serguey immediately regretted not being able to distinctly see his brother's expression or Alida's. He'd have no memory of it, no image to return to, no picture to paint Anabel. The entire ordeal felt rushed. Now he had the rest of his life for everything to slow down.

Mario's cousin spooled the rope with his hand and elbow, leaving enough for him and Serguey to enclose their waists. As they began the trek back to the cars, Serguey was vexed that he hadn't double-checked if Victor's money hadn't slipped out of his pants. Small things like that could make a difference. He thought again about the size of the dinghy. He didn't recall seeing a motor.

"That's a small boat," he said. "How far are they going?"

Mario's cousin slashed away with his machete, clearing a path. "The bigger boat will meet them at an outer island. It's too noisy to come all the way in here."

"How big is it?"

"Medium-sized, but the motor's strong. They'll be in the Keys before noon."

The rope was pulling Serguey along—short, vehement tugs—as the cousin assailed the boughs and shrubs. "What if something breaks down?"

"They got food and water. They've made a lot of trips."

"Are they friends of yours?"

The cousin stopped momentarily, the rope slack between them. The blade of his machete glinted above his head as he appeared to wipe sweat from his brow. "Better they go like this than with ten or fifteen people," he said earnestly. "Anyway, it's harder for the coastguard to notice a dinghy."

Serguey had no idea if any of it was true, but he chose to trust the man for his own peace of mind.

By the time they exited the mangroves, Serguey could feel a stinging, prickling sensation in various parts of his body. He was sure he was bleeding somewhere. Mario's cousin unhooked the rope and placed it back in the trunk. He looked at Serguey and Kiko inquisitively, but they had nothing to say. Seconds later, he drove away, sticking his hand out the window as a farewell gesture.

"Was that Mario's cousin?" Kiko asked.

Serguey swabbed the sweat from his forehead. "You could say that."

Chapter 28

Kiko didn't speak as he worked his way out of the remote roads. When he finally located the main street, he leaned into his seat and breathed profoundly. Serguey checked the rearview mirror on the passenger side: no patrol cars were tailing them. Out in front, each passing pair of headlights felt portentous. Serguey kept anticipating the colorful display of a siren, followed by a screeching U-turn, but they never came. After a few kilometers, he got used to the cars' transitory nature, standard weeknight traffic in the margins of Havana. He was able to convince himself, as they entered the city, that perhaps they were in the clear.

"Thank you," he said to his friend.

"You're lucky I found the right place. I'd never driven to that part of the coast in Marhondo."

"Victor and I owe you."

"Someone's got to do it. Besides, I'm scared of your wife."

The statement revolved like a jumbled pile of consonants and vowels somewhere on the fringes of Serguey's comprehension. It took him catching a glimpse of a timorous smirk on Kiko's lips for the phrase to pierce the realm of sense. There was only one logical response: "Why?"

"Let's just say she's expecting me to deliver you safe and sound."

Serguey realized that he hadn't told Kiko what he'd decided at some interval earlier in the night. "We're not going back to Mantilla."

His friend's smirk evaporated. "What do you mean?"

"Take me back to my Dad's house."

"What for? They might be watching the place."

"If they're going to come for me, let them do it now. I don't want to embarrass Anabel and my in-laws if I don't have to."

Kiko seemed to contemplate whether he should give up his assessment on the matter. His fingers twitched restlessly on the wheel. "You'll be safer with them. There'll be witnesses."

Serguey looked at him, his gaze charged with conclusive clarity. "Kiko, take me to the house."

Kiko grunted in protest. "I'm spending the night with you then."

"Don't be ridiculous."

"I promised Anabel I'd take you back." His friend's eyes skipped from the road to Serguey, then back to the asphalt. "You have to understand that if you get in trouble, all of us are going to feel responsible. I know your brother and father left, and you're in a fragile state and all that, but you can't lose your damn mind."

"I'll call Anabel. I know what I'm doing. I *need* to go to the house."

"What if I refuse?"

In his own mind, Serguey smiled, but the signal never reached his lips. "You won't."

"Your brother's right." Kiko shook his head and reclined once more in his seat. He was forfeiting. "You're as stubborn as he is."

They drove on in silence. Serguey intersected his arms and sloped his body against the window. His temples felt like the walls of an inflating balloon. The pressure caused his eyelids to droop, though he didn't quite fall asleep. The adrenaline had dwindled. His stomach and bowels were like dried-up fruit, the air sucked out of them. There was an acidic taste at the bottom of his throat, jolting to the back of his tongue with every bump in the road. Parts of his skin itched with a stinging sensation. His muscles, and perhaps his bones, were sore.

"You look beat-up," Kiko said. "Like they put you through a grinding machine."

Serguey found the crack nostalgic—it reminded him of Victor. "I'm just glad it's over."

As the word "over" oozed from his tongue, he knew it was a fallacy. The night around them had contained more hours than it had a right to. It was like a dream from which he hadn't yet awakened. Kiko was traversing La Lisa, north of the police station where Montalvo had spilled the hot coffee on Victor's leg. Despite the disturbing memory, the familiarity of the buildings and neighborhoods gave him some calm, some lucidity. He unlocked his arms and rotated his shoulders, looking for his body to not shut down, not yet.

"I never went to see your parents," Serguey said.

"Maybe you'll be able to now."

Kiko didn't sound confident. Serguey didn't possess the strength to lie, so he said nothing, leaving open the possibility that he might visit Kiko's parents after all.

"Please tell Claudia again that I'm immensely grateful."

"I'm thinking of joining her."

Serguey waited for him to explain.

"I'm going to start blogging," Kiko said. "What she did with you guys, it really made a difference. I know the Church got it done, but her blog posts really helped."

"It's remarkable what she does."

Kiko began to describe technical details about maximizing readership, getting articles reposted, and finding key words to attract readers. "There's an art to being a social media activist," he said. Serguey's endorsement had catapulted him into a rapt conversation with himself. A surge of delight had overtaken him. Kiko was not only fascinated by Claudia but engrossed by what she did.

"You guys will make a good team," Serguey said.

Kiko chuckled. "Someone has to let the world know what goes on in here."

"Maybe you found your calling. I mean it."

"And it doesn't hurt that she and I make a good team."

"Claudia's a brave woman. If you really like her, that doesn't devalue the difference you can make."

Kiko stopped the car at a red light. They were in El Cerro, in Kiko's neighborhood, not far from their destination. "See, that's where you and your brother are different. Victor would've already made about ten sexual jokes."

"That's his way of saying that he's proud and thinks it's a good idea."

Where was his brother now? Had they swapped boats yet? Was there another round of waiting on the outer island Mario's cousin had mentioned?

"I'm going to miss that son of a bitch," Kiko said.

Serguey nodded. "He'll miss us too."

The light changed to green, and Kiko eased the car into first gear. "Victor in Miami. He's going to be up to a thousand things in no time."

"Hopefully Dad will end up there too. Not that he's the best role model."

Kiko made an incoherent sound, marooned somewhere between agreement and dissension. "Felipe's a good man. Artists sometimes tend to be a little complicated, that's all."

Serguey couldn't subscribe to such romantic views. "My father isn't the saint people think he is, Kiko. But better flawed and free than in prison."

Kiko made a couple of unhurried, meticulous turns, sweeping the curbs for unrecognizable cars, and pulled to the front of the house. With the porch light off, the door and front wall regressed from them into a deepening darkness. They waited until their eyes adjusted and they could see no one hiding behind the columns. There was no sign of vandalism, no splashed eggs, no accusations. It was a desolate home, excavated from some dream that now felt too real. Its size seemed too big for one person yet even bigger for none. Serguey had no legal claim on it. The keys in his pocket weren't an inherited responsibility, which he would've welcomed. They had been Victor's gesture of allowing him to say goodbye to the place where they had grown together. But Serguey couldn't keep from worrying that his eyes were deceiving him, that an officer was in fact hiding behind a column or a nearby bush, or that Montalvo was sitting on the living room sofa, salivating at the opportunity to spook him, drag him out, make another spectacle.

What Serguey wanted most, as he took hold of the car's door handle, was to be left alone.

"I spoke with you brother's buddy," Kiko said. "He's acting as if he doesn't have his stuff. I think he figured Victor's in serious trouble and wants to keep the money."

"Let him have it. We owe Yunior anyway."

"You sure?"

"Unless he has a box of gold watches, it isn't worth it."

"Your brother's deals were mostly with *pacotilla*. Nothing exuberant."

If he were to believe Victor's stories, Serguey knew that wasn't precisely true, but what did it matter now?

"Don't forget to call Anabel," Kiko said.

Serguey shook his friend's hand. "Thank you."

"You should be proud. You got your brother and father out of this godforsaken country."

"And we get to stay."

Kiko shrugged. He had no suitable response. "Get some sleep. I wasn't lying when I said you look like shit."

⁂

Serguey sat sluggishly on the front steps, leaning back on his elbows. The muted glow of the streetlamps cast a spotlight on him. He didn't want to hide, to prevent being detected. As the hum of Kiko's car faded, the neighborhood turned silent. If a vehicle were to approach, he'd be able to hear it as far out as Via Blanca Avenue. If there were State Security officers hidden behind columns, let them come, he now thought. They wouldn't be arresting a defeated man, a fearful man. They'd be taking the man who beat them.

He flipped his phone from hand to hand, debating whether he should call Anabel. With her, he would be susceptible, exposed. He would tell her that he *was* afraid. With time to grasp what he'd be losing, he was terrified. But if it wasn't going to end well for him, he wanted it to end soon. He was exhausted. His thoughts were rambling. He couldn't muster up the energy to do much else. If he could be more coherent, he'd tell her how much he loved her, what she meant to him. He nodded to himself as a way of expressing these things, as if she could actually see him, read his mind.

He put the phone in his pocket, walked up the steps onto the porch and then toward the door. He opened it and faced the house. It felt haunted—not quite abandoned yet not quite livable. The kitchen and bedrooms were dark, concealing the phantoms of memories and events, moments that transpired before Serguey's time, before Felipe's. He shut his eyes and heard Irene in the kitchen, telling Victor amidst bursts of laughter, "No, don't spit it out!" Victor cackled himself to a cough, then a labored breath, as Irene gave him a glass of water, a plastic cup Victor clumsily held with two hands too close to the bottom, often spilling water down his chin.

The empty bookshelves nearer to him still vibrated with a modicum of life. At his father's request, he had assisted in alphabetically organizing Felipe's library once. He must've been nine or ten.

"This one," Felipe had said, raising *The Old Man and the Sea*, "was written by an American author named Ernest Hemingway. It's about a Cuban fisherman and his struggle with a marlin and sharks. It got Hemingway the Nobel Prize because of his prose style. I've gone on a tour of his house here in Havana. He used to have orgies there, you know. An American came to Cuba to have orgies and to fish, and they gave him a Nobel for it."

Felipe had paused several times while arranging the books to share similar anecdotes.

"Lezama Lima, you've heard the name, right?"

"Yes," Serguey said.

Felipe showed him the hefty tome that was *Paradiso*. "There's a chapter here about a penis. Most people only read that chapter and then claim to know Lezama."

When they reached the playwriting section, Felipe pointed out that Meyerhold, after revolutionizing theater, had been killed by the Soviets.

"They won't tell you that in school here, of course. The saddest part is that they pardoned him later. They figured out he was innocent after they'd shot him. Meanwhile, Dostoevsky was about to be killed, his grave dug up next to him, when he got his pardon. Can you imagine what that must be like, to be moments away from certain death and survive?"

Serguey remembered staring at his father, terror and excitement charging through him in equal measure.

"Art always gets its tragedies and triumphs from real life," his father told him. "Don't believe everything's made-up."

Serguey had seen his own mother murdered. He knew it all too well. Yet Felipe saw nothing but the innocence of his son's age, of his childish mind. At the time, all Serguey could think was that his father had, if only for an afternoon, allowed him into his world. Nothing was as exhilarating, not even attending his father's plays.

He considered lying on the sofa. There could be comfort, however temporary, in spending one last night inside his childhood home. But he didn't want to be arrested in his sleep, dragged from the house as if it were being snatched away from him. The sense of loss should be experienced on his own terms. He shut the door and paced across the porch, returning to the front steps. Once more, he sat, wearied. The air was balmy, the streetlights softer. There was distant traffic but none in his direction. He watched his block through blurred eyes, listening to the quiet of its collective slumber. In his tiredness, he still felt present, more than he had felt anywhere else. He had caused ripples. He mattered. His father had been liberated, was now safe in another continent, his file already accumulating dust in one of Montalvo's drawers. Victor and Alida were racing toward Florida, buoyant about their futures. What a month before had seemed so dangerous and unattainable was now a simple reality. The price Serguey had paid wasn't really a price. He'd freed himself from the traps of a delusion and returned home. He'd been a bull like Joaquin, his grandfather. He'd staked his claim, defied the authorities, risked everything for his family, and he'd won.

The faint glimmer of the streetlights was soon replaced by the dimness of Serguey's dreams. He saw Gimenez coming out of a plane, dressed in Mario's getaway outfit, and descending the stairs into a tarmac crowded with State Security agents. He saw Alida diving off the rocks into inky water, her giggles mixing with the waves. He showed off his diving skills for her, only to find it was Anabel and not her sister who'd jumped before him. He then heard a ringing sound, similar to a melody he'd heard in a movie, and woke with a start to realize it was his phone.

Serguey stared at the screen. It was Anabel. He declined the call, searching instead for missed messages. There were none. He returned to the main screen and looked at the time: 7:05 a.m. He pocketed the phone and pushed himself from the steps. The sky to his right was radiant, like the flash of a faraway explosion. The flow of cars on Vento and Lacret and Via Blanca sounded steady. He peered down the sidewalk and saw no one of interest. He felt a slight pain on his cheek and temple, from leaning his face against the porch railing. His fingers could trace narrow lines of indent on his skin. His dry eyes were in urgent need of water. He filled his lungs with early morning air and groaned, allowing his body a moment to become aware of itself. He didn't want to speak with Anabel until he was fully awake. He had no news from Victor or Alida to share, and she would surely reprimand him when she found out where he'd spent the night.

He entered the house and went to the bathroom to urinate. When he finished, he turned on the faucet and watched it spurt feebly, agonizingly. The water had been shut off. He flushed the toilet with what was left in the tank and headed to Victor's apartment. It was locked, no way to climb through a window. He considered whether he should smash his way in, take anything his brother might have if given the chance. Finally he decided to leave it. He walked through the house once more, inspecting each room, as he'd done at Gimenez's apartment. If there were any ghosts the previous night, they had already made their departure.

He found himself at the front door, suddenly anxious about who might be on the other side. Maybe this had been the game: to let him believe he was safe, forgotten, that he'd not only succeeded, but that he would be able to enjoy his success. Maybe they had watched him sleep, allowed him to dream, and now they were waiting with detestable smiles, ready to take him to Montalvo, who was sharpening whatever tools he saw fit for the Blanco who hadn't slipped through his fingers. This sensation—this particular instant—if Serguey were lucky, would be the rest of his life: a ceaseless, dreadful inferring about the loud knock on his door, the car sputtering toward the curb, the reticent passerby.

Spending the night at his father's had accomplished little except postpone the fear of a probable arrest. Serguey thought about political prisoners, marked by the government, constantly hounded. In the grand scheme of things, Felipe and Victor had been fortunate. Perhaps it was only right that *he* pay the price. Too many things had gone their way. Too many pebbles on their side of the scale.

He stepped out onto the street, encountering no unfamiliar faces, no strange vehicles. The sun was beginning to sear the pavement with a yellowish gleam. He called Anabel's number, thinking of what he should tell her—not just about Alida or Victor, about his decision to stay at the house—but about how he intended to provide for her, to make it work with Antonio and Julia. The best way to defy fear was to plan for the future. He listened to the line ring as he walked, another wave of exhaustion burdening his body. He looked at the slabs of fractured sidewalk that lay ahead, tiny weeds beginning to sprout from the grooves. He fought not to lift his gaze, waiting, with subdued desperation, to hear his wife's voice.

BIOGRAPHICAL NOTE

Dariel Suarez was born in Havana, Cuba, and immigrated to the United States with his family in 1997. His debut story collection, *A Kind of Solitude*, received the 2017 Spokane Prize for Short Fiction and the 2019 International Latino Book Award for Best Collection of Short Stories. Dariel is an inaugural City of Boston Artist Fellow and Education Director at GrubStreet. His prose has appeared in numerous publications, including the *Threepenny Review*, *Prairie Schooner*, the *Kenyon Review*, and the *Caribbean Writer*, where he was awarded the First Lady Cecile de Jongh Literary Prize. Dariel earned his MFA in Fiction at Boston University and currently resides in the Boston area with his wife and daughter.